TAER

DUN PYR

LADOTYN

BOBYR

CAER ICEL

CERRGONNEY

AVERBY

TAER
ANGWIDD

PREN CLUDAN

CAMYN YRAEN

CANTRAE

LYN EBYN

GADDMYR

DUN
CANTRAE

AVER NAIDDYR

HENDYR

DUN
HIRAEDD

GWER-
CONEDD

DUN DEVER

PECL

BUCCBRAEL

MWBBR

CYN

DEVERRY

DRAU

CERRMO

AVER BEL

AVER GW

TAB

TH

NIS

DUN
TONAU

METON

AD MOCYCL

MOR

Darkspell

Also by Katharine Kerr

DAGGERSPELL

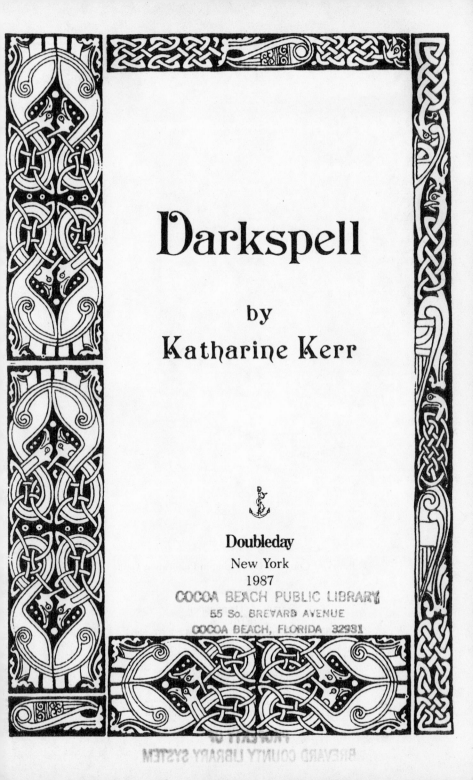

Darkspell

by

Katharine Kerr

Doubleday

New York

1987

Library of Congress Cataloging-in-Publication Data
Kerr, Katharine.
Darkspell.

Sequel to: Daggerspell.
I. Title.
PS3561.E642D35   1987   813'.54   87–6862

ISBN: 0-385-23109-1
Printed in the United States of America
First Edition

For my father, Sgt. John Carl Brahtin (1918–44),
who died fighting to free Europe from a worse
evil than anything a novelist could invent.

Acknowledgments

A thousand thanks to all my friends and relations, too numerous to list, who have had to put up with my fits of absentmindedness, compulsive writing stints, and downright obsession with this imaginary world. Most of all, though, my thanks go to my husband, Howard Kerr, who has to live with me, after all, when I'm working.

A Note on the Pronunciation
of Deverry Words

The language spoken in Deverry is a P-Celtic language. Although closely related to Welsh, Breton, and Cornish, it is by no means identical to any of these actual languages and should never be taken as such.

Vowels are divided by Deverry scribes into two classes: noble and common. Nobles have two pronunciations; commons, one.

A as in *father* when long; a shorter version of the same sound, as in *far,* when short.

O as *bone* when long; as in *pot* when short.

W as the *oo* in *spook* when long; as in *roof* when short.

Y as the *i* in *machine* when long; as the *e* in *butter* when short.

E as in *pen.*

I as in *pin.*

U as in *pun.*

Vowels are generally long in stressed syllables, short in unstressed. Y is the primary exception to this rule. When it appears as the last letter of a word, it is always long, whether that syllable is stressed or not.

Diphthongs have one consistent pronunciation.

AE as the *a* in *mane.*

AI as in *aisle.*

AU as the *ow* in *how.*

EO as a combination of *eh* and *oh.*

EW as in Welsh, a combination of *eh* and *oo.*

IE as in *pier.*

OE as the *oy* in *boy.*

UI as the North Welsh *wy,* a combination of *oo* and *ee.*

Note that OI is never a diphthong, but is two distinct sounds, as in the name Benoic (BEHN-oh-ik).

Consonants are as in English, with these exceptions:

C is always hard as in *cat*.

G is always hard as in *get*.

DD is the voiced *th* as in *breathe*, but the voicing is considerably more pronounced than in English. It is opposed to *TH*, the unvoiced sound as in *breath*. Note well: dd and th are *always* considered single letters.

R is well and truly rolled.

RH is a voiceless R, approximately pronounced as if it were spelled hr. The distinction is a subtle one, and in Eldidd tends to be increasingly ignored.

DW, GW, and TW are single sounds, as in *twit*, most of the time; but there are exceptions.

Y is *never* a consonant.

I before a vowel may be consonantal, particularly at the beginning of words and in the plural ending *-ion* (pronounced yawn).

Doubled consonants are both sounded clearly. Note that DD and RR are considered single consonants, as are the two "m's" in the name of the god Wmm.

Accent is generally on the penultimate syllable, but compound words and place names are often exceptions to this rule.

On the whole, I have transcribed both Elvish and Bardekian names and words according to the above system of orthography, which is quite adequate to the Bardekian, at least. As for Elvish, in a work of this sort it would be both confusing and overly pedantic to use the full apparatus by which scholars try to represent this most subtle and nuanced of tongues. To the average human ear, for instance, distinctions such as those between A, Å, and Å are lost in the hearing. Why then should we try to distinguish them in print? The reader should, however, remember that Elvish words are accented quite differently than Deverrian and Bardekian ones. Since Elvish is an agglutinative language, the various components of a name may receive stress according to their meaning rather than to their place in the pattern of syllables. Canbaramelim, for instance, which is composed of the morphemes for rough + name marker + river, is pronounced CAHN-BAHR-ah-MEH-lim.

Darkspell

Prologue
Winter, 1062

Every light casts a shadow. So does the dweomer.
Some men choose to stand in the light; others, in
the darkness. Be ye always aware that where you
stand is a matter of choice, and let not the shadow
creep over you unawares . . .

The Secret Book of Cadwallon the Druid

They met deep in the Innerlands in a place where only those who had mastered the heart of the dweomer could go. In various towns in the kingdom of Deverry, their physical bodies lay asleep in trance, leaving their minds free to assume a new form and travel far to the ancient grove of oaks that stood under a dim, pleasant sun. For a thousand years so many dweomer-masters had imagined this grove, had pictured it with trained minds and discussed its details among themselves, that now the images lived by themselves in the astral plane. They were always there when those who knew how came to them.

Those who met had chosen simple images for their minds to wear. Their faces looked like their physical ones, but their bodies were thin, curiously attenuated, and dressed in a stylized version of ordinary clothes, the men in white brigga and shirts, the women in white ankle-length dresses. There was no particular significance to the color white; it simply took less energy to maintain than bright colors. One at a time they appeared in the grove until at last the full company of thirty-two stood there, drifting above the insubstantial grass and waiting for the man who'd called this meeting to speak.

He was tall, quite old, with a shock of thick white hair and piercing blue eyes. Although he held the title of the Master of the Aethyr, he preferred to be known as Nevyn, a name that held a jest, because it meant "no one." Beside him stood a short, slender man with gray hair and dark eyes that dominated his face. His name was Aderyn, and technically he had no right to come to the grove, because his Wyrd lay not with his own humankind, but with the elven race, the Elcyion Lacar, who lived to the west of Deverry. Yet he had testimony to offer about the strange events that they were meeting to discuss.

"We're all here, then?" Nevyn said at last. "Now, you've all heard somewhat about what happened this summer."

The assembly nodded in agreement, their images mimicking the movements their bodies would have made. The news had spread that in a remote corner of Eldidd province, a lord named Corbyn had risen up in rebellion against his overlord, Tieryn Lovyan of Dun Gwerbyn. Normally this would have been of no concern to the dweomer; rebellions and bloodshed happened all the time in Deverry, and overlords had armies to deal with such things. But Corbyn had been ensorceled by a dweomerman gone mad, Loddlaen by name, who was half-elven, Aderyn's apprentice. Now Loddlaen was dead, the rebellion crushed, but the matter was far from settled.

"As soon as I joined Aderyn here to defeat Loddlaen," Nevyn went on, "I realized that someone had ensorceled him and was using him to work harm. Now, that someone had to be a master of the dark dweomer. Once he realized that he was facing me, he fled. As far as I can tell, he took ship for Bardek."

The assembly stirred uneasily. Caer, a tall, rangy man whose hazel eyes were green at the moment, drifted forward to speak.

"What exactly was the goal of the dark master? Did you ever find that out?"

"Only in the most vague terms. Tieryn Lovyan has a son named Rhodry. Years ago, I was given an omen that his Wyrd is crucial to Eldidd, and so I've been watching over him. It seems that the whole point of this cursed war was to kill him. He was leading his mother's army as cadvridoc, you see."

"The dark masters must have discovered the lad's importance, then," a woman named Nesta said. "Do you know what his Wyrd may be?"

"Not in the least, and that's part of the trouble. No doubt our enemies know more about it than I do. They're the ones who are always troubling their hearts about the future. The likes of us trust in the Light."

They nodded in agreement. The Great Ones who stand behind the dweomer, the Lords of Wyrd and the Lords of Light, never communicate clearly and directly with their servants, for the simple reason that those disincarnate spirits exist on a plane unimaginably removed from the physical world. It's impossible for them to reach down far enough to do more than send vague hints, feelings, dream images and warnings to the minds of those trained to receive these brief messages. For those who walk in the Light such hints are enough, but the dark dweomer is always picking at the future like a scab.

"I hope you're guarding the lad well," Caer said. "They'll doubtless make another try on him."

"Well, that's somewhat of a puzzle." Nevyn spoke slowly as he thought things out. "I've spent many an hour meditating, but I've received no warnings that he's still in danger. It's doubly odd, because after the war was over, Rhodry was sent into exile by his elder brother."

"What?" Nesta said. "Who's the elder brother? I don't know Eldidd politics at all well."

"My apologies. This is all of such great moment to me that I forget others aren't so interested. Rhodry's mother is Lovyan, and she rules the tierynrhyn of Dun Gwerbyn in her own right through the Clw Coc clan. His father was Tingyr, a Maelwaedd of Aberwyn, and now Rhodry's eldest brother, Rhys, is gwerbret of Aberwyn."

They all nodded, as if saying that the information was enough to get on with. Understanding the complicated web of bloodlines and landholds among the noble-born took all the long training of a bard or priest.

"Now, Rhys and Rhodry have hated each other for years. It has naught to do with dweomer or Wyrd; it's just one of those nasty things that happen between blood kin. So, one night in Aberwyn, Rhys insulted his brother so badly that Rhodry started to draw his sword on him—and remember that Rhys is a gwerbret."

"Rhodry's lucky his brother didn't hang him," Caer said.

"Just so. Rhys saw his chance to get rid of his hated kinsman and took it. Now Rhodry's riding the roads as a silver dagger."

"Indeed?" Nesta broke in. "I'm surprised you let him go for a mercenary soldier."

"I had naught to say about it, I assure you, or I wouldn't have.

But Rhodry's only the least part of our troubles. Now, Nesta here tracked the dark master when he came through Cerrmor, and neither she, I, nor any of our elemental spirits recognized the man. Here we'd been thinking we knew every fool who practiced this wretched craft. Well, we've all been too smug."

"And he made his escape easily, too," Nesta picked it up. "Just as if he had refuges ready all along his way. He must have been laying this scheme for a long time, right under our noses."

Several of the men muttered quite unenlightened oaths under their breaths. Aderyn stepped forward to speak.

"What frightens me is that he could ensorcel Loddlaen so easily. Loddlaen's mind was more elven than human. Do you see what that means? Our enemy must have a good knowledge of elven ways, but I'm as sure as I can be that no dark dweomerman has ever traveled in the elven lands."

"Bad news, indeed," Caer said. "Well, then, the hard truth of the matter is that we haven't been vigilant enough. That has to change."

"Exactly," Nevyn said. "We can work out the details among ourselves later, but there's one more thing I want to put to the full Council of Thirty-Two. During this war, hundreds of men saw dweomer worked openly."

For a moment the assembly was shocked into silence; then the talk burst out, just as when a summer storm gathers, the sky leaden gray, growing heavier as the birds hush; then suddenly with a crack of thunder comes the rain. Nevyn turned to Aderyn.

"It's time for you to leave us. I'll contact you later through the fire."

"Well and good, then. Truly, you've all got much to discuss."

Aderyn's image was abruptly gone from the grove. Slowly the assembly quieted itself.

"Well, now, this is a grave thing," Caer said at last. "Of course, no one outside of western Eldidd will believe them. In time, the tale will die away."

"Provided no one stirs it up again with more dweomer."

"Ye gods! Do you think that was part of the dark ones' scheme, to flush us out into the open?"

"It's a possibility, isn't it?"

The assembly turned uneasy, and with good reason. Once, back in the Dawntime when the people of Bel had first come to

Deverry from their original homeland across the eastern seas, the priests of the oak groves known as drwiddion had openly worked dweomer. Men feared them, flattered them, and groveled before them until the inevitable corruption set in. The priests grew rich and held great demesnes; they shaped the laws to their advantage and wielded power like lords. Slowly, of its own accord, the dweomer left them, until their rituals became empty shows and their words of power, mere chatter. Such are the temptations of temporal power that the priesthood forgot that it had ever had the true dweomer. By Nevyn's time, they too dismissed tales of wonder-working priests as mere fancies, fit for a bard's song and nothing more.

Yet the dweomer survived, passed down from master to apprentice in secret. The dweomerfolk swore strict vows to live quiet lives, hiding their skills, lest they too be corrupted by flattery and riches. Caer was the head groom of the gwerbret of Lughcarn's stables; Nesta, the widow of a Cerrmor spice merchant. Nevyn himself lived the simplest life of all, because he was a herbman, wandering the kingdom with a mule and tending the ills of folk too poor to afford apothecaries and chirurgeons. If those long years of secrecy came to an end, it was likely that, sooner or later, the dweomer-masters might succumb to the same temptations that had drawn the priests from the true path.

"And there's another thing," Caer said. "Most people in the kingdom would label us witches. What if they take it into their minds to hunt us down?"

Nesta shuddered. As an elderly woman, she was extremely vulnerable to such a charge.

"True enough," Nevyn said. "And so we—" He stopped, struck by a thought so urgent that he knew it came from beyond himself, and when he spoke again, his mind-voice rang with prophecy. "The time has come for the dweomer to show itself, only a little at first, but the time comes when all shall work openly."

Those assembled heard the ring and knew that the Lords of Light had spoken through their servant.

"Oh by the hells!" Caer whispered. "Never did I think to see this day come."

They all agreed, especially Nevyn.

"This calls for long hours of meditation," he remarked. "I

promise you all that I'll put them in, too. We've got to move as cautiously as a cat in a bathhouse."

For some time they discussed the prophecy, until they decided that Nevyn would work out this strange idea while the rest of them lived as they always had. The council broke up, the body-images winking out like blown candles, but Caer and Nevyn lingered in the peaceful stillness of the astral grove. Around them the enormous trees nodded as if in a wind as the astral tides began to change, a gentle stirring that they felt in their minds.

"It's a strange thing we've heard this day, oh Master of Earth," Nevyn remarked. "But I intend to pursue the idea, no matter how long it takes me."

"Oh, I'm not worried about that. You've always been as stubborn as a pig on market day."

They exchanged a smile of sincere affection. Once, some four hundred years earlier, Caer had been Nevyn's master when he struggled through his apprenticeship in the dweomer. Although Rhegor, as his name was then, had followed the normal pattern for dweomerfolk and died to be reborn, many times over now, Nevyn himself had lived one single life, sustained by the elemental forces he commanded. Although most people would have coveted such a long life, it was a harsh Wyrd for him to bear, because during his apprenticeship he'd made a grave mistake that had resulted in the deaths of three innocent people, and a rash vow that never would he rest until he'd redeemed his fault.

"Tell me somewhat," Caer said. "Do you think you're close to fulfilling your vow?"

"I don't know, I truly don't. So many times before I thought I was, only to have things slip away from me. But I can tell you this: Gerraent and I have come to terms between us. Part of the chain's broken once and for all."

"Thanks be to every god, then. I tried to warn you about swearing that—"

"I know, I know, and you're exactly right: I'm too stubborn for my own wretched good. Ah ye gods, poor Brangwen! You know, I still think of her by that name, even though she only bore it for a few pitiful years. I failed her so badly, and Blaen, too, but when I swore I'd make it up to her, I never thought it would take four hundred beastly years!"

"Well, don't take all the blame upon yourself for that. It's been many a lifetime now, and they've all had a hand in tangling their own Wyrds. I take it they're making a bigger mess of things in this life?"

"True spoken. Brangwen—I mean Jill, curse it—is off on the roads with Rhodry."

"Whom, I take it, is the same soul who once was known as Lord Blaen of the Boar."

"Just that. Did I forget to tell you? My apologies, but ye gods, I grow so muddled as the years stretch out. I wonder how the elves manage to keep their memories straight, I truly do."

"They have minds fit to do so. Our folk don't."

"Sometimes I wonder how long I'll be able to go on."

Caer's image looked at him sharply with a concern no less deep for being so shrewd. Nevyn looked away, up at the ancient trees, nodding gently in a world that knows no decay or change. At times he was so weary that he wished he could turn into a tree like the sorcerers in the ancient legends, who at last found peace by merging with the oaks they worshiped.

"Now here," Caer said. "If ever you need my aid, it's yours."

"My sincere thanks. I may take you up on that."

"Good. By the way, is there any chance you'll come through Lughcarn before winter sets in? It's always good to see old friends in the flesh."

"So it is, but maybe next spring. I have to stay in Eldidd."

"More dark doings afoot?"

"There's not, at that. I've been invited to a wedding."

At that time, Eldidd province was one of the more sparsely settled parts of Deverry, and in its western reaches, towns were rare. The biggest was Dun Gwerbyn, which held some five hundred round thatched houses, a couple of inns, and three temples inside its high stone walls. On a hill in the center of town stood the dun, or fort, of the tieryn. Another set of stone walls sheltered stables and barracks for the tieryn's warband of a hundred men, a collection of huts and storage sheds, and the broch complex itself, a four-story round stone tower with two shorter towers attached at the sides.

On that particular morning, the open ward around the broch was a-bustle with servants, carrying supplies to the cookhouse or stacks of firewood to the hearths in the great hall, or rolling big barrels of ale from the sheds to the broch. Near the iron-bound gates, other servants bowed low as they greeted the arriving wedding guests. Cullyn of Cerrmor, captain of the tieryn's warband, assembled his men out in the ward and looked them over. For a change, they were all bathed, shaved, and presentable.

"Well and good, lads," Cullyn said. "You don't look bad for a pack of hounds. Now remember: every lord and lady in the tierynrhyn is going to be here today. I don't want any of you getting stinking drunk, and I don't want any fighting, either. This is a wedding, remember, and the lady deserves to have it be a happy one after everything she's been through."

They all nodded solemnly. If any of them forgot his orders, they'd regret it—and they knew it.

Cullyn led them into the great hall, an enormous round room that took up the full ground floor of the broch. Today there were freshly braided rushes on the floor; the tapestries on the walls had been shaken out and rehung. The hall was crammed with extra tables. Not only were there plenty of noble guests, but each lord had brought five men from his warband as an honor escort. Servants sidled and edged their way through the crowd with tankards of ale and baskets of bread; a bard played almost unheard; the riders diced for coppers and joked; up by the honor hearth, the noble-born ladies chattered like birds while their husbands drank. Cullyn got his men settled, repeated his order about no fighting, then worked his way through to the table of honor to kneel at the tieryn's side.

Tieryn Lovyan was something of an anomaly in Deverry, a woman who ruled a large demesne in her own name. Originally her only brother had held this dun, but when he died without an heir, she'd inherited under a twist in the laws designed to keep big holdings in a clan even if a woman had to rule them. Forty-eight that year, she was still a good-looking woman, with gray-streaked raven black hair, large cornflower blue eyes, and the straight-backed posture of one quite at home with rulership. That particular day, she was wearing a dress of red Bardek silk, kirtled in with the red, white, and brown plaid of the Clw Coc clan.

"The warband is in attendance, my lady," Cullyn said.

"Splendid, Captain. Have you seen Nevyn yet?"

"I haven't, my lady."

"It would be like him to stay away. He does so hate crowds and suchlike, but if you do see him, tell him to come sit with me."

Cullyn rose, bowed, and returned to his men. From his seat, he could see the honor table, and while he sipped his ale, he studied the bride at this wedding, Lady Donilla, a truly beautiful woman with a mane of chestnut hair, clasped back like a maiden's now for the formality of the thing. Cullyn felt sorry for her. Her first husband, Gwerbret Rhys of Aberwyn, had recently cast her off for being barren. If Lovyan hadn't found her a husband, she would have had to return to her brother's dun in shame. As it was, her new man, Lord Garedd, was a decent-looking fellow some years older than she, with gray in his blond hair and thick mustache. From what the men in his warband said, he was an honorable man, soft-spoken in peace and utterly ruthless in war. He was also a widower with a pack of children and thus more than glad to take a beautiful young wife, barren or not.

"Garedd looks honestly besotted with her, doesn't he?" Nevyn remarked.

With a yelp, Cullyn turned to find the old man grinning at him. For all that Nevyn's face was as lined as an old leather sack, he had all the vigor and stamina of a young lad, and he stood there straight-backed, his hands on his hips.

"Didn't mean to startle you," he said with a sly grin.

"Here, I never saw you come in!"

"You weren't looking my way, that's all. I didn't turn myself invisible, although I'll admit to having a bit of a jest on you."

"And I took the bait, sure enough. Here, the tieryn wants you to come sit with her."

"At the honor table? What a cursed nuisance. It's a good thing I put on a clean shirt."

Cullyn laughed. Usually Nevyn dressed like a farmer in shabby brown clothes, but today he'd actually put on a white shirt with Lovyan's red lion blazon at the yokes and a pair of patched but respectable gray brigga.

"Before you go," Cullyn said. "Have you had any . . . well, news of my Jill?"

"You mean: have I scryed her out lately. Come with me."

They made their way over to the second hearth, where an

entire hog was roasting on a spit. For a moment Nevyn stared intently into the flames.

"I see Jill and Rhodry looking in good spirits," he said at last. "They're walking through a town on a nice sunny day, going up to a shop of some sort. Wait! I know that place. It's Otho the Silversmith's in Dun Manannan, but he doesn't seem to be in at the moment."

"I don't suppose you can tell if she's with child."

"She's not showing the babe if she is. I can understand your concern."

"Well, it's bound to happen, sooner or later. I just hope she has the wit to ride home when it does."

"She's never lacked for wit."

Although Cullyn agreed, worry ate at him. Jill was, after all, his only child.

"I just hope they have enough coin for the winter," the captain remarked.

"Well, we gave them plenty between us, if Rhodry doesn't drink it all away, anyway."

"Oh, Jill won't let him do that. My lass is as tight as an old farmwife with every cursed copper." He allowed himself a brief smile. "At least she knows the long road cursed well."

Because the mattress was full of bedbugs, Rhodry sat on the floor of the tiny innchamber while he watched Jill frowning in concentration as she mended a rip in his only shirt. She was dressed in a pair of dirty blue brigga and a lad's plain linen overshirt, and her golden hair was cropped short like a lad's, too, but she was so beautiful, with her wide blue eyes, delicate features, and soft mouth, that he loved simply looking at her.

"Ah by the black hairy ass of the Lord of Hell!" she snarled at last. "This'll just have to do. I *hate* sewing."

"You have my humble thanks for lowering yourself enough to mend my clothes."

With another snarl, she threw the shirt into his face. Laughing he shook it out, once-white linen stained with sweat and rust from his mail. On the yokes were the blazons of the red lion, all that he had left of his old life when he'd been heir to the tier-ynrhyn of Dun Gwerbyn. He pulled the shirt on, then buckled his swordbelt over it. At the left hung his sword, a beautiful blade of the best steel with the handguard worked in the form of a dragon, and at the right, the silver dagger that branded him as a dishonored man. It was the badge of a band of mercenaries who wandered the roads either singly or in pairs and fought only for coin, not loyalty or honor. In his case, it branded him as something even stranger, which was why they'd come to Dun Manannan.

"Do you think the silversmith will be in by now?" he said.

"No doubt. Otho rarely leaves his shop for any length of time."

Together they went out into the unwalled town, a straggling collection of round thatched houses and shops along a river. On the bank were fishing boats, an old and shabby lot, and from the look of them barely seaworthy.

"I don't see how these folk make a living from the sea," Rhodry remarked.

"Hush." Jill glanced around and made sure that no one was nearby, but still she dropped her voice to a whisper. "They make the boats look bad for a reason. There's more than one kind of cargo that comes in under the mackerel."

"Ye gods! You mean we're staying in a den of smugglers?"

"Keep your voice down! Just that."

Otho's shop was on the very edge of town, across a dirt path from a field of cabbages. Rhodry was pleased when he saw that the door was no longer padlocked. When Jill opened it, silver bells tinkled overhead.

"Who's there?" bellowed a deep voice.

"Jill, Cullyn of Cerrmor's daughter, and another silver dagger."

Rhodry followed her into an empty chamber, a small wedge of the round house set off by dirty wickerwork panels. In one panel was a frayed green blanket that did duty for a door, because Otho shoved it aside and came out. Although he was only four and a half feet tall, he was perfectly proportioned and muscular at that, with arms like a miniature blacksmith. He had a heavy gray beard, neatly cropped, and shrewd dark eyes.

"Well, Jill it is," he said. "And it gladdens my heart to see you again. Where's your Da, and who's this lad?"

"Da's in Eldidd. He won himself a place as captain of a tieryn's warband."

"Did he now?" Otho smiled in sincere pleasure. "I always thought he was too good a man to carry the silver dagger. But what have you done? Run off with this pretty face here?"

"Now here!" Rhodry snarled. "Cullyn gave her leave to go."

Otho snorted in profound disbelief.

"It's true," Jill broke in. "Da even pledged him to the silver dagger."

"Indeed?" The smith still looked suspicious, but he let the matter drop. "What brings you to me, lad? Have some battle-loot to sell?"

"I don't. I've come about my silver dagger."

"What have you done, nicked it or suchlike? I don't see how any man could bruise that metal."

"He wants the dweomer taken off it," Jill said. "Can you do that, Otho? Remove the spell on the blade?"

The smith turned, openmouthed in surprise.

"I know cursed well it's got one on it," she went on. "Rhoddo, take it out and show him."

Reluctantly Rhodry drew the dagger from its worn sheath. It was a lovely thing, that blade, as silky as silver, but harder than steel, some alloy that only a few smiths knew how to blend. On it was graved the device of a striking falcon (Cullyn's old mark, because the dagger had once belonged to him,) but in Rhodry's hand the device was almost invisible in a blaze and flare of dweomer-light, running like water from the blade.

"Elven blood in your veins, is there?" Otho snapped. "And a good bit of it, too."

"Well, there's some." Rhodry made the admission unwillingly. "I hail from the west, you see, and that old proverb about there being elven blood in Eldidd veins is true enough."

When Otho grabbed the dagger, the light dimmed to a faint glow.

"I'm not letting you in my workshop," he announced. "You people all steal. Can't even help it, I suppose; it's probably the way you were raised."

"By every god in the Otherlands, I'm not a thief! I was born and raised a Maelwaedd, and it's not my cursed fault that there's wild blood somewhere in my clan's quarterings."

"Hah! I'm still not letting you into my workshop." He turned and pointedly spoke only to Jill. "It's a hard thing you're asking, lass. I don't have true dweomer. This spell is the only one I can weave, and I don't even understand what I'm doing. It's just somewhat that we pass down from father to son, those of us who know it at all, that is."

"I was afraid of that," she said with a sigh. "But we've got to do somewhat about it. He can't use it at table when it turns dweomer every time he draws it."

Otho considered, chewing on his lower lip.

"Well, if this were an ordinary dagger, I'd just trade you a new one without the spell, but since it was Cullyn's and all, I'll try to unweave the dweomer. Maybe working it all backward will blunt the spell. But it's going to cost you dear. There's a risk in meddling with things like this."

After a couple of minutes of brisk haggling, Jill handed him five silver pieces, about half of the smith's asking price.

"Come back at sunset," Otho said. "We'll see if I've been successful or not."

Rhodry spent the afternoon looking for a hire. Although it was too close to winter weather for warfare, he did find a merchant who was taking a load of goods back to Cerrmor. For all their dishonor, silver daggers were in much demand as caravan guards, because they belonged to a band with a reputation that kept them more honest than most. Not just any man could even become a silver dagger. A warrior who was desperate enough to take the blade had to first find another silver dagger, ride with him a while, and prove himself before he was allowed to meet one of the rare smiths who served the band. Only then could he truly "ride the long road," as the daggers referred to their lives.

And if Otho could blunt the spell, Rhodry would no longer have to keep his dagger sheathed for fear of revealing his peculiar bloodlines. He hurried Jill through her dinner and hustled her along to the silversmith's shop a little before sunset. Otho's beard was a good bit shorter, and he no longer had any eyebrows at all.

"I should have known better than to do a favor for a cursed elf," he announced.

"Otho, you have our humble apologies." Jill caught his hand and squeezed. "And I'm ever so glad you didn't get badly burned."

"*You're* glad? Hah! Well, come along, lad."

When Rhodry took the dagger, the blade stayed ordinary metal without the trace of a glow. He was smiling as he sheathed it.

"My thanks, good smith, a thousand times over. Truly, I wish I could reward you more for the risk you ran."

"So do I. That's the way of your folk, though: all fine words and no hard coin."

"Otho, please," Jill said. "There's not even that much elven blood in him."

"Hah! That's what I say to that, young Jill. Hah!"

All day, the People arrived at the alardan. To a grassy meadow so far west of Eldidd that only one human being had ever seen it, they came in small groups, driving their herds of horses and flocks of sheep before them. After they pastured the animals, they set up leather tents, painted in bright colors with pictures of animals and flowers. Children and dogs raced through the camp; cooking fires blossomed; the smell of a feast grew in the air. By sunset well over a hundred tents stood there. As the last fire was lit, a woman began to sing the long wailing tale of Donabel and his lost love, Adario. A harper joined in, then a drummer, and finally someone brought out a conaber, three joined reedy pipes for a drone.

Devaberiel Silverhand, generally considered the best bard in this part of the elven lands, considered unpacking his harp and joining in, but he was quite simply too hungry. He got a wooden bowl and spoon from his tent, then wandered through the feast. Each riding group, or alar to give them their Elvish name, had made a huge quantity of one particular dish. Everyone strolled around, eating a bit here and there of whatever appealed to them, while the music, talk, and laughter went on. Devaberiel was searching for Manaverr, whose alar traditionally roasted a whole lamb in a pit.

Finally he found them near the edge of the camp. A couple of young men were just digging the lamb up, while others brought over leaves to make a clean bed to receive it. Manaverr himself hurried over to greet the bard. His hair was so pale that it was almost white, and his cat-slit eyes a deep purple. They each put their left hand on the other's right shoulder in greeting.

"It's a big gathering," Manaverr said.

"They all knew you'd be here to do the lamb."

Manaverr laughed with a toss of his head. A small green sprite popped into manifestation and perched on his shoulder. When he reached up to pat her, she grinned, revealing a mouthful of pointed teeth.

"Have you seen Calonderiel yet?" Manaverr said.

"The warleader? No. Why?"

"He's been asking every bard here about some obscure point of somebody's genealogy. He'll probably work his way around to you sooner or later."

The sprite suddenly pulled his hair, then vanished before he could swat her. The alardan was filled with Wildfolk, rushing around as excitedly as the children. Sprite, gnome, sylph, and salamander, they were the spirits of the elements, who at times took on a solid appearance, even though their home lay elsewhere in the many-layered universe. Devaberiel was not quite sure where; only dweomerfolk knew such things.

With one last heave, the men got up the lamb, wrapped in charred coarse cloth, and flopped it onto the leaves. The smell of the roast meat, heavily spiced and baked with fruit, was so inviting that Devaberiel moved closer without even being aware that he was doing so, but he had to wait for his portion. Calonderiel the warleader strode over and hailed him. He looked much like Manaverr, his cousin.

"What's this mysterious question?" the bard asked him.

"Just a point of curiosity," Calonderiel said. "You know that I rode with Aderyn when he was off chasing Loddlaen, don't you?"

"I heard something of the story."

"All right, then. I met a human warleader called Rhodry Maelwaedd, a lad of twenty. Strangely enough, he's got a good bit of our blood in his veins. I was wondering if you knew how it had gotten into his clan."

"A woman of the People married Pertyc Maelwaedd in . . . oh, when was that . . . well, say two hundred years ago."

"That long? But I saw Rhodry handle a piece of dwarven silver, and it blazed in his hands."

"Really? Then it can't just be that distant relationship. What was his father's name?"

"Tingyr Maelwaedd, and his mother is Lovyan of the Clw Coc."

Devaberiel went very still. When had that been? He could still see her face in his mind, a beautiful lass for all her blunt ears and round eyes, and she'd been so melancholy about something. But when? that unusually dry summer, wasn't it? Yes, and it was twenty-one years ago, all right.

"Oh by the Dark Sun herself!" Devaberiel burst out. "Here I never even knew I'd gotten Lovva with child!"

"And isn't that a fine jest?" Calonderiel said with a crow of laughter. "I certainly picked the perfect bard to answer my question. You have a peculiar fondness for round-ear women, my friend."

"There haven't been *that* many."

When Calonderiel started to laugh, Devaberiel threw a punch his way.

"Stop howling like a goblin! I want to know about this son of mine. Every detail you can remember."

Not many days later, Rhodry was the subject of another discussion, this one in Bardek, far across the Southern Sea. In an upstairs room of an isolated villa, deep in the hill country of the main island, two men lounged on a purple divan and watched a third, sitting at a table littered with parchment scrolls and books. He was grossly fat, as saggy and wrinkled as a torn leather ball, and only a few wisps of white hair clung to his dark-skinned skull. Whenever he glanced up, his eyelids drooped uncontrollably, half-covering his brown eyes. He had immersed himself so thoroughly and so long in the craft of the dark dweomer that he no longer had a name. He was simply the Old One.

The other two men were both from Deverry. Alastyr, who looked fifty but was actually closer to seventy, was a solid sort with a squarish face and gray hair. At first sight he looked like a typical Cerrmor merchant, with his checked brigga and nicely embroidered shirt, and indeed, he took great pains to act the part. The other, Sarcyn, had just turned thirty. His thick blond hair, dark blue eyes, and regular features should have made him handsome, but there was something about the way he smiled, something about the burning expression in his eyes, that made most people find him repellent. They both spoke not a word until the Old One looked up, tipping his head back so that he could see them.

"I have gone over all the major calculations." His voice was like the rasp of two dead twigs rubbed together. "There's some hidden thing at work here that I don't understand, some secret, some force of Destiny, perhaps, that has interfered with our plans."

"Could it simply be the Master of the Aethyr?" Alastyr said. "Loddlaen's war was going splendidly until he intervened."

The Old One shook his head no and picked up a parchment sheet.

"This is the horoscope of Tingyr, Rhodry's father. My art is very complex, little Alastyr. A single horoscope reveals few secrets."

"I see. I didn't realize that."

"No doubt, because few know the stars as I do. Now, most fools think that when a man dies, his horoscope is of no more use, but astrology is the art of studying beginnings. Whatever a man begins in his life—like a son, for instance—is influenced by his stars, even after his death. Now, when I correlated this horoscope with certain transits, it seemed clear that this summer Tingyr would lose a son through deceit on someone's part. The other brother's chart showed that he was in no danger, so obviously Rhodry had to be the son lost."

"Well, the year's not over yet. It would be easy to send assassins after him."

"Easy and quite useless. The omens clearly show that he will die in battle. Have you forgotten everything I ever told you?"

"My humble apologies."

"Besides, the Deverry year ends on Samaen. We have less than a month now. No, it's as I say. Some hidden thing is at work here." He let his glance linger on the heaped table. "And yet, it seems that I had all the information I could possibly need. This may bode ill—for all of us. No, Alastyr, we'll send no assassins, nothing so hasty until I unravel this puzzle."

"As you wish, of course."

"Of course." The Old One picked up a bone stylus and idly tapped another parchment. "This woman puzzles me, too. Very greatly does Jill puzzle me. There was nothing in the omens about a woman who could fight like a man. I wish more information about her, her birthdate if possible, so that I can scribe out her stars."

"I'll make every effort to find it for you when I return."

With a nod of approval that set his chins trembling, the Old One shifted his bulk in his chair.

"Send your apprentice to fetch me my meal."

Alastyr gestured at Sarcyn, who rose and obediently left the room. The Old One contemplated the closed door for a moment.

"That one hates you," he said at last.

"He does? I wasn't aware of it."

"No doubt he's taken great pains to hide it. Now, it's fit and right that an apprentice struggle with his master. How best does a true man learn but by fighting for knowledge? But hatred? It's very dangerous."

Alastyr wondered if the Old One had seen an omen that indicated Sarcyn was a real threat. The master would never tell except for a stiff price. The Old One was the greatest expert alive in one particular part of the dark dweomer, that of wresting hints of future events from a universe unwilling to reveal them. His personal perversion of astrology was only part of the art, which involved meditation and a dangerous kind of astral scrying as well. Since he was scrupulously honest in his own way as well as valuable, he commanded a respect and loyalty rare among dark dweomermen and was, in a limited sense, as much of a leader as their "brotherhood" could ever have. Since his age and bulk confined him to this villa, Alastyr had struck a bargain with him. In return for the master's aid with his own plans, he was doing such portions of the Old One's work that required traveling.

In a few minutes Sarcyn returned with a bowl on a tray, set it down in front of the Old One, then took his place at Alastyr's side. The bowl held raw meat, freshly killed and mixed with the still warm blood, a necessary food for aged masters of the dark arts. The Old One scooped up a delicate fingerful and licked it off.

"Now, as for your own work," he said. "The time is growing ripe to obtain what you seek, but you must be very careful. I know you've taken many precautions, but consider how carefully we worked to eliminate Rhodry. You know full well how that ended."

"I assure you that I'll be constantly on guard."

"Good. Next summer, a certain configuration of planets will lie adversely in the horoscope of the High King of Deverry. This grouping in turn is influenced by subtle factors beyond your understanding. All these omens taken together indicate that the King might lose a powerful guardian if someone worked to that end."

"Splendid! The jewel I seek is just such a guardian."

The Old One paused for another scoop and lick.

"This is all very interesting, little Alastyr. So far, you've kept your side of our bargain, perhaps even better than you can know. So many strange things." He sounded almost dreamy. "Very, very interesting. We'll see, when you return to Deverry, if more strange things come your way. Do you see what I mean? You must be on guard every single moment."

Alastyr felt an icy cold clench his stomach. He was being warned, no matter how circumspectly, that the Old One could no longer trust his own predictions.

Devaberiel Silverhand knelt in his red leather tent and methodically rummaged through a wall bag embroidered with vines and roses. Since it was quite large, it took him a while to find what he was looking for. Irritably he scrabbled through old trophies from singing contests, the clumsy first piece of embroidery his daughter had ever done, two mismatched silver buckles, a bottle of Bardek scent, and a wooden horse given to him by a lover whose name he'd forgotten. At the very bottom he found the small leather pouch, so old that it was cracking.

He opened it and shook a ring out into his hand. Although it was made of dwarven silver, and thus still as shiny as the day he'd put it away, it had no dweomer upon it, or at least, none that any sage or dweomerperson had been able to unravel. A silver band, about a third of an inch wide, it was engraved with roses on the outside and a few words in elvish characters but some unknown language on the inside. In the two hundred years he'd had this ring, he'd never found a sage who could read it.

The way he'd come by it was equally mysterious. He was a young man, then, just finished with his bardic training and riding with the alar of a woman he particularly fancied. One afternoon a traveller rode up on a fine golden stallion. When Devaberiel and a couple of the other men strolled out to greet him, they received quite a surprise. Although from a distance he looked like an ordinary man of the People, with the dark hair and jet-black eyes of someone from the far west, up close it was hard to tell just what he did look like. It seemed that his features changed constantly though subtlely, that at times his mouth was wider, then thinner, that he became shorter, then taller. He dismounted and looked over the welcoming party.

"I wish to speak with Devaberiel the bard," he announced.

"Then here I am."

"Excellent. I have a present for one of your sons, young bard, for sons you'll have. When each is born, consult with someone who knows the dweomer. They'll be able to tell which one receives the gift."

When he handed over the pouch and the ring, his eyes seemed more blue than black.

"My thanks, good sir, but who are you?"

The stranger merely smiled, then mounted his horse and rode off without another word.

Over the intervening years, Devaberiel had learned nothing more about the ring or its mysterious giver, not from sage nor dweomer-master. When each of his two sons was born, he'd dutifully consulted with the dweomerfolk, but each time the omens had been wrong to pass the gift on. Now, however, he'd gained a third son. Holding the ring, he walked to the door of the tent and looked out. A cold, gray drizzle fell over the camp, and the wind was brisk. He was going to have an uncomfortable journey, but he was determined to find the dweomerwoman who seemed to have the most affinity for the ring. His curiosity was not going to let him rest until he found out if it belonged to young Rhodry ap Devaberiel, who still thought himself a Maelwaedd.

Driven by a bitter-cold wind, the rains slashed down hard in the gray streets of Cerrmor. There was little for Jill and Rhodry to do but hole up like foxes in their inn by the north gate. Since they had enough coin to stay warm and fed all winter, Jill felt as rich and happy as a lord, but Rhodry fell into the black mood that can only be given the untranslatable name of hiraedd, a painful longing for some unobtainable thing. He would sit in the tavern room for hours, slumped down and staring into a tankard of ale while he brooded over his dishonor. Nothing Jill could do or say would rouse him out of it. Eventually, although it ached her heart to do it, she let him have his silence.

At least at night, when they went up to their chamber, she

could use kisses and caresses to bring him round. After their lovemaking he would be happy for a while, talking with her as they lay tight in each other's arms. When he drifted off to sleep, often she would stay awake and look at him as if he were a puzzle to be studied out. Rhodry was a tall man, heavily muscled but built straight from shoulder to hip, with long, sensitive hands that hinted at his elven blood. He had the raven-dark hair and cornflower blue eyes so typical of Eldidd men, but there was nothing typical about his good looks. His features were so perfect that he would have looked girlish if it weren't for the various small scars and battle-nicks on his face. Since she'd met some of the Elcyion Lacar, Jill knew that they too were as handsome. She would wonder over that trace of elven blood in his clan, which had, or so Nevyn assured her, merely all come out in him, a throwback. Logically, it seemed improbable.

One night her long pondering brought her the answer to the problem. Every now and then, Jill had true dreams, which were actually dweomer-visions beyond the control of her conscious mind. Generally they came, as this one did, when she'd been thinking over a problem for some time. On a night when the rain beat upon the shutters and the wind howled around the inn, she fell asleep in Rhodry's arms and dreamt of the Elcyion Lacar. It seemed that she flew above the western grasslands on a day when the sun broke through clouds only to vanish again. Far below her in a green sea of grass stood a cluster of elven tents, glowing like many-colored jewels.

Suddenly she stood on the ground among them. Bundled in a red cloak, a tall man strode past her and into a purple and blue tent. On a whim, she followed. The tent was elaborately decorated with woven hangings, embroidered wall bags, and Bardek carpets for floor cloths. Sitting on a pile of leather cushions was an elven woman, her pale blond hair bound into two long braids that hung behind her ears, which were as long and delicately pointed as seashells. Her visitor pressed his palms together and bowed to her, then doffed the cloak and sat down on the carpet nearby. His hair was as pale as moonlight, and his dark blue eyes were, like all elven eyes, slit vertically with a pupil like a cat's. Yet Jill thought that he was as handsome as her Rhodry in his alien way and also oddly familiar.

"Very well, Devaberiel," the woman said, and although she

spoke in Elvish, Jill could understand her. "I've been studying my stones, and I have an answer for you."

"My thanks, Valandario." He leaned closer.

At that point Jill realized that a cloth, embroidered in geometric patterns, lay between them. At various points on the web of triangles and squares lay spherical gems: rubies, yellow beryls, sapphires, emeralds, and amethysts. In the middle of the cloth lay a simple silver ring. Valandario began moving the gems along the various lines, finally bringing one of each color into the center to form a pentagon around the ring.

"Your son's Destiny is encircled by this ring," she said. "But I know not what that Destiny may be, except to say that it lies somewhat in the north and somewhat in the air. Doubtless all will be revealed in due time."

"As the gods desire. You have my solemn thanks for this. I'll see to it that Rhodry gets the ring, then. I might ride to Dun Gwerbyn myself to have a look at this lad of mine."

"It would be unwise to tell him the truth."

"Of course. I don't want to meddle with the political successions of all Eldidd. I just want to see him. After all, it's quite a surprise to learn you've got a full-grown son you never even knew existed. Though Lovyan could hardly have sent me word, of course, with her still married to her powerful warleader."

"I see your point." Valandario suddenly looked up, right at Jill. "Here! Who are you, to come spying upon me in the spirit?"

When Jill tried to answer, she found that she couldn't speak. In exasperation, Valandario threw up one hand and sketched a sigil in the air. All at once Jill found herself awake, sitting up in bed with Rhodry snoring beside her. Since the room was cold, she lay down and hurriedly snuggled under the blankets. That was a true dream, she thought, oh by the Goddess of the Moon, my lover's half an elf!

For a long while she lay awake, thinking over the dream. Of course Devaberiel would look familiar since he was Rhodry's father. She was honestly shocked to find out that Lady Lovyan, whom she much admired, had put horns on her husband's head, but then, Devaberiel was an exceptionally handsome man. She had the brief thought of telling Rhodry about the dream, but Valandario's warning stopped her. Besides, finding out that he was no true Maelwaedd, but a bastard, would only drive Rhodry deeper into his hiraedd. She could barely put up with his fits of it as it was.

And then there was the silver ring. Here was another proof of what Nevyn had told her, that Rhodry's Wyrd was deep and hidden. She decided that if she ever saw the old man again, she would tell him of the omens. As she was drifting back to sleep, she wondered if her path would ever cross his again. For all that his dweomer frightened her, she was very fond of Nevyn, but the kingdom was very large, and who knew which way the old man would choose to wander.

On the morrow, the full significance of the dream came to her as she and Rhodry sat in the tavern room. Yet once again, the dweomer had irrupted into her mind, taken her over with no warning. For a moment she shrank into herself, just as when the hare hears dogs baying and crouches frozen in the bracken.

"Is somewhat wrong, my love?" Rhodry said.

"Naught, naught. I was just . . . oh, thinking about Lodd-laen's war last summer."

"It was a strange thing, sure enough." He dropped his voice to a whisper. "All that cursed dweomer! I pray to every god we're never touched by the dweomer again."

Although she nodded her agreement, Jill knew that he was praying for the impossible. Even as he spoke, her little gray gnome manifested onto the table and sat down by Rhodry's tankard. All her life, Jill had been able to see the Wildfolk, and this particular skinny, big-nosed little creature was a close friend. Oh my poor Rhoddo, she thought, you ride with dweomer all around you! She felt both angry and frightened, wishing that her peculiar talents would go away, fearing that they never would.

Yet once, last summer, Nevyn had told her that if she refused to use her talents, they would eventually wither and be gone. Although she hoped that the old man was right—indeed, he knew far more about the matter than she did—she had her doubts, especially when she considered how dweomer had swept her into Rhodry's war and Rhodry's life that last summer. She'd been an utterly obscure person, the bastard daughter of a silver dagger, until her father had taken what seemed to be a perfectly ordinary hire, guarding a merchant caravan that was traveling to the western border of Eldidd. Yet from the moment that the merchant had offered Cullyn the job, she'd known that some-

thing unusual was going to happen, felt with an inexplicable
certainty that her life had reached a crossroads. How right she'd
been! First the caravan went west to the land of the Elcyion
Lacar, the elves, a people who were supposed to exist only in
fairy tale and myth. Then, with some of the elves in tow, they'd
returned to Eldidd and ridden right into the middle of a dweomer war.

Just in time for her to save Rhodry's life by killing a man who,
or so the dweomer seemed to declare, was invincible—Lord
Corbyn will never die by any *man's* hand, or so a prophecy
declared. Like all dweomer-riddles, this one had two sharp sides,
and a lass's hand had slain him, sure enough. As she thought
about it, it all seemed entirely too neat, too clever, as if the gods
shaped a person's Wyrd the way a Bardek craftsman shapes a
puzzle box with its precise little workings that mean absolutely
nothing in the long run. And then she remembered the elves,
who were not men in any true sense, and Rhodry himself, who
was only half a one. She saw then that Rhodry might have slain
his enemy himself, if only he'd believed he could, and that her
coming, while convenient, need not be foreordained anymore
than a snowstorm that appears in winter could be said to be a
mighty act of dweomer.

Yet dweomer had brought her to him; that she was sure of, if
not to save his life, then for some obscure purpose. Although she
shuddered at the thought, she also found herself wondering why
dweomer should frighten her so badly, why she was sure that
following the dweomer road would lead her to her death. Suddenly she saw it: she was afraid that if ever she tampered with
dweomer, it would bring not only her death, but Rhodry's. Even
though she told herself that the idea was stupid, it was a long time
before she could shake the irrational feeling off.

Deverry, 773

All men have seen the two smiling faces of the Goddess, She who gives good harvests and She who brings love to men's hearts. Some have seen Her stern face, the Mother who at times must chastise her erring children. But how many have ever seen the fourth face of the Goddess, which is hidden even to most women who walk the earth?

The Discourses of the Priestess Camylla

The rider was dying. He slid off his horse to the cobbles, staggered once and fell to his knees. Gweniver flung herself down and grabbed him by the shoulders before he fell on his face. Warm blood oozed through his shirt onto her hands as Claedd peered cloudy-eyed at her.

"Lost, my lady. Your brother's dead."

Blood welled into his mouth and broke in a bubble of death. When she laid him down, his foundered horse tossed its head once, then merely trembled, dripping gray sweat. She got to her feet just as a stable lad came running.

"Do what you can for that horse," she said. "Then tell all the servants to pack up and flee. You've got to get out of here or you won't live the night."

Wiping her hands on her dress, Gweniver ran across the ward to the tall broch of the Wolf clan, which would burn that night beyond her power to save it. Inside the great hall, huddled by the honor hearth, were her mother, Dolyan, her younger sister, Macla, and Mab, their aged serving woman.

"The Boar's men must have caught the warband on the road," Gweniver said. "Avoic's dead, and there's an end to the feud."

Dolyan threw back her head and keened out a wail for her husband and three sons. Macla burst into moist sobs and clung to Mab.

"Oh, hold your tongues!" Gweniver snapped. "The Boar's

warband is doubtless riding here right now to claim us. Do you want to end up as trophies?"

"Gwen!" Macla wailed. "How can you be so cold-hearted?"

"Better cold-hearted than raped. Now hurry, all of you. Get the things you can carry on one horse. We're riding to the Temple of the Moon. If we live to reach it, the priestesses will give us refuge. Do you hear me, Mam, or do you want to see me and Maccy handed over to the warband?"

The deliberate brutality forced Dolyan silent.

"Good," Gweniver said. "Now hurry, all of you!"

She followed the others as they puffed up the spiral staircase, but she went to her brother's chamber, not her own. From the carved chest beside his bed she got a pair of his old brigga and one of his shirts. Changing into his clothes brought her a scatter of tears—she'd been fond of Avoic, who was only fourteen—but there was no time for mourning. She belted on his second-best sword and an old dagger. Although she was far from being a trained warrior, her brothers had taught her how to handle a sword, simply because in those days one never knew when a woman would have to swing one in her own defense. Finally she unclasped her long blond hair and cut it off short with the dagger. At night she would look enough like a man to give any lone marauder pause about attacking her party on the road.

Since they had over thirty miles to go to reach safety, Gweniver bullied the other women into riding fast, trotting, and occasionally galloping in short bursts. Every now and then, she would turn in her saddle and scan the road for the dust cloud that would mean death chasing them. Shortly after sunset, the full moon rose to shed her holy light to guide them. By then, her mother was swaying in the saddle with exhaustion. Gweniver saw a copse of alders off to one side of the road and led the others there for a brief rest. Dolyan and Mab had to be helped down from their saddles.

Gweniver walked back to the road to stand guard. Far away on the horizon, in the direction from which they'd come, a golden glow flared like the rising of a tiny moon. It was most likely the dun burning. She drew her sword and clutched the hilt while she stared unthinking at the glare. Suddenly she heard hoofbeats and saw a rider galloping down the road. Behind her in the copse the horses nickered a greeting, unknowing traitors.

"Mount!" she screamed. "Get ready to ride!"

The rider pulled up, then dismounted and drew his sword. As he strode toward her, she saw his bronze cloak pin glittering in the moonlight: a Boarsman.

"And who are you, lad?" he said.

Gweniver dropped to a fighting crouch.

"A page of the Wolf from your silence. And what are you guarding so faithfully? I hate to kill a slip of a lad like you, but orders are orders, so come now, turn the ladies over to me."

In utter desperation Gweniver lunged and struck. Taken off-guard, the Boarsman slipped, his sword swinging up wildly. She cut again and sliced him hard on one side of his neck, then struck back on the other, just as her older brother Benoic had taught her. With a moan of disbelief, the Boarsman buckled to his knees and died at her feet. Gweniver nearly vomited. In the moonlight the sword blade was dark wet with blood, not shiny clean like in the practice sessions. Her mother's shriek of terror brought her back to her senses. She ran for the Boarsman's horse, grabbed the reins just as it was about to bolt, then led it back to the copse.

"That ever it would come to this!" Mab sobbed. "That a lass I tended would be forced to turn warrior on the roads! Oh holy gods all, when will you have mercy on the kingdom?"

"When it suits them and not a minute before," Gweniver said. "Now get on those horses! We've got to get out of here."

Deep in the middle of the night, they reached the Temple of the Moon, which sat at the top of a hill with a good stone wall around its compound. Along with his friends and vassals, Gweniver's father had given the coin to build the wall, a far-sighted generosity on his part that was now saving his wife and daughters. If any battle-drunk warrior were insane enough to break geis and risk the Goddess's wrath by demanding entry, the wall would keep him out until he'd come to his senses. At the gates, Gweniver screamed and yelled and kept it up until at last she heard a frightened voice call back that its owner was on the way. A priestess draped in a shawl yanked the gates open a bare crack, then shoved them wider when she saw Dolyan.

"Oh my lady, has the worst come upon your clan?"

"It has. Will you shelter us?"

"Gladly, but I don't know what to do about this lad with you."

"It's only Gwen in her brother's clothes," Gweniver broke in. "I thought we'd best pretend to have a man with us."

"Well and good, then," the priestess said with a nervous laugh. "Now ride in quickly, all of you."

Dark and shadowed in the moonlight, the vast temple compound was crowded with buildings, some of stone, others hastily thrown together out of wood. Priestesses with cloaks thrown over their nightdresses clustered around the refugees and helped the older women dismount in a chatter of soothing whispers. Some took the horses to the stables; others led Gweniver and her party to the long wooden guest house. Once an elegant place for visiting noblewomen, it was now crowded with cots and chests, because women of all ranks were sheltering there. The blood feud that had reduced the Wolf clan to three women was only one thread in a hideous tapestry of civil war.

By the light of a candle lantern the priestesses found the newest arrivals empty cots in a corner. In the midst of the whispers and confusion, Gweniver lay down on the nearest one and fell asleep, boots, sword belt, and all.

She woke to find a silent, empty dormitory flooded with light from the narrow windows near the roof. She'd come to this temple so often that for a moment she was confused: was she here to pray about her vocation or to represent her clan at the harvest rite? Then the memory came back, sharp as a sword thrust.

"Avoic," she whispered. "Oh, Avoic!"

Yet no tears came, and she realized that she was hungry. Sore and stretching, she got up and wandered through a doorway at the end of the dormitory into the refectory, a narrow room crammed with tables for desperate guests. A neophyte in a white dress kirtled with green screamed aloud.

"My apologies, Gwen," she said, laughing. "I thought you were a lad for a moment. Sit down, and I'll fetch you porridge."

Gweniver unbuckled the sword belt and slung it on the table next to her as she sat down. She ran one finger down Avoic's second-best scabbard, which was chaped in tarnished silver and inlaid with spirals and interlaced wolves. By all rights under the law, she was the head of the Wolf clan now, but she doubted if she could ever claim her position. For her to inherit in the female line she would have to overcome more obstacles than Tieryn Burcan of the Boar.

In a few minutes Ardda, high priestess of the temple, came in to sit beside her. Although she was close to sixty, with gray hair and web of lines around her eyes, Ardda's step and carriage were as lithe as a young lass's.

"Well, Gwen," she said. "You've been telling me for years that you want to be a priestess. Has the time come upon you now or not?"

"I don't know, my lady. You know that I've always had doubts about my calling . . . well, if I have any choice in the matter now."

"Don't forget that you've got the Wolf lands for a dowry. When the news spreads, I'll wager that many a man among your father's allies will want to come fetch you out."

"But oh ye gods, I've never wanted to marry!"

With a little sigh, Ardda unconsciously reached up and touched her right cheek, which was covered with the blue tattoo of the crescent moon. Any man who touched in lust a woman with that mark was put to death. Not only the noble lords, but any freeborn man would have slain the defiler, because if the Goddess were wrathful, the crops would fail and no man ever sire a son again.

"You'd have to marry to keep the Wolf lands," Ardda remarked.

"It's not that I want the lands. I want to keep my clan alive, and there's my sister. If I swore to the Goddess, then the right of inheritance would pass to Maccy. She always had lots of suitors, even when she only had a small dowry."

"But could she rule the clan?"

"Of course not, but if I pick her the right husband—oh, listen to me! How am I going to get to the King to lay my petition? I'll wager that the Boar's riding this way right now to make sure we're penned here like hogs."

Her prediction came true not an hour later. Gweniver was restlessly pacing round and round the grounds when she heard the sound of many men and horses riding their way. As she ran toward the gates, priestesses joined her, yelling at the gatekeeper to close them up. Gweniver was just helping slam the iron bar into the staples when the horsemen arrived in a clatter of hooves and jingle of mail. Ardda was already up on the catwalk over the gates. Trembling with rage, Gweniver climbed up and joined her.

Down below, milling around a respectful twenty yards away, was the seventy-man warband of the Boar. Burcan himself edged his horse out of the mob and insolently rode right up to the gates. A man in his late thirties, he had a thick streak of gray in his raven-dark hair and heavy mustache. As she leaned onto the rampart, Gweniver hated him, the man who had killed her clan.

"What do you want?" Ardda called out. "To approach the Holy Moon ready for war is an insult to the Goddess."

"No insult meant, Your Holiness," he called back in his dark, gravelly voice. "It's only that I rode in haste. I see that Lady Gweniver is safe here with you."

"And safe she'll remain, unless you want the Goddess to curse your lands into barrenness."

"What kind of a man do you think I am, to violate the holy sanctuary? I came to make the lady an offer of peace." He turned in the saddle to look up at Gweniver. "Many a blood feud's ended with a wedding, my lady. Take my second son for your man and rule the Wolf lands in the name of the Boar."

"I'd never let kin to you lay one filthy finger on me, you bastard!" Gweniver yelled at the top of her lungs. "And what do you expect me to do, follow that false king you serve?"

Burcan's broad face flushed in rage.

"I make you a vow," he snarled. "If my son doesn't have you, then no man will, and that goes for your sister, too. I'll cursed well claim your land by right of blood feud if I have to."

"You forget yourself, my lord!" Ardda snapped. "I forbid you to remain on temple land for another minute. Take your men away and make no more threats to one who worships the Goddess!"

Burcan hesitated, then shrugged and turned his horse away. Yelling orders, he collected his men and withdrew to the public road at the foot of the hill. Gweniver clenched her fists so hard that they ached as the warband spread out in the meadow on the far side of the road, technically off the demesne that supported the temple but in a perfect position to guard it.

"They can't stay there forever," Ardda said. "They'll have to go to Dun Deverry soon to fulfill their obligation to their king."

"True spoken, but I'll wager they stay there as long as they can."

Leaning back against the rampart, Ardda sighed. Suddenly she looked very old, and very weary.

The civil wars had come about in this wise. Twenty-four years past, the High King died without a male heir, and his daughter, a sickly young lass, died soon after. Each of his three sisters, however, had sons by their high-ranking husbands, Gwerbret Cerrmor, Gwerbret Cantrae, and the Marked Prince of the kingdom of Eldidd. By law, the throne should have passed to the son of the eldest sister, married to Cantrae, but the gwerbret was heavily suspected of having poisoned the king and princess both to get at the throne. Gwerbret Cerrmor worked that suspicion to claim the throne for his son, and then the Prince of Eldidd laid a further claim on the basis of his son's doubly royal blood. Since Gweniver's father never would have declared for a foreigner from Eldidd, the Wolf clan's choice was made when the long-hated Boars supported the Cantrae claim.

Year after year, the fighting raged around the true prize, the city of Dun Deverry, taken by one side one summer only to fall to another a few years later. After so many sieges, Gweniver doubted if there were much left of the Holy City to claim, but taking it was crucial to holding the kingship. All winter it had been in Cantrae hands, but now it was spring. Everywhere across the torn kingdom the claimants to the throne were mustering their vassals and reaffirming their alliances. Gweniver was certain that by now her clan's allies would be in Cerrmor.

"So listen, Maccy," she said. "We may have to stay here all summer, but eventually someone will bring his warband and get us out."

Macla nodded miserably. They were sitting in the temple gardens, on a little bench among the rows of carrots and cabbages. Macla, who was sixteen, was normally a pretty lass, but today her blond hair was pulled back in an untidy knot, and her eyes were red and puffy from weeping.

"I just hope you're right," Macla said at last. "What if no one thinks our lands are worth having? Even if they married you, they'd still have to fight with the rotten old Boar. And you can't afford to give me any dowry now, and so I'll probably rot in this awful old temple for the rest of my whole life."

"Don't natter like that! If I take the holy vows, then you'll have all the land for your dowry that any woman could want."

"Oh." Hope came into her eyes. "You always did talk about being a priestess."

"Just that. Now don't worry. We'll find you a husband yet."

Macla smiled, but her flood of complaints had raised doubts in her sister's mind. What indeed if no one wanted to take the Wolf lands because they brought the Wolf's feud with them? Since for all of her life Gweniver had listened to the constant talk of war, she knew something that the more innocent Maccy didn't: the Wolf lands lay in a bad strategic position, right on the Cantrae border and so far east of Cerrmor that they were hard to defend. What if the king in Cerrmor decided to consolidate his frontier?

She left Maccy in the garden and went for a restless walk. If only she could get to Cerrmor and petition the king! By all accounts, he was a scrupulously honorable man and might well listen. If she could get there. She climbed up the catwalk and looked out. After three days, Burcan and his men were still camped in the meadow.

"How long are you going to stay there, you bastards?" she muttered under her breath.

Not much longer, as it turned out. The next morning, when she climbed to the ramparts just after dawn, she saw the warband saddling up and loading their provision carts. Yet when they pulled out, they left four men and one cart behind, a guard over her provisioned to stay for months. Gweniver swore with every foul oath she'd ever heard until she was panting and out of breath. Finally she told herself that she should have expected no less. All at once, she felt hopeless. Even if Burcan had taken all his men away, she never could have travelled alone the hundred and eighty miles to Cerrmor.

"Unless I went as a priestess?" she remarked aloud.

Once she had the blue tattoo on her cheek, she would be inviolate, as safe on the roads as an army. She could go to the king with her holy vows lending her force and beg for the life of her clan, find some man to take Maccy and keep the Wolf's name alive. Then she could return here and take up her life in the temple. Turning, she leaned against the rampart and looked down at the compound. Already the neophytes and lower-ranked priestesses were working out in the garden or carrying firewood to the kitchens. A few strolled in meditation near the round temple itself. Yet for all the activity it was silent in the warm spring sun. No one spoke unless necessary, and then only in a quiet voice. For a moment she felt as if she couldn't breathe, just from the stifling vision of her future here.

All at once she felt a blind, irrational rage. She was trapped, a wolf in a cage, chewing and raging at the bars. Her hatred of Burcan rose up as strong as a lust and then spilled over on the king in Cerrmor. She was caught between them, begging one to let her have what was rightfully hers, begging the other to take her vengeance for her. Like a madwoman she trembled and threw her head from side to side as if to say nay to the whole universe. She was caught by a feeling that was far beyond her understanding, because its roots lay far in the past, far in another life, in fact, where once before she'd been caught between two men through no fault of her own. The memory, of course, was lost to her, but the core of feeling remained, as bitter and hard as a splinter of glass in her throat.

Slowly she calmed herself again. Giving in to mad rages would do her no good.

"You've got to think," she told herself. "And pray to the Goddess for her aid."

"The main body's pulled out," Dagwyn said. "But they left four men behind."

"Bastards!" Ricyn snarled. "Treating our lady like she was a prize horse or suchlike, there for the stealing!"

Camlwn nodded grimly. The three of them were the last men left alive from the Wolf's warband, and for days they'd been camping in the wooded hills behind the Temple of the Moon, where they could watch over the woman that they considered their sworn lord. All three of them had served the Wolf clan from boyhood; they were prepared to go on serving it now.

"How good a watch are they standing?" Ricyn said. "Armed and ready for a scrap?"

"Not on your life." Dagwyn paused for a grim smile. "When I snuck up on them, I saw them sitting around in the grass, as happy as you please, and dicing with their shirt sleeves rolled up."

"Oh, were they now? Then let's hope that the gods make their game a nice long one."

The free men who worked the temple's lands were extremely loyal to the high priestess, partly because she took far less of their crops in taxes than a noble lord would have, but mostly because they considered it an honor for them and their families to serve the Goddess. Ardda was sure, or so she told Gweniver, that one of the men would make the long trip to Dun Deverry for her with a message.

"This has got to stop! I can't order those men off land that doesn't belong to me, but cursed if I'm going to let them sit there all summer. You're not a criminal, come here for sanctuary, but we all know they'd murder you if they could. We'll see if this king Burcan serves can make him call his men off."

"Do you think the king will listen to your petition?" Gweniver said. "I'll wager he wants our lands in the hands of one of his vassals."

"He'd best listen! I'm asking the high priestess in the Dun Deverry temple to intercede personally."

Gweniver held the bridle of Ardda's palfrey as she mounted, adjusting her long dresses over the sidesaddle, then walked beside her horse as she rode down to the gates. Since the four Boarsmen had shown no inclination to try entering the temple, the gates were standing open. Gweniver and Lypilla, the gatekeeper for the day, stood together and watched as Ardda rode out, sitting straight and defiantly in the saddle. As she reached the road, the Boarsmen scrambled to their feet and made her deep, respectful bows.

"Bastards," Gweniver muttered. "They're keeping to every letter of the law while tearing out its heart."

"Just that. I wonder if they'd even murder you."

"Take me to Burcan for a forced marriage, more like. I'd die first!"

They shared a troubled glance. Gweniver had known Lypilla, who was in her early forties, all her life, just as she'd always known Ardda. They were as close to her as aunts or elder sisters, yet she doubted deep in her heart if she could bear to share their ordered life. Out on the road Ardda turned round the curve of a hill, riding north, and disappeared. The Boarsmen sat down and returned to their dice game. Gweniver found herself remembering the man she'd killed on the road and wishing that she could deal those four the same Wyrd.

Although she could have gone back and made herself useful in the kitchen, Gweniver lingered at the gates for a while, idly talking with Lypilla and staring out at the freedom of hill and meadow denied her. All at once, they heard distant hoofbeats, riding fast from the south.

"I suppose Burcan's sending messengers or suchlike to his men," Lypilla remarked.

The Boarsmen in the meadow seemed to agree, because they rose, idly stretching, and turned toward the sound. Suddenly, out of a stand of trees burst three riders in full mail and with swords at the ready. The Boarsmen stood frozen for a moment, then yelled and cursed as they drew swords: the riders were charging straight into them. Gweniver heard Lypilla scream as a Boarsman went down with his head cut half off his shoulders. A horse reared and staggered, and Gweniver saw the rider's shield full-on.

"Wolves!"

Without thinking she was running, sword in hand, down the hill while Lypilla screamed and begged her to come back. The second Boarsman fell as she ran; the third was being mobbed by two riders; the fourth broke and ran straight up the hill, as if in his panic he was trying to reach the sanctuary of the temple that his very presence was desecrating. When he saw Gweniver racing straight for him, he hesitated, then dodged to one side as if to go around her. With a howl of unearthly laughter that sprang out of her mouth of its own will, she charged and swung, catching him across the right shoulder before he could parry. When the sword slipped from his useless fingers, she laughed again and stabbed him in the throat. Her laughter rose to a banshee's shriek as the bright blood ran, and he fell.

"My lady!" It was Ricyn's voice, cutting through her laugh. "Oh by the Lord of Hell!"

The laughter vanished, leaving her sick and cold, staring at the corpse at her feet. Dimly she was aware of Ricyn dismounting and jogging toward her.

"My lady! My lady Gweniver! Do you recognize me?"

"What?" She looked up, puzzled. "Of course I do, Ricco. Haven't I known you half my life?"

"Well, my lady, that's not worth a pig's fart when a man goes berserk like you just did."

She felt as if he'd thrown icy water in her face. For a moment she stared half-witted at him while he looked her over in bemused concern. Just nineteen, her own age, Ricyn was a broad-faced, sunny-looking blond who was, according to her brothers, one of the most reliable men in the warband, if not the kingdom. It was odd to have him watching her as if she were dangerous.

"Well, that's what it was, my lady," he said. "Ye gods, it made my blood run cold, hearing you laugh."

"Not half as cold as it made mine. Berserk. By the Goddess herself, that's what I was."

Dark-haired, slender, and perpetually grinning, Dagwyn led his horse up and made her a bow.

"Too bad they left four men behind, my lady," he remarked. "You could have handled two all by yourself."

"Maybe even three," Ricyn said. "Where's Cam?"

"Putting his horse out of its misery. One of those scum could actually swing a sword in the right direction."

"Well, we've got their horses now, and all their provisions, too." Ricyn glanced at Gweniver. "We've been up in the woods, my lady, waiting to make our strike. We figured that the Boar couldn't sit here all cursed summer. Here, the dun's razed."

"I was cursed sure of that. What of Blaeddbyr?"

"It still stands. The folk there gave us food." Ricyn looked away, his mouth slack. "The Boar caught the warband on the road, you see. It was just dawn, and we were only half-dressed when the bastards came over the hill without so much as a challenge or the sound of a horn. They had twice as many men as we did, so Lord Avoic yells that we're to run for our lives, but we couldn't do it fast enough. Forgive me, my lady. I should have died there with him, but then I thought about you, well, you and all the womenfolk, I mean, so I thought it'd be better to die in the ward defending you."

"So did we," Dagwyn chimed in. "But we were too late. We had to be cursed careful with Boars all over the roads, and by the time we reached the dun, it was burning. And we were all half-mad, thinking you slain, but Ricco here says you could have gotten to the temple."

"So we headed here," Ricyn picked up. "And when we found the cursed Boar camped at the gates, we knew you had to be inside."

"And so we were," Gweniver said. "Well and good, then. You lads get those horses and that cart of supplies up here. There's some huts round back for the husbands of women who come just for a day or two. You can stay there while I decide what we'll do next."

Although Dagwyn hurried off to follow orders, Ricyn lingered, rubbing his dirty face with the back of a dirtier hand.

"We'd better bury those Boars, my lady. We can't leave that for the holy ladies."

"True enough. Huh . . . I wonder what the high priestess is going to say about this. Well, that's for me to worry about, not you. My thanks for rescuing me."

At that he smiled, just a little twist of his mouth, then hurried off after the others.

Although Ardda was not pleased to have four men slain at her gates, she was resigned, even remarking that perhaps the Goddess was punishing the Boar's impiety in the matter.

"No doubt," Gweniver said. "Because it was She who killed that one lad. I was naught but a sword in Her hands."

Ardda looked at her sharply. They were sitting in her study, a spare stone room with a shelf of six holy books on one wall and a table littered with temple accounts on the other. Even now, with her decision coming clear in her mind, Gweniver debated. Once her highest ambition had been to be high priestess here herself and to have this study for her own.

"All afternoon I've been praying to Her," Gweniver went on. "I'm going to leave you, my lady. I'm going to swear to the Moon and turn the clan over to Macla. Then I'm going to take my men and go to Cerrmor to lay the Wolf's petition before the king. Once I have the tattoo, the Boar will have no reason to harm me."

"Just so, but it's still dangerous. I hate to think of you out on the roads with just three riders for an escort. Who knows what men will do these days, even to a priestess?"

"Not just three, my lady. I'm the fourth."

Ardda went still, crouched in her chair as she began to pick up Gweniver's meaning.

"Don't you remember telling me about the fourth face of the Goddess?" Gweniver went on. "Her dark side, when the moon turns bloody and black, the mother who eats her own children."

"Gwen. Not that."

"That." With a toss of her head, she rose to pace about the chamber. "I'm going to take my men and join the war. It's been too long since a Moon-sworn warrior fought in Deverry."

"You'll be killed." Ardda got to her feet. "I shan't allow it."

"Is it for either of us to allow or disallow if the Goddess calls me? I felt Her hands on me today."

As their eyes met, as they locked stares in a battle of will, Gweniver realized that she was no longer a child, but a woman, when Ardda looked away first.

"There are ways to test such inspirations," Ardda said at last. "Come into the temple tonight. If the Goddess grants you a vision, it's not for me to say you nay. But if She doesn't . . ."

"I'll be guided by your wisdom in the matter."

"Very well, then. And what if She grants you a vision, but not the one you think you want?"

"Then I'll swear to Her anyway. The time has come, my lady. I want to hear the secret name of the Goddess and make my vow."

In preparation for the ceremony, Gweniver fasted that evening. While the temple was at its dinner, she fetched water from the well and heated herself a bath by the kitchen hearth. As she was dressing afterward, she paused to look at her brother's shirt, which she'd embroidered for him the year before. On each yoke, worked in red, was the striding wolf of the clan, surrounded by a band of interlacement. The pattern twined so cleverly around itself that it looked like a chain of knots made up of many strands, but in fact there was only one line to it, and each knot flowed inevitably into the next. My Wyrd's just such a tangle, she told herself.

And with the thought came a cold feeling, as if she had spoken better than she could know. As she finished dressing, she was frightened. It was not that perhaps she might die in battle;

she knew that she would be slain, maybe soon, maybe many years hence. It was the way of the Dark Goddess, to call upon her priestesses to make the last sacrifice when She decided the time had come. When Gweniver picked up the sword belt, she hesitated, half-tempted to throw it to the floor; then she buckled it on with a toss of her head.

The round wooden temple stood in the center of the compound. At either side of the door grew twisted, flamelike cypress trees, brought all the way from Bardek and nursed through many a cold winter. When Gweniver walked between them, she felt a surge of power as if she passed through a gate into another world. She knocked nine times on the oak door and waited until nine muffled knocks answered from inside. Then she opened it and went into the antechamber, dimly lit by a single candle. A priestess robed in black waited for her.

"Wear those clothes into the temple. Take in your sword as well. The high priestess has so commanded."

In the inner shrine, the polished wood walls gleamed in the light of nine oil lamps, and the floor was spread with fresh rushes. By the far wall stood the altar, a boulder left rough except for the top, which had been smoothed into a table. Behind it hung a huge circular mirror, the only image of Her that the Goddess will have in Her temples. Dressed in black, Ardda stood to the left.

"Unsheathe the sword and lay it on the altar."

Gweniver curtsied to the mirror, then did as the high priestess ordered. Through a door to the side three senior priestesses entered without a word and stood at the right. They would witness her vow.

"We are assembled to instruct and receive one who would serve the Goddess of the Moon," Ardda went on. "Gweniver of the Wolf is known to us all. Are there any objections to her candidacy?"

"None," the three said in unison. "She is known to us as one blessed by Our Lady."

"Well and good, then." The high priestess turned to Gweniver. "Will you swear to serve to the Goddess all your days and nights?"

"I will, my lady."

"Will you swear never to know a man?"

"I will, my lady."

"Will you swear never to betray the secret of the holy name?"

"I will, my lady."

Ardda raised her hands and clapped them together three times, then three more, and finally a third three, measuring out the holy number in its just proportion. Gweniver felt a solemn yet blissful peace, a sweetness like mead that flowed through her body. At last the decision was made, and her vow given over.

"Of all the goddesses," Ardda went on, "only Our Lady has no name known to the commonfolk. We hear of Epona, we hear of Sirona, we hear of Aranrhodda, but always Our Lady is simply the Goddess of the Moon." She turned to the three witnesses. "And why should such a thing be?"

"The name is a secret."

"It is a mystery."

"It is a riddle."

"And yet," Ardda said after the answers, "it is a riddle easy to solve. What is the name of the Goddess?"

"Epona."

"Sirona."

"Aranrhodda."

"And," this said in unison, "all the rest."

"You have spoken true." Ardda turned to Gweniver. "Here then is the answer to the riddle. All goddesses are one goddess. She goes by all names and no names, for She is One."

Gweniver began to tremble in a fierce joy.

"No matter what men or women call her, She is One," Ardda went on. "There is but one priestesshood that serves Her. She is like the pure light of the sun when it strikes the rain-filled sky and turns to a rainbow, many colors, but all One at the source."

"Long have I thought so," Gweniver whispered. "Now I know."

Again the high priestess clapped out the nine knocks, then turned to the witnesses.

"There is a question of how Gweniver, no longer lady but now priestess, shall serve the Goddess. Let her kneel in petition at the altar."

Gweniver knelt in front of the sword. In the mirror she could see herself, a shadowy figure in the flickering light, but she barely recognized her face, the cropped hair, the mouth set grim, the eyes glowing with lust for vengeance. Help me, oh Lady of the Heavens, she prayed, I want blood and revenge, not tears and mourning.

"Look in the mirror," Ardda whispered. "Beg Her to come to you."

Gweniver spread her hands on the altar and took up her watch. At first, she saw nothing but her face and the temple behind her. Then Ardda began to chant a high wailing song in the old tongue. It seemed that the oil lamps flickered in time to the long sprung rhythms as the chant rose and fell, winding through the temple like a cold north wind. In the mirror, the light changed, dimmed, became a darkness, a trembling dark as cold as a starless sky. The chant sobbed on, wailing through ancient words. Gweniver felt the hair prickling on the back of her neck as in that mirror-darkness appeared the stars, the wheel and dance of the endless sky. Among them formed the image of Another.

She towered through the stars, and her face was grim, blood-besotted as she shook her head and spread a vast mane of black hair over the sky. Gweniver could hardly breathe as the dark eyes looked her way. This was the Goddess of the Dark Time, Whose own heart is pierced with swords and Who demands no less from those who would worship Her.

"My lady," Gweniver whispered. "Take me as a sacrifice. I'll serve you always."

The eyes considered her for a long moment, fierce, gleaming, utterly cold. Gweniver felt the presence all around her, as if the Goddess stood beside and behind as well as in front of her.

"Take me," she said. "I'll be naught but a sword in your hand."

On the altar, her sword flared and ran with bloody colored light, casting a glow upward that turned the mirror red. The chant stopped. Ardda had seen the omen.

"Swear to her." The priestess's voice shook. "That in her service you'll live . . . ," her voice broke, "and die."

"So do I swear, from deep in my heart."

In the mirror, the eyes of the Goddess radiated joy. The light on the sword danced up like fire, then fell back. As it faded, the mirror darkened to the turning stars, then only to blackness.

"Done!" Ardda clapped her hands together, a boom and echo in the temple.

The mirror reflected Gweniver's pale, sweating face.

"She has come to you," the high priestess said. "She has given you the blessing that many would call a curse. You have chosen, and you have sworn. Serve Her well, or death will be the least of your troubles."

"Never will I betray Her. How can I, when I've looked into the eyes of Night?"

Ardda clapped her hands together nine times, measured out three by three. Still trembling, Gweniver rose and took up her sword.

"Never did I think She would accept you." Ardda was close to tears. "But now all I can do is pray for you."

"I'll treasure those prayers no matter how far I ride."

Two more priestesses entered the temple. One carried a silver bowl of blue powder, the other a pair of fine silver needles. When they saw the sword in Gweniver's hands, they exchanged startled glances.

"Give her the mark on her left cheek," Ardda said. "She serves Our Lady of the Darkness."

Thanks to the provisions they'd captured from the Boarsmen, Ricyn and the others had a good hot breakfast for the first time in days, barley porridge and salt bacon. They ate slowly, savoring every bite, savoring even more the temporary safety. They were just finishing when Ricyn heard someone leading a horse up the hut. He was on his feet and out in a hurry, with his sword drawn in case the Boar had sent a spy, but it was Gweniver, dressed in her brother's clothes and leading a big gray warhorse. In the morning sun her left cheek looked burned, it was so puffy red, and in the center of the discoloration was the blue crescent of the Moon. All three stared unspeaking while she smiled at them impartially.

"My lady?" Dagwyn said at last. "Are you staying in the temple, then?"

"I'm not. We're packing up and riding for Cerrmor today. Load up as many provisions as the captured horses can carry."

All three nodded in unquestioning obedience. Ricyn couldn't look away from her face. Although no one would ever have called Gweniver beautiful (her face was too broad and her jaw too strong for that), she was attractive, tall and slim, with the grace of a wild animal when she moved. For years he had been hopelessly in love with her, when every winter he would sit on one side of her brother's hall and watch her, unobtainable on the other. Seeing that she'd sworn the vow was grimly satisfying. Now no other man would ever have her.

"Is somewhat wrong?" she said to him.

"Naught, my lady. If it's my place to ask, I was only wondering about the tattoo. Why is it on the left side of your face?"

"You've got every right to know. It marks me as a moon-sworn warrior." When she smiled, she seemed to change into a different woman, cold, hard-eyed, and fierce. "And here you all thought that such existed only in bard songs, didn't you?"

Ricyn was as startled as if she'd slapped him. Dagwyn caught his breath in a gasp of surprise.

"Lady Macla's the head of the Wolf clan now," she went on. "She's made me captain of her warband until such time as she marries and her husband brings her riders of his own. If we're still alive by then, you'll all have a choice: to pledge to her new man, or to follow me. But for now, we're going to Cerrmor for the summer's fighting. The Wolf swore to bring men, and the Wolf never breaks its word."

"Well and good, then, my lady," Ricyn said. "We may not be much of a warband, but if anyone says one wrong word about our captain, I'll slit the bastard's throat."

When they rode out, they went cautiously, in case some of the Boarsmen were lurking on the roads. Dagwyn and Camlwn took turns riding point as they made their way along the bypaths through the hills. Although Cerrmor was a good ten days ride away, safety lay much closer in the duns of the Wolf's old allies to the south and east. For two days they skirted the Wolf demense, not daring to ride on their own lands in case the Boars were patrolling them. On the morning of the third, they crossed the River Nerr at a little-used ford and headed more east than south, aiming for the lands of the Stag clan. That night they camped on the edge of a stretch of forest that the Stags and the Wolves used jointly as a hunting preserve. Seeing the familiar trees brought tears to Gweniver's eyes as she remembered how her brothers had loved to hunt among them.

While the men tethered the horses and set up camp, Gweniver paced restlessly around. She was beginning to feel grave doubts. It was one thing to talk of riding to war herself, another to look at her tiny warband and realize that their lives depended on how well she led them. On the excuse of looking for dead wood for a fire, she went into the forest and wandered through the trees until she found a small stream, running silently over rock between fern-lined banks. Around her the old oaks cast shadows that seemed to have lain there since the beginning of time.

"Goddess," she whispered. "Have I chosen the right path?"

In the flickering surface of the stream, she saw no vision. She drew her sword and stared at the blade, which had run with fire on the Goddess's altar. Then it seemed she felt the ghosts of the dead gather around her, Avoic, Maroic, Benoic, and last of all, her father, Caddryc, those tall grim men whose lives had dominated hers, whose pride had summed up her own.

"I'll never let you lie unavenged."

She heard them sigh at the bitterness of their Wyrd, or maybe it was just the wind in the trees, because they left as silently and quickly as they'd gathered. Yet she knew that the Goddess had given her an omen, just as She had when She blessed the sword.

"Vengeance! We'll deal it for the Goddess's sake, but vengeance we'll all have."

Sword still in hand, Gweniver started back to her men, but she heard a twig snap and a footfall behind her. She spun around and raised the sword.

"Come out!" she snapped. "Who disturbs a sworn priestess of the Darktime?"

Dressed in torn, filthy clothes, their faces stubbled, their hair matted, two men with swords at the ready stepped out of the underbrush. When they looked her over with narrowed eyes, Gweniver felt the Goddess gathering behind her, a tangible presence that raised the hair on the nape of her neck. She looked them over with a cold smile that seemed to appear on her face of its own will.

"You never answered me," Gweniver said. "Who are you, and what are you doing here?"

The dark-haired, slender fellow glanced at the other with a trace of a smile; the redhead, however, shook his head in a no and stepped forward.

"And is there a temple near here, my lady?" he said. "Or are you a hermit in this forest?"

"I carry my temple in my saddlebags. You've never met a priestess of my rite before, and doubtless you won't again."

"She's got the mark on her face, sure enough," the dark-haired man broke in. "But I'll wager she—"

"Hold your tongue, Draudd," the redhead snarled. "There's somewhat cursed strange about this. Now here, my lady, are you truly out in this cursed forest all alone?"

"What's it to you if I am? The Goddess sees sacrilege no matter how far from the eyes of men it happens."

When Draudd started to speak, Gweniver stepped forward, swinging the sword point up as if in challenge to a duel. She caught his glance and held it, stared him down while she felt the Goddess as a dark shadow behind her and the smile locked on her mouth. Draudd stepped back sharply, his eyes wide with fear.

"She's daft," he whispered.

"I said: hold your tongue!" the redhead snapped. "There's daft, and then there's god-touched, you ugly bastard! My lady, my apologies for disturbing you. Will you give us your Goddess's blessing?"

"Oh, gladly, but you don't know what you're asking for." All at once she laughed, a cold upwelling of mirth that she couldn't suppress. "Come with me, and then we'll see about the blessing."

Gweniver turned on her heel and strode through the trees. Although she heard them following, Draudd protesting in whispers, she never looked back until she reached the camp. When Ricyn saw the men following her, he called out and ran forward, his sword in hand.

"There's naught amiss," Gweniver said. "I may have found us a pair of recruits."

The men all looked at each other for a stunned moment.

"Draudd! Abryn!" Ricyn burst out. "What by the name of all the gods has happened to you? Where's the rest of the warband?"

Only then did Gweniver notice the barely visible blazons on their muddy shirts: stags.

"Dead," Abryn said, his voice cold and flat. "And Lord Maer with them. A cursed big band of Cantrae riders struck us hard some five days ago. The dun's razed, and cursed if I know what's happened to our lord's lady, and the children, too."

"We were trying to get to the Wolf, you see," Draudd broke in. He paused for a bitter, twisted smile. "I take it that it wouldn't have done us one cursed jot of good."

"None," Gweniver said. "Our dun's razed, too. Here, are you hungry? We've got food."

While Abryn and Draudd wolfed down hardtrack and cheese as if it were a feast, they told their story between mouthfuls. Some hundred and fifty of the false king's own men fell upon the Stag just as they were leaving their dun to start for Cerrmor. Just as Avoic had done, Lord Maer ordered his men to scatter, but Abryn and Draudd had both had their horses killed as they tried to fight free. The Cantrae men hadn't pursued them; they'd headed straight for the dun and swept in without warning before the gates could be shut.

"Or so they must of," Abryn finished up. "It was taken, anyway, when we made our way back there."

Gweniver and her men nodded solemnly.

"Well," she said at last. "It sounds to me like they'd planned this raid in conjunction with the one on us. I can see what the piss-poor little weasels have in mind: isolating the Wolf lands so it'll be easier for the cursed Boars to keep them."

"It's going to be hard for the swine to take the Stag lands," Abryn said. "Lord Maer's got two brothers in the king's service."

"No doubt they won't risk trying to hold your clan's lands," Gweniver said. "They're too far south. But by razing the dun and killing your lord, they've taken our closest ally away. Now they'll try to establish a strong point on the Wolf demesne and nibble at the Stag later."

"True spoken." Abryn looked at her in sincere admiration. "My lady understands matters of war, sure enough."

"And when have I ever known anything else but this war? Now here, we've got extra horses. Join up with us if you like, but I warn you, the Goddess I serve is a goddess of darkness and blood.

That's what I meant about Her blessing. Think well before you take it."

They did think on the matter, staring at her all the while until at last Abryn spoke for them both.

"What else have we got, my lady? We're naught but a pair of dishonored men without a lord to ride for or a clan to take us in."

"Done, then. You ride at my orders, then, and I promise you, you'll have your chance for vengeance."

In sincere gratitude they smiled at her. In those days, a warrior who lived through a battle in which his lord died was a shamed man, turned away from everyone's shelter and mocked wherever he went.

As the warband made its way south to Cerrmor, they picked up other men like Abryn and Draudd, some other survivors from the Stag's warband, some who were stubbornly closemouthed about their past, but all of them desperate enough to lay aside their amazement at finding a priestess at the head of a warband. Eventually Gweniver had thirty-seven men, just three short of the number that Avoic had pledged to bring. In fact, they pledged to her so gladly and accepted her so easily that she was surprised. Their last night on the road, she shared a campfire with Ricyn, who waited upon her like an orderly.

"Tell me somewhat," she said to him. "Do you think these lads will still follow my orders once we're down in Cerrmor?"

"Of course, my lady." He seemed surprised that she would ask. "You're the one who took them off the roads and gave them the right to feel like men again. Besides, you're a priestess."

"Does that matter to them?"

"Oh, twice over. Come now, we've all heard those tales about Moon-sworn warriors, haven't we? But it's twice a marvel to actually see one. Most of the lads think it's an omen, you see. It's like dweomer, and you're dweomer-touched. We all know it's bound to bring us good luck."

"Luck? Oh, it won't bring that, but only the favor of the Moon in Her Darktime. Do you truly want that kind of favor, Ricyn? It's a harsh thing, a cold wind from the Otherlands."

Ricyn shuddered as if he felt that wind blowing. For a long time he stared into the campfire.

"Harsh or not, it's all I have left to me," he said at last. "I'll follow you, and you follow the Goddess, and we'll see what she brings us both."

Cerrmor lay at the mouth of the Belaver, the watercourse that was the natural spine of the kingdom, where the estuary had cut a broad harbor out of the chalky cliffs. With over eighty thousand people sheltering behind its high stone walls, it was the second biggest city in the kingdom now that Dun Deverry had been laid waste. From a long line of piers and jetties, the city spread out upriver in a sprawl of curved streets like ripples from a stone thrown into a pond. As long as its gwerbrets kept it safe, its trade with Bardek kept it rich. A fortress within a fortress, Dun Cerrmor stood on a low artificial hill in the middle of town not far from the river. Inside a double ring of walls were the stone broch complex, stone outbuildings, and barracks, all with slate roofs; nowhere was there a scrap of wood that might be fired with a flaming arrow. Outside the main gate were barbicans, and the gates themselves were covered with iron, opened and shut with a winch.

When Gweniver led her warband through to the cobbled ward, cheers rang out: it's the Wolf! By all the gods, it's the Wolf! Men poured out of broch and barrack to watch, and pages in the king's colors of red and silver ran to greet them.

"My lord," a lad burst out. "We heard you were slain!"

"My brother was," Gweniver said. "Go tell the King that the Lady Gweniver is here to honor Lord Avoic's vow."

The page stared goggle-eyed at her tattooed face, then dashed back into the broch. Ricyn rode up beside her and gave her a grin.

"They thought you were a ghost from the Otherlands, my lady. Shall I have the men dismount?"

"Just that. Here, you've been acting like the captain for days. It's about time I told you that you officially are."

"My lady honors me too highly."

"She doesn't, and you know it. You were never humble, Ricco, so don't pretend to be now."

With a laugh he made her a half-bow from the saddle and turned his horse back to the men.

Gweniver stood beside her horse and nervously looked over the broch complex while she waited for the page to return. Although her brothers had told her of the splendor of Cerrmor, she'd never been there before. A full seven stories high, the massive tower joined to three lower half-brochs, the dark gray complex like the fist of a giant turned to stone by dweomer. Nearby were enough barracks and stables to house hundreds of men. Over it all flew a red and silver flag, announcing proudly that the king himself was in residence. When she glanced around at the swelling crowd, she saw all the noble lords watching her but afraid to speak until the king gave his judgment on this strange matter. Just as she was cursing the page for being so slow, the ironbound doors opened, and the king himself came out with a retinue of pages and councillors in attendance.

Glyn, Gwerbret Cerrmor, or king of all Deverry as he preferred to be known, was about twenty-six, tall and heavyset, with blond hair bleached pale and coarsened with lime in the regal fashion so that it swept back from his square face like a lion's mane. His deep-set blue eyes bore a perpetually haunted expression, because he took his responsibilities as seriously as he took his rights. When Gweniver knelt before him, she felt an honest awe. All her life she'd heard about this man, and now here he was, setting his hands on his hips and looking her over with a small bemused smile.

"Rise, Lady Gweniver," Glyn said. "May I not sound like a churl, but never did I think to see the day when a woman would bring me men."

Gweniver made him a curtsy as best she could in brigga.

"Well, my honored liege, never has the Wolf clan broken its sworn vow, not once in all these long years of war."

"I'm most mindful of that." He hesitated, picking careful words. "I'm informed that you have a sister. Later, no doubt, when you've rested, you'll wish to speak to me about the fate of the Wolf."

"I will, my liege, and I'm honored that you would turn your attention to the matter."

"Of course. Will you shelter with me a while as an honored guest, or do you need to return straightaway to your temple?"

Here was the crux, and Gweniver called upon the Goddess in her heart.

"My liege," she said. "The most holy Moon has chosen me to serve Her as a Moon-sworn warrior. I've come to beg you a boon, that you'll let me keep the place I have as head of my warband, to ride with you in your army and live at your command."

"What?" He forgot all his ritual courtesy. "Here, you must be jesting! What would a woman want with battles and suchlike?"

"What any man wants, my liege: honor, glory, and a chance to slay the enemies of the king."

Glyn hesitated, staring at the tattoo as if he were remembering the old tales of those who served the Darktime Goddess, then turned to the warband.

"Now here, men," he called out. "Do you honor the lady as your captain?"

To a man, the warband called out that they did. At the back of the line, Dagwyn boldly yelled that Gweniver was dweomer.

"Then I'll take it as an omen that a Moon-sworn warrior has turned up at my court," Glyn said. "Well and good, my lady. I grant your boon."

At a wave of Glyn's hand, servants descended like locusts. Stableboys ran to take the horses; riders from the king's personal warband hurried over to Ricyn to take him and the men to the barracks; councillors appeared at Gweniver's side and bowed; two underchamberlains trotted up to escort her into the great hall. The sight of it amazed her. Big enough to hold over a hundred tables for the warbands, it had four enormous hearths. Red and silver banners hung among fine tapestries on the walls and, rather than straw, colored slate tiles covered the floor. Gweniver stood gawking like the country lass she was as the head chamberlain, Lord Orivaen by name, hurried to greet her.

"Greetings, my lady," he said. "Allow me to find you accommodations in our humble broch. You see, since you're both noble born and a priestess, I'm honestly not sure what rank that gives you. Perhaps the same as tieryn?"

"Oh, my good sir, as long as the room has a bed and a hearth, anything will do. A priestess of the Dark Moon cares not for rank."

Orivaen kissed her hand in honest gratitude, then took her to a small suite in a side tower and sent pages to bring up her gear. Once she was alone again, she paced restlessly around while she wondered if the king would consider the Wolf lands worth holding now that the Stag clan had suffered such losses. In a few minutes there was a knock at the door, and a possible weapon in her battle to save the clan walked in. Lord Gwetmar was a lanky, lantern-jawed young man with an untidy mop of dark hair. Although his birth was noble enough, his family was land-poor and considered somewhat disreputable among the great clans. Gweniver's kin, however, had always treated him as an equal. He grabbed both of her hands in his and squeezed them hard.

"Gwen, by all the gods, it gladdens my heart to see you alive. When the news came in of Avoic's death, I was sick, wondering if you and your sister had come to harm. I would have ridden north straightaway, but our liege wouldn't allow it."

"Doubtless he didn't want to lose you and your men along with ours. Maccy's safe in the temple, and Mam along with her."

With a grin, Gwetmar draped himself into a chair. Gweniver perched on the windowsill and considered him.

"Now here," he said. "Are you truly going to ride with us?"

"I am. I want a chance at vengeance even if I die for it."

"I understand that. I pray to every god that they'll let me cut down Avoic's killer. Listen, if we live till fall, I'll join my men to yours and help with this feud."

"My thanks. I was hoping you'd say somewhat like that, because I've been thinking about the Wolf lands. They're Maccy's now, or they will be if the King grants my petition to let them pass in the female line. But I'm still the elder as well as a priestess, and she's cursed well going to marry the man I pick for her."

"And no doubt you'll pick a good one." Gwetmar looked away, suddenly melancholy. "Maccy deserves no less."

"Listen, you dolt, I'm talking about you. I know Maccy's always been a coldhearted little snip to you, but now she'd marry the Lord of Hell himself to get out of that temple. I have no intention of telling any other land-hungry lord where she is until you've had a chance to send her messages."

"Gwen! I happen to honestly love your sister, not just her lands!"

"I know. Why do you think I'm offering her to you?"

He tossed his head back and laughed, as bright as the sun breaking through storm clouds.

"Never did I think I'd have a chance to marry her," he said at last. "Taking the Wolf's name and the Wolf's feud seem a cursed small price to pay."

Gwetmar escorted her down to the great hall. Along one side

was a raised dais, where the King and the noble-born ate their meals. Although Glyn was nowhere to be seen, a number of lords were sitting there, idly drinking ale while they listened to a bard play. Gweniver and Gwetmar sat down with Lord Maemyc, an older man who'd known Gweniver's father well. He stroked his gray mustaches and looked her over sadly, but to her relief he said not a word about the road she'd chosen to ride. Now that the King had given his approval, no one would dare question her choice.

The talk turned inevitably to the summer's fighting ahead. Things promised to be slow. After the bloody campaigns of the last few years, Cerrmor simply didn't have enough men to besiege Dun Deverry, nor did Cantrae have enough to make a real strike at Cerrmor.

"A lot of skirmishing ahead, if you ask me," Maemyc pronounced. "And maybe one good strike north to avenge the Stag and Wolf clans."

"A quick couple of raids and little else," Gwetmar agreed. "But then, there's Eldidd to worry about on the western border."

"Just so." He glanced at Gweniver. "He's been getting bolder and bolder, raiding in deep to bleed both us and Cantrae. I'll wager he holds back his full force until we're both worn down."

"I see. It sounds reasonable, truly."

On the far side of the dais there was a bustle at the small door that led to the King's private stairway. Two pages knelt ceremoniously while a third swung the door open wide. Expecting the King, Gweniver got ready to rise, but another man came through and paused to look over the assembled company. Blond and blue-eyed, he looked much like Glyn, but he was slender where the King was heavyset. His long swordsman's arms were crossed tight over his chest as he watched the lords with narrowed contemptuous eyes.

"Who's that?" Gweniver whispered. "I thought the king's brother was dead."

"His true brother is," Gwetmar said. "That's Dannyn, one of the old gwerbret's bastards, the only lad among the lot. The King favors him highly, though, and made him captain of his personal guard. After you see him fight, you can't begrudge him his birth. He swings a sword like a god, not a man."

His thumbs hooked into his sword belt, Dannyn strolled over, gave Gwetmar a pleasant if distant nod, then looked Gweniver over. On the yokes of his shirt was embroidered the ship blazon of Cerrmor, but all down the sleeves was a device of striking falcons.

"So," he said at last. "You're the priestess who thinks she's a warrior, are you?"

"I am. And I suppose you're a man who thinks he can tell me otherwise."

Dannyn sat down beside her and turned to slouch against the table. When he spoke, he looked out over the hall instead of at her.

"What makes you think you can swing a sword?" he said.

"Ask my men. I never boast about myself."

"I already spoke with Ricyn. He had the gall to tell me that you go berserk."

"I do. Are you going to call me a liar?"

"It's not my place to call you anything. The King ordered me to take you and your men into his guard, and I do what he says."

"And so do I."

"From now on you do what I say. Understand me, lass?"

With a flick of her wrist, Gweniver dumped the contents of her tankard full into his face. As the lords at table gasped and swore, she swung herself free and rose, staring at Dannyn, who looked up blandly, the ale running down his face unnoticed.

"Listen you," she said. "You're a son of a bitch, sure enough, but I'm the daughter of a wolf. If you want to test my skill so badly, then come outside."

"Listen to you. Feisty little wench, aren't you?"

She slapped him across the face so hard that he reeled back.

"No man calls me a wench."

The great hall turned dead silent as everyone in it, from page to noble lord, turned to watch.

"You forget to whom you speak," she went on. "Or are you blind and unable to see the tattoo on my face?"

Slowly Dannyn raised his hand to his cheek and rubbed the slap, but his eyes never left hers. They were cold, deep, and frightening in their intensity.

"Will my lady accept my apology?"

When he knelt at her feet, the entire hall gasped with a sound like sea waves.

"I'm most truly sorry I insulted you, Your Holiness. Truly, a madness must have taken my heart. If any man dares call you a wench again, then they'll have to answer to my sword."

"My thanks. Then I forgive you."

With a small smile Dannyn rose and wiped his ale-struck face on his shirt sleeve, but still he looked at her. For the briefest of moments, she was sorry that she'd sworn the vow of chastity. His fluid way of moving, his easy stance, his very arrogance struck her as beautiful, as strong and clean as the cut of a sword blade in the sun. Then she remembered the dark eyes of the Goddess, and the regret passed.

"Tell me somewhat," he said. "Do you ride at the head of your warband?"

"I do. I'd rather die than have it said of me that I lead my men from the rear."

"I expected no less."

Dannyn bowed, then walked slowly and arrogantly through the lords to the door. Once it shut behind him, the hall burst into a rustle of whispers.

"Ye gods!" Gwetmar wiped the sweat from his forehead. "I truly thought your last hour had come. You're the only person in the kingdom who's crossed Dannyn and lived five minutes longer."

"Oh nonsense," Gweniver said. "He's doubtless got more sense that to injure a sworn priestess of the Moon."

"Hah!" Maemyc snorted. "Dannyn does his killing first and his thinking afterward."

It was some minutes later that a page came to Gweniver and told her that the King wished to speak with her privately. Mindful of the enormous honor being paid her, she followed him up to the second floor of the main broch, where Glyn had a suite of apartments furnished with carved chairs and tables, hung with tapestries, and carpeted with fine Bardek weavings. The king was standing at a hearth of pale sandstone, carved with ships and interlacements. When she knelt before him, he bade her rise.

"I was thinking of all your kin who've died serving me," Glyn said. "This matter of the Wolves lies heavily upon me, Your

Holiness. Do you wish to petition me to hand the lands and name down in the female line?"

"I do, my liege. Now that I've sworn my vows, I can own naught but what I can carry in one large sack, but my sister will soon be betrothed to a man who's willing to take on our feud with our name."

"I see. Well, let me be honest. I may not be able to move as quickly as I like in this matter of your lands, but I'm quite willing to grant that the name pass down to your sister's sons. As much as I'd like to remove the Boars from your demesne, much depends on the progress of the summer's fighting."

"My liege is most honorable and generous. I understand that my clan's woes are only one thing among many to him."

"Unfortunately, Your Holiness, you speak true. I only wish it were otherwise."

As she was leaving the King's presence, Gweniver met Dannyn, opening that most private of doors with no announcement or ceremony. He gave her a thin twitch of a smile.

"Your Holiness," he said. "My heart aches for the death of your kin. I'll do my best to avenge them."

"Lord Dannyn is most kind, and he has my thanks."

Gweniver hurried down the corridor, but at the staircase she glanced back to see him still watching her, his hand on the door. All at once she shuddered with cold and felt danger like a clammy hand along her back. She could only assume that the Goddess was sending her a warning.

On the morrow, Gweniver was walking around the outer ward with Ricyn when she saw a shabby old man leading two pack mules through the gates. Although he was dressed in dirty brown brigga and a much-mended shirt with Glyn's blazons upon it, he stood as straight and walked as vigorously as a young prince. Several pages came running to help him with the mules, and she noticed that they treated the old man deferentially.

"Who's that, Ricco?"

"Old Nevyn, my lady, and that's truly his name. He says his da named him 'no one' in a fit of spite." Ricyn looked oddly in awe of the old man as he spoke. "He's an herbman, you see. He finds wild herbs and brings them in for the chirurgeons, and then he grows some here in the dun, too."

The pages were taking the mules away. An underchamberlain who was passing by stopped to bow to the herbman.

"Now here," Gweniver said. "Obviously our Nevyn is a useful sort of servitor to have, but why do people treat him like a lord?"

"Uh well." Ricyn looked oddly embarrassed. "There's just somewhat about the old man that makes you respect him."

"Indeed? Out with it! I can tell you're hiding somewhat."

"Well, my lady, everyone says he's dweomer, and I half believe it myself."

"Oh nonsense!"

"It's not, my lady. Here, the King's been known to go down to old Nevyn's garden and talk with him for hours."

"And does that mean he's dweomer? No doubt the King needs to lay aside affairs of state from time and time, and the old man probably just amuses him or suchlike."

"If my lady says so." But it was plain that he didn't believe a word of what she said.

At this point Nevyn himself walked over with a friendly greeting for Ricyn, who promptly bowed to him. When the old man looked at Gweniver, his eyes turned as ice cold as the north wind and seemed to pierce into her very soul. Suddenly she was sure that she knew him, that in some strange way she'd been waiting to find him, that her entire life had led her here to this shabby herbman. Then the feeling faded, and he gave her a pleasant smile.

"Good morrow, my lady," he said. "Your fame has spread through the whole dun."

"Has it now?" Gweniver still felt shaken. "Well, I suppose that gladdens my heart."

"Well, a Moon-sworn warrior's a rare thing, but truly, the times are dark enough for Her of the Sword-Struck Heart."

Gweniver frankly stared. How did a man know that secret name? Nevyn bowed gravely to her.

"You'll excuse me, Your Holiness. I have to make sure those pages unpack the herbs carefully. No doubt we'll meet again."

When he strolled away, Gweniver stared after him for a long time. Finally she turned to Ricyn.

"Oh well and good, then, Captain," she snapped. "He's dweomer, sure enough."

At about the same time, the King was sitting in council in the narrow council chamber, which was bare except for a long table and a parchment map of Deverry on the stone wall. At the head of the table, Glyn sat in a high-backed chair draped with the ceremonial plaid of the kingship. Dannyn sat at his right, and the councillors in their black robes perched on stools like crows around spilled grain. This particular morning, the King had invited Amain, high priest of Bel in Cerrmor, to attend. While the councillors rose one at a time to give solemn advice on matters of war, Dannyn stared out the window and thought of other things, because the real decisions would be hammered out later between the King and his warrior-vassals. Toward the end of the meeting, though, the discussion hit upon a matter that caught Dannyn's attention. Saddar, an old man with white side whiskers and trembling chin, rose and bowed to the King.

"My most humble apologies, my liege, for questioning you," he said. "But I was wondering why you took the Lady Gweniver into your warband."

"After all her clan's done for me," Glyn said, "I didn't feel I could deny her the boon she begged for. I'm sure Dannyn here can keep her from coming to any real harm, and soon enough she'll tire of riding to war."

"Ah." The old man paused, glancing at the other councillors for support. "We were thinking that perhaps she could be spared the rigors more simply, you see, by simply coercing her back to her temple, then telling her men later."

Dannyn pulled his jeweled dagger and threw, hitting the table directly in front of Saddar. With a gasp, the councillor leapt back as the dagger stuck, quivering in the wood.

"Tell me somewhat," Dannyn remarked. "How can a coward like you judge a warrior like her?"

When the King laughed, all the councillors forced out laughs, too, even Saddar.

"Dannyn thinks highly of her spirit, good sirs," Glyn said. "I trust his judgment in such matters."

"Never would I question Lord Dannyn in matters of war, my liege. I was merely thinking of the propriety of the thing."

"You can shove that up your behind," Dannyn snapped.

"Hold your tongue!" The King intervened sharply. "Good

councillor, I assure you that I respect your wisdom far more than my arrogant brother here does, but I've already given the lady my sworn word of honor. Besides, I've invited His Holiness here to the council to explain this matter for us."

Everyone turned to the priest, who rose with a nod of recognition all round. Like all of Bel's vassals, his head was shaved clean, and he wore a gold torque around his neck and a simple linen tunic, belted at the waist with a bit of plain rope. From the belt hung a small golden sickle.

"The King wished to know of the status of Lady Gweniver's worship," Amain said in his soft, dark voice. "It's a most legitimate one, going back to the Dawntime, when as the chronicles record women were forced to become warriors by the cruel press of circumstance. The worship of the Moon in Her Darktime is by no means to be confused with the rites of either Epona or Aranrodda." At the mention of the second name, he paused to cross his fingers in the sign of warding against witchcraft. Many of the councillors did the same. "Now, truly, I was surprised to find that the knowledge of the warrior rites remains alive, but I gather the holy ladies of the temples have kept the lore of such things intact."

As Amain sat back down, the men looked uneasily among themselves.

"So you see, good Saddar," Glyn said, "that I can't cross the will of the Holy Goddess in this."

"Of course not, my liege, and may She forgive me for ever questioning the lady's purpose."

The council broke up in conciliatory nods and bows all round. As Glyn strode out of the room, Dannyn lingered just long enough to retrieve his dagger from the table. While he sheathed it, Saddar watched with poisonous eyes. Dannyn hurried after the King and followed him up to his private apartments. Glyn had a page bring them each a tankard of ale, then sat down in a chair by the hearth. Although Dannyn took the chair his brother offered him, he would have gladly sat by his feet like a dog.

"Now here, Danno," the King said. "That pack of blowhards wearies me as much as they weary you, but I've got to have their loyalty. Who else is going to run this piss-poor excuse for a kingdom when we're gone on campaign?"

"True spoken, my liege, and you have my apologies."

With a sigh, Glyn sipped his ale and stared into the empty hearth. Lately he'd been slipping into these dark moods; they troubled his brother deeply.

"What aches your heart, my liege?" Dannyn said.

"Lord Avoic's death, and the deaths of all his brothers, too. Ah by the hells, there are times when I wonder if I can be king, when I think of all the death that my claim's brought to the kingdom."

"What? Here, only a true king would have such doubts. I'll wager Cantrae doesn't give a pig's fart who dies in his cause."

"You believe in me, don't you, Danno?"

"Ah by the hells, I'd die for you."

"You know," Glyn looked up, his eyes cloudy with something suspiciously like tears, "there are times when I think I'd go mad without you."

Dannyn was too shocked to speak. With a toss of his head, Glyn rose.

"Leave me," he snapped. "We would be alone."

As much as he wanted to stay, Dannyn hurried out at this direct order. His heart heavy, he wandered out to the ward. His one consolation was that Glyn's dark mood would probably break once they rode out to the war, but it was a shallow one. It was quite likely that there would be little direct fighting this summer. He himself would probably lead what raids there were while the King stayed in his dun and brooded, because he was too important to risk to a chance wound in some insignificant action.

His aimless walking eventually brought him to the barracks area. Out in front of their stable, the Wolf's warband were grooming their horses. Lady Gweniver herself perched on the tongue of a wooden cart and watched them. For all her cropped hair and men's clothing, Dannyn could only think of her as a woman, and as an attractive one at that. Her large, luminous eyes dominated her face and sparkled like beacons that drew him toward her. The way she moved attracted him, too: every gesture definite yet fluid, as if she drew upon a hidden source of energy. When she saw him, she slid off the wagon tongue and came over to meet him.

"Lord Dannyn, my men need blankets and clothes."

"Then they'll have them today. You're part of the King's

household now, so remember that what you and your men need is part of your maintenance."

"My thanks, then. Our liege is truly most generous."

"He is. I've got more reason than most to praise his generosity. How many bastard sons have ever been given a title and a place at court?"

When she winced, he smiled. He liked getting the delicate subject of his birth out in the open and shoving it into the faces of the noble born before they could use it against him. For a moment he considered, remembering Amain's lecture on her worship, but something seemed to drive him to speak.

"That moon on your cheek, does it mark a true vow?"

"And what else would it be?"

"Well, a ruse, I thought, a way to travel safely, and never would I blame you. A woman on the road with a warband had better have the Goddess's protection—or make men think she does."

"That's true enough, but this crescent embraces my whole life now. I swore to Her, and I stay faithful to Her."

The quiet coldness in her voice was giving him a message.

"I see," he said hurriedly. "Well, far be it from me to question how a priestess has her visions. There's somewhat else I wanted to ask you. Does your sister have a suitor that you favor for her? I'll speak to the King on his behalf."

"Would you? That's an enormous favor you're offering me."

"What? What makes you say that?"

"Oh come now, my lord, don't you see what a treasure you've got in the eyes of the court? You've got more influence with the King than any man alive. If you don't value it, it could turn into a curse."

Dannyn merely smiled, puzzled by the urgency in her voice. It always amazed him when women carried on about unimportant details.

"Well," she went on, "the suitor I favor is Lord Gwetmar of the Alder clan."

"I've fought beside him, and he's a good man. I'll mention him to the King."

"My thanks."

With a little curtsy, Gweniver walked away, leaving him with a dark hiraedd for this woman he could never have.

Lord Dannyn kept his promise about speaking to the king much sooner than Gweniver had expected. That very afternoon, Saddar the councillor came to her chamber with important news. As a deference to his age, she sat him down in a chair by the hearth and poured him a small serving of mead, then took the chair opposite.

"My thanks, Your Holiness," he said in his thin, dry voice. "I wanted to tell you personally that it gladdens my heart that the Wolf clan will live."

"And my thanks to you, good sir."

He smiled and had a dainty sip of mead.

"Now, the King himself asked me to come speak to you," he went on, stressing the words "the King himself." "He has made an important decision, that Lord Gwetmar shall lay aside his allegiance to the Alder clan and marry your sister."

"Splendid!" Gweniver pledged him with her goblet. "Now all we've got to do is get Macla out of the temple safely."

"Ah, I have further news on that. The King wishes you to fetch her soon. He'll be lending you and Gwetmar two hundred men from his personal guard to add to your warbands."

"By the hells! Our liege is most generous."

"So he is. Lord Dannyn will accompany you at their head."

Saddar paused, as if expecting some momentous reaction. Gweniver cocked her head to one side and considered him.

"Ah well," the councillor said at last. "And what does Her Holiness think of Lord Dannyn, if I may ask?"

"My men tell me that he's splendid in battle, and truly, good sir, that's all that matters to me."

"Indeed?"

Something about the old man's smile made her remember the odd warning she'd received from the Goddess, but still she said nothing.

"Well," Saddar said, "it's not my place to question those of holy vows, my lady, but let me give you a small warning from one whose long years at times make him frank. Lord Dannyn is a very impetuous man. I would keep my eye on him, if I were you." He paused to finish the mead in his goblet. "Ah, it gladdens my heart to see you here, Your Holiness. No doubt your Goddess has sent you as a mark of Her favor to our king."

"Let's hope not. Her favor is as dark and harsh as a blooded blade."

Saddar's smile froze on his lips. In a moment he rose, made her a polite bow, and hurriedly took his leave.

For some time, Gweniver thought over the councillor's oddly troubling words. She wanted to turn to the Goddess and ask Her advice, but in truth, she was unsure of how to go about it. What she knew of the Darktime rite was very little indeed, because very little had been preserved. The temple priestesses knew several chants and rituals to be worked at the waning of the moon; there were odd scraps of lore from the Dawntime about certain battlefield prayers; nothing more. Without a temple with mirror and altar, Gweniver simply didn't know how to approach her Goddess. In her saddlebags she had a letter of introduction from Ardda to the high priestess of the Cerrmor temple, but she was afraid to go to that citywise and courtbound lady with her odd talk of the Moon in Her Dark.

The mirror-working, however, was crucial. Later Gweniver did go down into the city, but instead of the temple, she went to the market and bought herself a bronze mirror with a silvered face, small enough to fit into a saddlebag. After dinner that night, she shut herself up in her chamber with only a candle-lantern for light and propped the mirror up against a chest while she knelt in front of it. Silvery and distorted, her face looked back at her.

"My lady," she whispered. "My lady of the Darkness."

In her mind she pictured her vision in the temple, a mere memory image only, and dead. Over the past weeks she'd brooded so much over this memory that the image held still and firm in her mind, a clear picture that she could examine from many different angles, as she looked first at her sword on the altar, then at the mirror or at Ardda, standing nearby. If only there was a way I could see it in this mirror, she told herself, then maybe it would move. As she tried to build the image on the silver surface, it stayed stubbornly blank. All at once, she felt foolish. Doubtless what she wanted was impossible, but some stubborn instinct drove her to try to force the image of the Goddess out through her eyes and onto the gleaming silver.

It was also very late, and she was yawning, finding it hard to focus her eyes as she worked. All at once, she stumbled onto the trick in her mind, just as when a child struggles to learn how to roll a hoop with a stick, and it seems that no matter how hard she tries, the hoop will always fall—then suddenly, without conscious effort, the hoop rolls, and never again will she fail in the attempt. First she saw a flickering trace of a picture on the mirror. Then all at once the image of the Goddess appeared, lasting only a moment, but there.

"Praise be to my Lady's name!"

Gweniver was no longer tired. For half the night she stayed before the mirror, with her knees and back cramped and aching, until she could see the Goddess as clearly as if the image were painted on the silver. At last the vision moved, and the dark eyes of night looked her way yet once again. The Goddess smiled, blessing her only worshipper in the whole wide kingdom of Deverry. Gweniver wept, but in pure, holy joy.

Since the plan was a simple one, Dannyn was sure it would work well. While he escorted Gweniver and her men to the Temple of the Moon, the two brothers of Lord Maer of the Stag would lead a punitive raid deep into Cantrae-held territory, striking at the Boar's demesne if at all possible.

"That will keep them too busy to worry about the Wolf's lands," Glyn remarked.

"So it will, my liege. They don't have to raid any longer than it takes to make the false king give up Lord Maer's lady. By then, we'll be well on our way back to Cerrmor."

"A good plan all round." Glyn considered for a moment. "And, no doubt, the real fighting over the Wolf demesne won't come till fall, when the Boar has the leisure to take up his blood feud."

After the king dismissed him, Dannyn went to the women's quarters to look in on his son. Some years before, Glyn had found him a wife from a noble clan that was willing to ignore his bastardy in return for royal favor. Although Garaena had died of childbed fever, the baby had been born healthy. Now Cobryn was four years old, and already chattering of weapons and warfare. That afternoon, Dannyn took him out of the royal nursery and into the ward to see the horses. Since the warbands were returning after a day's exercises on the roads, the ward was full of men and horses. Dannyn picked his lad up and settled him against his shoulder like a sack of grain. He was a pretty child, his hair as fair as flax, his eyes dark blue like his father's. Cobryn threw his arms around his father's neck and hugged him.

"I love you, Da."

For a moment Dannyn was too surprised to answer, because he'd grown up hating his own father.

"Do you now?" he said at last. "Well, my thanks."

As they strolled through the ward, Cobryn chattering about every horse he saw, Dannyn saw Gweniver talking to a group of lords by the main gate. When they went over, Cobryn twisted in his arms and pointed her out.

"Da, that's a lady!"

When everyone laughed, the lad turned shy and buried his face in Dannyn's shoulder. Gweniver strolled over to get a better look at him.

"What a beautiful child!" she said. "He's not yours, is he?"

"He is. I was married once."

"Now, that's a surprise. I thought you were the kind of man who never marries."

"You misjudge me badly, my lady."

Gweniver went as wary as a startled doe. As he watched her, as the moment dragged on in awkward silence, Dannyn was cursing himself for stubbornly wanting this woman beyond his reach. At last Cobryn piped up and rescued him.

"You know what? The King's my uncle."

"So he is." Gweniver turned her attention to the child in some relief. "Do you honor him?"

"I do. He's splendid."

"More splendid than this cub of mine can realize at his age," Dannyn said. "Our liege has formally taken my lad into the line of succession, right after his own sons. It's not often a bastard's spawn gets to be a prince."

"By the black ass of the Lord of Hell! Well, young Cobryn, you're right enough. He's very splendid indeed."

During the evening meal, Dannyn found himself watching Gweniver greedily, even though his very thoughts were impiety. An old proverb neatly summed up his plight: a man who loves a lass sworn to the Moon had best put many a mile between him and his hopelessness. Her golden hair shone in the candlelight as she clasped a silver goblet between slender fingers, so lovely and delicate that he found it hard to believe that she could really swing a sword. From what Ricyn had told him, she'd made her kills out of luck alone, and luck has a way of deserting a man in battle.

After they were done eating, Dannyn got up and went to her table, where he hunkered down in front of her on the floor, forcing her to lean over to speak to him privately.

"I've been meaning to ask you somewhat," he said. "Do you have a coat of mail?"

"I don't. You know, I've never even worn any."

"What? Oh ye gods, then you've got no idea how heavy it is, do you now?"

"No doubt I'll get used to it. My Goddess will protect me as long as She wants me alive, then let me be slain when She wants me dead. It won't matter when that time comes if I'm wearing the best mail in the kingdom."

"That's true enough, no doubt, because when a man's Wyrd comes upon him, it comes, but a good set of mail turns aside many a bit of bad luck."

When she smiled, their eyes met, and at that moment he felt they understood each other in a dangerously deep way. He stood up quickly.

"But you're not dying this summer if I can help it, Your Holiness. Doubtless it'll ache your heart to take orders from a bastard, but once we're back from claiming your sister, you're going to train with me like a thirteen-year-old rider, new to his warband. A good many of them live to grow up, don't they? Do what I say, and so will you."

Her eyes snapping in rage, she started to rise, but he ducked back out of her way.

"Good night, my lady, and may all your dreams be holy ones."

He hurried away before she could challenge him to a fight. He could see it coming in her eyes.

Nevyn was not quite sure when the King had begun to suspect that his shabby old servitor had the dweomer. When he'd come to offer his services at Dun Cerrmor, some six years ago now, he'd dealt only with an underchamberlain and been given quarters in a typical servant's hut. As the year passed, he'd seen Glyn only from a distance, usually during some ceremonial parade. The anonymity suited Nevyn well; he was there only to keep an eye on events, not meddle in politics, or so he saw it, and he'd chosen Glyn's court only because he could not abide Slwmar of Cantrae, who was sly, treacherous, and suspicious to the point of paranoia.

Yet, since Glyn was gracious to those who served him, at some point during the second year he'd found out about the man who'd ridden in to offer such valuable services and called Nevyn into the great hall for a formal audience to thank him for growing medicines sorely needed in a war. The audience was very short, of course, and Nevyn shared it with several other servitors, but he must have said something that caught the king's attention, because not long after, Glyn had actually visited the herb garden out behind the stables and talked with him again. It became something of a habit; whenever the King had an odd moment, he would come out and ask various questions about this herb or that, about the cycle of the seasons and the growing of things. It seemed to give him some relief from the pressures upon and the intrigues around him.

In the third year, Nevyn had been given a pleasant chamber of his own in one of the side brochs, with no explanation but that he deserved a bit of privacy. Soon after came a place down on the floor of the great hall at a table with more courtly servitors. The King's visits became longer, too, especially in winter when he had more leisure, and at times the liege asked the servitor for blunt advice about the doings of the court. Although Nevyn was always cautious with his answers, they seemed to please the King, who on occasion dropped little hints about knowing that Nevyn was more than the grubby old man he seemed to be.

Now, it seemed, the King had decided that the time had come to be blunt. On the morning when the men of the Stag led out a small army to start their raid against the Boar, Nevyn was weeding a row of comfrey plants when a page came, announcing that the King wished to see him in the council chamber. Hurriedly Nevyn washed his hands in a leather bucket of water and followed the lad into the broch.

In the narrow chamber Glyn was alone, sitting casually on the edge of the table and staring at the parchment map, struck with sunlight through the window. Cut from an entire calfskin, the map was worn, the writing faded in places. Here and there, lines had been drawn in red ink, then scraped away again, the old frontiers and battle lines showing through, a bleeding palimpsest. Seeing it made Nevyn feel wry: it was his kingdom that other men were fighting for. Of anyone in Deverry, he had the best claim to the Wyvern throne, if, of course, he'd been able to convince anyone that Prince Galrion was still alive after all these years.

"I called you here to ask you somewhat," Glyn said abruptly. "You're the only man I can trust to hold your tongue about it. Even priests talk among themselves like old women."

"Old women hold their tongues better, my liege."

"Yet this question of mine takes a priest's kind of knowledge to answer." And here Glyn paused. "I was hoping the dweomer might be able to advise me."

"And does my liege think I have such knowledge?"

"He does. Is your liege wrong?"

"He's not."

Glyn smiled in triumph, very briefly.

"Then answer me this," he went on. "If a man or a woman has sworn a vow in a temple, is there any way that the oath can be foresworn without offending the gods?"

"Well, only in rare circumstances. Suppose someone swore a wrong thing with the connivance of a corrupt priest, then that priest's superior could pronounce the vow invalid. It might also be possible for the person who swore the vow to renounce it by devoting the rest of their life to the god's service, but that would be a tricky matter indeed."

"That's hardly the case here."

"Oho! I take it my liege has noticed his brother pining after a forbidden thing."

"He has, at that. It doesn't take dweomer to see a horse in a chamber, good sorcerer."

"True enough. I only hope that no one besides us has seen it, my liege. There are plenty of men who envy Dannyn."

With a sigh, Glyn nodded his agreement.

"If an old man may offer his liege advice," Nevyn went on. "The king had best speak to his brother about this. It would be a terrible and impious thing for Dannyn to seduce Gweniver into breaking that vow."

Glyn sighed and looked at the map.

"I should arrange for Dannyn to marry again," he said. "I had thoughts of settling Lady Macla and the Wolf lands upon him, but I didn't want him so far from my court all winter. Perhaps my selfishness was all for the best. No doubt Gweniver will visit her sister often."

"No doubt, my liege. May I be so presumptuous as to ask you why you favor Lord Dannyn so highly? I find him worthy of your favor, mind, but most men don't see their father's bastards so clearly. Most prefer not to see them at all."

"True enough. Well, you see, since my father claimed the throne for me when I was just a babe in arms, I was raised to be king. It sounded splendid to a lad: I'd claim the Holy City after glorious battles, I'd be the ruler of all I could survey, I'd save the kingdom from war. But one day I was out in the ward, and I saw the stable lads tormenting this other lad. He was just about six, then, and I was eight. They were mocking him for a bastard, and when he tried to hit one of them, they mobbed him and started beating him. So I ran over and ordered them to stop. I felt most generous, kingly indeed, defending this poor little creature." He smiled in overscrupulous self-mockery. "So I picked the lad up and wiped his bloody nose for him, and by every god in the sky, I might as well have been looking into a mirror. I suppose it goes without saying that no one had ever told the young king that his father took fancies to kitchen maids. Well, I found out that morning. So I went storming into Father's chamber like the king I felt myself to be and demanded to know what he thought he was doing. It's a pity you couldn't have seen the look on his face."

Nevyn allowed himself a laugh.

"But at any rate," Glyn went on, "I insisted on having Dannyn come live with me, because he was my brother, no matter what our father thought about it. And a bit at a time, he told me what he'd gone through, living mocked and scorned as a scullery lad, made to feel grateful for having scraps to eat. And so I began to think about what rulership means, good sorcerer, in my childish way. I made a solemn vow to Great Bel that never would I put my will above all else and worship it the way my father did. For that alone I'd honor Dannyn. He gave me a gift worth more than a hundred horses. But beyond that, he's the only man in this court who loves me for what I am, not for the influence and land he can get out of me. Do I sound a fool for caring about such things? I must, I suppose."

"My liege is not a fool. My liege is one of the sanest men I've ever met, and lest you think that idle flattery, let me add that sanity is a curse in mad times like these."

"Is it now?" The King looked away, slack-mouthed for a moment. "True enough, I suppose. Well, my thanks, good sir, for your counsel. If things allow, I'll come down to the garden one of these days and see how it's getting on."

Rather than returning to his weeding, Nevyn went back to his chamber after he left the King. His heart was troubled, wondering if Glyn were meant to rule as the only king in Deverry, hoping that such was his Wyrd, yet knowing that the future was closed to him. After he barred the door to ensure that he wouldn't be disturbed, he stood in the center of his small chamber and imagined that his right hand held a sword of blue fire. Slowly he bent his will to the image until it lived apart from his will, no matter where he turned his attention. Only then did he use it to trace a circle of blue fire around him, imaging the flames until they, too, lived of their own will.

Laying aside the sword, he sat down in the center of the leaping, glowing circle and built up before him the mental image of a six-pointed star, glowing also with gold fire, a symbol of the center and balance of all things, and the source of the true kingship. Invoking the Kings of the Element of Aethyr, he stared into the hexagon formed in the center of the interlaced triangles and used it to scry the way clumsier dweomerfolk use a stone or a mirror.

The visions came cloudy, barely forming before they dissolved, thrown together and torn apart like clouds in a high wind, and he saw naught there of Glyn's Wyrd. Even in the Innerlands, the currents were troubled, the forces out of balance, the light shadowed. For every kingdom or people, there's a corresponding part of the Innerlands—people think of it as a place, which will do for an image—that's the true source of the events that come to the kingdom on the outer plane, just as every person has their secret and undying soul, which determines what that person calls his will or his luck. The Deverry folk saw wars raging between ambitious men; those men saw themselves as the authors of their actions; Nevyn saw the truth. The petty squabbles of would-be kings were only symptoms of the crisis, like the fever is only the symptom of the disease, a painful thing in itself, but not the true killer. Out on the Innerlands, the dark forces of Unbalanced Death were out of control, sweeping all into chaos, with only a handful of warriors who served the Light to pit themselves against them. Although Nevyn was only the humble servant of those Great Ones, he had his own part of the war to fight in the kingdom. After all, a fever may kill a patient if it's allowed to burn unchecked.

Now, mind that you never think of these forces of Unbalanced Death as persons, some sort of evil army led by beings with a recognizable soul. On the contrary, they were forces as natural in their own way as falling rain, but out of control like a river in flood tide, swelling over its banks and sweeping farms and towns before it. Every people or kingdom has a streak of chaos in its soul, weaknesses, greeds, small prides and arrogances, which can be either denied or given in to. When indulged, they release energy—to use a metaphor—which flows to the appropriate dark place in the Innerlands. So it was with Deverry in that troubled time. The forces were swollen and sweeping down, exactly like that river.

Nevyn was simply unsure of how far he could intervene on the physical plane. The work of the dweomer is subtle, a thing of influences, images, and slow inner working. Direct action in the world is normally so foreign to a dweomer-master that Nevyn was afraid to intervene until the time was exactly right. A wrong action, even to the right end, would only score another victory for Chaos and the Dark. Yet it ached his heart to wait, to watch the death, the sickness, the suffering, and the poverty that the wars were spreading across the kingdom. The worst thing of all was knowing that here and there were the evil masters of the dark dweomer, gloating over the suffering and sucking up the power released by the Chaos tide for their own dark ends. Their time will come, he reminded himself, for them is the dark at the end of the world, the curse at the end of the ages of ages.

But he as servant couldn't send them to the dark before their time, any more than he could see if Glyn would someday rule a peaceful kingdom in Dun Deverry. With a sigh, he broke off his fruitless meditations and banished the star and the circle. He went to his window and leaned out, watching the warriors hurry across the ward far below on their way to the great hall for dinner. Seeing them laughing and jesting stabbed guilt into his heart. His old fault had ripened the war, or so he saw it. Long ago, when he'd been a prince of the realm, he'd been given the choice between marrying Brangwen of the Falcon clan and thus making slower progress in learning dweomer (since he would have a wife and children to care for), or casting her off and devoting himself to the craft. In his clumsy attempt to have the best of both choices, he'd brought three people to their deaths: Brangwen herself, her brother Gerraent, who'd loved her with an incestuous and unholy passion, and Lord Blaen of the Boar, an honorable suitor who'd had the bad luck to be entangled with Gerraent's madness.

If he'd only married Brangwen, he reproached himself, they would have had heirs, who would have had heirs in their turn to inherit the throne cleanly, and prevent the civil war. Perhaps. He warned himself that no man could know the truth of that. On the other hand, this matter of the Boars was more closely related to his mistake. Even since they'd been given the Falcon lands as retribution for Blaen's death, the Boars had swelled with pride and arrogance until they'd urged Gwerbret Cantrae to make a claim on a throne that he was never meant to have.

And now all the actors in that ancient tragedy were gathered here in Cerrmor. That night at dinner, Nevyn looked around the hall and marked them all: Blaen, eating with the rest of the Wolf riders as Ricyn, their captain; Gerraent, sitting at Glyn's left as his brother; Brangwen, with the blue tattoo of a Moon-sworn rider on her cheek. They were all twined together still, but it was Gweniver's lot in this life that ached his heart the most.

Nevyn was seated at a table on the floor of the hall with the scribe and his wife, the head groom and his, two underchamberlains, and the widowed Master of Weaponry, Ysgerryn. That particular evening, Ysgerryn noticed Nevyn watching the Lady Gweniver as she ate and mentioned that earlier Dannyn had brought her in to be fitted with a coat of mail.

"Fortunately, I'd saved some mail that used to fit Lord Dannyn when he was about fourteen," Ysgerryn went on. "It could have been broken apart and reworked to a larger size, of course, but it was such a nice bit of work I kept it for one of the young princes someday. It came in handy now."

"So it did. And what did the lord think of having the lady wear his old armor?"

"Oddly enough, he was pleased. He said somewhat about it being an omen."

I'll just wager he did, Nevyn thought, curse him!

Once the meal was over, Nevyn started to leave the hall, but he noticed Dannyn coming over to sit with Gweniver at her table. He lingered below the dais to eavesdrop, but Dannyn was only asking her an innocent question about the mail.

"Oh ye gods," she said with a laugh. "My shoulders ache like fire from wearing the thing! It must weigh a good two stone."

"It does, at that," Dannyn said. "But keep wearing it, every cursed minute you can stand to have it on. I'd hate to lose a man of your spirit just because of a lack of training."

With a drunken grin, young Lord Oldac leaned across the table, a beefy, blond lad with entirely too high an opinion of himself.

"A man?" he said. "Here, Dannyn, what's happened to your eyes?"

"They can see the blue tattoo on her face. As far as anyone under my command is concerned, she's a man, or as much like one as matters."

"True spoken, of course." Oldac wiped his mead-soaked mustache on the back of his hand. "But here, Gwen, there's no denying that you're a good-looking enough wench to make a man forget."

As fast and straight as a grouse breaking cover, Dannyn rose and leaned over to grab Oldac by the shirt. While goblets rolled and spilled and men shouted, he hauled the kicking, yelling lord across the table. With a last heave, he dumped him at Gweniver's feet.

"Apologize," Dannyn snarled. "No one calls a lady and a priestess a wench."

Dead silent, every man in the hall was watching. Oldac gasped for breath and hauled himself up in a kneel.

"Go on." Dannyn prodded him with one foot.

"Most humbly I apologize," Oldac panted. "Never will I call you that again, Your Holiness. I beg your Goddess to forgive me."

"You're a fool," Gweniver said. "But your apology is accepted."

Oldac got up, smoothed down his mead-soaked shirt, and turned on Dannyn.

"May the Goddess forgive my slight," he said. "But as for you, bastard . . ."

When Dannyn laid his hand on his sword hilt, men rose from their seats.

"Does his lordship wish to offer me a formal challenge?" Dannyn's voice was as mild as a lady's maid.

Trapped, Oldac looked this way and that, his mouth working as he debated the choice between broken honor and certain death. Dannyn waited, smiling. At the table of honor, the King rose.

"Enough!" Glyn yelled. "A pox on both of you for fighting in my hall! Danno, get back here and sit down. Oldac, I wish to speak with you later in my apartments."

Blushing in shame, Oldac spun on his heel and ran out of the hall. His head down like a whipped hound, Dannyn slunk back to his brother's side. As Nevyn left, he was wondering about Gerraent, as he tended to think of him in weak moments. It seemed that he was determined to treat Gweniver honorably and to ignore that long-buried passion which had to be working its way to the surface. More power to the lad, Nevyn thought, maybe he'll get free of it in this life. And yet with the thought came a clammy touch of dweomer-cold down his back. There was danger working here, danger of which he was unaware.

At the head of a small army, Gweniver returned to the Temple of the Moon late on a spring day when the setting sun washed the high walls with golden light. Leaving the men at the foot of the hill, she and Gwetmar walked up to the gates, which opened a crack to reveal Lypilla's face.

"It is you, Gwen!" she sang out. "When we saw the army, we thought it might be those wretched Boars coming back or suchlike."

"It's not, at that. We've come to fetch Maccy. I promised her a wedding, and that's what she's going to have."

"Splendid! The poor little thing's been so heartsick. Come in, come in. It gladdens my heart to see you."

When Gweniver came inside, Macla ran to meet her and

threw herself into her sister's arms. The temple ward was full of women, watching with sentimental smiles as Maccy wept in joy.

"I've been so worried, thinking you might be dead," she sobbed.

"Well, here I am. Now pull yourself together, Maccy. I've brought you a husband, and everything's going to be all right. You're going to have a big wedding down in the court itself."

Macla shrieked with joy and clasped her hands over her mouth.

"So go get your things together while I talk with Ardda," Gweniver went on. "Lord Gwetmar's waiting for you."

"Gwetmar? But he's homely!"

"Then you won't have to worry about him siring bastards on your serving women. Listen, you little dolt, he's the only man in court who would have married you because he loves you, not for the dowry, so start counting up his qualities. You won't see his face when he blows the candle out, anyway."

Macla groaned dramatically, but she trotted off for the dormitory. Only then did Gweniver notice their mother, standing on the edge of the crowd. Dolyan stood with her arms crossed across her chest as if she were hugging grief, her eyes half-filled with tears. Gweniver went over hesitantly.

"You've made your sister a good marriage," Dolyan said in a trembling voice. "I'm proud of you."

"My thanks, Mam. Are you well?"

"As well as I can be, seeing you like this. Gwen, Gwen, I beg you. Stay here in the temple."

"I can't, Mam. I'm the only honor the clan has left."

"Honor? Oh, is it honor now? You're as bad as your father, bad as all your brothers, talking of honor until I thought I'd go mad, I truly did. It's not the honor that pleases you, it's the slaughter." All at once, she tossed her head, and the words poured out in a rage-tide. "They never cared that I loved them; oh, it didn't matter half as much as did their cursed honor, riding out, bleeding the clan white, and all to work grief on the kingdom! Gwen, how can you do this to me? How can you ride to war like they did?"

"I have to, Mam. You have Maccy, and soon you'll be dowager, back on our lands."

"Back on what?" She spit the words out. "A burnt home and

ravaged lands, and all for the honor of the thing! Gwen, please, don't ride!" And then she was weeping, sobbing aloud.

Gweniver could neither speak nor move. The other women rushed to Dolyan's side, swept her up, and hurried her away, but all the while they looked daggers back at this ungrateful wretch of a daughter. As Gweniver fled through the gates, she heard Dolyan keen, a long high wail of grief. I'm dead to her already, she thought. Yet because it was the will of the Goddess, she could not weep, as much as she longed for tears.

"What's so wrong?" Gwetmar asked.

"Naught. Maccy'll be out shortly." She turned away and looked downhill, searching to see Ricyn among her men. "By the black hairy ass of the Lord of Hell, it'll gladden my heart to get back to Cerrmor."

Wherever Ricyn was, she couldn't pick him out, but she saw Dannyn, sitting easily on horseback at the head of the King's riders. Soon she would be riding to war under his command, and she thought to herself that the Goddess had sent her a splendid master in the arts of death.

Although Nevyn had several apprentices in the art of herbcraft, the most capable was a young woman named Gavra, a tall, slender lass with raven-dark hair and hazel eyes. Since she'd been born the daughter of an innkeep down in Cerrmor, she was used to hard work and also determined to better herself in life. In the two years she'd studied with him, she'd made excellent progress in learning the multifarious herbs and their uses. Accordingly, he allowed her to help him every afternoon when he tended the minor illnesses or accidents of the palace servants, who were below the notice of the official chirurgeons. Gavra also used her mind to good advantage when it came to court intrigue. Dannyn and Gweniver had been back in the dun only two days when the apprentice brought Nevyn an interesting bit of news.

"Lord Oldac stopped me to speak with me today," Gavra remarked.

"Indeed? Has he been pressing his attentions on you again?"

"Well, he was ever so polite, but I think me he had somewhat dishonorable on his mind. Master, would you speak to him? It's cursed hard to insult one of the noble-born, but the last thing I want in life is one of his bastards—or any man's, for that matter."

"Then speak I will. You're as much under my protection as if you were my daughter, and I'll cursed well go to the King if I have to."

"My thanks and twice over. But it wasn't only his drunken smiles that troubled my heart. He had the gall to insult Lady Gweniver. I think she's splendid, and I won't hear that sort of talk from anyone."

"And just what did he say?"

"Oh, he was insinuating things, more like, about the way she and Lord Dannyn spend so much time on the practice ground."

Nevyn snarled under his breath.

"He said it more against his lordship than Her Holiness," Gavra went on. "Asking me didn't I think it strange that his lordship was so eager to teach Lady Gweniver his sport, but it vexed me none the less. I told him that a common-born servant like me was below having thoughts about his lordship one way or another, and then I marched off."

"Good lass. I'll have to speak to Oldac about more things than one, I see. If it gets back to Gweniver's ears that he's been insulting her, he may die quite suddenly."

"Well, it wouldn't ache my heart if he did."

The very next afternoon Gweniver and Dannyn came to their afternoon surgery. They'd just finished putting salve on the underfalconer's scratched hand when the two strode in with the rattle and clang of full mail. Dannyn held a bloody rag pressed to his cheek.

"Would you tend the captain here, good herbman?" Gweniver said. "He's too embarrassed to go to the chirurgeon."

"If I could call a priestess a bitch," Dannyn mumbled through the rag, "I would."

Gweniver merely laughed. When the captain took the rag away, his cheek was scraped raw, swelling badly, and dripping blood from two small nicks.

"We were using blunt blades," Gweniver explained. "But they can still raise a good bruise, and he refused to wear a helm for our lesson."

"Stupidity," Dannyn said. "Mine, I mean. I never thought she'd get near me."

"Indeed?" Nevyn remarked. "It seems that the lady has

more talent for this sort of thing than either of us would have thought."

Dannyn gave him so insolent a smile that Nevyn was tempted to wash the wounds with the strongest witch hazel he had. As an act of humility, he used warm water instead, forcibly reminding himself that Dannyn was not Gerraent, that while the soul was the same at root, the personality was different, and that Dannyn had excuses for his arrogance that Gerraent had never had. Yet every time the captain's cold eyes flicked Gweniver's way, Nevyn was furious. When he left, Nevyn allowed himself a sigh for the foolish pride of men, which could hold a grudge for a hundred and thirty years.

Gweniver herself lingered, looking curiously over the herbs and potions and chatting idly with Gavra, who mercifully said nothing about Lord Oldac's slight. Although the lady seemed oblivious of them, Wildfolk followed her around the room, at times plucking timidly at her sleeve, as if asking her to see them. For some reason that Nevyn didn't truly understand, the Wildfolk could always recognize someone with dweomer-power, and the little creatures found such fascinating. Finally they vanished with disappointed shakes of their heads. Nevyn suddenly wondered if Gweniver had stumbled across her latent dweomer-talents and was using them in the service of her Goddess. The thought made him turn cold with fear, and something of it must have shown on his face.

"Is somewhat wrong, good herbman?" Gweniver said.

"Oh, naught, naught. I was just wondering when you'd be riding on campaign."

"Soon, after Maccy's wedding. We're going to sweep the Eldidd border on patrol. We might not even see any fighting, or so Lord Dannyn tells me, so don't trouble your heart, good sir."

When she smiled, he felt the fear again, clutching his heart, but he merely nodded and said nothing more.

The wedding festivities lasted all day, with mock combats and horse races, dancing and bard-song. By evening, those few souls who were still sober were stuffed with food to the point of drowsiness. Before Gwetmar and Macla retired to their chamber for their wedding night, one last formality remained. Glyn summoned the couple, Gweniver, and a handful of witnesses to his chamber to oversee the signing of the wedding contract. Although normally the King himself would have had nothing to do with such a matter, the passing down of a great clan through the female line was an important affair. When Gweniver arrived, she was quite surprised to see Nevyn among the witnesses, Dannyn, Yvyr, and Saddar.

The King's scribe read out the decree that turned Gwetmar into the head of the Wolf clan and bestowed Macla's dowry upon him on the terms that he would rule as the Wolf and give all his loyalty to that clan. First Gwetmar made his mark on the parchment; then Gweniver signed her name as her last act as the head of the Wolf. After Dannyn made his mark, the other witnesses signed.

"Done, then," Glyn said. "Gwetmar of the Wolf, you have our leave to take your bride to your chambers."

In a great flurry of bowing and curtsies, the wedding pair and the councillors left the chamber, but Glyn motioned to Gweniver and Nevyn to stay with him and Dannyn. A page brought ale in silver tankards, then discreetly retired.

"Well, Your Holiness," the King said. "I've kept my promise to you about the Wolf's name. I sincerely hope that your father and brothers will hear of this in the Otherlands."

"I echo that hope, my liege. You have my humble thanks, and I'm well-pleased by your generosity to one far below you."

"Well, I find it hard to think of a sworn priestess as being below me."

"My liege is most pious, and the Goddess will honor him for it." Gweniver made him a curtsy. "But priestess or not, I ride at his command."

"Or at mine, once we're on campaign," Dannyn broke in. "I trust my lady will remember that."

They all turned to look at him, Glyn with a cold warning in his eyes. Dannyn was frankly drunk, his face mead-flushed, his mouth slack.

"I ride at my Goddess's orders in all things," Gweniver made her voice as cold as she could. "I trust Lord Dannyn will remember *that.*"

"Oh now here." Dannyn paused for a most unnecessary sip of ale. "All I want to do is serve your Goddess by keeping you alive. Can't say the rites when you're dead, can you? Besides, you're too cursed valuable to lose. Everyone knows it's a good omen you're here."

Glyn started to speak, but Nevyn got in before him.

"His lordship speaks the truth," the old man said. "But he had best mind how he phrases his word when he speaks to one of the Holy Ladies."

"Ah, what's it to you, old man?"

"Danno!" the King snapped.

"My apologies." Dannyn turned cloudy eyes Gweniver's way. "And to you, too, my lady, but I just wanted to warn you. I know you fancy yourself a warrior, but—"

"Fancy myself?" Gweniver got to her feet. "The Goddess has marked me out for blood, and don't you think that you're going to keep me from it."

"Indeed? Well, we'll see about that. I'd argue with the Lord of Hell himself to advance my brother's cause, and so I'll argue with your Goddess if I have to."

"Dannyn, hold your tongue," Nevyn broke in. "You don't know what you're saying."

Dannyn went scarlet with rage. The King grabbed for his arm, but too late: with an oath, Dannyn flung the tankard of ale straight at Nevyn's head. The old man barked out one incomprehensible word. In midair the tankard stopped as if grabbed by an invisible hand while ale spilled all over the floor. Gweniver felt the blood drain from her face and leave it as cold as the winter snow. The unseen hand set the tankard down on the floor quite neatly, top upward. Dannyn stared at it, tried to speak, then started to shake all over, scared into near-sobriety. Glyn, however, laughed.

"When he recovers himself, good Nevyn," he said, "My brother will apologize."

"No need, my liege. A drunken man's not quite responsible for his lapses. My apologies, my liege, for that mess on the carpet. Spirits can't think too well, you see, so it never occurred to them to catch the cursed thing right-side-up."

Spirits? Gweniver thought, ye gods, this room must be full of them, if Nevyn has dweomer! Although she looked around uneasily, she saw none. Muttering something about calling a page to clean up the ale, Dannyn got up and fled the chamber.

"There's more than one way to make a man mind his courtesies," the King remarked. "My lady, allow me to apologize."

"It's no fault of yours, my liege. As Nevyn says, a drunken man's not quite himself."

Although they stayed with the King for a few more moments, the awkward incident soon forced them to leave. Gweniver supposed that the King would have a few sharp words for his brother later. As she walked down the corridor with Nevyn, she was wondering why a man with his powers would be content with so humble a place at court, but she was too frightened to ask him outright.

"Well, good sorcerer," she said at last. "I take it that our liege will be king of all Deverry soon, with a man like you to aid him."

"I wouldn't wager hard coin on it."

She stopped walking and turned to stare at him. Nevyn gave her a weary smile.

"Who knows what the gods have in store?" he went on. "The Goddess you serve has a dark heart, as well you know. It's possible that She sent you here to preside over a bloody defeat."

"Perhaps so." She felt sick at the thought, but it was a logical one. "I'll pray it's otherwise."

"So will I. Glyn is a good man and a splendid king, but it's not given to me to see the end of this. My lady, I'll beg you to keep my dweomer a secret from the rest of the court."

"As you wish, then. I doubt me if anyone would believe me if I told them, anyway."

"Perhaps not." He paused, considering her. "I trust Lord Dannyn is going to treat you with all the respect your position deserves."

"He'd better. I assure you, I have no intention of breaking my vow."

When he looked startled, she laughed.

"It behooves a priestess to be blunt at times," she said. "My sister can tell you that I've never spared my tongue."

"Good. Let me be blunt, too. It aches my heart to see you ride to war. I'll pray your Goddess protect you."

As she went on her way, Gweniver felt flattered, that a man with his power would be concerned for her.

Torchlight flared on the walls as the army mustered in the ward. Yawning from a short night's sleep, Ricyn walked among his men, yelling orders to keep them hurrying. Loaded with provisions, carts rumbled by, the sleepy carters cracking long whips. Ricyn smiled at everything. He'd always dreamt of this day, when he'd be riding to war as a captain, not merely a common rider. One at a time, his men led their horses into line at the watering trough. Ricyn found Camlwn, who was holding the reins to Dagwyn's horse as well as to his own.

"And where's Dagwyn?" Ricyn said.

For an answer he jerked his thumb at the nearby stable, where Dagwyn and a kitchen lass were embracing passionately in the shadow of a wall.

"One last sweet farewell," Camlwn said, grinning. "I don't know how he does it. I'll swear he's ensorceled a lass in every dun we've ever been in."

"If not two. Daggo, come on! Save it for when we ride home!"

The soft silvery notes of Lord Dannyn's horn drifted through the dun. When Dagwyn tore himself away from the lass, the warband hooted and jeered. Calling orders, Ricyn mounted his horse. The familiar scuffling jingle as the warband followed his example was sweeter than any bard-song. He led them around to the front of the dun, where the rest of the army, over three hundred men in all, waited by the gates with the carts, packhorses, and servants off to one side. Gweniver turned her horse out of the confusion and rode over to fall into place at Ricyn's side.

"Good morrow, my lady." He made a half-bow from the saddle.

"Morrow. This is splendid, Ricco. I've never been so excited in my life."

Ricyn grinned, thinking that she was like a young lad on his first ride out. It seemed impossible that she would be there, wearing mail like the rest of them, with the hood pushed back to reveal the soft cropped curls of her golden hair and the blue tattoo on her cheek. The sky turned gray with dawn and paled the torchlight below. Up at the gates, servants began to attach the chains to the winch. Lord Dannyn rode his stocky black

gelding down the line, paused here and there to speak to someone, then finally jogged up to Gweniver.

"You're riding at the head of the line with me, Your Holiness."

"Oh, am I now? And to what do I owe this honor?"

"Your noble birth." Dannyn gave her a thin-lipped smile.
"It's a cursed sight better than mine, isn't it?"

As they rode away, Ricyn stared at Dannyn's back and hated
him.

All that morning, the army ambled west along the coast
road, which hugged the sea cliffs. Ricyn could see the ocean,
sparkling turquoise, flecked with white, running slow waves onto
the pale sand far below. Off to the right were the well-tended
fields of the King's personal demesne, stubbled golden, where an
occasional peasant walked along, bent double as he gleaned the
last few grains of the first harvest. Ordinarily, Ricyn would have
been whistling as they rode, just because it was a lovely day and
they were headed for glory, but today he rode wrapped in his
thoughts, alone at the head of the warband instead of next to a
familiar riding partner. Every now and then, when the road
curved, he would see Gweniver far ahead and wish that she was
riding next to him.

Yet that night, when the army camped in the broad meadows along the cliffs, Gweniver came to his campfire with her
arms full of her gear. He jumped up and took the burden from
her.

"You should have let me tend your horse, my lady."

"Oh, I can stake out a horse if I have to. I'll be sharing your
fire."

"That gladdens my heart. I was wondering just how long
Lord Dannyn would keep you at his side."

"And just what do you mean by that?"

"Naught but what I said, my lady. I'll go fetch you some
dinner from the carts."

As he hurried off, Gweniver watched him with her hands set
on her hips. He cursed himself for his big mouth. When he returned, she was sitting by the fire and going through her saddlebags for something, but she laid them aside to take the bread and
beef jerky from him. While they ate in silence, he was aware of
her watching him narrow-eyed. Finally she spoke.

"And just why did you say that about our bastard? I want the truth out of you."

"Well, me and the whole cursed army honor your vow. Does he?"

"He's not going to have any choice. What's making you think otherwise?"

"Naught, my lady. My apologies."

She hesitated, still looking at him with that deep-eyed suspicion, then turned away and brought out a pair of dice from her saddlebags, tossing them in one hand like a hardened rider.

"Are you game?" she said. "We can play for splinters of firewood."

"Of course, my lady. Have the first roll."

With a toss she threw them into the firelight.

"Five, by the hells!" she groaned. "Your roll, then, but I hope it's the last cursed five I see from now on."

They played dice all evening, and never once did she mention Lord Dannyn's name again. Yet in the morning she went to speak to the king's captain, then came back with the news that she'd be riding with her own men from then on.

The morning was thick with sea fog, which turned the air as cold as winter and dampened their heavy wool cloaks as the army rode along, strangely silent in the heavy damp. Although Gweniver grumbled about it as loudly as any of her men, in the end it turned out to be something of a blessing. Close to noon they came to Morlyn, a small harbor town some thirty miles from the Eldidd border, and found the gates shut against them. When Dannyn hailed them in Glyn's name, guards leaned over the ramparts on top the stone walls.

"Cerrmor men, by the gods!" yelled one. "Open the gates, lads! And aren't we glad to see you, my lord Dannyn."

"Why? Has there been trouble?"

"Trouble and twice trouble. Eldidd ships cruising along outside the harbor, and Eldidd raiders firing farms along the roads up north."

Ricyn suddenly loved the fog, which was keeping the warships becalmed out at sea where they couldn't raid in and burn the harbor. When they rode in the gates, they found the town looking like a market fair. From miles around, farmers had fled into the walls and brought their families, cattle, and pigs with them. Every street was a camp where women made do in rough tents, and children ran around among the cooking fires with dogs trailing after them. Dannyn tried to find somewhere to draw up his men, then settled for letting them trail down alleys crowded with tethered livestock. Ricyn followed Gweniver as she made her way through the confusion to Dannyn's side.

"Well, my lady," Ricyn said. "It looks like we're going to have a bit of sport after all."

"I'll pray so." She gave him an open, sunny smile.

From a nearby tavern, a stout gray-haired man emerged, pulling a long black ceremonial robe over his shirt and brigga. He clutched Dannyn's stirrup as a sign of fealty and introduced him as Morlo, the town mayor.

"And when did you see these ships?" Dannyn said.

"Three days ago, my lord. The fishermen come in with the news, a big merchantman, they say, and two galleys with her."

"I see. Well, then your harbor's probably safe enough. I'll wager those ships are there only to provision the raiders. Where's your local lord? Tieryn Cavydd, isn't he?"

"He is." Morlo paused to run a worried hand over his eyes. "But we haven't seen a trace of him or his men this past two days, and that's a bad omen, says I. We been afraid to send him a messenger."

With an oath, Dannyn turned to Gweniver.

"Let's get our lads out of here. If Cavydd isn't dead, he's under siege. We'd better send a messenger back to Cerrmor, too, and get some ships out here to chase the Eldidd scum away." He glanced around and saw Ricyn beside her. "Your captain might be a good man for the job."

"He's not." Gweniver spoke firmly. "My lord."

Dannyn flushed scarlet. Only Ricyn's long years of military discipline kept his hand away from his sword.

"As you wish, my lady," Dannyn said at last. "I'll send some of my own lads back."

In a disorganized mob, the army picked its way through town, then reformed on the north-running road. Reluctantly Gweniver rode beside Dannyn when he ordered her, leaving Ricyn alone with his dark thoughts until Dagwyn broke ranks and rode up to join him. For some ten miles they traveled fast, leaving the supply train to follow at its own slow pace, then halted in a big cow pasture. Ricyn could see Dannyn sending scouts out.

"What do you think this means?" Dagwyn said.

"Trouble. What else? By the asses of the gods, I didn't want our lady to see a scrap this soon."

"Ah horseshit, Ricco. She's the safest one among us. The Goddess has Her hands upon her night and day."

He spoke with such quiet conviction that Ricyn was reassured. After half an hour or so the scouts rode back. From one man to the next, the news passed down the line: Tieryn Cavydd's dun was besieged by a hundred Eldidd men, and it lay just two miles away. Without waiting for orders, the men armed, pulling their shields into position on their left arms, loosening swords in scabbards, drawing up the hoods of their mail, and reaching for javelins. Ricyn saw Gweniver arguing furiously with Dannyn until, with a hurled oath, she pulled her horse out of line and trotted back to her warband.

"That arrogant bastard!" she snarled.

"What's he done, my lady?" Ricyn said. "Ordered you to keep us in the rear as a reserve?"

"Just that. How did you know?"

"Makes sense, my lady. Our band has never ridden together before. It makes somewhat of a difference."

"Oh, that's all very well, but he mocked me, curse him! If my lady would be so kind, says he, to stay out of the way? If my three hundred can't slaughter a third as many Eldidd dogs, says he, then we'll need your Goddess's help very badly."

"By the hells!"

"Just so. It's the insult to the Goddess more than to me. If the King didn't honor him so cursed much, I'd kill him here and now."

When the army moved out, Gweniver's warband rode in the rear. They trotted across fields that had recently been set to the torch, the black stubble mute witness to the raids, then forded a stream and climbed up a low hill. From the top Ricyn could see the dark broch tower within its earthworks, and the siege camp spreading out across a meadow. Screaming a war cry, Dannyn drew his sword and led his army down at a breakneck gallop as the enemy camp suddenly came alive with shouting. The reserve trotted decorously after.

Below the camp turned into a swirl of dust and clamor, men shouting, running for horses, fighting desperately on foot as Dannyn's charge swept over them. Even if Gweniver broke orders, Ricyn reflected, there wasn't much of a way they could join in the unequal fight, because Dannyn's men seemed to cover the field like a breaking wave. Just then the dun gates opened and Cavydd's men slammed into the besiegers from the rear. The shouting rang out as the mob plunged back and forth, horses rearing, swords flashing. Gweniver smiled as she watched. Ricyn was suddenly frightened of her.

With war cries that were closer to screams of terror, one little clot of Eldidd men broke free from the melee and in their panic fled straight toward the reserve. Ricyn had just time to draw his sword before Gweniver howled out a challenge and spurred her horse straight for them. With a shout, he went after her. Although he heard the men following him, he kept his eyes on her as she plunged into the middle of the desperate mob.

"Ah shit!" He spurred his horse hard.

He saw her blade flash up bloody, and a man fall from his saddle, but there were three others around her. Howling a war cry, he charged the mob from the rear. He swung hard, slashing one horse, getting a good blow on a man's back, slashing back and forth as if he were beating hounds off a deer with a whip. Off to his right, Dagwyn made a kill. An Eldidd man pulled his horse around clumsily. Ricyn stabbed in, getting him so hard that he shattered his mail and killed him clean. When he pulled the sword free, the dead man rolled off his horse and under the hooves of Ricyn's mount, which reared. As it came down, he heard Gweniver laughing, howling, shrieking like a fiend, and he saw that she'd made another kill. Then the Wolf riders were all around them, and the fight over.

As merry as if she'd just heard a splendid jest, Gweniver trotted up to him.

"I got two," she announced, crowing over it. "What's so wrong, Ricco? You look frightened or suchlike."

"By all the hells, the next time you ride into hopeless odds, at least take me with you! You little dolt! I never thought I'd see you alive again. I mean . . . well, uh . . . my lady."

"I knew you'd have the sense to follow, and you did, didn't you?"

The warband clustered round to stare at her in awe.

"Look at that," Dagwyn said. "Her horse doesn't even have a scratch on him."

The men whispered among themselves, a superstitious ripple that was as much fear as awe.

"It was the Goddess," she said. "She rode with me."

In a flurry of whispered oaths, the men edged their horses back—but only a little way, because her god-touched power was like a fire, spreading warmth. Ricyn had never seen a smile like hers, as tight and cold as if it were a smile carved on the face of a statue of a god. Yet at a familiar shout from behind them, her smile disappeared. The men parted to let Lord Dannyn through to the lady's side.

"So your men saw a bit of sport, did they?" he said. "Did you lead that charge, Ricco? I hope to all the hells that she had the sense to stay out of it."

The entire warband wheeled around, eyes flashing in rage, and mobbed him. When Dannyn's hand went to his sword hilt, Ricyn drew.

"Get back!" Gweniver yelled. "Leave him be!"

Swearing under their breaths, they edged their horses back, except for Ricyn, who rode up to the lord's side and made him a half-bow from the saddle, though his sword was still in hand.

"His lordship forgets that he speaks to a priestess. Me and my men most humbly beg that his lordship remembers it from now on. My lady led that charge, my lord. We all saw her hold off four men before we reached her, and she killed two of them."

White-faced, Dannyn swung Gweniver's way.

"I wasn't truly riding at your orders," she said. "You may quibble with the Moon over questions of command if you wish. And as for you, Ricco, you fought like a fiend from hell yourself. I swear you're half-a-berserker."

As he realized that she spoke the truth, Ricyn felt caught by feelings he couldn't sort out. He'd never been that kind of fighter before, preferring to mark his man well and pay strict attention to the strategy of things. It seemed to him that her Goddess had reached out and laid Her hands upon him, and he shuddered as if he were cold.

A slender blond who was no more than twenty, Tieryn Cavydd laughed as much as he talked, half hysterical with his unexpected rescue. Over a hasty meal in his great hall, he told Gweniver and Dannyn the story at his table of honor, while the Cerrmor army sat on the floor for want of enough benches. His pregnant young wife sat beside him and listened, her food untouched before her.

"I've never known them to be so cursed bold," Cavydd said. "We always have raids, well, you know that, but never this many. By the Lord of Hell, there were three hundred of them at my gates, at least, maybe four, and all at once. Then they left part of the army to keep me pinned and rode off. I was sure as sure they were heading for Morlyn, but if I'd sallied with only fifty men, we never would have lived to reach the town. I've been praying that some of my allies would get wind of it and come relieve me."

"They've doubtless got their hands full," Dannyn said. "Well, we'll be riding north after them tomorrow."

"I'll have to leave men behind on fort guard, but I'll ride with you myself, of course."

"Not necessary and most unwise. They might swing back here to pick up the men they left on siege. I'll leave fifty men to reinforce you."

"It's not going to be me and my warband," Gweniver broke in. "Lord Dannyn may banish the idea from his mind."

When he turned her way with an icy stare, Gweniver smiled, remembering the way her men had mobbed him on the field. Dannyn seemed to remember it as well.

"As my lady wishes," he said. "Well, this bodes ill, Your Grace. Looks like Eldidd's planning on pushing the western border hard from now on."

The wife rose and fled the hall with her hands clasped so tightly that her knuckles turned bloodless.

"How far away are your nearest vassals?" Dannyn remarked.

"Fifteen miles north, and then there's another one sixteen miles to the west—or I should say, there was. Who knows if his dun still stands?"

When Dannyn swore aloud, Cavydd's mouth twisted in what might have been a smile.

"When you return to court," he said levelly, "tell our liege somewhat for me, will you? I don't know how much longer we can hold out. When you ride north, my lord, look around you. Once there were demesnes all the way between here and the Eldidd border, all the way north along the Aver Vic. Just look around and see how many Deverry lords are left."

"I have no doubt our liege will remedy the situation."

"He'd better. I swore I'd die for our King, and I will if it comes to that, but there are some who are ready enough to make their peace with Eldidd if it'll put a stop to these raids."

Dannyn slammed both hands palm down on the table and leaned forward.

"Then let me tell you somewhat," he growled. "If anyone turns traitor, then he'll have me and my men raiding his lands. Ask your grumbling friends which would be worse."

He swung himself free of the bench, turned on his heel, and stalked off without another word. Cavydd sighed and picked up his tankard of ale.

"Do you know Dannyn well, Lady Gweniver?" he said.

"Not truly, Your Grace. I'd never met him before this spring."

"Then you have a very interesting time ahead of you."

On the morrow, the army rode north through deserted farms, stripped of food, that were as good as the tracks in the road for tracing the Eldidd raiders. At sunset, they came to a village, burned to the ground. A tangle of charred timbers, still smoking, lay among black trees and a tumble of cracked stone from the village well.

"Looks like the folk escaped in time, my lady," Ricyn said.

"So it does. Look!"

Next to the ruins was a meadow, the village commons, lined with a thick stand of poplars. Among the trees were women with children huddled against them, men with crowbars, pitchforks, sticks, whatever impromptu weapons they'd managed to grab when the raiders swept over them. Gweniver dismounted and joined Dannyn as two old men came to meet them. They stared at Gweniver's tattoo, then knelt.

"You be Cerrmor men," one stated.

"We are," Dannyn said. "When were you raided? How many men were there?"

"Two days ago now, your lordship." The old man sucked his teeth in thought. "And as to how many, well, it's hard to say, because they just comes riding out of nowhere. Young Molyc was out with the cows, you see, and if it weren't for him, we'd be dead, but he sees them coming, so he runs back."

"And how did Molyc know they were enemies?"

"They had these blue shields, with these silver dragons on them, and Molyc's never seen any such thing in his life, so he figures it means no good."

"He was right enough." He glanced at Gweniver. "Do you know what those shields mean? These raiders are part of the King's own men, and they never ride unless a prince of the realm is with them."

"A prince?" The old man spat on the ground. "He must be a poor kind of prince if he needs our cows that bad. They took everything we had, my lord. Our cows, our chickens, every cursed scrap of food we had."

"No doubt. Well, you'll eat well for a while. We'll leave you all the food we can spare, and a packhorse or two that maybe you can trade for seed grain."

The old man kissed his hand, then began to sob in convulsive shudders. Gweniver stared in amazement, because she'd expected Dannyn to care even less about peasants than most lords would, which was cursed little. The captain turned to her with a twisted smile.

"I know what it's like to have naught," he said. "I remember it every day of my life. That's somewhat you wouldn't understand, is it? My most noble lady."

In embarrassment Gweniver strode away, but the first order she gave was for the carters to unload food for the villagers.

Once the army was settled in for the night and the guard posted, Gweniver joined Dannyn at his fire for a council of war. In the dancing light of the fire, his face was grim with shadows as he drew a plan of the river valley in the dirt.

"Sooner or later they have to turn south to meet their ships," he said. "Then we have them, if not before."

"So we do. Here, if we take this prince alive, we're going to have a nice prize to take home."

"What? I'd rather have his head on a pike."

"Don't be a dolt. If we hold a prince of the realm hostage, we can stop these raids without swinging a sword."

Dannyn whistled under his breath and looked up.

"Well, my lady, whatever I may have thought of your skill with a sword, there's no doubt you understand war. Done, then. We'll do our best to snare this prince like a rabbit."

On the morrow, scouts on the best horses rode ahead, wheeling and circling in front of the army like seagulls around a ship entering harbor. Just past noon, they found the place where the raiders had camped the night before. Amid the flattened grass and the usual detritus of a big warband were two fire pits and the scattered remnants of beef bones. Two of the village cows would never come home again, but the tracks made it clear that the raiders were still traveling with about fifty head of cattle.

"And that's their death warrant," Dannyn cheerfully remarked. "We can travel faster, even with the cursed carts, than they can if they're driving stock. Once we get close, here's our plan. We leave the carts behind and ride out early to catch them on the road. The prince is going to be at the head of the line, of course, so we send a wedge of my best men straight into the line behind him and cut him off while the rest of the lads shove the line of march into their baggage train. You, me, and a handful of picked men go right for the prince and mob him. Try not to knock him off his horse. If he's trampled to death, so much for our hostage."

"Sounds splendid. It gladdens my heart that you're including me and my men in this."

"We need every man we've got. Even if one of them's a woman."

For the rest of the day, Dannyn kept the army moving fast by riding in the rear and bullying the carters. Up in solitary splendor at the head of the line, Gweniver received the reports from the scouts and meekly led the men where they told her. By the time they camped, about an hour before sunset to let the horses graze, the scouts were sure that the Eldidd raiders were only some five miles ahead of them. Best of all, they hadn't met any enemy scouts at all, a heartwarming bit of arrogance on the prince's part.

While Gweniver and Ricyn diced for splinters of firewood at their campfire, she told him the news.

"Well, my lady, then we'll have some proper sport on the morrow."

"So we will. You'll be riding with me when we go after the prince."

He smiled and threw the dice, rolling a five that lost him the game. When he handed her two splinters, she remembered him handing her the first violets of spring, shyly, without ever saying a word, when he must have spent hours hunting for them. She wondered how she could have been so blind to never suspect that a common-born rider would love her for all those years.

"Are you going to throw?" he said. "I'm too far behind to let you weasel out of the game now."

As she threw, she was thinking that she didn't mind in the least when he forgot to call her "my lady" or when he yelled at her for doing something stupid. It was odd, considering that her brothers would have had him flogged for such impertinence. It made her wonder if, in her own way, she loved him, too, but it was too late for such wonderings. Now she belonged to the Goddess alone, and forever.

On the morrow the army rose with the dawn. Dannyn sorted the men out, picked temporary captains, and gathered up the twenty-five who would ride with him and Gweniver for their strike on the prince. The bright summer sun lay on green meadows when they rode. She felt perfectly calm, as if she were floating through the air instead of wearing nearly thirty pounds of mail. As she made a long silent prayer to the Goddess, she began to smile. Since she'd put long hours of work into the mirror-scrying, in her mind the image built up effortlessly of the night-dark eyes and terrible beauty of the Goddess, who trembled in lust for the bloodletting ahead. Gweniver heard chanting, a sobbing wail in quarter-notes, so old, so strange, that she was sure she was remembering it from a very long time ago, when the worship of the Dark Moon flourished. The chant became so real and so loud that she was startled when Dannyn called out the order to halt.

Dazed, she looked around to find the warband near a woodland. Once it must have been part of a lord's hunting preserve, because it was open forest, mostly larches and maples, with little underbrush to hold the riders back. Calling orders, Dannyn broke his army's line and led them scattered into the cover. On the other side lay the road, and far down to the north she saw a cloud of dust coming. The army settled shields and drew javelins as slowly the Eldidd raiders sauntered toward the ambush.

They were only a quarter mile away before some sharp-eyed lad in their warband noticed something odd about the woodlands ahead. A cry spread like wildfire among the raiders as they pulled to a confused halt. Gweniver could see the cattle, lowing miserably at the rear of the line.

"Now!" Dannyn yelled, forgetting his horn. "Get 'em!"

Like a sweep of arrows the ranks broke free of cover and charged the enemy line. Javelin points winked in the sun as they showered down on the Eldidd line—except at the front, where a lucky hit might rob them of the prince. As the raiders swirled to meet them, the first troop hit, swords in hand, near the vanguard. A whirling chaos of men and horses, the battle spread out on either side of the road.

"For the prince!" Dannyn yelled.

Howling a war cry, Dannyn charged for the head of the line, his picked men streaming after. When Gweniver tried to yell, her voice broke into laughter. This time it was so cold, so hollow, that she knew it was the Goddess, using her voice, using her body, speaking and fighting through Her priestess. Ahead, in the rising dust, ten Eldidd men were galloping to meet them. When she saw a dragon shield rimmed with silver and set with jewels, she knew that the prince's gallantry was playing into their hands.

"Ricco!" she yelled. "There he is!"

The laughter grabbed her voice as the two packs broke into each other, spreading out and wheeling their horses round. She made a slash at an Eldidd horse, nicked it, and saw bright blood on her sword point. The entire world suddenly flared a hazy red. Laughing and howling, she slashed, pressed her horse forward, struck again, and parried a clumsy answering strike. Through the red haze she saw her enemy's terror-struck face as he parried and struck in return while her laughter rose like the chant she'd heard in her mind. His very fear made her hate him. She feinted, got him to reach out too far, then risked a dangerous thrust and cut him across the face. Blood welled and wiped his fear from her sight. She let him fall, then thrust on forward to Ricyn's side.

Outnumbered as they were, the Eldidd men clustered around their prince and desperately tried to fend the Cerrmor squad away from him. Gweniver saw Dannyn pressing in from the rear, fighting a man who threw himself in the way to block his path to the prince. In two quick cuts Dannyn killed first the horse, then the rider, and surged farther in, yet all the time he fought he was silent, his mouth a little slack as if all this slaughter bored him. As the group around the prince tried to reform, Gweniver had her chance. She slammed into an Eldidd man from the side and killed him through the joining of his mail at his armpit. Her laughter rose to a banshee shriek as she turned on the raider beside him.

The silver shield swung to meet her as the pure white horse carried its prince to the hopeless charge. Gweniver saw his corn-flower-blue eyes, cold and determined, as he swung cleanly at her. The blow was so hard and so well-placed that it cracked her shield in half, but she swung from underneath and caught his gauntleted wrist with the flat of her blade. With a yelp, he dropped the sword. His dead-white face told her that his wrist was broken. From the side Dannyn swung with his shield and smacked him on the side of the head. Stunned, gasping, the prince reeled in the saddle. Gweniver sheathed her sword and grabbed the silver rim of the shield, forcing him to swing around toward her. At that moment, Ricyn grabbed the reins of the milk-white horse, and the prince was trapped.

"Well played!" Dannyn yelled. "Get him away!"

His eyes drunken with shock and pain, the prince suddenly grabbed at the dagger in his belt with his left hand, but Gweniver got it before him.

"No suicides," she said. "Ever have a fancy to see Cerrmor, lad?"

Dannyn and the rest of his men wrenched their horses around and rode back to the battle, which was screaming and swirling behind them. With Dagwyn falling in with them, Gweniver and Ricyn took the prince in the opposite direction down the road and paused in the shade of a treet.

"Get that gauntlet off him, Ricco," Gweniver said. "If his wrist swells in there, it'll take a blacksmith to cut the cursed thing free."

The prince pulled off his helm with his left hand and threw it hard into the dirt. When he looked at her with tear-filled eyes, she realized that he was no more than seventeen. As Ricyn pulled off the gauntlet, he grunted, biting his lower lip so hard that it

bled. All at once, Gweniver felt a cold shudder down her back:
danger. With a yell, she turned in the saddle and saw Eldidd men
galloping straight for them, a squad of some ten raiders with
Cerrmor men right behind them, but Eldidd had the lead by a
couple of lengths.

"Ah shit!" Dagwyn said. "They must have seen the prince's
cursed horse!"

Gweniver wrenched her horse around, then drew her sword
as she charged straight toward the oncoming riders. Howling
with laughter, she saw the blood-red mist come down again. The
two men in the lead swung right around her and headed toward
the prince. She started to turn, but another dragon shield was
riding straight for her. Her laughter rose to a wail as she threw
every cautious lesson aside and lunged, leaning dangerously in
her saddle, stabbing with no thought of parrying. Her cracked
shield fell away under his blow, but the Goddess guided her
sword. She thrust so hard that his mail split. As he slid dead from
the saddle, she turned her horse. All she could think of was Ricyn,
back there outnumbered.

By then the Cerrmor men had caught up, and in a howling
charge they swept toward the prince. Gweniver could see the
white horse, rearing and bucking under its helpless rider. Swords
flashed, and she heard Ricyn's war cry as she charged into the
mob.

"Ricco! Dagwyn!" she yelled. "I'm here!"

It was ridiculous, maybe, but Dagwyn yelled back a war cry
and fought like a fiend. Nose to tail, he and Ricyn were parrying
more than cutting, desperately trying to stay mounted in a mob
of Eldidd swords. Gweniver slashed one enemy across the back,
swung in the saddle, and barely parried a strike from the side.
She heard Cerrmor voices behind her, around her, but she thrust
on, laughing, always laughing, swinging hard, feeling blows
glance off her mail, striking in return, until she'd fought her way
to Ricyn's side. His horse was dying under him, and his face ran
with blood.

"Get up behind me!" she yelled.

Ricyn threw himself clear of the saddle as his horse went
down. She blindly slashed and fended as he scrambled up behind
her, the horse snorting and dancing under them. An Eldidd man
charged in, then screamed, twisted, as a Cerrmor strike got him

from the rear. Swearing at the top of his lungs, Dannyn shoved his way through the mob and grabbed the reins of the prince's white horse. Slowly the little eddy of death died away as the Cerrmor men chased the last of the raiders down the road. Suddenly Gweniver felt the Goddess leave her. She wept like a child who falls asleep in its mother's lap only to wake up alone in a strange bed.

"By the hells!" Dannyn snapped. "Are you cut?"

"I'm not. One minute the Goddess had Her hands on me, but the next, She'd gone."

"I saw Her," Ricyn said, his voice faint. "When you ride into a fight, Gwen, you are the Goddess."

She twisted around to look at him. He had one hand pressed over the bloody cut on his face, and his eyes were narrow with pain. The quiet conviction in his voice was frightening.

"I mean it," Ricyn said. "You *are* the Goddess to me."

TWO

Some four weeks after she'd ridden out untried, Gweniver came back to Dun Cerrmor a warrior. Since he wanted to keep most of the army on the Eldidd border for a while, Dannyn had sent her and her warband back as an escort for their royal prize, who turned out to be Prince Mael of Aberwyn, the youngest son of the dragon throne. When she rode into the ward and looked at the towering broch complex, she realized that she belonged there. It was no longer overwhelming because its splendor meant nothing more than a place to live between campaigns. She acknowledged the swarm of servants and pages with a small nod and nothing more, then dismounted and helped Ricyn cut the captured prince's ankles free from his saddle. Just as Mael was dismounting, Saddar the councillor hurried over and bowed. The prince stood stiffly, looking at both councillor and dun with a small contemptuous smile.

"Our liege is in his reception chamber, Your Holiness," Saddar said. "We received your messages, and his highness is most anxious to see the prince."

"Good. I'll be cursed glad to get rid of him, I tell you. He was rotten company on the road."

Four men of Glyn's guard led them into the echoing reception chamber inside the main broch. At one end was a small dais, spread with carpets and backed by two enormous tapestries, one depicting King Bran founding the Holy City, the other showing the same king leading a battle charge. In a high-backed chair waited King Glyn, dressed in ceremonial clothes: a pure white tunic, richly worked, a golden sword at his side, and the royal plaid, fastened at the shoulder with the enormous ring-brooch that marked him king. Freshly bleached, his pale hair swept back from his face as if he were looking into a private wind. He acknowledged the entrance of Mael and Gweniver, both filthy and tattered from the road, with a small wave of a ringed hand. When Gweniver knelt, Mael remained standing and looked steadily at Glyn, who was, after all, no more than his equal in rank.

"Greetings," the King said. "Although I disclaim and dispute your clan's claim on my throne, I'm quite mindful of your right to yours. I assure you that you'll be treated with every courtesy during your stay here."

"Indeed?" Mael snapped. "Such courtesies as your rough court can offer, anyway."

"I see that the prince has a strong spirit." Glyn allowed himself a small smile. "I'll be sending heralds soon to your father's court to formally announce your capture. Do you wish any messages to go along with them?"

"I do, a letter to my wife."

Gweniver was honestly surprised. Although it was common practice among the blood royal to marry their heirs off young, he looked like such a lad, standing there in his dirty clothes, that it was hard to believe him married. Mael made her a bow.

"My wife was due for her childbed when I rode away, Your Holiness. Perhaps such things would be of no interest to you, but her well-being weighs heavily upon me."

"My own scribe will come to you later," Glyn said. "Tell your lady what you wish."

"Simple pen and ink will be enough. The men of *my* house know how to read and write."

"Very well then." The King smiled again. It was easy to be immune to insults when he was the captor, not the captive. "I'll be informing you now and again of the progress of the negotiations. Guards."

Like a hand clasping over a jewel, the guards surrounded the prince and marched him away.

Up at the top of the central broch, the prince's chamber was a large round room with its own hearth, glass in the windows, a Bardek carpet on the floor, and decent furniture. Whenever Nevyn visited him, Mael would pace round and round like a donkey tied to a mill wheel. The guards told Nevyn that he paced that way half the night, too. Although the dweomerman visited him first to tend his broken wrist, as the month wore on he kept coming out of simple pity. Since the prince could read and write, Nevyn brought him books from the scribal library and lingered to spend an hour or two discussing them. The lad was unusually bright, with the kind of wits that might develop into wisdom if he lived long enough. The prospect for that, however, was doubtful, because under all of Glyn's courtesy lay the real threat that if Eldidd didn't ransom his son, Mael would hang. Since he himself had once been a third and thus superfluous prince, Nevyn doubted that Eldidd would humble himself unduly when it came to saving Mael's life. Mael had his own doubts.

"I wish I could have killed myself before they captured me," he remarked one afternoon.

"That would have been a shameful thing. A man who flees his Wyrd has a harsh reckoning to make in the Otherlands."

"Would it have been any harsher than hanging like a horse thief?"

"Oh come now, lad, your father might ransom you yet. Glyn's not inclined to be greedy over the ransom, and your father would feel shamed if he just let you die."

Mael flung himself into a chair and slouched down, his long colt's legs stuck out in front of him, his raven-black hair a rumpled mess.

"I can bring you another book," Nevyn went on. "The scribes have a copy of Dwvoryc's *Annals of the Dawntime*. It has some splendid battles in it, or would reading about war ache your heart?"

The prince shook his head in a no and stared out the window at the blue sky.

"You know what the worst thing was?" he said after a moment. "Being captured by a woman. I thought I'd die of shame when I looked at her and saw she was a woman."

"Well, not just any female, your highness. There's no shame in being captured by a Moon-sworn warrior."

"So I'll hope, then. But truly, I've never seen anyone fight like her. She was laughing." Mael paused, his mouth slack with the memory. "It truly was like seeing a goddess come over the field, the way she was laughing and cutting. One of her men called her the goddess, and you know, I almost believed him."

Nevyn felt sick at the thought of her being so bound up in battle lust.

"Good sir, you seem wise," the prince went on. "I thought it was impious for a woman to take up arms."

"Now, that depends on which priest you choose to listen to. But it's an act of piety to Lady Gweniver's goddess. Every man she kills is a sacrifice to the dark of the moon."

"Indeed? Then her goddess must have been glutted after that scrap, and her holy battle ravens, too."

"No doubt. Now, back in the Dawntime there were many battle maidens, all sworn to the Dark Moon. The cursed Rhwmanes thought it impious, but then, all their silly women did was sit and spin."

"You mean back in the Homeland, then, before the great exile."

"Just that, long before King Bran led his people to the Western Isles. But once they were here, cut off from the Homeland, well, I suppose a childbearing woman was simply too valuable to risk in battle. I don't truly understand it, but the cult of the Dark Moon died away then. There's somewhat about it in that book I mentioned."

"Then I'd truly like to read it. It makes it better, knowing I wasn't captured by the only one."

That very same day, heralds came in from Eldidd. The court was abuzz with gossip, wondering how much the foreign king was offering for his son, and if Glyn would take it. The eager ears did hear one bit of news straightaway, that Mael's wife had been delivered of a fine, healthy son. Nevyn wondered how much the king would care about Mael now that he had still another heir. Quite a bit, as it turned out. Nevyn heard the tale from the King, when Glyn summoned him to his private chambers that night, as he'd grown accustomed to doing, just to hear the long view that the dweomer could offer him.

"Eldidd's promised me a cursed large amount of gold," Glyn said. "But I don't need coin as much as I need a quiet border. I'm planning on dragging the negotiations out as long as possible, and I've warned him that his son will hang if he raids while I have him."

"Doubtless he'll respect that, my liege, at least for a time."

"So I hope. I'd hate to actually hang a helpless prisoner. After all, Eldidd can press his claim to the throne by attacking Cantrae lands. They share a long border to the north." The King smiled gently. "Let Slwmar see how it feels to be a morsel of meat between a pair of jaws."

One of those jaws was, of course, Dannyn and the King's Guard, who were raiding up in the north. Every time a messenger returned, Nevyn questioned him for news of Gweniver, and every time the man said in awe that not only was she well, but an inspiration to the entire army. God-touched, they called her. Nevyn supposed that most people would see her that way, one of those fortunate few whom the gods directly favor with power and luck. He, of course, saw it differently, because he knew what the gods are: vast centers of force in the Innerlands, which correspond to part of either the natural world or the human mind. For thousands of years, worshippers have built up the images of the gods and poured power into them, until they seem to be persons in their own right. Anyone who knows how to build the appropriate mental images and chant the correct sort of prayers—they hardly need to be exact—can contact the centers of force and draw off power for their own use. The priest contacts those centers in blind faith; the dweomer-person, coldbloodedly, knowing that he creates the god more than the god creates him; Gweniver had stumbled into a dark corner of the female mind that women had been forced to bury for the past seven hundred years. Without a temple of the Dark Rite to teach her, she was like a child who tries to pick up a burning fire because it's so pretty, and he worried constantly.

Yet, even though he knew that her true Wyrd lay with the dweomer, he was forbidden by his vows to interfere boldly in her life. All he could do was win her confidence, make casual hints, and hope that someday she would ask him the right questions. If,

of course, she lived long enough. He could only pray that the
winter would come early that year. Once they were all in the dun
together, with the campaigning over for the season, he would
have a chance to become her friend.

For a month more, the Cerrmor raiders struck with impu-
nity along Cantrae's southern border, because Slwmar was
forced to siphon off troops to march west and deal with the new
threat from Eldidd. Every now and then they faced a sizable
army, but Dannyn generally withdrew before battle, preferring
to bleed Cantrae's sources of supply rather than lose men of his
own. Finally, though, Slwmar was desperate enough to force
battle, backing Dannyn's men up against the Belaver by some
shrewd manoeuvering. Although the outcome was technically a
Cerrmor victory that sent Slwmar's men rushing back north toward the Holy City, the losses were high.

As he walked through the battlefield that evening, where his
men were still working at finding and bringing in the wounded,
Dannyn knew that another pitched fight would destroy them.
With him was Gweniver, as filthy and sweaty as any of them, with
blood spattered on her face and shoulders. As they walked, she
looked on the slaughter with an indifference that frightened him.
For all that he loved battle glory and combat, he hated to see his
men killed. His ideal of battle was something out of an old saga,
where the noble-born challenged each other to single combat
while their troops cheered them on.

"We're going to have to withdraw," he said abruptly.

"Whatever you think best, as long as we come back."

"We might, we might not. With Eldidd in this truce, I could
maybe strip Dun Cerrmor of the fort guard, but I'm not sure I
want to. The King will have to make the final decision, of course."

She turned her head to look at him in exasperation.

"Her Holiness had best remember that we need men to send
against the Boar this fall. There'll be more slaughter then, maybe
even enough to glut her."

With a toss of her head at the insult, she left him, striding
away to her warband. For a moment he watched her go and
wished that he could find her repellent, could stop thinking of
her as a woman at all, as her holy vow should have made him do.
Although he was far from a pious man, Dannyn believed in the

gods, and he knew that he was risking their wrath by wanting a sworn priestess in his bed. Yet at times she would smile at him, or simply walk by, and his lust would be so strong that he would find it hard to breathe for a moment. He promised himself that if ever the time came to field two armies, he would make sure that she was in one, and he, the other.

He would have found his longing easier to forget if it weren't for Ricyn. At times, during their slow march south to Cerrmor, he would notice the way that she and her captain talked together, so intimately, so closely, that he wondered if perhaps she'd already broken her vow, and with a common-born rider at that. The jealousy ate at him until he started hating Ricyn, a man he'd always liked before. He'd admired Ricyn, even, for his steadiness, his calm courage, his easy way with the men beneath him. Now he at times had long daydreams of sending Gweniver's captain out to certain death on a hopeless charge.

Once they were back in Dun Cerrmor, without even the distraction of battle, Dannyn found his feelings for her even harder to ignore. He did his best to avoid her, but there remained their lessons in swordcraft. Although he mocked his feelings for her, telling himself that he was nothing more than a stallion in rut, he honestly loved her enough that the thought of her eventual death terrified him. He was determined to teach her every trick he knew to compensate for her lack of weight and reach.

Every morning they sparred for several hours. Although they were only using blunt blades and light training shields, at times the contest turned into a real fight. Something would set her off, and rather than scoring light touches, she would go berserk and start landing hits, hard slaps of the blade that set off his fury to match hers. For a few minutes they would battle, then break off by some semiconscious mutual consent and resume a more civilized lesson. Although he always won those fights, Dannyn never felt that he was mastering her. He could give her bruises all morning, but the next day she would start it again, pushing him over the edge with a hard blow. He was beginning to think that she was determined to master him.

Being back in the dun also made it hard for him to ignore Ricyn. Often he saw them together, laughing at some joke, Ricyn leaning close to her as they strolled in the ward, even dicing for coppers like a pair of riders. At times Ricyn would come watch them spar. He'd stand at the edge of the practice ground like a chaperone, saying nothing, then escort her away when they were done. Since he had no justifiable reason to order away the captain sworn to another noble, Dannyn had to put up with it.

Dannyn was furious enough one afternoon to go over and join them when they were out by the stables. He simply didn't like the way Ricyn was smiling at her and strode over in time to overhear an odd jest about rabbits.

"Good morrow," Dannyn said. "What's all this about rabbits, my lady?"

"Oh, Ricco's good at snaring them with these wires he always carries, so I was just saying that maybe he can snare me a few Boars."

Dannyn liked hearing her use Ricyn's nickname even less. "Somewhat that you learned on the farm?" he snapped.

"It was, my lord," Ricyn said. "You learn a lot, being a farmer's son. Like how to tell a purebred horse from a nag."

"And just what do you mean by that?" Dannyn laid his hand on his sword hilt.

"Just what I said." Ricyn did the same. "My lord."

With an oath, Dannyn drew. He saw a flash of metal; then his wrist burned, and his sword was flying from his hand. Cursing, he stepped back just as Gweniver slapped Ricyn's arm down with the flat of her blade. She'd outdrawn them both.

"That's enough, both of you!" Gweniver snarled. "What do you think I am, a bitch in heat?"

Ricyn sheathed his sword and stepped back.

"By all the gods," she went on. "I'll kill the first one of you that starts this up again, even if I hang for it. Do you both understand me?"

Ricyn turned and ran, heading back for the barracks. Dannyn rubbed his aching wrist and scowled at his retreating back until Gweniver tapped his chest with the point of her sword.

"If you run him hard in the field, and if he dies from it, then I'll kill you."

There was no doubt that she meant it. Refusing to reply, he retrieved his sword from the cobbles. Only then did he notice the crowd of onlookers, watching, grinning, no doubt thinking that the bastard had it coming to him. In blind rage, Dannyn strode back to the dun and ran upstairs to his chamber. He flung himself down on his bed and lay there shaking in fury. Yet slowly the rage left him to be replaced a cold hopelessness. Well and good, then, if the bitch preferred her stinking farmer, then let her have him! The Goddess would punish both of them soon enough, if they were bedding together. With a sigh he sat up, realizing that they were probably doing no such thing. He would have to keep his jealousy well in hand from now on, he told himself, lest he give in to a rage stronger even than his lust.

For the rest of that day, Ricyn avoided Gweniver, but at the evening meal in the great hall, he found himself watching her as she sat on the dais with the rest of the noble-born. It was a real torment to remember how he'd shamed himself in front of her. He'd forgotten the Goddess. It was as simple as that—for one moment he'd thought of her only as a woman, not as the sacred priestess she truly was. That Dannyn made the same mistake was no real excuse. The Goddess had taken and marked her, and that was that. When he was done eating, Ricyn got a second tankard of ale and drank it slowly while he considered what he was going to do to make retribution, not to Gweniver, but to the Goddess. He had no desire to die in his next battle because She wanted him slain.

"Coming back to the barracks?" Dagwyn said. "We could have a game of dice."

"Oh, I'll follow you in a bit. I was thinking of having a word with the old herbman."

"What for?"

"Naught that concerns you."

With a shrug, Dagwyn got up and left. Ricyn wasn't sure why he thought Nevyn would know about the Dark Goddess, but the old man seemed so wise that it was worth a try. Halfway across the hall, Nevyn was finishing his meal and engrossed in conversation with the Master of Weaponry. Ricyn decided to wait until he was done, then follow him out. A few at a time, the other Wolf riders left the table until he was alone in a small island of quiet in the noisy hall. He got a third tankard, sat back down, and cursed the Master of Weaponry for talking so much.

"Captain?" someone said from behind him.

It was Lord Oldac, his thumbs hooked into his sword belt.

Although Ricyn had never forgiven him for calling Gweniver a wench, he rose and bowed as Oldac's rank forced him to do.

"I'd like a word with you. Let's step outside."

Ricyn followed him out the back door into the cool ward. They stood in a spill of light from a window while Oldac waited for a pair of serving lasses to walk past out of earshot.

"What was that little scrap between you and Lord Dannyn today?" Oldac said.

"Begging his lordship's pardon and all, I don't see where it's any affair of his."

"Oh, no doubt it isn't. Just cursed curious. One of the pages said Lord Dannyn insulted her holiness, and that you defended her."

It was tempting to lie and let this less-shameful story get around.

"Well, my lord, that's not true. I said somewhat that Lord Dannyn took wrong, and my lady intervened."

"Well, our bastard's certainly a touchy sort, isn't he?" Oddly enough, Oldac looked disappointed. "Well, just wondering."

When he returned to the hall, Ricyn found Nevyn already gone. Cursing Oldac in his mind, he found a page who told him that the old man had retired to his chamber. Ricyn hesitated, afraid to disturb a man everyone said had dweomer, but after all, if he didn't placate the Goddess properly, his life was at stake. He went up to Nevyn's chamber, where he found the old man sorting out herbs by lantern light.

"Here, good sir," Ricyn said. "Could I have a word with you?"

"Of course, lad. Come in and shut the door."

Since Nevyn had only one chair, Ricyn stood uneasily by the table and looked at the sweet-smelling herbs.

"Don't you feel well or suchlike?" Nevyn said.

"Oh, I haven't come for your herbs. Here, you seem like a truly wise man. Do you know if the Dark Goddess would take prayers from a man?"

"I don't see why not. Bel listens to a woman's prayers, doesn't he?"

"Good. I can't ask my lady, you see. I'm afraid that I've offended the Goddess, but I cursed well know I've offended her. So I thought maybe I could make it up to the Goddess on my own, because I don't want to die on my next ride. It's cursed hard when She doesn't even have a proper temple I can go to."

Nevyn considered him with a puzzling look that was halfway between exasperation and admiration.

"Well, no doubt the Goddess understands that," Nevyn said. "In a way, She needs no temple, because all night is Her home and the darkness Her altar."

"Here, sir, did you used to be a priest?"

"Oh, I didn't, but I've read many a book on sacred lore."

"Well and good then. Shouldn't I sacrifice somewhat to Her? The gods always seem to like that."

"So they do." Nevyn thought for a moment with an impressively solemn expression. "I'll give you a bit of mandrake root, because it's forked like a man and has dweomer. You go down to the river in the dead of night, throw it in, and then pray that She takes it in your stead and forgives you."

"My thanks, good sir, truly, my humble thanks. I'll pay you for the bit of root, too."

"Oh, no need, lad. I don't want to see you slip up and get killed because you believe the Goddess has turned against you."

Ricyn wrapped the precious mandrake in a bit of cloth and hid it in his shirt, then went back to the barracks. He lay on his bunk and thought of what he was going to say to the Goddess, because he wanted to get the words exactly right. Knowing that he too could worship Her filled him with a solemn peace. Darkness is Her altar—he liked the way old Nevyn had put it. Someday, when his Wyrd came upon him, he would sink into Her arms and lie quiet and spent, at rest in the dark, with all the surge and pain of this endless war behind him.

"Dagwyn?" Gweniver said. "Where's Ricyn?"

Dagwyn turned and hastily looked over the stable.

"Cursed if I know, my lady," he said. "He was here not but a minute ago."

Gweniver hurried out into the bright morning sunlight and walked round the stables. He was deliberately avoiding her again, she supposed, a supposition proved correct when she finally caught up with him. He gave her one startled glance, then looked only at the ground.

"Come walk with me, Ricco."

"If my lady orders it."

"Oh by the hells! Don't keep slinking around like a whipped dog! Here, I was never even that angry with you, but if I was going to put Dannyn in his place, I had to be fair about it, didn't I?"

Ricyn looked up and smiled, a quick flash of his usual good cheer. She loved seeing him smile that way.

"Well, so you did," he said. "But I've been eating my heart away over it, anyway."

"It's over now, as far as I'm concerned."

Together they strolled through the storage sheds and empty carts out behind the stables until they found a quiet sunny spot by the dun wall. They sat down, backs to a shed, and looked at the towering rise of dark stone, shutting them in as much as it shut enemies out.

"You know," Gweniver said, "you should find yourself some lass in the dun. We'll be here the rest of your lives."

Ricyn winced as if she'd slapped him.

"What's so wrong?" she said.

"Naught."

"Nonsense. Out with it."

Ricyn sighed and rubbed the back of his neck as if it helped him think.

"Well, suppose I did get a lass. How would you take it? I was hoping you'd—ah, curse it!"

"Hoping I'd envy her? I would, but that's my burden, not yours. I'm the one who chose the Goddess."

He smiled at the ground in front of him.

"You truly would envy her?"

"I would."

He nodded and stared at the cobbles as if he were counting them.

"I've been thinking about that," he said at last. "There's a lass or two around that I sort of fancy, and one of them fancies me well enough. Just yesterday it was, she was talking with me, and I knew I could bed her easy enough if I didn't mind sharing her with a couple of the other lads, and I've never minded that before. But all at once, I didn't give a pig's fart if I ever had her or not, so I walked away." He was silent for a few minutes. "It's never going to be any good with some other lass. I love you too much. I have for years."

"Oh now here, you just haven't found the right lass."

"Don't jest with me, Gwen. I'm not going to live long enough for that. You're minded to die, aren't you? I can see it in your eyes, whenever we ride to a scrap. Well, I'm not going to live a minute longer than you. I've been praying to the Goddess, and I promised Her that." Finally he looked at her. "So I was thinking, I might as well swear the same vow as you."

"Don't! There's no need, and if you broke it—"

"And don't you think I've got as many guts as you?"

"That's not what I meant. There's just no reason to."

"There is, at that. What do most men give the lass they love? A home, and plenty to eat, and a new dress every now and then. Well, I'll never be able to give you any of that, so I'll give you what I can." He smiled at her as easily, as sunnily, as he always did. "Whether you care or not, Gwen, you'll never see me with another woman, or hear about it, either."

She felt like a woman who's been using an old pot in her kitchen, only to polish it one day and find it solid silver.

"Ricco, I'll never break this vow. Do you understand that?"

"And if I didn't, would I be swearing one of my own?"

When she caught his arm, she felt the Goddess making her speak.

"But if I ever did, you'd be the one, not Dannyn. You're twice the man he is, for all his rank."

He wept, two thin trails of tears, hastily stifled.

"Oh ye gods," he whispered. "I'll follow you to the death."

"You will, if you follow me at all."

"The Goddess will have us all in the end, anyway. Why by every hell should I care when?"

"Well and good, then. I love you."

He caught her hand and twined his fingers through hers. For a long while they sat that way, unspeaking; then he sighed heavily.

"It's a pity I can't save up my wages and buy you a betrothal brooch," he said. "Just to give you somewhat, like, to mark this."

"I feel the same. Wait, I know. Swear a blood vow with me, like they did in the Dawntime."

He grinned, nodding his approval. When she gave him her

dagger, he made a small cut on her wrist, then on his own, and laid the bloody wounds together to let them mingle. As she stared up into his eyes, she felt like weeping, just because he looked so solemn, and because this was the only wedding they'd ever have. Then she felt the Goddess, a cold presence around her. She knew that the Dark Lady was pleased, that their love was as clean and harsh as another sword to lay upon Her altar. He bent his head and kissed her, just once, then let her go.

It was later that same morning that an aimless walk brought them to Nevyn's herb garden, and to Nevyn himself, who was down on his knees and fussing over his plants. When they hailed him, he rose, wiping muddy hands on his brigga.

"Good morrow," he said. "I hear from the gossip that you two will be riding back to the Wolf lands soon."

"We will," Gweniver said. "And we're going to rid them of vermin, too."

Nevyn cocked his head to one side and looked back and forth between them, his eyes suddenly cold.

"What's that on your wrist, Ricco?" he said. "It looks like your lady has a cut to match it."

With a laugh, she held up her hand to display the dried smear of blood.

"Ricyn and I have sworn a vow together. We'll never share a bed, but we'll share a grave."

"You stupid young dolts," Nevyn whispered.

"Now here," Ricyn said. "Don't you think we can keep it?"

"Oh, of course. No doubt you'll fulfil your vow splendidly and have exactly the reward you want, too, an early death in battle. No doubt bards will sing of you for years and years to come."

"Then why look so troubled?" Gweniver broke in. "We'd never ask for anything better."

"I know." The old man turned away. "And that's what troubles my heart. Ah well, it's your Wyrd, not mine."

And without another word, he knelt down and went back to his weeding.

That night Nevyn had no heart to sit in the great hall where he would see Gweniver. He retired to his chamber, lit candles, then paced back and forth while he wondered what there was about his race that made it take pleasure in suffering, that made it love death the way that other races loved comfort and riches. There were Gwen and her Ricyn, thinking that they loved each other while all the time they loved the dark streak in the Deverry soul.

"Ah ye gods," Nevyn said. "It's no affair of mine now."

The candle guttered as if shaking its golden head in a no. It *was* his affair, whether he managed to help them in this life or whether he was forced to wait till their next, not only Gweniver now, but Ricyn as well. Whether they broke their vow or kept it, they were binding themselves together with a chain of Wyrd that would take the wisdom of a King Bran to untangle and the strength of a Vercingetorix to break. Thinking of those two Dawntime heroes blackened Nevyn's mood further. A cursed blood vow, something right out of an old saga! He wanted to explain to them, to force them to see that it's always easier to fall than to climb, that letting go for the fall brings a wonderful feeling of ease and power. She would never listen. It was probably too late.

Nevyn threw himself into a chair and stared at the empty hearth. He felt the whole kingdom slipping back as the civil wars broke and trampled all those long years of culture, the learning, the courtly honor, the concern for the poor—all those civilized things that so many men had spent so many years trying to build into the Deverry soul. How long will it be before they start taking heads again? Nevyn bitterly wondered. For the first time in his unnaturally long life, he wondered if his service to the Light was worthwhile, wondered if there truly could be any Light to serve, since things could slip back into darkness so easily. Never before had he been so aware of how fragile civilization is, that it floats like oil on the black ocean of men's minds.

As for Gweniver, Nevyn had one last desperate hope. If only he could make her see it, the dweomer offered greater power than anything else on earth, and she loved power. Perhaps he could get her away from court—and Ricyn, too, because she would never leave him behind—and retreat to the wild north country or even Bardek. There he could help her throw off the burden she'd taken upon herself and make her see clearly again. That very night, he went to her chamber for a talk.

Gweniver poured him mead and sat him down in her best

chair. In the lantern light her eyes were glowing, her smile bright and fixed, as if it had been cut into her face with a knife.

"I can guess why you're here," she announced. "Why is your heart so troubled about the vow Ricyn and I swore?"

"Mostly because it seems shortsighted. It's best to think carefully before committing yourself to a single path. Some roads travel through many different lands and offer many different views."

"And others run straight and short. I know that, but my Goddess has chosen my road for me, and I can't turn back now."

"Oh, of course not, but there are more ways of serving Her than with a sword."

"Not for me. I truly don't care, good Nevyn, that my road's going to be a short one. It's . . . oh, it's like having only so much firewood. Some people eke it out a stick at a time so they have a little puny fire all night. Others like to heap it up and have a good roaring blaze while it lasts."

"And then they freeze to death?"

She frowned into her goblet.

"Well," she said at last. "I didn't pick the best way of saying that, did I? Or, here, it's good enough. Not freeze to death—then they throw themselves into the fire."

When she laughed at her own jest, Nevyn finally saw what he'd been refusing to see for a very long time: she was mad. Long ago she'd been pushed over the edge of sanity, and now madness glowed in her eyes and smirked in her tight smile. Yet there's madness and madness; in this world gone mad, she would be considered splendid, heaped with honor and glory by men only slightly less mad than she. Sitting there and continuing to chat was one of the hardest things Nevyn had ever done. Even though she talked of her plans for Blaeddbyr and the Wolf clan, she was a walking suicide.

Eventually he made a polite escape and returned to his chamber. He could never bring her to the dweomer now, because studying magicks demands the sanest of all possible minds. Those who are the least bit unbalanced when they begin dweomer-study soon find themselves torn apart by the powers and forces they invoke. In this life, he knew, she would never have her true Wyrd. As he paced around his chamber, Nevyn suddenly began to tremble. He sank into a chair and wondered if he were ill until he realized that he was weeping.

The summer rains had turned the dun of the Wolf clan into a pool of muck. The gutted roofless broch rose in the middle of black mud, ashes, and charred timbers, all cracking on the cobbles, clogging the well, and stinking with the sickly-sweet stench of burning and rot. Here and there in the shade of the walls molds and mildews lay clammy, like diseased snow. Gweniver and Gwetmar sat on horseback in the opening that had once been the gate and looked it over.

"Well," Gweniver said. "You're a great lord now, sure enough."

"Will Your Holiness partake of the hospitality of my splendid hall?" He made her a mock bow. "We might as well ride on and take a look at the village."

"Truly. You won't have time to rebuild Dun Blaedd before winter."

They rode back downhill to the waiting army. Besides their own warband, about seventy men in all, they had two hundred of the King's Men, led by Dannyn. Glyn's generosity extended to a long baggage train of supplies and a contingent of skilled craftsmen to fortify whatever buildings they found still standing. As they rode across the Wolf's lands, Gweniver began to wonder if the demense could be saved, because the bondsmen who worked the fields had all fled. Twice they passed the site of one of their villages to find the rough huts burned, as if the bondsfolk had decided to show their contempt for their former masters as they escaped. The village, however, which had been held by freemen, still stood, even though the inhabitants were gone, driven in their case by fear of the Boar, not the Wolf. The weeds grew thick and green around the village well and down the paths. Under the apple trees, the ungathered fruit lay rotting like gouts of blood. The houses seemed to be crouching together, the shuttered windows sad eyes, reproaching those who'd deserted them.

"I'll be a fine lord indeed with no folk to rule," Gwetmar remarked with a false-ringing jest in his voice.

"The villagers will come back in time. Send messengers to the south and east, where they have kin. As for your own lands, my friend, I think me you'll have to be content with rents from free men—if you can find some who want to settle here."

Gwetmar unceremoniously broke the padlock on the black-smith's house and claimed it as his own, simply because it was the biggest. Since there was no time to build a proper stone wall, the master mason and the master carpenter decided on a earthwork and ditch to ring an inner palisade of logs. While the slow work got underway, the army rode constant small patrols along the border between the Boar and the Wolf lands. Yet it was a fort-night before the trouble came. Gweniver was leading a squad through deserted meadows when she saw, far down the road, a cloud of dust announcing that men rode toward them. She sent a messenger back to Dannyn and the main body of the army, then drew her warband up in battle order across the road.

Slowly the dust resolved itself into ten riders, coming at an easy jog. When they saw the squad, they halted and formed into a rough line. They were on their side of the border; the Wolves were on theirs; the situation hung on heartbeats as the leader edged his horse out of the pack to meet Gweniver halfway.

"Wolves, are you?" he said.

"We are. What's it to you?"

The leader's eyes flicked to her twenty-four men and counted up hopeless odds. With a shrug, he wheeled his horse and led his troop off in retreat. As they turned, she saw that one rider was carrying a shield blazoned with the green wyvern of the Holy City.

"So," she said to Ricyn. "I see why Glyn sent his men along with us."

"Just that, my lady. Slwmar of Cantrae isn't going to let this much land go without a fight."

"We'd best get back and tell the others."

Back at Blaeddbyr, the ditch was finished and the earthwork piled up, though not yet tamped and reinforced. In a rough circle, the logs for the palisade lay like a shark's teeth on the ground just inside. Gweniver found Gwetmar and Dannyn talk-ing with the master carpenter and led them aside to tell her news.

"So I'll wager Burcan will know by sunset that we're back," she finished up.

"Just that," Dannyn said. "They know we couldn't be at the

ruined dun, so I'll wager they ride straight here. We'd best meet them on the road. If we're badly outnumbered, we'll fall back to the village, and the earthwork will even the odds for us."

"If we have to retreat," Gwetmar joined in. "We should do it as soon as we realize we have to. We don't want to get cut off."

"Of course," Dannyn said. "But you're staying here to hold the village."

"Now just one moment! I intend to ride in defense of my own lands."

"The intention is noble, my lord, but the thought is poor. The only reason that me and my lads are here is to keep you alive."

When Gwetmar flushed in rage, Gweniver intervened.

"Don't be a dolt!" she snapped. "How do we know if that child Maccy's carrying is a lad or a lass? If you die in battle, and if it doesn't live or suchlike, then there isn't any Wolf clan until Maccy remarries. We'll have to go through this whole cursed thing again."

"Exactly." Dannyn gave Gwetmar a smile that was meant to be conciliatory. "You produce the heirs, my lord, and we'll get the land for them."

On the morrow, Dannyn woke the men early and led them out as the gray dawn was brightening, because if Burcan marched fast, he would reach the village by late afternoon. In the middle of the morning they crossed the border between the two demesnes and marched on through deserted countryside, depopulated by the constant feuding between the two clans. At noon they came to a large meadow with a thick stand of trees to one side. Dannyn sent out scouts, then let the main body rest their horses for a short while before he formed up the battle line. Two thirds of the men drew up across the road; the others hid among the trees, where they would wait until the battle was joined, then fall on Burcan's flank.

They were waiting in the hot sun when the scouts came back, bearing the news that they'd met with scouts from the Boar. Gweniver turned to Ricyn with a smile.

"Well and good. They're on their way. Remember to leave Burcan himself to me."

"I will, my lady. And if I don't see you alive tonight, then I'll see you in the Otherlands."

When she drew a javelin, her men followed her lead, the points flashing like a line of fire across the road. Again they waited, the horses stamping restlessly, the men utterly silent. Suddenly Gweniver felt a cold touch ripple down her spine. When she looked around, she saw her father, her brothers, and her uncles, sitting on shadowy horses as insubstantial as they, off to one side of the battle line. They watched her gravely, as silent as the living men as they waited to see either the victory or the death of their clan.

"Is somewhat wrong?" Ricyn said.

"Can't you see them? Look. There."

Utterly puzzled, he peered in the direction she pointed out, while the ghosts smiled, as if thinking that good-hearted Ricyn had changed very little since last they'd seen him. Just at that moment someone raised a shout. Down the road a cloud of dust appeared, the Boars, riding to the challenge. Some fifty yards away, they halted and formed a rough wedge. There were about two hundred of them, and they thought that they were facing a warband of only a hundred and fifty. Dannyn edged his horse forward as Burcan did the same.

"Cerrmor men, are you?" the Boar yelled. "But I see Wolf blazons with you."

"You do, because the Wolves have appealed to the true king to defend their ancestral lands."

"Hah! The true king in Dun Deverry has awarded me these lands by right of blood feud."

"It all comes down to king against king, doesn't it?" Dannyn gave a good-humored laugh. "You piss-poor excuse for a noble swine."

With a howl, Burcan hurled his javelin straight at him, Dannyn calmly bounced it off his shield into the dirt. Shouting, screaming, the Boarsmen charged as javelins arched up and whistled in the sun. As she spurred her horse forward, Gweniver drew her sword. She wanted Burcan himself, curse him, and curse Dannyn, too, who was trading blows with the lord in the midst of the battle. The lines met, the men peeling off, whirling around each other in a hacking, shouting mob of single combats. Gweniver's laughter started as she cut and slashed her way through. Just as she reached Dannyn's side, the hidden warband broke free of the trees and plunged onto the Boar's rear. A shout went up, but there was no way that the Boarsmen could escape the trap.

"Gwen!" Dannyn shouted. "He's yours!"

Guarding himself with a fling of his shield, Dannyn wrenched his horse around and let her close with Burcan. She heard her hatred well out of her mouth in a long laugh as she caught his swing on her shield and thrust in, only to have him parry with his blade. For a moment their swords hung locked as she stared him in the face and laughed. She saw him turn pale with fear and, as always, the sight of cowardice drove her into a red fury. She broke free, thrust again, and realized that everything had turned very slow. Slowly she glided her sword round to cut up from below; slowly Burcan's blade drifted toward hers and turned it back. It was as if they moved in a dance, some courtly grave circling that made every movement, every moment, preternaturally sharp.

A noise like wind swept over them, a dark night wind howling and sweeping the battle sound away. As he made a clumsy thrust that she blocked on her shield, she realized that he was out of time to the dance. Ever so slowly, his horse tossed its head and blocked its master's thrust. Urging her horse with her knees, she leaned and crept round to the flank position. Before he could turn properly, she struck in a leisurely drift. Her blade floated down onto his shield arm so slowly, so lightly, that it seemed unbelievable when he swore, swayed, and dropped the shield. The wind whined and moaned as she thrust forward, her arm and sword like a single spear biting into his side. With a choking scream of pain, he wrenched his horse's head around as if to flee, but again he misjudged the dance.

She was there to block his way. Leaning in the saddle, clutching the peak with both hands, he stared at her while blood oozed ever so slowly down his side.

"Mercy," he whispered. "I'll cede your claim."

Gweniver hesitated, but she saw her father, riding next to her and watching with sorrowful eyes. With a straight cut she slashed the Boar across the eyes, heard him scream, slashed back from the other and saw him fall, sliding off his horse, hitting the ground hard as around them horses reared and bucked to avoid trampling him. Her father saluted her with a shadowy sword, then disappeared. At that instant, the world came back, the wind turning into the screaming, shouting battle noise.

"Gweniver!" It was Ricyn's voice. "To Gweniver!"

Suddenly her men were all around her, fighting hard, yelling, driving back the Boarsmen who were on the verge of mobbing her. Then silver horns sang out as the enemy line broke and fled in rout, with most of Dannyn's men riding hard after them.

"Well played, my lady!" Ricyn crowed. "Oh, well played!"

So it was over, then. Her long summer's hatred lay trampled with Burcan on the bloody field. As dazed as if she'd been struck on the head, she lowered her sword and wondered why she wasn't weeping in joy. All at once she knew that she would never weep again, and that the Goddess had claimed her utterly.

After the army had rested from the battle, Dannyn left fifty men with Gwetmar as reinforcements, then led the rest back to Cerrmor. As they rode through the gray, rain-slick streets of the city, he felt melancholy settle around him like his wet cloak. Unless the new head of the Boars did something unusually foolish, the summer's campaigning was at an end. When they reached the dun, he made his report to the King, then went up to his chamber and took a bath. He was just dressing again when Saddar the councillor came to the door to request a word with him.

"Show him in," Dannyn said to his page. "We'll see what the tedious old fart has to say for himself."

Grinning, the lad did as he was bid, but Saddar told him to stay out in the corridor while he and the captain talked.

"Now here," Dannyn snapped. "Why did you order my lad away?"

"Because what I have to say is too grave a thing to trust to young ears." The councillor sat himself down unasked in a chair and smoothed his black robes. "I know, of course, that I can trust Lord Dannyn's discretion in this. Indeed, I've come here in the hopes that you'll lay my suspicions to rest and tell me that I'm quite mistaken to have them."

If that's true, Dannyn thought to himself, then it'll be the first time in his useless life that he wanted to hear he was wrong.

"What suspicions?" he said aloud.

"Ah, the thing is so vile that I can hardly bear to say it aloud."

Saddar did indeed look quite distressed. "A matter of sacrilege, or I should say, possible sacrilege. Far be it from me to insult a lady who might well be blameless."

He looked at Dannyn as if he expected him to understand exactly what he meant.

"What lady?" Dannyn said.

"Lady Gweniver, of course. I see that I'd best be blunt, no matter how deeply it pains me to do so. Now you've been in her company for months, my lord. Have you noticed how . . . well, on what intimate terms she seems to be with her captain? It would be a grave and horrible thing if she broke her sacred vows. I'm sure that doom would come upon us all if the Dark Goddess were wrathful. Please, I beg you to tell me that their friendship is only the sort of close tie that warriors often have with a fellow."

"As far as I know it is. By the hells, old man, her men would murder her, I'll wager, if they thought she was committing sacrilege. They know their lives depend upon her."

"Ah, well, then that relieves my heart." He sighed dramatically. "It was just that matter of the blood vow, you see, that . . ."

"What? What do you mean?"

"Why, Lady Gweniver swore a blood oath with young Ricyn. Surely you knew that."

Dannyn felt his rage flare up like an oil-soaked fire.

"I didn't, at that," he snarled.

"Oh. Well, I did wonder, seeing as his lordship is often distracted by matters of war. But you can see my concern."

With an inarticulate growl, Dannyn paced to the window, grabbed the sill with both hands, and stared blindly out while he trembled in fury. No matter what he'd said to the councillor, he was sure now that she'd broken her oath of chastity, sure that she and Ricyn had profaned themselves, and probably many a time. He never even saw the councillor leave, which was a pity, because Saddar was smiling to himself in a most undistressed way.

It was only later, when he was calm again, that Dannyn took the somewhat maddened next step in his line of thinking. If Gweniver had already broken the vow, why by all the gods shouldn't he have her, too?

In was a few days later that Nevyn happened to be crossing the ward as Gweniver was assembling her warband near the gates. He paused to watch as she and Ricyn mounted their horses. They made a handsome pair, in a way, both golden-haired and young. And doomed, he thought to himself. Oh ye gods, how long can I bear to stay here and watch their Wyrd? As he walked on, his heart was so heavy with his brooding that he nearly ran into Dannyn.

"My apologies," Nevyn said. "I was just thinking about somewhat."

Dannyn's eyes widened in awe.

"Not mighty spells or suchlike, my lord," Nevyn said.

"Well and good, then." He forced out a smile meant to be pleasant; it made Nevyn think of a wolf begging for table scraps. "Do you know where Lady Gweniver is going?"

"I don't. I assume that she and her men are just going to exercise their horses."

"Most like, truly."

By then the warband was clattering out of the gates. Dannyn watched Gweniver with such intensity that Nevyn was troubled.

"Now listen, lad," he said. "She's forbidden to you and to any other man as well. You should have the sense to realize that."

Dannyn turned toward him so sharply that Nevyn ducked back, summoning the Wildfolk in case the captain tried violence, but Dannyn, oddly enough, looked more hurt than enraged. For a moment he hesitated, as if there were something he wanted to ask, then turned on his heel and walked off fast. Dolt, Nevyn thought after him. Then he put the matter out of his mind and went up to visit Prince Mael.

Up in the silent tower room, the lad was leaning on the windowsill and looking down, watching the tiny figures of the last of the Wolf warband filing down the hill into the town.

"When I was a lad," Mael said, "I had some toys that came all the way from Bardek, little silver horses and warriors. That warband looks just the same size from here. I used to line them up and long for the day I'd lead men to battle. Oh by the hells, that day came and went so fast."

"Now here, Your Highness, you might be ransomed yet."

Mael gave him a bitter smile and flung himself into a chair by the hearth, where a small fire crackled to take off the chill. Nevyn sat down opposite and held out his hands to the warmth.

"There won't be any more heralds till spring," the prince said with a sigh. "Oh ye gods—a whole winter here! You know, my wife wanted to come and share my imprisonment, but Father wouldn't let her. He's right, I suppose. It would only give Glyn somewhat to hold over over her clan."

"You seem fond of her."

"I am. Father arranged our match when I was ten and she was eight, and she lived with us at court while we were betrothed. It was her training, you see, for being a prince's wife. And then we married three years ago. You get used to someone, and then you miss them. Oh here, good sir, my apologies. I'm babbling today."

"No apologies needed, lad."

For a long while the prince merely stared into the fire, but at last he roused himself.

"I've finished that book of chronicles," he said. "It's cursed strange. I'm going to be the best-educated prince that Eldidd ever had, and it won't do my kingdom the least bit of good."

"Now, now, it's much too soon to give up hope."

Mael swung around to face him.

"Here, good Nevyn, all the guards swear that you're dweomer. Answer me somewhat, honestly. Will I ever leave here for anything but my hanging?"

"That hasn't been given to me to know."

Mael nodded slowly, then want back to staring at the fire. Nevyn had to speak to him several times before he answered, and then it was only to discuss his reading.

Like a silver dancing wall, the rain swept over Dun Cerrmor. In the council chamber it was damp with a fine exhalation of cold from stone walls. Gweniver wrapped her plaid tightly around her as the councillors droned on. Across the table, Dannyn fiddled with his dagger. The King leaned forward in his chair with an expression of such serious attention that she wondered what he was really thinking about.

"Temperance and a slow pace are always best in all things, my liege," Saddar was saying. "And even more so in this matter of the Prince of Aberwyn. We must keep Eldidd in constant wonderment for as long as possible."

"Just so," Glyn said. "And most well put."

With a little smile, Saddar sat down again.

"Now, honored sirs," the King went on. "I plan to give Lord Gwetmar of the Wolf leave from the war next summer so that he may rebuild his dun and find farmers to tend his lands. Do you think this plan wise?"

Bowing, Yvyr rose to speak.

"Most wise, my liege. I doubt me if even a single one of your vassals will grumble. Everyone knows that the Wolf lands are an important salient."

"Good." Glyn turned to Gweniver. "Well, there you are, Your Holiness. The matter is settled as you wished it."

"My most humble thanks. My liege is most generous, and his councillors most wise."

With a nod all round, Glyn rose and ended the council. As Gweniver left, she realized that Dannyn was following her, but from a distance. She hurried down the corridor and the staircase to the great hall, but he caught up with her before she could reach the dais. The barely suppressed rage in his eyes was terrifying.

"I want a word with you," he said. "Outside."

"There's naught that you have to say to me that you can't say here."

"Indeed? I think otherwise, my lady."

Suddenly she felt the cold warning, telling her that she'd best let him have his talk before he made some kind of scene right there in the hall. Reluctantly she followed him out to the imperfect shelter of the overhanging roof of a storage shed.

"I've been thinking of what to say for three days," he snarled. "I can't wait any longer. I hear you've sworn a blood oath with Ricyn."

"I have, at that. What's it to you? We've sworn to share a grave, not a bed."

"I'm not sure I believe that."

"You'd best, because it's true."

For a moment he hesitated on the edge of believing her; then he smiled in a twisted sort of way. For the first time she realized that in his own harsh way he honestly cared for her, not merely lusted after her.

"Danno, look," she said, softening her voice. "If ever I broke any vow I swore to the Goddess, I'd die the day after. I'm sure of it. She'd find a way to strike me down."

"Indeed? What are you, then, a ghost from the Otherlands?"

"I have *not* broken my vow. And if you're so sure I have, why aren't you publicly proclaiming my sacrilege?"

"That should be cursed obvious."

The soft way he smiled made her step back, yet he made no move toward her.

"It gripes my very soul to say this," he went on. "But I love you."

"Then my heart aches for you, because that's a burden you'll have to bear alone."

"Let me tell you somewhat. I've never turned down a challenge when one was thrown my way."

"It's not a challenge, but the simple truth."

"Indeed? We'll just see about that."

Over the next few days, Gweniver felt as if she were doing a deadly dance to stay away from Dannyn. Whenever she came into the great hall, he would come over and sit with her as if he had every right to be there. Whenever she went out to the stables, he followed. Whenever she was on her way to her chambers, she met him in the corridor. He was setting himself to be charming, and it was painful to watch such a proud man trying to be courtly and seductive. During the day, Gweniver took to spending as much time as possible with Ricyn. At night, she would visit Nevyn in his chamber or shut herself up in hers with her maidservant for company.

On an evening when the wind moaned in the stone corridors, Gweniver went to Nevyn's chamber to find that he'd acquired a couple of chairs. On his table he'd spread a cloth and put out a flagon of mead and three goblets.

"Good eve, my lady," he said. "I'd like to invite you to stay, but I've got a couple of guests coming. I've been minding my courtesies and making friends out of Saddar and Yvyr."

"That's doubtless wise. No doubt they'd only resent your influence with the King if you didn't."

"I had thoughts that way myself, truly."

Gweniver had taken only about five steps down the corridor when she saw Dannyn, leaning against the wall and waiting for her. With a sigh, she strolled over.

"Leave me alone, will you?" she said. "It's cursed tedious to have you following me everywhere."

"Ah Gwen, please. I'm heartsick for the love of you."

"Then go ask Nevyn for some physic."

When she walked on by, he caught her shoulder.

"Get your hands off me! Leave me alone!"

Her voice was too loud, ringing in the empty corridor. His face scarlet with rage, Dannyn started to speak, but someone was coming toward them. Gweniver knocked his hand away and ran, brushing against Saddar with a curt apology. She hurried down the stairs and burst into the great hall, where she could sit with her warband and be safe. That evening, she toyed with the thought of laying a charge against him, but he was simply too important to the welfare of the kingdom for her to be easily believed.

All the next day, Dannyn seemed to be going out of his way to avoid her. She was as puzzled as she was relieved until Nevyn mentioned that he'd had a word with the captain and warned him to leave her alone. Yet eventually the warning seemed forgotten. One rainy morning, as she was coming back from the stables, he caught her out back behind the broch with no one else in sight.

"What do you want?" she snapped.

"Just a few honest words with you."

"Then here they are: you'll never share my bed."

"So, it's different with your common-born farmer lad, is it?"

"I've told you the truth about that. And it's not for the likes of you, anyway, to question a priestess about her vows."

When he made a grab at her wrist, she dodged, running back to the broch as fast as she could.

Gweniver's maidservant was a pale plain lass named Ocladda, who honestly loved working at court mostly because the work was so much easier than slaving on her father's farm. She took an odd pride in her lady being so eccentric and kept Gweniver's sparsely furnished chambers scrupulously clean. Since Gweniver had no long hair for her to comb and arrange or fancy clothes to tend, Ocladda made the best of her situation by endlessly polishing her lady's weapons and saddle-soaping her horse gear. While she worked, she would chatter over all the gossip from servants' quarters and queen's chamber alike, never mindful of how little her lady listened. One cold afternoon, then, it was a bad omen when Ocladda worked silently, laying a fire with never one word.

"Now here," Gweniver said at last. "What's wrong?"

"Oh my lady." She turned from the hearth. "I just pray you believe me. When a servant says one thing and a lord another, no one calls the lord a liar. I just know he'd deny every word of it."

Gweniver's first thought was that someone had gotten the lass pregnant.

"Now, now," she said soothingly. "Tell me who."

"Lord Dannyn, my lady. He met me out in the corridor this morning, and he offered me a bribe. He said he'd give me a silver coin if I left you alone in your chamber tonight. And I said that I'd never do such a thing, so he slapped me."

"Oh by the hells! Now here, I believe you well enough." In sheer fury, Gweniver began to pace back and forth. "Go back to your work while I think about this."

At the evening meal, she was constantly aware of Dannyn watching her with a smug smile. She ate fast and left her table before he could finish and join her, but she was afraid to go back to her chamber. If he followed and made some unpleasantness in front of Ocladda, soon every servant in the dun would hear about it. Obviously he considered the lass too far beneath him to consider that grim possibility. Finally she went down to the floor of the great hall and sought out Nevyn, who was talking with Ysgerryn over a tankard of ale.

"I want to invite you to my chamber, good Nevyn," she said. "It's time I returned your hospitality. Perhaps Ysgerryn would care to join us for a bit of mead, too."

Nevyn's bushy eyebrows shot up, as if he knew cursed well that something was afoot. Ysgerryn was all smiles at the thought of being invited to drink with the noble-born.

"I'd be most honored, Your Holiness," said the Master of Weaponry. "I just have to have a word with the chamberlain, and then I'll be free to join you."

"So shall I," Nevyn said. "My thanks."

Leaving the two of them to follow, Gweniver hurried back

to her chamber and sent Ocladda off to the kitchen to fetch mead and something to drink it in. She lit two candle lanterns with a splint of burning kindling from the hearth and was just putting them down when there was a knock on the door.

"Come in, good sirs," she called out.

Dannyn stepped in and shut the door behind him.

"What are you doing here?"

"Just coming to see you. Gwen, please, your heart can't be as cold to me as you pretend."

"My heart has naught to with what's on your mind. Now, listen, get out of here! I have two—"

"Don't you give me an order."

"It's not an order but a warning. I've got guests—"

Before she could finish, he caught her by the shoulders and kissed her. She twisted out of his hands and slapped him across the face. At the blow, all his careful pretense of courtesy shattered.

"Gwen, curse you! I'm sick of all this fencing."

He moved so fast that she couldn't dodge. He grabbed her by the shoulders and pinned her against the wall. Although she struggled and kicked and punched, his weight was too much for her to shove away as he pressed against her by brute force. Swearing, he held on, his hands bruising her shoulders, then tried to kiss her again.

"Let me go! You bastard, let me go!"

He slammed her so hard against the wall that she could barely breathe. Suddenly she heard a scream, slicing through the chamber. Dannyn let her go and spun around just as Nevyn and Ysgerryn ran in. In the doorway Ocladda screamed over and over again in high-pitched yelps.

"Sacrilege!" Ysgerryn was whispering in horror. "Oh dear Goddess, forgive us!"

"You fool, Danno!" Nevyn said. "You utter dolt."

Out of breath, shaken, Gweniver felt her back and shoulders aching like fire, but the pain was nothing compared to the sick coldness in her stomach. She'd nearly been polluted by brute force. Ysgerryn turned to Ocladda.

"Stop that screaming, lass! Run, get a page. Send for the guards. Hurry!"

When still sobbing the lass ran, Dannyn spun toward the door. Nevyn calmly stepped in front of him.

"Are you going to cut down two old men to get out of this chamber?" he said quietly. "I think you have more honor than that."

In silence Dannyn started shaking, trembling like a poplar in the wind. Gweniver wanted to scream. She clasped her hands over her mouth and watched him tremble. All her glory, her power on the battlefield and her pride in her sword, had been stripped away from her. Dannyn's brute strength had turned her into an ordinary frightened woman, and for that she hated him most of all. Ysgerryn laid a paternal hand on her arm.

"My lady, how do you fare? Did he hurt you?"

"Not badly," she choked out.

Out in the corridor men shouted. Four of the King's guards burst into the chamber with drawn swords and stopped, staring at their leader as if they thought themselves in a nightmare. Dannyn tried to speak, then went on shaking. After an eternity of painful minutes, Glyn himself hurried in with Saddar trailing after. At the sight of his brother, Dannyn broke, falling to his knees and weeping like a child. Saddar drew back with a dramatic gasp.

"Sacrilege!" the councillor cried out. "And here I've been fearing it for ever so long. Lady Gweniver, oh, what an abominable thing!"

"Now wait a moment," Glyn said. "Danno, what is all this?"

His face running tears, Dannyn drew his sword and handed it to the King hilt first, yet still he could not speak.

"My liege, Nevyn and I saw it," Ysgerryn said. "He was trying to force the lady."

"Oh ye gods," Saddar said. "What terrible curse will the Goddess visit upon us now?"

With a violent shudder, the guards drew back from the man who would have profaned a priestess. The disgust in their eyes made it plain that their piety was sincere, no matter what Gweniver thought of the councillor's.

"Danno," the King said. "It can't be true."

"It is." At last he forced out words. "Just kill me, will you?"

Dannyn tipped his head back to expose his throat. With an oath, Glyn threw the sword across the chamber.

"I'll judge this matter in the morning. Guards, take him to his chamber and keep him there. Take that dagger away from him, too." He glanced at the white-faced witnesses. "I wish to consult with her holiness. Alone."

While the guards were marching Dannyn away, Glyn stared fixedly at the wall. One at a time, the others hurried out, Saddar trailing at the last. The King slammed the door behind him, then flung himself into a chair and stared at the leaping fire in the hearth.

"In this, Your Holiness," he said, "you're the monarch and I the subject. I'll submit Lord Dannyn to any punishment that the Goddess demands, but as a man, I'll beg you for my brother's life." He paused, swallowing heavily. "The law says I should flog a man for meddling with a priestess. Publicly flog him, then hang him."

Gweniver sat down and pressed her shaking hands together. She was going to enjoy every stripe the executioner gave him; she would enjoy watching him hang, too. Then she felt the Goddess gathering behind her, a cold dark presence like winter wind through a window. She realized that if she used the holy laws for personal vengeance, she would be committing an impiety just as much as if she ignored them for the King's sake. She lifted up her hands and prayed silently to the Goddess while Glyn stared into the fire and went on waiting.

Every man in the great hall knew that something was wrong when a frightened page raced onto the dais and grabbed the King's arm. After Glyn left, riders and noble-born alike speculated in a whispering flood of gossip. What could possibly be so wrong for the lad to have forgotten his courtesies that way? Ricyn considered the matter no affair of his and went on drinking. Soon enough, he figured, everyone would know all about it. Things were just settling down when Lord Oldac made his way through the tables and tapped him on the shoulder.

"Come with me, Captain. Councillor Saddar wants to speak to you."

At the foot of the staircase stood Saddar, rubbing his hands together repeatedly.

"A terrible thing's happened, Captain," the councillor said. "Lord Dannyn has tried to rape the Lady Gweniver."

Ricyn felt as if the world froze and trapped him motionless, like a dead leaf caught in ice.

"I thought you should know," the old man went on. "I'm frankly terrified that our liege will pardon him contrary to all justice. If he should, please beg your lady to spare the city from the curse of the Goddess."

"By the hells," Ricyn snarled. "If our liege tries to weasel out of this, I'll kill the bastard myself."

Oldac and Saddar exchanged the briefest of smiles. Ricyn ran up the staircase, raced down the corridor, and came face to face with two guards outside Gweniver's door.

"You can't pass by. The King is in there."

Ricyn grabbed him by the shoulder and shoved him against the wall.

"I don't care if the Lord of Hell is in there. I've got to see my lady."

Just as the other guard made a grab at him, the door was flung open: Gweniver, pale, shaken, but unharmed.

"I thought I heard your voice," she said. "Come in."

When Ricyn stepped inside, he saw the King, rising from a chair. Never before had he been so close to the man he worshipped second only to her. In awe, he dropped to his knees.

"What's this?" Glyn said. "How did you hear about it?"

"Councillor Saddar told me about it, my liege. You can flog me if you want to for intruding, but I had to see my lady safe with my own eyes."

"No doubt." He glanced at Gweniver. "Councillor Saddar, was it?"

"And Lord Oldac," Ricyn added.

Gweniver considered this. He knew that the Goddess was upon her by the ramrod-straight way she stood and the cold power in her eyes.

"Tell me somewhat, Captain," the King said. "How are the men going to take this news?"

"Well, my liege, I can't speak for Lord Dannyn's men, but my men and me would fight the Lord of Hell himself to defend our lady's honor. We can't just take this calm, like."

"Especially not with the councillor stirring everyone up, my liege," Gweniver said. "You know, somewhat's coming clear to me about Councillor Saddar—not that we'd ever be able to prove a thing."

"Indeed?" Glyn glanced Ricyn's way. "Leave us."

Ricyn rose, bowed, and backed out of the chamber. He spent a long anxious night lying on his bunk and wondering what his lady and his king were deciding between them.

In the morning, Gweniver came to the barracks to fetch him. By her special request, Ricyn was allowed to witness the judgment in the audience chamber. Up on the dais, Glyn sat in his ceremonial clothes with a golden sword in his hand. Four councillors, including Saddar, stood behind him, and two priests of Bel stood to his right. The witnesses stood at the foot of the dais, Gweniver among them. At the sound of a silver horn, four guards marched Dannyn in. From the dark circles under his eyes, Ricyn judged that he hadn't slept all night. Good, he thought. Let the bastard taste every bitter drop of this.

"We have before us a charge of sacrilege," Glyn announced. "Lord Dannyn is accused of attempting to profane the person of Gweniver, lady and priestess. Let the evidence proceed."

"My liege," Dannyn called out, "let me spare you that. I confess. Just take me out and kill me. If ever I've done you any service, do it now and swiftly."

Glyn considered him with eyes so cold that he might have been looking at a stranger. Saddar smiled to himself.

"Lady Gweniver," the King said, "step forward."

Gweniver came to the foot of the throne.

"We offer you a choice of retribution, to take as the Goddess advises and desires. Death or banishment. The banishment will be from our court and our lands. We will strip Lord Dannyn of all rights, rank, and privilege, yet will we retain his child, to be raised as our son, out of pity for one too young to share his father's shame. This sentence would spare his life only because the crime was uncompleted. If the Goddess desires otherwise, we will have him given fifty lashes, then hanged until dead in the market square of our city of Cerrmor. In your Goddess's name, speak and sentence this man."

Although Ricyn knew what she was going to say, he had to admire the way Gweniver looked as she pretended to debate the question, all solemn and profound. Saddar looked as if he had a mouthful of vinegar as he began to guess what was coming. Finally Gweniver curtsied to the King.

"Banishment, my liege. Although the affair was grave and sacrilegious at root, the Goddess can be merciful when a crime is freely confessed, and when the criminal has been driven to mad actions by things beyond his control."

She paused and let her eyes meet Saddar's. The old man turned very pale indeed.

"Done, then." Glyn raised the golden sword high. "We hereby pronounce the aforesaid sentence of banishment against Dannyn, no longer lord. Guards! Take him away to prepare for his journey out of my city. Let him have no more than the clothes he wears, two blankets, a dagger, and the two pieces of silver due a banished man."

As the guards dragged the prisoner away, the audience in the crowded chamber began whispering in a sound like rushing water. Since he had an errand to run, Ricyn slipped out a side door and hurried to Dannyn's chambers. In the middle of the floor, Dannyn was kneeling and rolling up a cloak into his bedroll. He glanced Ricyn's way, then went on working.

"Have you come to kill me?" he said.

"I haven't. I've brought you somewhat from the lady."

"It's a pity she didn't just let me hang. The flogging would have been better than this."

"Don't talk like a dolt." Ricyn took the prepared message tube out of his shirt. "Ride to Blaeddbyr and give this to Lord Gwetmar. He needs a good captain with all the cursed Boars on the border."

Dannyn looked at the proffered tube for a moment, then took it and slipped it inside his shirt.

"She's most generous to those she conquers, but taking her favor is the cursed worst thing of all. Tell me somewhat and honestly, Ricco, for the sake of the battles we've ridden together. Are you bedding her or not?"

Ricyn's hand seemed to find his swordhilt of its own accord.

"I'm not, and never would I."

"Huh. So you'll be her little lapdog, will you? I thought you were more of a man than that."

"You're forgetting the Goddess."

"Huh." It was more a snort than word.

Ricyn found his sword in his hand without his being aware that he'd drawn it. Dannyn sat back on his heels and smirked at him. With a wrench of will, Ricyn sheathed the sword.

"Clever bastard, aren't you? But I'm not going to kill you and spare you your shame."

Dannyn went as limp as a sack of meal. Ricyn turned on his heel and left, slamming the door behind him.

The ward was packed with people from wall to wall, every lord, every rider, every servant, all whispering and waiting. Ricyn found Gweniver and Nevyn down by the gates, where a pair of the King's Guard held Dannyn's black gelding, saddled and ready. When Dannyn came out of the broch, the crowd parted to let him pass. His head held high, he swung his bedroll from one hand as easily, as cheerfully as if he were going out on campaign. The whispers rose around him, but he smiled at the guard, patted his horse's neck, and tied his bedroll to the saddle while he ignored the tittering laughter, the pointing kitchen wenches. When he mounted, a few jeers of bastard rose about the whisper. Dannyn turned in the saddle and bowed to his taunters, and all the while he smiled.

Drawn by some impulse that Ricyn couldn't understand, Gweniver followed Dannyn when he rode out the gates. Ricyn caught Nevyn's eye and motioned for the old man to come along as he hurried after her. All during Dannyn's slow ride through the crowded streets, the folk turned to stare at him, to whisper, to call him bastard, but he sat straight and proudly in the saddle. At the city gates he bowed to the guards, then kicked his horse to a gallop and raced down the open road. Ricyn let out his breath in a sigh of relief. In spite of himself, he felt a stab of pity.

"My lady?" he said to Gweniver. "Why did you follow him?"

"I wanted to see if he'd break. Pity he didn't."

"Ye gods, Gwen!" Nevyn snapped. "I was hoping you'd find it in your heart to forgive him."

"Now, that's the first stupid thing I ever heard you say, good sir. Why by all the hells should I? I allowed the King to banish him for his sake, not Dannyn's, and our liege was cursed lucky that he got that much out of me."

"You know," the old man said with some asperity, "hatred binds two people together even more tightly than love. You might reflect upon that."

The three of them strolled along the north-running road, bordered with the green meadowland of the King's personal demesne. In the cold clear sky, white clouds piled up and scudded before the rising wind. Ricyn was just thinking that he'd like to get back to the warmth of the great hall when he saw the horse, trotting toward them down the road. It was Dannyn's black, riderless, with the reins tied to the saddle peak. With an oath, Ricyn ran over and grabbed the reins. All of its master's gear was still tied to the saddle.

"Oh ye gods," Nevyn said. "Gwen, take that horse back to the dun and tell the guards how you found it. Bring them back with you. Ricco, come along. He can't be far."

Ricyn found out that Nevyn could run surprisingly fast for a man his age. They jogged down the road for about half a mile to a small rise with a single oak growing at its top. Someone was sitting under the tree. Swearing, Nevyn raced up the hill, and Ricyn panted after him. Dannyn was slumped over, his bloody dagger still tight in his hand. He'd cut his own throat not a mile away from the King he loved. When Ricyn turned away, he could see Dun Cerrmor rising about the town, the red and silver banners flapping in the wind.

"Ah shit!" Ricyn said. "The poor bastard."

"And is this enough vengeance for you?"

"Too much. He's got my forgiveness, if it'll do him any good in the Otherlands."

Nodding a little, Nevyn turned away.

"Well and good," he said. "Then that's one link on this chain broken, anyway."

"What?"

"Oh, naught, naught. Look. Here come the city guards now."

THREE

Nevyn stayed for another year in Cerrmor, but the time came when he could no longer bear to see Gweniver ride to war or to wait with the dread that she'd never ride home. One wet spring day he left the dun and rode aimlessly north to do what he could for the common folk of the kingdom. Although at first he thought of Gweniver often, he had so much else to trouble his heart that soon her memory faded. Year after year, the wars raged, and plague followed in their wake. Everywhere he went, Nevyn tried to counsel lords toward peace and the ordinary folk toward their own survival, but he felt that he was doing so little good, no matter how grateful were the people he helped, that he gave in to despair. In his heart, he reached the Dark Paths, where even the dweomer turns to dust and ashes, no comfort nor a joy. Out of duty to the Light, he kept up his work, but the last cruel mockery was that he was serving out of duty alone instead of his former love.

In the fifth spring, when apple blossoms were coming out in deserted orchards, some chance thought made him remember Gweniver, and once he'd thought of her, his curiosity got the better of him. That night he knelt by his campfire and focused his mind on the flames. Vividly he saw Gweniver and Ricyn, walking across the ward in Dun Cerrmor. They looked so unchanged that he thought he was only having a particularly vivid memory, but then she turned her head and he saw a scar sliced through the blue tatto. He ended the vision, but once he'd seen her, he couldn't forget her again. In the morning, with a sigh for the follies of men, he took the road to Cerrmor.

On a day when the soft breeze and the smell of fresh-growing grass mocked the kingdom's sufferings, Nevyn rode through the gates of the city. As he was dismounting to lead his horse and pack mule through the busy streets, he heard someone hail him and turned to find Gweniver and Ricyn, leading horses as they hurried over.

"Nevyn!" she sang out. "It gladdens my heart to see you."

"And mine to see you, and Ricco here, too. I'm flattered that you remember me."

"What? Oh now, here, how could we ever forget you? Ricco and I were just going out for a ride, but let us stand you a tankard of ale instead."

At Gweniver's insistence, they went to the best inn in Cerrmor, an elegant place with polished wood floors and white-washed walls. She also insisted on buying them the best ale with that easy warrior's generosity that cares little for coin a man might not live to spend. Once they were settled, Nevyn studied her while she told him the latest news of the war. Although she was hardened, as if her entire body were a weapon, her movements were firm yet graceful in a way that lay beyond the categories of male or female. As for Ricyn, he was as sunny and bland as ever, shy as he drank his ale and watched her.

Every now and then, when their eyes met, they smiled at each other, an exchange that was as full of tension as it was of love, as if their hearts were goblets filled to the brim, the liquid trembling but never spilling over to release. The link between them was so strong that it was visible to Nevyn's dweomer-touched sight as a web of pale light, all their normal sexual energy transmuted to a magical bond in their auras. He had no doubt that power flowed between them, too, that somehow they would always know where the other was in the worst press of battle, that thoughts passed between them so instinctively that they were unaware of it. Seeing her dweomer-talent so ill-used made him heartsick.

"Now here, good Nevyn," she said at last. "You've got to come up to the dun. Did the dweomer bring you back to us?"

"Not truly. Why? Is somewhat wrong?"

"Somewhat like that." Ricyn glanced around and lowered his voice. "It's our liege, you see. He's been having these black moods, and no one can bring him out of them."

"He broods on things," Gweniver put in, also in a whisper. "And he says things like he can't be the true king after all and other utter nonsense. The Queen's half afraid he's going mad."

They both looked at him in expectant faith that he would solve everything. He felt so helpless that their trust came close to making him weep.

"What's so wrong?" Gweniver said.

"Ah well, I'm just so cursed weary these days, seeing the land in turmoil, and there's naught I can to stop the suffering."

"Well, by the gods, it's not yours to stop. Don't vex yourself so deeply. Don't you remember what you told the King when he was so heartsick over Dannyn's death? You said it was only vanity that makes a man think he can turn aside someone else's Wyrd."

"Vanity? Well, so it is."

In her unthinking way she'd given him the very word he needed to hear. A vanity much like Glyn's, he thought. In my heart I'm still the prince, thinking that the kingdom still revolves around me and my doings. When he reminded himself that he was only a servant, waiting for a command, he was suddenly sure that the command would come. Someday he would see the Light shine again.

When they went up to the dun, servants came running and clustered round him as if he were indeed a prince. Orivaen insisted on giving him an elegant chamber in the main broch and accompanied him up personally. While Nevyn unpacked, the chamberlain gave him various bits of gossip. Lord Gwetmar and Lady Macla had two sons; Prince Mael was still in the tower; Gavra, his old apprentice, was now an herbwoman in the city.

"And what of our liege?" Nevyn said.

Orivaen's eyes darkened.

"I'll arrange a private audience this evening. Once you've seen him, we can speak further."

"I see. And what about Saddar? Is he still at court, or did he finally take his humbling to heart and leave?"

"He's dead. Strange, in way. It happened directly after you left us that summer. He developed a strange congestion of the stomach."

When Nevyn swore under his breath, Orivaen's expression turned completely bland. Nevyn wondered if the King himself had ordered the old man poisoned, or if some loyal courtier had taken the little task on himself, once the only herbman who could have saved the councillor was far away.

In the afternoon Nevyn went down into Cerrmor and found Gavra, who was living with her brother's family over his inn. She fell laughing into his arms, dipped him up some ale, and took him up to her chamber for a chat. She'd grown into an imposing young woman, still pretty and sleek, but with a depth of feeling and shrewdness in her dark eyes. Her chamber was stacked with herbs, jars of salve, and the other tools of her trade, neatly arranged around the furniture, a single bed, a wooden chest, and by the hearth, a cradle. Asleep inside was a pretty little lass about ten months old.

"Your brother's youngest child?" Nevyn said.

"She's not, but mine. Do you despise me for it?"

"What? Whatever made you think I would?"

"Well, my brother was none too pleased at having a bastard in the family. I'm just lucky I can bring in the coin to feed us."

As if she knew she was being discussed, the baby yawned, opened cornflower-blue eyes, and fell back asleep.

"Why hasn't the father married you?"

"He's married to someone else. I know I'm not a fool, but I love him all the same."

Nevyn sat down on the wooden chest. He'd never expected that his clever Gavra would have gotten herself into this sort of mess. She leaned on the windowsill and looked out at her narrow view, the side of another house, a small dusty yard with a chicken coop.

"Prince Mael," she said abruptly. "My poor captive love."

"Ye gods!"

"I beg you, don't tell a soul. They might kill my babe if they knew that Eldidd had a royal bastard here in town. I've told everyone that her father was one of the King's riders, Dagwyn his name was, who was killed in last year's fighting. Lady Gweniver's been helping me, you see. I guess Dagwyn was quite a lad with the lasses, and everyone believed it of him without thinking twice."

"Is Gweniver the only one who knows?"

"Just that, not even Ricyn." She paused to look into the cradle with a wry smile. "I had to tell someone, and Gweniver is a priestess, no matter what else she may be. It's sad, though. Ricyn comes here sometimes and gives me coin for his friend's daughter. Little Ebrua seems to mean much to him."

"Then it's best that he never learn the truth. But here, how did this happen? Can you fly through the air like a bird?"

"Oh, I climbed the stairs to the tower, sure enough," she said, half laughing. "But not long after you left, the prince got a fever, and all the chirurgeons were gone with the army. So Orivaen sent for me to keep their bit of booty alive. Ye gods, I felt so sorry for Mael, and Orivaen allowed me to visit him like you used to. Mael offered to teach me to read and write, you see, just to have somewhat to pass his time. So I had my lessons, and we grew to be friends, and well—" She gave an eloquent shrug of her shoulders.

"I see. Does he know about the child?"

"Oh, how could he not know? My poor captive love."

When he returned to the dun, Nevyn made a point of going up to the tower to see the prince. Although his pleasant chamber had changed not at all, Mael was a man now. Tall, filled out, he paced gravely around the room instead of throwing himself about in an agony of impatience. He was also dead pale, his alabaster skin making his raven hair look even darker. With start, Nevyn realized that it had been seven years since the prince had been out in the sun.

"You can't know how much it gladdens my heart to see you," Mael said. "I missed my tutor badly when he left."

"My apologies, but the dweomer calls a man down many a strange road. I seem to have left you some comfort, though. I've spoken to Gavra."

The prince turned scarlet and looked away.

"Ah well," he said after a moment. "It's strange, truly. There was a time when I would have thought that a common-born woman was beneath my notice. Now I wonder what Gavra could possibly want with a wretch like me."

"Your highness has had a harsh Wyrd, truly."

"Oh, not as harsh as many. I've grown tired of pitying myself, you see. Some men are like hawks, dying young in battle. I'm a little finch, kept in a royal cage and dreaming of trees. But it's a nice cage, and there's plenty of seed in my bowl."

"True enough."

"The books you left me have become more and more of a comfort, too. And Gavra found me an interesting thing down at the bookseller's in the temple of Wmm. It's a compendium of a philosopher named Ristolyn, who wrote in the Dawntime. Was he a Rhwman?"

"He wasn't, but one of a tribe called the Greggycion, a wise folk judging from what little we have of their books. I believe that the cursed Rhwmanes conquered their kingdom, much as they did the one belonging to our ancestors back in the Homeland. Ristolyn always struck me as a writer worthy of much thought. I've read part of his *Ethics of Nichomachea*."

They passed a pleasant hour discussing things that Nevyn hadn't heard so much as mentioned in years. Although the prince talked with the eagerness of a born scholar, when it was time for Nevyn to leave, melancholy settled over Mael like a sea fog. He wasn't a scholar, after all, but a desperate man clinging to whatever would keep him sane.

Leaving Mael's silent room and going into the great hall was like walking into another world. Since the army was mustering, the hall was filled with lords and warbands: men shouting, men laughing, yelling for ale, and throwing jests like daggers at one another. Nevyn sat at Orivaen's table with the King's councillors just below the dais. As the meal was being served, Glyn came through his private door with Gweniver. When he went to the honor table, however, she left the dais and went to eat with King's guards and her Ricyn.

"Lady Gweniver seems to hold her nobility in contempt," Nevyn remarked to Orivaen.

"She does. I've spoken to her about it ever so often, but one simply can't argue with the god-touched."

During the meal, Nevyn watched Glyn, who seemed to have changed not all, still as straight and gracious as ever as he smiled at a jest or listened to the conversation of his honored lords. Yet the change came clear later, when a page took Nevyn to the King's private apartments. Glyn was standing by the hearth. Candlelight shone and sparked on silver, gleamed on the rich colors of the hangings and carpets, and picked out the hollow shadows under his eyes. Although he insisted that Nevyn take a chair, he paced restlessly by the hearth as they talked. At first they exchanged little more than news and pleasantries, until slowly, a bit at a time, the regal presence wore away, and Glyn leaned wearily against the mantel, a heartsick man.

"My liege seems to honor Lady Gweniver highly," Nevyn remarked.

"She's worthy of honor. I've given her the place at the head of my Guards, you see. No one will dare envy a god-touched warrior."

There it was, the memory they would have to face.

"Does my liege still miss his brother?"

"I doubtless will every day of my life. Ah ye gods, if only he hadn't killed himself! We could have met now and then in secret, or perhaps I could even have recalled him someday."

"Well, his pride wouldn't let him wait."

With a sigh, Glyn sat down at last.

"So many men who've served me have come to grief," he said. "There's no end in sight, either. Ah by the Lord of Hell himself, sometimes I think I should just let Cantrae have the cursed throne and be done with it, but then everyone who's died for me would have died for naught. And my loyal friends—Cantrae might slaughter the lot." He paused for a weary, twisted smile. "How many people here at court have told you that I'm going mad?"

"Several. Are you? Or are they merely mistaking sanity for madness?"

"I'd prefer to think the latter, of course. Ever since Danno died, I've felt besieged. I could talk to him, and if he thought I was babbling like a fool, he'd say so. Now what do I have? Flatterers, ambitious men, jackals, half of them, and if I don't throw them enough scraps of meat, well, then they bite. If I try to ease my mind of some dark thought, they cringe."

"Well, my liege, their lives depend on you, after all."

"I know. Oh, ye gods, I know that so well! I wish I'd been born a common rider. Every man in the court envies the King, but do you know whom the King envies? Gweniver's Ricyn. I've never seen a happier man than Ricco, farmer's son or not. No matter what he does, no matter what happens to him, he calls it the will of his Goddess and gets a good night's sleep." Glyn paused briefly. "Do you think I'm mad? Or am I just a fool?"

"The King has never been a fool, and he would be happier if he were mad."

Glyn laughed in a way that suddenly reminded Nevyn of Prince Mael.

"Nevyn, I'd be most grateful if you'd rejoin my court. You see things from very far away. The King humbly admits that he needs you badly."

Because he saw nothing but grief ahead of him, Nevyn wanted to lie and claim that the dweomer forbade him to stay. He liked all these people too much to stay aloof from their inevitable sufferings. Yet suddenly he saw that he had a role to play, that he'd deserted Glyn, Mael, and Gavra when he'd fled for his own selfish reasons.

"I'm most honored, my liege. I'll stay and serve you as long as you have need of me."

And so, utterly reluctantly, Nevyn received what many men would have killed to get: a position as a royal councillor and the personal favor of the King. It took him two difficult years to untangle the web of envy that his sudden elevation created, but after that time, no one questioned his place. Everyone in the kingdom knew that the center of court power rested with this shabby old man with his eccentric interest in herbs, but few, of course, knew why.

And during those two years, and on into the third, the war dragged on, a sporadic thing of raids and feints.

The rain caught them a good forty miles from the main camp. A slantwise driving storm with a cold wind that cut through cloaks turned the road to muck. Even though the situation was desperate, it was impossible for the horses to go at more than a walk. The one good thing about the rain, Ricyn reflected bitterly, was that it was slowing the enemy down, too. He made a point of saying so to the thirty-four men left out of the hundred and fifty who'd ridden out. No one responded with more than a grunt. Ricyn rode up and down the line twice, spoke to everyone by name, yelled at the slackers and praised the few who had the least bit of spirit left. He doubted if it was doing any good. When he said as much to Gweniver, she agreed.

"The horses are in worse shape than the men," she said. "We have to stop soon."

"And if they catch us?"

Gweniver merely shrugged. Neither of them had the slightest idea of how far behind them the Cantrae warband was. The one thing they could be sure of was that they were being chased. The hard-won victory that had reduced their warband to this weary fragment was just the sort of battle that Cantrae would feel honor-bound to avenge.

Close to sunset, they met a pair of farmers who were struggling with a cart pulled by a balky milk cow for want of a horse. In the darkening light, Ricyn could just see that the cart was full of furniture, tools, and barrels. When the warband surrounded them, the farmers looked up in blank exhaustion, as if they didn't even care if they were slaughtered on the road.

"Where are you fleeing from?" Gweniver said.

"Rhoscarn, my lady. The dun fell yesterday, and we're trying to get south."

"Who razed it?"

"These men with green beasts, like, on their shields."

Ricyn swore under his breath: the Cantrae wyvern.

"They didn't raze the dun, you dolt!" the second farmer said. "We didn't see any smoke, like, did we now?"

"True enough," said the first. "All the cursed same to me. We saw a powerful lot of them on the roads, my lady."

Gweniver pulled the warband off the road to let the weary farmers trudge past.

"What do you say to this, Ricco? We could ride to Rhoscarn and have a roof over our heads. If they've been there already, they won't ride back."

And so they rode straight into the trap. Later, Ricyn was to think how cleverly it had been laid, how well Cantrae's men had played the part of farmers, how nicely Cantrae had judged their minds. At the time, he was only glad to find shelter for the horses. When they reached the dun, they found the stone wall breached in three places. Tieryn Gwardon's body lay headless among the rubble of stone. Although there were plenty of other corpses, it was too dark by then to count them. Since this dun had been taken and burned several times before, there was no stone broch, merely a big wooden roundhouse in the middle of a muddy ward.

It may have been primitive, but the roundhouse was dry inside. The men stabled the horses at one side, laid down their gear at the other, then split up the furniture and built fires in the hearths. Once the horses were at their last nosebags of oats, the men broke out what was left of their rations. Ricyn was just about to mention to Gweniver that they'd have to try to forage on the morrow when he felt danger, a cold touch down his back. From the way that she shuddered, he knew she'd felt it, too. In wordless agreement they ran out of the house to the ward.

Ricyn stayed below as she climbed the wall. In the darkness he saw her shape crest the top; then she turned and yelled.

"The men! Guard the breaches! Attack!"

As he ran back, he heard the distant noise of horses, coming fast toward the dun. Yelling orders, he burst inside and got his men moving. Grabbing swords, swearing, the warband spread out around the wall and filled each breach. By then, the sound of an army surrounded them like ocean waves pounding on the shore. Through a breach he saw he saw men dismounting and circling the walls.

"Penned," Gweniver said idly. "Think we can hold this siege for a whole day?"

"Not by half. Here, I'm surprised the Goddess didn't warn us when we were talking to the farmers."

"I'm not. I always knew the day would come when She wanted us dead."

She reached up and kissed him on the mouth, just once before she walked away to start giving her orders.

Since it was unlikely that the enemy would attack in the rainy darkness, they set guards at the breaches and slept in rotating shifts. About an hour before dawn, the rain stopped, and a cold wind sprang up to clear the sky. Ricyn woke the men, who armed in utter silence. Everyone looked at their friends in a way that said farewell without need of words. While Gweniver kept watch at the breach that was once the gates, Ricyn posted the warband at the others.

"It's to the death," he said, over and over. "All we can do is make them pay high."

Over and over, the men nodded their silent agreement. Down by the back wall Ricyn found Alban, just fourteen that summer and brand new to the Cerrmor riders. Although the lad stood as straight and bravely as any man there, Ricyn was determined to spare his life if he could.

"Now listen, lad," he said. "I've got an important mission for you. I'm choosing you because you're the shortest man in the pack and the least noticeable. We've got to get news of this back to the King. You're taking the message."

Wide-eyed in the rising dawn, Alban nodded.

"What you do is this," Ricyn went on. "Crouch down behind this pile of rubble and hide until you see a Cantrae man fall where you can grab his shield. Once the action sweeps past you, you slip out, pretend you're wounded, and mingle with the enemy. Then steal a horse if you live that long and ride like the hells were opening under you."

"I will, and if they catch me out, then I'll dine with the rest of you in the Otherlands."

As he walked away, Ricyn begged the Goddess to let this clumsy ruse work.

When he rejoined Gweniver at the gates, he found the squad that would fight behind them already in position.

"There's over a hundred," Gweniver remarked. "They're just drawing up for their charge now. On foot, at least."

"Why waste horses killing rats in a hole?"

As he took his place beside her, they exchanged a smile.

Beyond the breach he saw men climbing slowly uphill, then
fanning out to the breaches. Inside it was dead silent except for
the occasional clink of a sword or shield. As the eastern sky
brightened, Ricyn felt his heart pounding, but it wasn't truly a
fear, more a wondering what the Otherlands would be like. I'll
see Dagwyn again, he reminded himself, and tell him about his
daughter. The dawn light brightened on metal, sword and mail,
helm and shield boss. From far back in the Cantrae line, a silver
horn cried out. With a yell, the Wyvern shields surged forward. It
had started.

Cerrmor held the breaches far longer than any of them had a
right to expect. Gweniver and Ricyn themselves, fighting side by
side, could have held off a large force alone in that size of a
breach—if only there had been no gaps behind them. As it was,
they fought grimly, barely aware of how high the sun was climbing. Screaming, the mob swirled for them, but Ricyn kept swinging, thrusting forward and falling back in perfect rhythm with
the perfect partner. The dead began to pile up, hampering the
Cantrae charges. Ricyn felt sweat streaming down his back and
wished for a drink of water as he fought on and on. Next to him a
Cerrmor man fell; another stepped forward to kill the Cantrae
man who'd dropped him. Suddenly Ricyn heard screams from
behind him—warning, despair.

"Fall back!" Gweniver yelled. "They've broken through behind."

One cautious step at a time, the line retreated, swinging,
parrying, trying to fan out as the Cantrae men poured through
the gates. The ward was a madhouse of running men as the other
Cerrmor squads tried to reform their lines. Ricyn began cursing,
a steady stream under his breath, but he heard Gweniver laughing and howling in her berserker's fit. Suddenly the sun dimmed.
As Ricyn made a quick thrust at an enemy, he smelled smoke, a
thick billowing cloud of it. Back and back toward the roundhouse, stumbling over the bodies of dead friends and enemies,
choking from the smoke and swinging thrusting slashing—still
Ricyn had time to look her way and hear her laughing as the mob
grew around them. They reached the house and held the door
while, one by one, what was left of the Cerrmor warband hob-
bled, crawled, and ran inside, all eight of them.

"Get in, Ricco!" Gweniver yelled.

He stepped in, dodging to make room for her to follow, then helped Camlwn swing the door shut and bar it. The roundhouse was sweltering hot from the burning upper story. The horses reared and screamed in panic as the men grabbed their reins and pulled them forward. Outside, Cantrae men were yelling for axes and pounding on the wooden shutters at the windows. At last the horses were gathered in a hysterical mob at the door. Ricyn and Camlwn flung it open as the men behind screamed at the herd and slapped them with the flat of their swords. Trampling and kicking, the horses tore out and plunged into the Cantrae men like living bludgeons.

Ricyn swung around and started to yell an order. Then he saw Gweniver, and his voice cracked in his throat.

She'd staggered back out of the way to die in the curve of the wall. In his battle fever, he'd never seen her struck. He ran to her, sank down on his knees, and saw that she'd been stabbed in the back through the joining of her mail. When he turned her over, her face was oddly calm, her lovely blue eyes wide open as her blood spread around her on the floor. Only then did Ricyn truly realize that he'd never live to see the noontide. He dropped his sword, grabbed hers like a talisman, and ran for the door. The smoke billowed down thick and swirled around the Cantrae men regrouping out in the ward.

"Let's charge, lads," Ricyn said. "Why die like rats?"

With one last shout of Glyn's name, his men fell in behind him. Camlwn gave him one last grin; then Ricyn raised the sword that once the Goddess had blessed and charged straight for the enemy. For the first time, he started laughing, just as coldly as she had, as if the Goddess were letting him for this little moment take Her priestess's place.

Ricyn stumbled over a dead horse and flung himself on the first Cantrae man that came his way. He killed him in one thrust, then spun around to meet the Wyvern shields ganging around him. He got a weak backhanded slash on an enemy, spun and lunged at another, then felt a bite of metal on his face, so sharp that for a moment he thought it was a bit of burning thatch, but blood welled up warm and salty in his mouth. When he staggered, a sword bit into his side. He threw his useless shield and turned, stabbed hard, and killed the man who'd wounded him. The fire was roaring, and the smoke as thick as sea fog. He staggered, swung again, choked on his own blood, and fell, trying to cough it back up. The enemies left him for dead and ran on.

Ricyn staggered to his feet and took a few steps, but only when he tripped over the lintel to the house did he realize he'd gotten turned around. The fire was already creeping down the walls inside. He got to his feet and stumbled toward Gweniver. Although every step stabbed him with pain, at last he reached her. He fell to his knees beside her, then hesitated, wondering if the Goddess would condemn him for this gesture. He doubted if She would care any longer. He threw himself down, reached out, and pulled Gweniver into his arms until he could rest with his head on her chest. His last thought was a prayer to the Goddess, asking forgiveness if he were doing a wrong thing.

The Goddess was merciful. He bled to death before the flames reached him.

Nevyn was in the King's tent at the encampment when he heard the shouting and hoofbeats that meant the army had returned. He grabbed a cloak and ran through the drizzling rain to the meadow, a mob of confusion as the men dismounted. He shoved his way through and found the King, handing over his reins to his orderly. Glyn's face was stubbled and filthy, with a streak of another man's blood on his cheek and a black smear of ashes on his pale, stiff hair.

"No one left alive," he said. "We buried everyone we could find, but there was no trace of Gweniver and Ricyn. The Cantrae bastards had fired the dun, so most likely they were inside the roundhouse. At least they had a pyre, just like in the Dawntime."

"They would have liked that. Well, so be it."

"But we caught the Cantrae warband on the road—what was left of them, anyway. We wiped them out."

Nevyn nodded, not trusting his voice. Gwen would have liked that best of all, he thought, vengeance. The King turned away and called for someone to bring Alban to him. So pale and exhausted that he was staggering, the lad came to the King's side.

"Can you do somewhat for him, Nevyn?" Glyn said. "I don't want him getting a fever or suchlike after the splendid way he rode that message."

The praise from the King himself broke Alban's last resistance. He tossed his head once, then began to sob like the young lad he was. As Nevyn led him off to the chirurgeon, he had trouble holding back his own tears. It will happen again and again, he reminded himself, that someone you love will die long before you. He wanted to curse his bitter Wyrd, but the most bitter thing of all was knowing that he had only himself to blame.

Interlude
Spring, 1063

A hunter who lays snares had better watch where he puts his feet.

Old Deverry proverb

In all the wide kingdom of Deverry, there were only two towns that the Elcyion Lacar ever visited, Cernmetyn and Dun Gwerbyn, and them only rarely. The townsfolk in both places had a curious reaction whenever the People rode their way. In a kind of unconscious conspiracy, they simply refused to admit how different the elves were. Any child who asked about elven ears was told that this savage tribe cropped their babies' ears. Any child who pointed out the strange cat-slit eyes was told to hold his tongue, or else his ears might get cropped the same way. The adults themselves, however, found it hard to look an elf in the eye, which was one reason that the People considered human beings to be shifty and untrustworthy.

Devaberiel, therefore, wasn't surprised when the guards at Dun Gwerbyn's gates first stared at him, then looked quickly away at the small crowd of beings behind him: Jennantar, Calonderiel, two packhorses dragging travois, and finally, a string of twelve riderless horses.

"Have you come here to sell those?" the guard asked. "There's taxes to pay if you have."

"I've not. I'm bringing them as tribute to the tieryn."

The guard nodded solemnly, because it was common knowledge that every now and then the Westfolk, as Eldidd people called the elves, gave some of their beautiful horses to gain the goodwill of the tieryns of Dun Gwerbyn and Cernmetyn both.

Although Jennantar and Calonderiel had been in Eldidd before, they'd never been inside the town, and Devaberiel noticed them looking scornfully at the grimy houses and dirty alleys as they led their stock along. Devaberiel himself felt faintly uneasy about the way everything was crammed in together. You simply couldn't get a clear view in a human town, no matter which way you looked.

"We're not going to stay here long, are we?" Calonderiel muttered.

"Not very. You can leave straightaway, if you like, after we get the horses to the dun."

"Oh, no. I want to see Rhodry again, and Cullyn, too."

Cullyn they saw immediately, because he happened to be standing in the open gates of the dun when they puffed up the hill. With a shout of greeting, he trotted down to meet them. Although Devaberiel had heard a good bit about the man who was considered the best swordsman in all Deverry, he was unprepared for the sight of him. Well over six feet tall, he was broad-shouldered and hard-muscled. An old scar slashed down his left cheek, and his blue eyes did nothing to dispel the grim impression. They were as hard and cold as a winter storm, even when he smiled and shook Calonderiel's hand.

"Now this is a gift from the gods," Cullyn said. "It gladdens my heart to see you again."

"And mine to see you," said the warleader. "We've brought tribute to Lady Lovyan and young Rhodry."

"Well, the lady will be glad to receive it." His eyes turned even grimmer. "But Gwerbret Rhys of Aberwyn sent Rhodry into exile last fall."

"What?" All three elves spoke at once.

"Just that. But come in, come in. I can tell you the tale over a tankard of the tieryn's hospitality."

As they led the horses up to the dun, Devaberiel felt as if he'd been kicked in the stomach.

"Cullyn?" he said. "Then where's Rhodry now?"

"Riding the long road as a silver dagger. Do you know what that means, good sir?"

"I do. Oh ye gods, he could be anywhere in the cursed kingdom!"

As they came into the ward, servants and grooms came running, exclaiming over the horses. The elven breed, known as Western Hunters in Deverry, stood sixteen to eighteen hands, with broad chests and delicate heads. Although they were usually gray, buckskin, or roan, a few were a rich golden color, and those were the most prized. Although Devaberiel had brought a golden mare for his son to use as breeding stock, now he was tempted to take her back again. Come now, he told himself, I owe Lovva something for giving me a son.

The clatter and the shouting outside had apparently aroused Lovyan's curiosity, because she came out of the broch and strolled over. Wearing a dress of red Bardek silk, kirtled in with her clan's red, white, and brown plaid, she walked as lithely as a young lass, but when she came close, Devaberiel's heart was wrung for the second time that day. She was growing old, her face slashed by wrinkles, her hair heavily streaked with gray. She glanced his way, stiffened slightly, then looked at him as blandly as if they'd never met. His heart ached for her, and he cursed himself as a fool or worse for coming. She was growing old, while he still looked like a lad of twenty. It was one of those rare times in his life when he could find nothing to say.

"My lady Lovyan," Calonderiel said with a bow. "Your Grace, tieryn of Dun Gwerbyn. We come to bring you tribute to your power and dominion."

"My thanks, good sir. I'm most pleased to receive such a splendid gift. Come in and take the hospitality of my hall."

Since there was no way out, Devaberiel followed along. As a favor to Cullyn, Lovyan allowed him to join her and the guests at the honor table. Once they'd all been served mead, the captain told the story in detail of Rhodry's exile. Although Calonderiel and Jennantar constantly interrupted to ask questions, Devaberiel found it hard to listen. He kept cursing himself for coming and causing such pain to both himself and to the woman he once had loved. When the tale was finished, everyone drank in silence for a moment. Devaberiel risked another glance at Lovyan only to find her looking at him. When their eyes met, for a moment her composure wavered, her eyes so haunted, her mouth so tense, that he feared she would weep. Then she looked away, and the moment passed.

"Well, good men of the Westfolk," she said, "will you shelter in my dun awhile?"

"My humble thanks for the honor, Your Grace," Devaberiel said. "But my folk are used to wandering through grassland and forest. It makes us uneasy to be within stone walls. Would it

displease Your Grace if we camped outside the town tonight, and
then went on our way?"

"How can I refuse a favor to men who've just brought me
such a splendid gift? Just two miles north I have a game preserve.
I'll give you a token for my forester, and you may camp there for
as long as you please."

And her eyes thanked him for taking himself away.

Yet they had a chance for a few private words while the
servants brought the elves' riding mounts and packhorses. Cullyn and the other two stood on the dun steps and talked among
themselves with the earnestness of old comrades, but Lovyan
gestured at the bard to follow her some paces away.

"Did you come here just to bring me horses?" she said.

"I didn't. I came to see our son."

"So. You know the truth about that, then?"

"I do. Lovva, please, forgive me. I never should have come,
and I swear to you that you'll never have to see me again."

"It would be for the best. Rhodry must never know the
truth. Do you realize that?"

"Of course. I only wanted a look at the lad."

She smiled briefly.

"He looks much like you, but he has the raven-dark Eldidd
hair. He's a handsome lad, our Rhodry."

He caught her hand and squeezed it, then let it go before
anyone could see.

"I wonder if I'll ever lay eyes on him," he said. "I don't dare
ride any farther east. They haven't learned how to ignore our
eyes and ears in the rest of the kingdom."

"True spoken. You know, I'd always heard that your folk
were long-lived, but I didn't realize how young you stayed." Her
voice caught. "Or is the old tale true, and you live forever?"

"Not forever, but for a cursed long time. And we do age, but
not until we're ready to die. That's how we know it's time to
prepare for our last ride."

"Indeed?" She looked away and unconsciously touched the
wrinkles on her cheek. "Perhaps we have the best of it, then,
because while we age early, we're never burdened with knowing
when we'll die."

He sighed, remembering his grief when his father's hair
began to turn white and his vigor fade.

"Truly," he said. "You may have the better bargain."

He walked quickly away, because tears were gathering in his throat.

When they rode out, Devaberiel said not a word to the others, and they allowed him his silence until they reached the hunting preserve. Lovyan's forester took them to an open dell where a stream ran and there was good grass for the horses, remarked that there were plenty of deer this year, then rode off rather fast to avoid spending time with Westfolk. They pitched the red tent, tethered the horses, then gathered a few sticks of firewood to add to their stock of dried manure for a fire, and still Devaberiel said nothing. Finally Calonderiel could stand it no longer.

"Coming here was a really stupid thing to do," he remarked.

"The warleader is known far and wide for his graceful tact," Devaberiel snapped. "By the Dark Sun herself, why do you have to pour bitter gall in a man's cup when he's thirsty?"

"Well, sorry, but—"

"You're forgetting the rose ring," Jennantar broke in. "The dweomer said Rhodry should have it."

"Now, that's true," Calonderiel said. "So I suppose Dev had some excuse."

Snarling under his breath, Devaberiel went to unpack a skin of mead from the travois. Jennantar followed, squatting down next to him.

"Don't take everything Cal says to heart. He's always like that."

"Then I'm cursed glad I don't march in one of his squadrons."

"It takes some getting used to. But I was wondering, how are you going to get that ring to your lad? Do you have any idea?"

"I was thinking about that on the ride here. I've got another son, you know, who had a Deverry mother. He looks more like her folk than he does ours."

"Of course—Ebañy." Jennantar looked worried. "But are you really going to trust him with the ring?"

"I know what you're thinking, and yes, I have my own doubts. Ye gods, he's a wild lad! Maybe I never should have taken him away from his mother, but the poor lass couldn't support a child on her own, and her father was livid with rage that she had one. I don't understand these Deverry men sometimes. They don't have to carry the babe, do they, so what business of theirs is it if their daughter's got one? But anyway, if I lay a father's charge on Ebañy to get the ring to his brother, he'll doubtless do it. It's just the sort of wild escapade that would appeal to him."

"Do you know where he is?"

"No, and that's the real problem, isn't it? You never know with that lad. I'll just have to put out the word that I want to see him and hope that it reaches him."

By this time, Cerrmor had grown to a city of some hundred and twenty thousand people. Not only did it stretch far up the river, but some rich merchants had built splendid houses on the cliffs above, far away from the noise and dirt of the town. The dun where once Glyn had ruled as king had been razed a hundred years before and a new, even larger, one built for the gwerbrets of Cerrmor. Down near the waterfront, however, was a section of town that had nothing splendid about it. Brothels, cheap inns, and taverns stood close together in a maze of winding streets and alleys that decent citizens never entered, except for the gwerbret's wardens, who entered there far more frequently than the inhabitants would have liked. It was called the Bilge.

Whenever he went to the Bilge, Sarcyn always walked quickly, kept his eyes moving, and wrapped his aura tight around him, a dweomer that made him very hard to notice. He wasn't truly invisible—anyone walking straight toward him would have seen that he was there—but rather he caught no one's attention, especially when he walked close to walls or in shadows. That particular afternoon it was overcast, and several people nearly bumped into him as they strode past, unmindful that they shared the street with someone else. Still, he kept his hand on his sword hilt.

Since it was late in the day, the streets were growing crowded. Sailors with pay to spend strolled along through street vendors hawking cheap food and cheaper trinkets. A few whores were already out, the kind known as "cobblestones" because they had only the dark back alleys to take their clients to. Here and there he saw a group of Bardek sailors, their brown faces neatly painted, their dark hair oiled for their night of liberty. Once, six city wardens marched past, keeping a tight formation and carrying their quarter-staves at the ready. Sarcyn ducked into a doorway and stayed there until they were well past. Then he went on his way, moving quickly through the confusing maze.

Although he hadn't been in Cerrmor for some time, he knew the Bilge well. He'd been born there.

Finally he reached his destination, a three-story stone roundhouse with a freshly thatched roof and neatly whitewashed walls. Gwenca could afford to keep her whorehouse up because she catered to a better class of clients than mere sailors. He paused at the door, released his aura, then stepped into the ground floor tavern. Arranged around the central spiral staircase were wooden tables, standing on clean straw. A peat fire smoldered on the hearth to take off the chill, because the young women sitting on cushioned benches were either naked or wearing only gauzy Bardek shifts. A lass wearing nothing but a square of black silk tied round her hips hurried over. Her blue eyes were lined with Bardek kohl, and her long blond hair smelled of roses.

"We haven't seen you in ever so long, Sarco," she said. "Do you have any?"

"I do, but your mistress is the one who'll be handing it out. Where's Gwenca?"

"In the cellar, but can't you let me have a little bit right now? You can come fish in my bucket if you do."

"I'll give you naught until your mistress says so."

The tavernman moved aside two ale barrels from the curve of the wall, then pulled up the trap door to let him go down into what seemed an ordinary cellar. Ale and mead barrels stood in profusion; hams hung from the ceiling amid nets of onions. But on the far side was a door, and when he knocked, a gravelly woman's voice snarled, asking who he was.

"Sarcyn, back from Bardek."

At that the door opened, and Gwenca stood smiling at him. About fifty, she was a stout woman with hennaed hair and brown eyes that looked out from a web of lines and pouches. On every finger she wore a jewelled ring, and round her neck a chain with a blue-and-silver charm against the evil eye. Sarcyn smiled inwardly; she knew him only as a drug runner and had no idea that he was exactly the sort of man who could cast the evil eye.

"Come in, pretty lad. I take it you've got somewhat to offer me."

"I do, at that, and good quality it is."

Gwenca's private chambers were oppressively stuffy. Although there were vents near the ceiling, the room reeked of scent and stale opium smoke, as if the tapestries and cushions exhaled the smell. She sat down at a small table, inlaid with glass in a gaudy spiral of red and blue, and watched while he unbuckled his sword belt, laid it close to hand on a chair, then pulled his shirt over his head. Slung from his neck like saddlebags were a pair of flat leather pouches. He took them off and tossed them down in front of her.

"Twenty-five silvers the bar. You'll see why when you open them."

With greedy fingers she untied the pouches and brought out the first bar, about three inches long by two wide. She unwrapped the oiled parchment and sniffed at the smooth, black opium.

"It looks good," she pronounced. "But I'm not saying a word more until I smoke some of it."

A burning candle-lantern stood on the table, next to a long white clay pipe and a stack of splints. She shaved off a pipeful with her table dagger, laid it in, then set fire to a splint. First she heated the pipe bowl, then coaxed the sticky opium to burn. The first mouthful made her cough, but she kept sucking at it.

"It's splendid," she said with a spew of smoke and another cough. "What's the price if I buy ten bars?"

"A Deverry regal. That's fifty silvers saved."

Reluctantly she laid the pipe down to let it go out.

"Done, then," she said. "A regal it is."

While Sarcyn counted out the bars, she disappeared into another chamber, finally returning with the heavy gold coin.

"Do you want one of the lasses while you're here?" She handed the coin over. "Free, of course."

"My thanks, but I don't. I've other business to attend to."

"Come back tonight if you want. Or is it that your tastes run to lads?"

"What's it to you?"

"Naught, except it seems a bit of a waste, with you so good-looking and all. Come now, lad. Why don't you be like some of them Bardek merchants and roll your dice with either hand? They get their good time out of both cheeks and fur that way."

Sarcyn stared straight at her.

"Old woman, you go too far."

Gwenca flinched back. While Sarcyn finished dressing, she crouched in a chair and fingered her amulet.

When he left the Bilge, Sarcyn walked upriver, keeping off

the main streets whenever possible. Although to avoid attention
he was staying at an inn in another poor section of town, he
refused to lodge anywhere near the Bilge, which held too many
painful memories for him. His mother had been an expensive
whore in a house much like Gwenca's. On some whim, she'd
actually borne two children out of her many pregnancies, Sarcyn
and his younger brother, Evy. She alternately spoiled and ignored them until she was strangled by a drunken sailor when
Sarcyn was seven and Evy three. The brothel-keeper kicked
them out into the streets, where they lived as beggars for months,
sleeping under wagons or in broken ale barrels, scrounging what
coppers they could and then fighting to keep the bigger boys
from stealing their food.

Then one day a well-dressed merchant stopped to give them
a copper and asked them why they were begging. When Sarcyn
told him, he gave them a whole silver piece, and that day their
bellies were full for the first time in months. Naturally, Sarcyn
began to keep an eye out for this generous fellow. Every time he
saw Alastyr, the merchant would give him more coins and stop to
talk with the lads, too. Even though Sarcyn was a prematurely
wise gutter rat, slowly Alastyr won his confidence. When the
merchant offered to let the boys come live with him, they wept in
gratitude.

For some time Alastyr treated them kindly but distantly.
They had nice clothes, warm beds, and all the food they wanted,
but they rarely saw their benefactor. When he looked back on
how happy he was then, Sarcyn felt only disgust for the innocent
little fool he'd been. One night Alastyr came to his bedchamber,
first coaxed him with promises and caresses, then coldly raped
him. He remembered lying curled up on the bed afterward and
weeping with both pain and shame. Although he thought of
running away, there was nowhere to go but the cold and filth of
the streets. Night after night he endured the merchant's lust, his
one consolation being that Alastyr had no interest in his younger
brother. Somehow he wanted to spare Evyn the shame.

But once they moved to Bardek to live, Alastyr turned his
attentions to the younger boy as well, especially after Sarcyn
reached puberty and became less interesting, at least in bed. The
year Sarcyn's voice changed, Alastyr began using him for dark
dweomer workings, such as forcing him to scry under the master's control or mesmerizing him so thoroughly that he had no

idea of what he'd done in the trances. Later, the master did the same to Evy, but this time he offered repayment for using them: lessons in the dark dweomer itself. Both of them grasped eagerly at the dweomer. It was all they had to assuage the ache of their helplessness.

Not, of course, that Sarcyn phrased it that way to himself. In his mind, he'd endured the first stages of a harsh apprenticeship in order to prove himself worthy of the dark power. And so they were both still bound to Alastyr, even though Sarcyn hated him so much that at times he dreamt of killing him, long detailed dreams. What Evy felt he didn't know—they no longer spoke of things like feelings—but Sarcyn supposed that he would agree that it was worth putting up with the master to gain the knowledge. At least he'd be free of Alastyr for some days now while he sold his wares. The master never stayed long in Cerrmor; there were too many people who might recognize him.

His way back to the inn took him through one of the many open squares in the city. Although there was no market that day, a good-sized crowd was gathered round a platform improvised from planks and ale barrels. On the platform stood a tall, slender man with the palest hair Sarcyn had ever seen and smoky-gray eyes. He was also very handsome, his regular features almost girlish. Sarcyn stayed to watch. With a flourish, the fellow pulled a silk scarf from his shirt sleeve, tossed it up, and made it disappear seemingly in midair. The crowd laughed its approval.

"Greetings, fair citizens. I am a mountebank, a traveling minstrel, a storyteller who deals in naught but lies, jests, and fripperies. I am, in short, a gerthddyn, come to take you for a few pleasant hours to the land of never-was, never-will-be." He made the scarf reappear, then vanish again. "I hail from Eldidd, and you may call me Salamander, because my real name's so long that you'd never remember it."

Laughing, the crowd tossed him a few coppers. Sarcyn considered simply returning to his inn, because this sort of nonsense had nothing to offer a man like him, who knew the true darkness of the world. On the other hand, the gerthddyn was very pretty, and he might agree to a tankard of ale after his show. He was also an excellent storyteller. When he launched into a tale of King Bran and a mighty wizard of the Dawntime, the crowd stood fascinated. He played all the parts, his voice lilting for a beautiful maiden, snarling for the evil wizard, rumbling for the mighty king. Every now and then, he sang a song as part of the tale, his clear tenor ringing out. When he stopped halfway and pleaded exhaustion, coins showered down on him to revive his flagging spirits.

Even though he felt foolish for doing so, Sarcyn enjoyed every minute of the tale. He was amused for more than the obvious reasons. Whenever the crowd shuddered with pleasurable fear at the abominable doings of the evil wizard, Sarcyn inwardly laughed. All that wanton slaughter and ridiculous scheming to do people useless harm had no place in the dark dweomer. Never once did the tale touch on the true heart of the working: mastery. First a man mastered himself until he was as cold and hard as a bar of iron, and then he used that iron soul to pry what he wanted from the clutches of a hostile world. True, at times other people died or were broken, but they were the weak and deserved it. Their pain was only incidental, not the point of the matter.

At last the gerthddyn finished his tale, and the ragged edge to his voice showed why he wouldn't do another, no matter how much the crowd pleaded. As the crowd broke up, Sarcyn worked his way through and pressed a silver coin into Salamander's hand.

"That was the best-told tale I've ever heard. Can I stand you a tankard of ale? You need somewhat to ease your throat."

"So I do." Salamander considered him for a moment, then gave him a faint smile. "But alas, I cannot take you up on your most generous offer. I have a lass here in town, you see, who's waiting for me at this very moment."

There was just enough stress on the word "lass" to convey a clear message without discourtesy.

"Well and good, then," Sarcyn said. "I'll be on my way."

As he walked off, Sarcyn was more troubled than disappointed. Either the gerthddyn had unusually good eyes, or he'd revealed more than he meant to of his interest. Finally he decided that a man who wandered the roads for his living had seen enough to know a proposition when he heard one. Yet on the edge of the square he paused for one last look at the handsome gerthddyn and saw a crowd of Wildfolk trailing after him as he walked away. Sarcyn froze on the spot. Although Salamander seemed unaware of his strange companions, their interest in him might have well meant that he had the dweomer of light. You were cursed lucky he turned down that tankard, he told himself.

Then he hurried off to his inn. He would make very sure that the gerthddyn never got another look at him while he was in Cerrmor.

On the morrow the overcast lifted, and the strong spring sun blazed on the harbor. As he stood on the poopdeck of his Bardek merchantman, Elaeno, master of the ship, was wondering how the barbarians could bear to wear wool trousers in this kind of weather. Even though he himself was dressed in a simple linen tunic and sandals, the heat was oppressively humid. On his home island of Orystinna, summer days were parched and easier to bear. Below him on the main deck, the crew of Cerrmor long-shoremen worked stripped to the waist. Nearby, Masupo, the merchant who'd hired the ship for this run, watched over every barrel and bale. Some of them contained fine glassware, specially made to sell to barbarian nobles.

"Sir?" the first mate called up. "The customs officials want to speak to you."

"I'll be right there."

Waiting on the wooden pier were three blond, blue-eyed Deverry men, as hard to tell apart as most of the Cerrmor barbar-ians were. As Elaeno approached, they looked startled, then carefully arranged polite expressions on their faces. He was used to that, because he drew those startled looks even in most of the islands that Deverry men lumped together under the name of Bardek. Like many of the men on his home island, he was close to seven feet tall, heavily built, and his skin was a rich bluish black, not one of the various common shades of brown. Orystinnians were proud of their difference from other Bardekians, who until a recent naval war had raided them for slaves.

"Good morrow, Captain," said one of the barbarians. "My name is Lord Merryn, chief of customs for his grace, Gwerbret Ladoic of Cerrmor."

"And a good morrow to you, my lord. What do you need from me?"

"The permission to search your ship after the cargo's been unloaded. I realize that it's somewhat of an indignity, but we've been having a bad problem with smuggled goods of a certain kind. If you wish, we'll exempt your ship, but if so, neither you nor any of your men can come ashore."

"I've got no quarrel with that. I'll wager his lordship means opium and poisons, and I'll have no truck with that foul trade."

"Well and good then, and my thanks. It's also my duty to warn you that if you have any slaves on board, we won't hunt them down for you if they seek freedom."

"The people of my island don't own slaves." Elaeno heard the growl in his voice. "My apologies, my lord. It's a touchy subject among us, but of course, you wouldn't realize that."

"I didn't, at that. My apologies to you, Captain."

The other two officials looked profoundly embarrassed. Elaeno himself felt uncomfortable. He was as bad as they were, he knew, always lumping all foreigners together unless he watched himself.

"I must compliment you on your command of our language," Merryn said after a moment.

"My thanks. I learned it as a child, you see. My family had taken in a boarder from Deverry, an herbman who came to study with our physicians. Since we're a trading house, my father wanted all his children to speak Deverrian well, so the old man traded lessons for his keep."

"Ah, I see. Good bargain, it sounds like."

"It was." Elaeno was thinking that the bargain had been a better one than ever these men could know.

Once the goods were unloaded onto the pier, one crew of customs men went through them and argued with Masupo about the duties while a second searched every inch of the ship. Elaeno stood on the poop, leaned comfortably onto the rail, and watched the sun sparkling on the gentle swell of the sea. Since water was his most congenial element, he reached Nevyn's mind easily and heard the old man's thought that it would take him a moment to find a focus. Soon the image of Nevyn's face built up on the sea.

"So," he thought to Elaeno. "You're in Deverry, are you?"

"I am, down in Cerrmor. We'll be in port for a fortnight, most like."

"Splendid. I'm on my way to Cerrmor now. I'll probably get there in a couple of days. Did my letter reach you before you left?"

"It did, and a grim bit of news it was. I asked around various harbors, and I've got information for you."

"Wonderful, but don't tell me now. We might be overheard."

"Indeed? Then I'll see you when you reach town. I'll be living abroad while we're in port."

"Very well. Oh here, Salamander's in Cerrmor. He's staying at an inn called the Blue Parrot, a fitting enough name."

"The Chattering Magpie would be even better. Ye gods, it's hard to believe that the lad has the true dweomer."

"Well, what do you expect from the son of an elven bard? But our Ebañy has his uses, wild lad or not."

Nevyn's image winked out. His hands clasped behind his back, Elaeno paced back and forth. If Nevyn was afraid of spies, the situation must be grave indeed. He felt angry, as he always did at the thought of the dark dweomer. It would be very satisfying to get his massive hands around the neck of a foul master one fine day, but of course, it was better to fight them with subtler weapons.

It was just three days later that Sarcyn was loitering outside a tavern just on the edge of the Bilge. With his aura wrapped tight around him, he leaned against the building and waited for the courier. He never told any of the various men who smuggled drugs and poisons into Deverry where he was actually staying in Cerrmor; they knew to find him here, and he would lead them to a safe place for their transaction. In some minutes he saw Dryn's stout figure coming along the narrow street. Sarcyn was just about to release his aura and reveal himself when six city wardens appeared from an alley and surrounded the merchant.

"Hold!" one barked. "In the gwerbret's name!"

"What's all this, good warden?" Dryn tried to muster a smile.

"You'll find out back in the wardroom."

Sarcyn waited to hear no more. He slipped back around the tavern, then walked fast—but not fast enough to attract undue attention—through the maze of the Bilge. Down alleyways, between buildings, in the front door of Gwenca's and out the back, his route twisted and turned until at last he was through the Bilge on the north side and heading back to his inn. He had no doubt that Dryn would spill everything he knew in an attempt to save his own skin.

But long before the wardens had beaten Sarcyn's name and description out of the merchant, Sarcyn was riding out the city gates and heading north to safety.

In his chamber of justice, Gwerbret Ladoic was holding full malover. At a polished ebony table he sat under the ship banner of his rhan, while the gold ceremonial sword lay in front of him. To either side sat priests of Bel. The witnesses stood to the right, Lord Merryn, three city wardens, Nevyn, and Elaeno. Before him knelt the accused, the spice merchant Dryn and Edycl, captain of the merchantman *Bright Star.* The gwerbret leaned back in his chair and rubbed his chin as he thought over the testimony that had been laid before him. At thirty, Ladoic was an imposing man, tall and muscled, with steely gray eyes and the high cheekbones common to southern men.

"The evidence is clear enough," he said. "Dryn, you approached the herbman and offered to sell him some forbidden merchandise. Fortunately, Nevyn is an honorable man and consulted with Elaeno, who immediately contacted the chief customs officer."

"I didn't approach the cursed old man, Your Grace," Dryn snarled. "He's the one who made hints to me."

"A likely tale, indeed, and it wouldn't matter if it were true. Can you possibly deny that the city wardens found four different kinds of poison on your person when you were arrested?"

Dryn slumped and stared miserably at the floor.

"As for you, Edycl." The gwerbret turned cold eyes his way. "It's all very well to claim that Dryn shipped the foul herbs without your knowledge, but why did the customs men find a cache of opium in the walls of your personal cabin?"

Edycl trembled all over, and sweat broke out on his forehead.

"I'll confess, Your Grace. You don't need to put me to the torture, Your Grace. It was the coin. He offered me so much cursed coin, and the ship needed repairs, and I—"

"That's enough." Ladoic turned to the priest. "Your Holiness?"

The aged priest rose and cleared his throat, then stared into space as he recited from the laws.

"Poisons are an abomination to the gods. Why? Because they can only be used for murder, never in self-defense, and so no man would want them unless there was murder in his heart. Therefore let none of these foul substances be found in our lands. From the *Edicts of King Cynan,* 1048." He cleared his throat again. "What is the fit punishment for the smuggler of poisons? None fitter than that he eat some of his own foul goods. The ruling of Mabyn, high priest in Dun Deverry."

As the priest sat down, Dryn wept, a silent trickle of tears. Nevyn felt sorry for him; he wasn't an evil man, merely a greedy one who'd been corrupted by the truly evil. The matter, however, was now out of his hands. Ladoic took the golden sword and held it point upright.

"The laws have spoken. Dryn, as an act of mercy, you will be allowed to pick the least painful poison from your stock. As for you, Edycl, I have been informed that you have four young children and that, indeed, poverty did drive you to this trade. You will be given twenty lashes in the public square."

Dryn raised his head, then broke, sobbing aloud, throwing himself from side to side as if he already felt the poison gnawing at him. A guard stepped forward, slapped him into silence, then hauled him to his feet. Ladoic rose and knocked the pommel of the sword onto the table.

"The gwerbret has spoken. The malover has ended."

Although the guards dragged Dryn away, they left Edycl crouched at the gwerbret's feet. Quickly the hall cleared until only Nevyn and Elaeno remained with the lord and the prisoner. Ladoic looked down on Edycl as if he were contemplating a bit of filth on the streets.

"Twenty lashes can kill a man," he remarked in a conversational tone of voice. "But if you tell these gentlemen what they want to hear, I'll reduce your sentence to ten."

"My thanks, Your Grace, oh ye gods, my thanks. I'll tell them anything I can."

"Last year you wintered in Orystinna," Elaeno said. "After making a very late crossing. Why?"

"Well, now, that was a cursed strange thing." Edycl frowned in thought. "It truly was late, and I was thinking about putting the *Star* in drydock, when this Bardek man approaches me and says that a friend of his, a very rich man, had to reach Myleton before winter. He offered me a cursed lot of coin to take them over, enough to turn a big profit even with the expense of wintering in Bardek, so I took them on. I wintered in Orystinna because it's cheaper than Myleton."

"I see. What were these men like?"

"Well, the one who hired me was your typical Myleton man, on the pale side, and his face paint marked him for a member of

House Onodana. The other fellow was a Deverry man. Called himself Procyr, but I doubt me if that was his real name. There was somewhat about him that creeped my flesh, but cursed if I know why, because he was well-spoken and no trouble. He stayed in his cabin mostly, because it was a rough crossing, and I'll wager that he was as sick as a pig the whole way across."

"What did this Procyr look like?" Nevyn broke in.

"Well, good sir, I'm not cursed sure. It's cold out to sea that time of year, and whenever he was on deck, he was muffled up in a hooded cloak. But he was about fifty, I'd say, a solid sort of man, gray hair, thinnish sort of mouth, blue eyes. But I remember his voice cursed well. It was oily, like, and too soft for a man. It creeped my flesh."

"No doubt," Nevyn muttered. "Well, there you are, Your Grace. Elaeno and I are as sure as we can be that this man Edycl described is very important to the drug trade."

"Then I'll keep an eye out for him," Ladoic said. "Or perhaps, considering his voice, keep my ears out."

The supposed Procyr was, of course, likely to be more than merely a drug courier. Nevyn was fairly sure that he must have been the dark dweomerman who started Loddlaen's war the summer before and who seemed to be determined to kill Rhodry. As he thought it over, he wondered why for perhaps the thousandth time.

Salamander, or Ebañy Salomonderiel tranDevaberiel, to give him his full Elvish name, was staying in one of the most expensive inns in Cerrmor. His reception chamber was spacious, with Bardek carpets on the polished wood floor, half-round chairs with cushions, and glass in the windows. When his visitors arrived, he poured them mead from a silver flagon into glass goblets. Both Elaeno and Nevyn looked around them sourly.

"I take it that your tales pay well these days," Nevyn said.

"They do. I know that you're always chastising my humble self for my admittedly vulgar, crude, extravagant, and frivolous tastes, but I see no harm in it."

"There's not. It's just that there isn't any good in it, either. Well, it's none of my affair. I'm not your master."

"Just so, although truly, I would have been honored beyond my deserving to have been your apprentice."

"That's true enough," Elaeno broke in. "The bit about 'beyond your deserving,' that is."

Salamander merely grinned. He enjoyed bantering with the enormous Bardekian, although he doubted if Elaeno liked the game as much as he did.

"I know my talents are modest," Salamander said. "Here, if I had the power of the Master of the Aethyr, I'd be as dedicated as he. Alas, the gods saw fit to give me only a brief taste of the dweomer before they snatched that honey-sweet cup from my lips."

"That's not exactly true," Nevyn said. "Valandario told me that you could easily make more progress—if only you'd work for it."

Salamander winced. He hadn't realized that his mistress in the craft had told the old man so much.

"But that's neither here nor there right now," Nevyn went on. "What I want to know is why you're in Deverry."

"The real question is: why not be in Deverry? I love to wander among my mother's folk. There's always somewhat to see along your roads, and I'm also far far away from my esteemed father, who is always and in the most perfect prose berating me for some fault or another, both real and imagined."

"Mostly the former, I'd say," Elaeno muttered.

"Oh, no doubt. But if I can be of any service to either you or the Master of the Aethyr, you have but to ask."

"Good," Nevyn said. "Because you can. For a change, your wandering ways might come in cursed handy. I have every reason to believe that there are several dark dweomermen abroad in the kingdom. I don't want you trying to tangle with them, mind. They're far too powerful for that. But they're also supporting themselves by smuggling drugs and poisons. I want to know where the goods are sold. If we can choke off this foul trade, it will hurt our enemies badly. After all, they have to eat like other men—or well, more or less like other men, anyway. I want you to be constantly alert for signs of this impious trade. A gerthddyn's welcome anywhere. You just might overhear somewhat interesting."

"So I might. I'll gladly poke my long elvish nose into the matter for you."

"Don't poke it so far that it gets cut off," Elaeno said. "Remember, these men are dangerous."

"Well and good then. I shall be all caution, wiles, snares, and deceits."

About ten miles east of Dun Deverry lived a woman named Anghariad, who'd been pensioned off on a little plot of land after many years of service in the King's court. None of her neighbors were sure of what she'd actually done there, because she was the closemouthed sort, but the common guess was that she'd been a midwife and herbwoman, because she knew her herbs well. Often the folk of the village would trade chickens and produce for her doctoring rather than make the long trudge into the city for an apothecary. Yet when they visited, they usually crossed their fingers in the sign of warding against witchcraft, because there was something strange about the old woman with her glittering dark eyes and hollow cheeks.

Apparently the noble-born hadn't forgotten the woman who once served them, either. It was a common sight to see a pair of fine horses with fancy trappings tied up by her cottage, or even a noble lady herself, talking urgently with Anghariad out in her herb garden. The villagers wondered what the noble-born could possibly have to say to the old woman. If they'd known, they would have been appalled. To the farmers, whose every child was a precious pair of hands to work on the land, the very idea of abortion was repellent.

Besides her abortifacients, Anghariad had other strange things for sale to the right customers. That afternoon, she was extremely displeased at the paucity of goods that Sarcyn had to offer her.

"I can't help it," he said. "One of our couriers was taken with all his goods down in Cerrmor. You're cursed lucky that I've got any opium at all."

The old woman picked up the black lump and scored it with her fingernail, then carefully examined the way it crumbled.

"I prefer it better refined than this," she snapped. "The noble-born have more fastidious tastes than some sot of a Bardek dockworker."

"I told you: you're cursed lucky to get any at all. Now, if you do me a favor, I'll give it to you for free."

Suddenly she was all smile and close attention.

"I know who some of your regular customers are." Sarcyn leaned closer. "And one of them particularly interests me. I want

to meet him. Send Lord Camdel news of the delivery and tell
him to come out here alone."

"Oh ye gods," Rhodry grumbled. "We finally find a tavern
with decent mead, and now you tell me that we can't afford it."

"Well," Jill said. "If you weren't too cursed proud to take a
hire guarding a caravan—"

"It's not just pride! It's the honor of the thing."

Jill rolled her eyes heavenward to ask the gods to witness
such stubbornness, then let the matter drop. Actually, they had a
fair amount of coin left from the winter, but she had no intention
of letting him know it. He was just like her father, drinking the
coin away or handing it over to beggars with never a thought for
what might lie ahead on the long road. Just as she'd done with
Cullyn, therefore, she let Rhodry think that they were close to
being beggars themselves.

"If you spend coin on mead now," she said, "how are you
going to feel when we're riding hungry without even a copper to
buy a scrap of bread? I'll wager the memory of the mead will
taste bitter enough then."

"Oh well and good then! I'll settle for ale."

She handed him four coppers, and off he went to get the ale.
They were in the tavern room of the cheapest inn in Dun Aedyn,
a prosperous trading town in the middle of some of the richest
farmland in the whole kingdom. When they left Cerrmor, they'd
ridden there because they'd heard rumors of a feud brewing
between the town's lord and one of his neighbors, but unfortunately it had been settled by the local gwerbret before they
arrived. Dun Aedyn was too important to the rhan for the overlord to sit by while it was ravaged by war. Rhodry returned with
two tankards, set them down on the table, then sat next to her on
the bench.

"You know," she said, "we could ride east to Yr Auddglyn.
There's bound to be fighting there this summer."

"True spoken, and it's a cursed lot closer than Cerrgonney.
Shall we ride straight through the border hills?"

Since the road through the hills was shorter than turning
south to take the road along the seacoast, Jill was about to agree
when she suddenly felt as if an invisible hand had clamped over
her mouth to silence her. Blindly and irrationally she knew that
they should head for Dun Manannan before going to the Audd-

glyn. Dweomer again, curse it! she thought. For a moment she struggled against it, decided that they'd cursed well go through the hills if they wanted to, but she knew stubbornly and fiercely that something of importance would meet them in Dun Manannan.

"Did you hear what I said?" Rhodry snapped.

"I did. My apologies. Uh, here, my love. I want to take the coast road. I know it's longer, but . . . ah well . . . there's somewhat I want to ask Otho the Smith."

"Very well, then. But do we have enough coin to take the longer way?"

"We would if you'd take that caravan job. They're going to the coast." She put her hands on his shoulders and smiled up into his eyes. "Please, my love?"

"Ah curse it, I don't—"

She stopped the grumble with a kiss.

"Oh very well," he said with a sigh. "I'll go look up that merchant straightaway."

After he left, she sipped her ale and wondered about the strange thought that had come into her mind of its own will. She also wondered why she'd given into it, but that answer was easy; simple curiosity. If they hadn't gone to Dun Manannan, she would have been always wondering what would have been there.

Since the High King would have been furious to find his noble-born retainers meddling with Bardek opium, those few who'd acquired this dangerous taste never indulged it inside his dun. Down in the city of Dun Deverry itself was a luxurious inn, the top floor of which was reserved for noble patrons who needed a chamber for some private reason. Many a pretty lass from the town had lost her virtue in that inn, and many a pipeful of opium had tainted its air. For his second meeting with Lord Camdel, Master of the King's Bath, Sarcyn had rented a chamber there.

Now the young lord was half-sitting, half-reclining against a pile of cushions on a Bardek-style divan and twirling an empty clay pipe between his long fingers. About twenty, Camdel was slenderly built, with a thick shock of brown hair, deep-set brown eyes, and an engaging smile. Although Sarcyn found him attractive, Anghariad's gossip made it clear that the lord's taste ran to lasses. If all went well, however, soon Camdel would be in no position to refuse Sarcyn anything.

"His lordship seems to be the kind of ambitious young man we've been looking for," Sarcyn said. "It could be quite profitable for you to join us."

With a little nod, Camdel looked up, his dilated eyes heavy-lidded. He thought very highly of himself, did this polished courtier, and was thus an easy fish to catch with flattery for bait.

"I wouldn't mind being shed of Anghariad altogether," Camdel said. "The stuff's cursed dear."

"Just so, and if you began marketing it yourself, you'd get a much better price from us. I'm sure I can trust you to be discreet, my lord."

"Of course. My own neck's in this noose, isn't it?"

Sarcyn smiled, thinking the image all too apt.

"But before I agree to anything," Camdel went on, "I insist on speaking to someone more important than a common courier."

"Of course, Your Lordship. I was sent only to find out if his lordship would be interested. I assure you that the man who commands us will speak to you personally. He'll reach Dun Deverry in another week."

"Good. You may tell him that he may arrange a meeting here."

Sarcyn inclined his head in a little gesture of humility. He'd been wondering how to get the lord together with Alastyr, but Camdel's own arrogance had just made the job easy.

It took the slow-moving caravan four days to reach Dun Manannan, but at last the long line of men and mules straggled into the open space in the middle of town that did service as a market square. After Rhodry got his hire, he and Jill led their horses down to the cheap little inn by the river where they'd stayed the fall before only to find it burnt out. A few black withes poked forlornly into the sky where once had been thatch, and half the wooden wall was gone, too. A passing townswoman volunteered the information that a couple of the local lads had gotten into a bit of a fight, which had ended when a candle-lantern got knocked into the straw on the floor.

"Oh curse it," Jill said. "Now we'll have to camp by the road."

"What?" Rhodry snapped. "There's a perfectly good inn on the other side of town."

"It's expensive."

"I don't care, my miserly love. After camping in the midst of those stinking mules, I want a bath, and I'm going to have one."

After a brief squabble, she gave in and allowed him to lead the way to the other inn. Although the innkeep there was less than pleased to take in a silver dagger, Jill managed both to mollify him and save money by suggesting that they could sleep out in the hayloft at a reduced price. Even she had to admit that, expensive or not, it was nice to have a proper bath instead of merely swimming in some cold stream. The tavern room was pleasant, too, and, unlike the ones she was used to, it didn't smell of moldy straw and unwashed dogs. They had a table to themselves, because when customers entered, they took one look at Rhodry, another at the pommel of his silver dagger, and sat elsewhere, a double insult when one considered that they were smugglers themselves.

In a few minutes, though, someone entered who was apparently a traveller, judging from the suspicious way that the locals looked him over. He was dressed in a fine green cloak, gray brigga of the softest wool, and a shirt thick with embroidery, and he tipped the innkeep's lad a silver piece to bring in his gear when a copper would have done. He also insisted that the innkeep show him the best chamber he had. As he followed the innkeep up the spiral staircase, Jill studied him curiously. Tall and slender, he had the pale hair and handsome features of someone with more than a touch of elven blood in his veins. He also looked oddly familiar, although she couldn't place where she'd seen him. The innkeep's lad noticed her interest and hurried over.

"That fellow's name is Salamander," he said. "And he's a gerthddyn."

"Is he now? Well, then, we'll have a splendid time listening to his tales later."

Jill supposed that at some point on the long road, she'd seen him perform somewhere. Later, however, he came back downstairs, paused, and looked at Rhodry with a small puzzled frown, as if he were thinking that he should know this silver dagger. Seeing the pair of them in profile made her realize the truth: the gerthddyn looked enough like her man to be his brother. At that point she remembered the strange thought that had driven her to Dun Manannan, and she shivered.

"Here, good sir," she called out. "Come join us if you'd like. A gerthddyn's always welcome to a tankard."

"My thanks, fair lady." Salamander bowed to her. "But allow me to stand you a round."

Once the ale was fetched and paid for, Salamander settled in companionably at their table. He and Rhodry considered each other for a moment, both puzzled. They only looked in a mirror once a day when they shaved, after all, and bronze mirrors never showed a man a good picture of himself.

"Here," Rhodry said. "Have we met before?"

"I was just wondering the same myself, silver dagger."

"Were you ever in Aberwyn?"

"Oh, many a time. Do you hail from there?"

"I do, so maybe I watched you tell a tale in the marketplace. My name's Rhodry, and this is Gilyan."

Salamander laughed and saluted him with his tankard.

"Then well-met indeed. I'm a good friend of old Nevyn the herbman."

"Are you now?" Jill broke in. "Have you seen him lately?"

"Just six days ago, over in Cerrmor. He looked as fit as always. I swear, he's the best advertisement for his herbs that ever a man could have. If I see him again, and I might well do so, I'll tell him that you're both well."

"Our thanks," Rhodry said. "Have you heard anything about local wars in this part of the kingdom? A gerthddyn always hears what news there is."

While Rhodry and Salamander talked over the local gossip, Jill paid little attention. Although it seemed that Salamander had no idea that Nevyn was dweomer, which made it unlikely that the gerthddyn had it himself, Wildfolk clustered around him. They sat on the table, they climbed in his lap, they perched on his shoulders and affectionately patted his hair. Every now and then, his eyes moved as if he could see them. Of course, all elves could see the Wildfolk, and he was at least half an elf, she was sure of it. Rhodry, however, couldn't see them. It was a puzzle, and she studied the pair of them carefully, noting all the little points of resemblance: the curve of their mouths, the way the corners of their eyelids drooped slightly, and above all, the shape of their ears, a sharper curve than normal for human beings. She remembered her true dream of Devaberiel, and truly, they both resembled him, too. Her curiosity stopped irking her and began to gnaw.

In a bit, when Rhodry left the table to fetch them more ale, her curiosity bit hard enough to force her to give in.

"You know," she said, "I spent a lot of time once on the western border of Eldidd."

"So Nevyn once remarked."

"Is the name of your father Devaberiel by any chance?"

"It is, at that. Fancy you knowing that!"

"Well, I just guessed." She found a convenient lie. "A man named Jennantar once mentioned in passing that a fellow he knew had a son who was a gerthddyn, and I thought it unlikely that there'd be two who were half-an-elf."

"By the gods, you have sharp eyes! Well, I have to confess, now that you've ferreted out my parentage so neatly, that I am indeed the son of that esteemed bard, for all that it seems to vex him deeply at times. I know Jennantar well, by the way. I hope he's well. I haven't been in the elven lands for . . . oh, two years now."

"He was the last time I saw him."

So, she thought, I'll wager he doesn't know Rhodry's his brother. She felt sad, knowing that she could never tell them the truth, but she held her tongue. It was truly best that Rhodry thought himself a Maelwaedd, for his sake as well as Eldidd's.

Later that night, when they were going out to the hayloft to sleep, Salamander went with them, for a word in private, or so he said. When she heard what he wanted to know, Jill was very glad that he had the sense to keep quiet about it in the tavernroom.

"Opium smugglers?" she said. "By the hells, don't tell me you're stupid enough to use that stuff."

"Not on your life," Salamander said. "Nevyn asked me to help track them down, and so I thought Dun Manannan would be a logical place to start."

"Oh, the lads here would never touch that kind of cargo. The smuggler lords have a certain amount of honor, you see."

"So much for that, then. It's cursed lucky I met up with you, because truly, for all that my tongue is glib and golden, I was having a hard time thinking up the right sort of questions to ask."

"And the wrong sort would have gotten your throat slit."

"The thought had occurred to me. Now here, Jill, from what

Nevyn tells me, you've traveled all over this kingdom and been in many a strange place, too. Do you have any idea who buys the vile distillation of peculiar poppies?"

"Brothel-keepers, mostly. They use it to keep their lasses in line."

Salamander whistled under his breath. Rhodry was listening as if he couldn't believe she'd said it.

"I never knew that," Rhodry said. "How do you?"

"Da told me, of course. He was always warning me about the tricks men use to seduce lasses into a brothel so I wouldn't fall for them. It's most common in Cerrmor, he said, but it happens all over."

"Oh by the black ass of the Lord of Hell!" Salamander said. "Here it's been under our noses the whole time! When I see Nevyn next, I must tell him that silver daggers know many a thing worth learning."

Floating above the fire, Nevyn's image looked as startled as if someone had just dumped cold water all over him.

"I never would have thought of that in a thousand years," the old man's thought came in a wave of bemusement. "And a vile and impious thing it is! Well, I'm almost to Eldidd. I think I'll have a long talk with our Cullyn."

"It seems a sensible thing to do," Salamander thought back. "And I'll return to Cerrmor if you like."

"Splendid, but don't make a move or say one thing until I tell you to. There's thugs mixed up in this trade as well as the dark dweomer, and we're going to have to move carefully and lay clever snares."

"Just so. You know, some brothels are secretly owned by men with considerable influence."

Nevyn's thought came like the growl of a wolf.

"No doubt! Well, we'll see what we can do. My thanks, lad. This is a very interesting bit of news."

After they broke the contact, Salamander put out the fire in the charcoal brazier with a wave of his hand. Through the window of his innchamber the gray dawn light was creeping in. When he glanced out, he saw Jill and Rhodry below, saddling up their horses. Hurriedly he pulled on his boots and went down to say farewell. Although he couldn't say why, he'd never met a man he liked as well as Rhodry on first meeting.

"I take it you leave on the wings of dawn," Salamander said.

"We do," Rhodry said. "It's a long ride up to Yr Auddglyn from here."

"So it is. It saddens my heart that our paths should cross only to part again. Ah well, mayhap we'll meet again on the long road."

"I'll hope so." Rhodry held out his hand. "Farewell, gerthddyn. Maybe the gods will allow us to sit over a tankard again."

As he shook hands, Salamander felt a dweomer-touched cold run down his back. They'd meet again, he knew, but not in the way that they were hoping. The dweomer-cold was so strong that he shivered convulsively.

"Here," Jill said. "Do you have a chill?"

"A bit of one. Ye gods, I hate rising early."

They all laughed and parted smiling, but all day, as he rode back west to Cerrmor, Salamander remembered the dweomer-cold.

In a splendidly appointed innchamber in Dun Deverry, Alastyr and Camdel sat at a small table and haggled over the price of twenty bars of opium. Sarcyn leaned against the windowsill and merely watched this meaningless charade. Although the money meant little to Alastyr, he had to pretend it did to keep Camdel convinced that he was nothing more than a midnight importer. Finally the deal was done, the coins handed over. It was time for the true purpose of this meeting. Sarcyn opened up his second sight to watch.

"My lord," Alastyr said, "you must realize that it's dangerous for me to come to Dun Deverry. Now that we've met, I'd prefer that you dealt directly with Sarcyn."

With a sneer of objection, Camdel looked up, but Alastyr sent a line of light from his aura, threw it around the aura of the lord, and sent the egg of light spinning like a top. Camdel swayed drunkenly.

"Sarcyn is very important," Alastyr whispered. "You can trust him like you can trust me. You will trust him. You will trust him."

"I will, then," Camdel said. "I trust him."

"Good. You will forget you've been ensorceled. You will forget you've been ensorceled."

Alastyr withdrew the line and let Camdel's aura settle.

"Of course I understand," Camdel said briskly. "Dealing with your lieutenant will be most satisfactory."

Sarcyn shut down the sight and escorted the lord out the door with a bow, then latched the heavy oak door after him. Alastyr chuckled under his breath and stood up, stretching his back.

"Done, then," the master said. "Now remember, work on him slowly. If you can, only ensorcel him when he's mead-drunk or smoke-drunk, so he never realizes that somewhat odd's afoot."

"Easily done, master. He boozes like a swine and sucks smoke like a chimney."

Alastyr chuckled again. Sarcyn couldn't remember a time when the master had been this pleased, but then, his long plot of years was finally going well. As an intimate in the King's chambers, Camdel was in a perfect position to steal them a thing that they could never reach themselves.

"I can see why the lad makes you itch so badly," Alastyr went on. "But then, you were always a little fiend for bed." Casually he patted the apprentice on the behind.

Sarcyn went stiff with shock. Never before had he realized that Alastyr thought he'd enjoyed the master's attentions, all those years ago.

"My apologies," Alastyr said, misunderstanding. "I shouldn't tease you at your age. But well and good, lad. Keep working on him until we can lead him like a horse—on a very long rein. Evy and I will be waiting outside the city. Once he's thoroughly ensorceled, ride out and join us. But remember, there's no rush. If it takes weeks, so be it."

After Alastyr left, Sarcyn spent a long time pacing back and forth. His hatred burned like a fever in his body.

For all his pose of a shabby old herbman, Nevyn was well-known in the great broch of Dun Gwerbyn. When he arrived at the gates one morning, the two men on guard both bowed to him, then called for servants to take his horse and pack mule to the stables. Out in the ward stood several large wagons, and servants, working slowly in the warm sun, were loading them with bundles and barrels.

"Is the tieryn leaving soon for her summer residence?" Nevyn asked.

"She is," the page said. "In just two days time we'll start for Cannobaen. Her grace is in the great hall right now."

Lovyan was sitting at the honor table with a scribe. Although they seemed to be going over important matters, she dismissed him as soon as she saw Nevyn and sat the old man down at her right hand. Straightaway he told her all the news he had of Jill and Rhodry, because he knew that her heart ached to hear it.

"And finally, I scryed them out last night," he finished up. "They're in the Auddglyn, looking for a hire. I must say that Jill knows how to squeeze a copper hard enough to polish it. They seem to have plenty of coin left from the winter."

"That gladdens my heart, but ah ye gods, the summer's just begun, and there's my poor little lad, selling his sword on the roads."

"Oh come now, Lovva. You must admit that the 'poor little lad' happens to be one of the very best swordsmen in the kingdom."

"Oh, I know. I suppose that there's no need for me to carry on so, but how can I not worry?"

"True-spoken, and for all my fine words to you, I worry myself."

"I know that, and here, of course, I forgot you wouldn't know yet! I'm worried about Rhodry for more than his sake these days. Nevyn, the most truly appalling thing's happened. Do you remember Donilla, the wife Rhys put aside for being barren?"

"Quite well."

"Well, her new husband was absolutely besotted with her, and he's been courting her as if she were a young lass. Apparently he's been quite successful, because she's with child."

"Oh by every god! Has Rhys heard the news yet?"

"He has. I rode to Aberwyn myself to tell him, thinking that it would be best if he heard it from me. He did not take it well."

"No doubt. You know, I can even find it in my heart to feel sorry for Rhys. The gossip must be spreading like wildfire."

"He's become the laughingstock of every lord in Eldidd. My heart absolutely aches for his poor little wife, being treated like a racehorse or suchlike. Here, people actually have been making bets on whether she'll conceive, and I take it the odds against are very high. Ah ye gods, how cruel men can be!"

"Just so. But I see what you mean about Rhodry. He's the last Maelwaedd heir for Aberwyn. We've got to get him back."

"With Rhys in this temper? You haven't seen him. He walks around in a fury all day long, and not a soul dares to mention the very word 'babe' in front of him. He'll never recall Rhodry now. Besides, there are too many ambitious men to feed his hatred for his brother, in the hope that if Rhys dies childless, their clan will have a chance at the gwerbretrhyn."

"That has the disgusting ring of truth."

"Of course. I'll wager that the scheming and jockeying among the Council of Electors has already begun." She gave him a faint, self-mocking smile. "I've already started my own scheming. When we go to Cannobaen, I'm going to take Rhodry's bastard daughter out of fosterage and keep her with me. Little Rhodda will be a pawn in this struggle, and I want to supervise her training myself. After all, the man who marries Rhodry's heir, bastard or not, will have a small claim to push before the Council."

"By the Goddess herself, I have to admire you. Most women would still be tearing their hair over their son's exile, but you're scheming fourteen years in advance."

"Most women have never held the power I do, not even ones of my rank."

For several minutes they sat in a troubled silence. Lovyan looked so weary and miserable that Nevyn surmised she was thinking about the bitter truth: Rhodry was no true Maelwaedd at all. Yet it was crucial that men think he was. Although Nevyn couldn't read the future clearly, of course, he was certain that Rhodry was meant to rule in western Eldidd, if not as Gwerbret Aberwyn, then at least as tieryn in Dun Gwerbyn. Neither he nor the Lords of Wyrd cared one jot who Rhodry's father was, but the noble-born would.

"Do you know what I fear most?" Lovyan said abruptly. "That things will come to open war when Rhys dies. It's happened, you know, when a disgruntled candidate feels himself wronged by the Council. Ah well, I'll be long gone myself by then, and past worrying over it."

Since Rhys was a healthy man of only twenty-nine, her remark was eminently reasonable, but Nevyn felt a sudden stab of dweomer-warning. It seemed likely that she would have to bury yet another son.

"Is somewhat wrong?" she said, reading his expression.

"Oh, just thinking that we've got to get Rhodry recalled."

"If words were gold coins, we'd all be as rich as the king."
She sighed heavily. "It's always hard to see the death of a great
clan, but it would be a true pity to see the end of the
Maelwaedds."

"It would indeed."

And a greater pity than she could know, in fact. The
Maelwaedd clan had always been important to the dweomer,
ever since its oddly humble beginning, close to three hundred
years before.

Cerrmor
and Eldidd
790-797

And are all things that happen in life preordained by the gods? They're not, for many things happen by blind chance. Mark this well: every man has a Wyrd, and every man has a Luck. The secret of wisdom is telling one from the other.

The Secret Book of Cadwallon the Druid

About a week's ride from Aberwyn, on what might as well have been the western border of Eldidd since no one lived beyond it, there was a dun standing on the wide grassy clifftop overlooking the ocean. A stone wall, badly in need of repair, ringed a big ward where grass poked up through the cobbles. Inside was a squat stone broch, a clutter of wooden sheds, and a narrow tower like a stork standing among chickens. Every afternoon, Avascaen climbed the hundred and fifty spiraling steps to the flat top of the tower. Using a heavy winch and pulley, he would haul up loads of firewood, which his sons had put in the sling far down below, and stack them under the little shelter above the beacon pit. Just at sunset, he would light a torch and fire the first load. Not far out to sea were submerged rocks, a little ripple of white water from his vantage, but virtually invisible to a ship sailing toward them. Any captain who saw the Cannobaen light knew enough to swing wide out to the safety of the open sea.

Not that there had been many ships in the last few years. Thanks to the war for the Deverry throne, trade was falling off badly. There were times, especially when the cold winter winds whipped under the shelter, when Avascaen wondered why he even bothered to keep tending the fire. But if just one ship founders, he would tell himself, just think of how you'll feel then. Besides, he'd been enjoined to keep this light by Prince Mael himself, all those years ago before the prince rode off to war and never returned.

Avascaen was training his two sons, Maryl and Egamyn, to take over the job of lighthouse keeper when he died. Maryl, a stolid sort of lad, was glad enough of the work and their somewhat privileged position in the village of Cannobaen. Egamyn, however, who was only fourteen, grumbled, cursed, and constantly threatened to run away to become a rider with the king's army. Avascaen would generally give him a cuff on the head and tell him to hold his tongue.

"The prince asked me and my family to tend the light," Avascaen would say. "And tend it we will."

"Oh here, Da," Egamyn always answered. "I'll wager you never see the cursed prince again."

"Maybe not, but if I do, then he'll hear I did what I said I was going to do. I'm like a badger. I hold on."

Avascaen, his wife, Scwna, and the lads all lived in the great hall of the broch, where they cooked, slept, and generally made do. The upper stories were shut up to save heat in the winter. Twice a year, Scwna aired out each chamber, shook off the dust covers on the furniture, and swept the floors, just in case the prince should return to his country lodge one fine day. Out in the ward, they had a kitchen garden, a few chickens, and some young hogs. The farmers in the nearby village supplied the rest of their needs as part of their taxes to the Cannobaen light. The farmers also supplied the firewood, which came from the vast primeval oak forests stretching to the north and west.

"We've got a good life," Avascaen would tell Egamyn. "You should thank the gods that things are peaceful, like."

Egamyn would only shake his stubborn dark head and mutter that things were tedious. Aside from the farmers, company rarely came to Dun Cannobaen.

It was, therefore, quite an event when someone did turn up at the gates one afternoon. Since he slept all morning, Avascaen was just starting his day with a stroll in the ward when he saw a rider on a chestnut horse coming up the road with two gray mules heavily laden with canvas packs. When the rider dismounted, Avascaen realized with a start that it was a woman, stout and middle-aged. Although she was wearing a dress, she had a pair of dirty brigga under it so she could ride astride like a man. Her gray hair was caught back in the clip of an unmarried woman, and her dark eyes brimmed with good humor. The oddest thing of all were her hands, which were a peculiar color—a dirty brownish blue, all the way up to her elbows.

"Good morrow, good sir," she said. "I'll wager you're surprised to see me riding up."

"Well, that I am, but you're most welcome, anyway," Avascaen said. "May I ask your name?"

"Primilla of Abernaudd, good sir. I'm out here looking for rare plants and suchlike for the dyer's guild in Abernaudd."

"Fancy that! Well, won't you take our hospitality? I can offer you a meal, if you don't mind having breakfast for your dinner, anyway."

Primilla minded not in the least. While Maryl tended her horse and mules, she agreeably pitched into a trencher of bacon and a bowl of barley porridge. She was full of precious news from Abernaudd, the royal city of Eldidd, and Scwna and Egamyn listened avidly as she described the goings-on in the town.

"And I don't suppose there's any news of my Prince Mael," Avascaen asked finally.

"Well, now, there is, and sad news at that. His wife just died, poor thing, of a fever." Primilla shook her head sadly. "A pitiful thing, her never getting to see her husband again."

Tears welled in Scwna's eyes. Avascaen felt a bit rocky himself. It was just like something in a bard's tale.

"And is there talk of disclaiming my prince and putting his son in his place?"

"Well, there is, and what will you think of that?"

"Mael's the prince I swore to serve, and serve him I will. I'm like a badger, good dame. I hold on."

Primilla smiled as if she found his loyalty delightful—a great relief after all the people who mocked him for it. As he considered her eyes, shrewd, really, for all the jolly look of her round face and pink cheeks, Avascaen wondered about her.

That night, when the moon was at its zenith, Primilla panted up the stone steps to join Avascaen on top of the tower. She helped lay the second load of wood on the beacon, then strolled over to the edge of the tower for a look at the view. Far down below them, the full moon was laying a silver road across the dark rippled sea, stretching out to the featureless horizon. In the clear spring air, the stars seemed to be a mere arm's reach above.

"Lovely, isn't it?" Avascaen said. "But few bother to come up for a look, except for me and my lads."

"You must have strong legs, good sir, from all these cursed steps."

"Oh, you get used to it in a bit, truly."

The flaring beacon cast a dancing golden light around them as the fresh wood caught. Primilla leaned comfortably on the stone guardrail and contemplated the beach far below, where the breakers rolled in like silver ghosts.

"Now, begging your pardon and all," Avascaen said, "but it's a rare thing to find a woman traveling alone. Aren't you afraid of danger on the roads?"

"Oh, I can take care of myself when I have to," Primilla said with a chuckle. "And besides, there's not a lot of folk out here to give me trouble. It's worth the trip, truly, to poke about in the woodlands and find my plants. You see, I've been a dyer all my life, and now I'm at the point of wanting to find better colors for my guild. We'll study what I've brought back, make up some bits of cloth dyed with it, and see how it washes and all. You never know when you'll find somewhat worth a small fortune." She held up her discolored hands. "Here's my whole life, good sir, stained right into my skin."

Since Avascaen was a great believer in taking pains to do things right, he could see her point. But occasionally, after Primilla was long gone, he would remember the woman with blue hands and wonder what she'd been up to.

The King's city of Abernaudd spanned the Elaver some two miles upstream from the seacoast and the harbor. Behind ramparted stone walls, cobbled streets marched up and down terraced hills. At the top of the highest hill stood the royal dun, flying the blue and silver banner of the Dragon throne, while down in the valleys huddled the stinking, close-packed huts of the poor. In Abernaudd, how high up one lived showed literally how high one was on the social scale. As head of the Dyers' Guild, Primilla lived on the crest of a low hill in a spacious compound that came with her position. With her in the three-story round-house lived her five apprentices, who waited on her to earn their training. Out in back in the cobbled yard were the long sheds that housed the master workrooms of the guild. The cloth produced there under her personal supervision went to the royal household.

Although Primilla had indeed found rare dye plants on her

trip to Cannobaen, she was annoyed at having to take the time away from guild affairs. Her duty to the dweomer, however, always took precedence over her duty to the dyers. It would have been most unseemly if she'd refused to help the leader of the Council of Thirty-Two when he asked. Although she didn't know why Nevyn was interested in the affairs of Mael, prince of Aberwyn and Cannobaen, she was willing to poke around and learn what she could. Now that she'd discovered that Cannobaen still stood loyal to him, she could concentrate on the more important matter of the prince's standing in court.

Fortunately, she would have plenty of access to court circles that summer, because the King was asking the city guilds for an enormous loan to continue his bid for the Deverry throne. Although normally the noble-born sneered at commerce, whenever the King needed hard coin, the guildsmen and merchants found themselves being courted by all the best people. The very night after her return, Primilla had the first of many meetings called by the guilds and merchants to select representatives to go the palace for the actual haggling. Since she wanted the job, she got a place on the council easily. Although the merchants vied for the positions, few of the craftspeople were willing to take the time away from their work.

Finally, after a week of meetings and lobbying, the guild commission of five, with Grotyr the moneylender at their head, met with four of the King's councillors in a narrow chamber on the second floor of the royal broch. While a scribe from each side took careful notes, they sat around a long oak table. Primilla was expecting a session of hedging and fencing, but the King's chief councillor, a dark-eyed paunchy fellow named Cadlew, flatly announced that the King wanted five thousand gold pieces.

"Ye gods!" Grotyr sputtered. "Do you realize, good sir, that the guilds would go bankrupt if such a loan weren't repaid promptly?"

Cadlew merely smiled, because everyone in the room knew that Grotyr was lying. While the haggling got underway in earnest, Primilla was pondering the size of the loan. If the King needed that much coin, it seemed that he was planning a major offensive, and such boded ill indeed for the captive prince in Cerrmor. The meeting ended inconclusively, as everyone knew that it would. As the guildspeople were leaving, Primilla lingered and asked Cadlew if he had a moment to show her the royal gardens.

"Of course, good dame. Doubtless they would interest you, since much of your work lies with plants."

"True spoken, and it's quite a treat for me to see flowers whole, since my work mostly shreds and boils them."

With a pleasant laugh, he led her off round the broch. A low brick wall, mostly there to keep horses out, set off a complex of tiny lawns twined round with flower beds, like green jewels set in colored wires. They passed a pleasant quarter hour discussing the various flowers before Primilla felt she could make her move.

"You know," she said, "a while back, I was hunting for rare plants near the western border, and I happened to stop at Cannobaen; you know, Prince Mael's country lodge."

"Ah. Do they even remember the prince out there?"

"Oh very well, indeed. A sad thing, Mael's Wyrd. I can't helping thinking that this loan means the King's going to cut him adrift."

"For your ears only, good dame, but you've guessed right enough. Our liege should have let Mael hang and gotten on with the war years ago, but the Princess Maddyan pleaded and kept her husband's case alive. Since she was raised here at court, the King always thought of her as a daughter."

"But now the princess is dead."

"Just so."

"And what of Mael's son?"

"Well, out of honor, Ogretoryc pleads for his sire, but ye gods, the lad was a babe when his father rode away. How long can a man be sentimental over someone he's never met?"

Especially when he stands to inherit that someone's place, Primilla thought to herself. It was time, she decided, to take some direct action rather than hoping for more hints from injudicious councillors. Later in the week, she selected several skeins of her finest blue embroidery threads and sent them as a gift to Ogretoryc's wife, Camlada. Her woad-dyed blue was always in great demand, because only a master dyer could ensure that the entire skein was an exactly even color, an important thing for courtly needlework. The gift earned her an audience with the lady on the next afternoon that she was at court.

A page took her to a surprisingly small chamber up on the third floor of one of the side brochs. Although the room was luxuriously furnished with carpets and cushioned chairs, it had a poor view out the one window. Camlada, a pretty blond lass of sixteen, received Primilla alone instead of in the company of the serving women that would have marked high status. Her only companion was a little terrier, who sat on her lap and growled at intervals throughout the interview.

"My thanks for the fine thread, good dame. It will be put to good use on one of my husband's shirts."

"Then, my lady, I'm most honored."

With a smile, Camlada gestured at a padded footstool near her chair. Primilla obligingly sat down and let the lady look her over.

"I've spent my whole life at court," Camlada remarked. "I doubt me if this gift is only a sweet thoughtfulness on your part. What sort of favor do you want from my husband?"

"A very small one. I only want him to be aware of my existence. You see, out on the western border are some very rare dye plants. I'd eventually like our guild to have the right to hunt for them, even though the Aberwyn guild has first claim. After all, the prince controls both Aberwyn and Cannobaen."

"Prince? He's hardly a prince yet."

"Well, more a prince than his father is, considering the circumstances."

Abruptly Camlada rose and paced to the window, her terrier keeping close to her skirts.

"Have I upset my lady?" Primilla said. "My humble apologies."

"It's just that you've reminded me of the truth. No one knows what my husband is or what's open to us. I don't suppose you ever met the Princess Maddyan."

"I never had that honor, truly, but I heard that she was a sweet and devoted wife."

"She was. Everyone adored her, but look at all the good it ever did her. I felt so sorry for her, and now she's dead."

"And by rights, you should have her rank."

"I have no rank at all, good dame, until my father-in-law is dead. Oh, that sounds so horrible of me, but I'm just so frightened. The same thing could happen to me as happened to Maddyan, just sitting around court, with no influence or anything, and the king doesn't even like me the way he likes her."

"I can understand my lady's fears."

Primilla understood something else, too: although Ogretoryc had never met his father, he saw his wife every night. She decided that she had best contact Nevyn straightway through the fire and tell him of this poisoned grain of news she'd gleaned.

As King Glyn's most trusted councillor, Nevyn had rights far beyond those of the usual courtier. As soon as he finished talking with Primilla, he went to the royal apartments without so much as sending a page ahead of him. In the past, he'd often wondered if it were a right thing to tell the King military information gleaned by dweomer. Now that he had some to offer, he decided that it was, simply because Eldidd's claim to the throne was so weak that he was clearly an usurper. He found a visitor there ahead of him, Prince Cobryn, now the leader of the King's Guard. At twenty-one, Cobryn was tall, slender, and handsome, looking so much like Dannyn that at times Nevyn and the King found it painful to look at him.

"Is your business urgent, my lord?" Cobryn said. "I can retire from our liege's presence."

"Urgent it is, but it concerns you, too." Nevyn bowed to Glyn, who was standing at the hearth. "Eldidd is taking out an enormous loan from the guildmasters of Abernaudd. I can think of only one place he'd want to spend so much coin: our borders."

"So," the King said. "I was wondering how long we could milk tears for one prince out of three. Well, Cobryn, that means we'll have to change our plans for the summer's fighting down to the last detail. Huh—I'll wager Eldidd was going to have his warband over our border before we received the formal message of disclamation. And I don't need dweomer to tell me that."

"Just so." Cobryn laughed, a cold wolf's mutter his breath. "But we're going to have a surprise waiting for the bastards."

"My liege," Nevyn broke in, "are you going to make good your threat and hang Prince Mael?"

Glyn rubbed his chin with the back of his hand while he thought the matter over. Always heavy, his face had turned square and stout with age, and a florid color lay across his cheeks.

"It would ache my heart to hang a helpless man, but Eldidd may leave me no choice. I'll do naught till I have the formal renouncement in my hand. Eldidd might change his mind, but there's no bringing the prince back from the dead once he's hanged."

That very week, Prince Cobryn led five hundred men along the coast road to the Eldidd border, and they were supported by grain ships and war galleys. After an anxious three weeks, messengers returned: they'd fought a major victory over a very surprised Eldidd army. Two days later, a herald arrived from the king of Eldidd with a letter formally renouncing Mael and putting his son, Ogretoryc, in his place. Nevyn went up straightaway to inform Mael.

He found the no-longer prince sitting at his writing desk, which was stacked with the prisoner's beloved books and scattered with pieces of parchment, the beginnings of Mael's commentary on the *Ethics* of the Greggyn sage, Ristolyn. Nevyn was sure that the commentary would be excellent, if only Mael lived to finish it. At thirty-four, Mael was going prematurely gray, thick streaks of it in his raven-dark hair.

"I've got some cursed bad news for you," Nevyn said.

"I've been renounced?" He spoke flatly, even dryly. "I thought that was in the wind when I heard the guards talking about war on the border."

"I'm afraid it's true."

"Well, Ristolyn's ideas about virtue are going to stand me in good stead. It seems that the entire goal or end of my life has been to make a good death down in the market square. I'd say that fortitude would be the most appropriate virtue to that end, wouldn't you?"

"Listen. You're not going to hang if I have one cursed word to say about it."

"Then that gives me hope. I suppose it's hope. Maybe it would be better to hang and ride free in the Otherlands than sit here and molder. You know, I've been here longer than I was a prince in Eldidd. Fancy that. Over half my life as Glyn's guest."

"I'll wager the freedom of the Otherlands won't look so attractive when the executioner's putting a noose around your neck. I'll return as soon as I've spoken to the King."

It was late in the afternoon before court affairs would allow Nevyn to have a private word with his liege. They walked out to the walled garden behind the broch. By the ornamental stream, a willow tree trailed long branches in the water; the roses were thick with blood-red blooms, the only touch of color in the tiny parkland, carefully tended to look untended.

"I've come to intercede for Mael's life, my liege," Nevyn said.

"I thought you might. I'm half-minded to release him and let him go home, but I see no way that I can, none. He'd be a bitter enemy there, and worst of all, how would Eldidd interpret my mercy? As a weakness, no doubt, and I can't afford that. It's the honor of the thing."

"My liege is right about not being able to release him, but he might be useful again in the future."

"He might, but again, will Eldidd take it as weakness?"

"The gods will count it as strength. Whose good opinion does my liege value more?"

Glyn plucked a rose, cupped it in his calloused, broad palm, and considered it with a slight frown.

"My liege?" Nevyn said. "I'll outright beg you for his life."

With a sigh, Glyn handed him the rose.

"Done, then. I can't deny you that after all you've done for me. Eldidd has a clutch of heirs like a sly old hen, but who knows? The day may come when he'll regret disclaiming Mael."

Since she enjoyed the favor and patronage of the King's most important councillor, Gavra's herb business had prospered down in the city. She now owned her own house and shop in the merchant's quarter and made plenty of coin to support herself and her two children, Ebrua and Dumoryc, the prince's bastards. For years, Gavra had endured the gossip that branded her as a slut who had children by any number of men she fancied, because it was better than having her children slain as heirs to an enemy line. Now that Mael was formally disclaimed, she considered telling the children the truth, but it was pointless. Even though he lived not two miles away, they had never seen their father.

She supposed that the men who guarded Mael knew perfectly well that she was his mistress, but they held their tongues, partly out of masculine sympathy for Mael's dull life, but mostly because they were terrified of what Nevyn would do to them if they spilled the secret. When she went up to the tower room that particular day, they even congratulated her about Mael's reprieve from the hangman.

As soon as she was inside, she flung herself into Mael's arms.

For a moment they merely held each other tightly, and she could feel him shaking.

"Thank every god you're going to live," she said at last.

"I've been doing somewhat of that, truly." He paused to kiss her. "Ah my poor love, you deserved a proper husband and a happy life, not a man like me."

"My life's been happy enough, just knowing that you love me."

When he kissed her again, she clung to him, feeling that they were two frightened children, clinging together in a dark full of nightmares. Nevyn will never let him hang, she thought, but oh dear Goddess, how long can our dear old man live?

TWO

After three years of hard fighting, the Eldidd border war came to a stalemate when, in the middle of that summer, something happened for which none of the three sides were prepared: the province of Pyrdon rebelled against the Eldidd throne. Glyn's spies brought the news back at a gallop that not only was it rebellion, but it looked to be a successful one. In Cwnol, formerly gwerbret of Dun Trebyc, the only large city in Pyrdon, the rebel forces had a leader so brilliant that his men whispered he was dweomer.

"Half of Pyrdon is still forest, too," Glyn remarked. "He can have his men fade into the trees if they're hard-pressed, then fade right out again to attack in ambuscade. He seems to have a large force. Huh. I wonder if he's getting coin from Cantrae?"

"I wouldn't be in the least surprised, my liege," Nevyn said. "And it would behoove us to send some, too."

For the rest of that summer, the Eldidd border stayed quiet, and by autumn it appeared that while Cwnol would be fighting for a long time, he had great chance of success. When Glyn sent the rebel messages, they went addressed to Cwnol, King of Pyrdon. As a final gesture, Glyn betrothed Prince Cobryn's six-year-old daughter to Cwnol's seven-year-old son, a mark of royal honor that Cwnol repaid by increasing his raids into Eldidd. Yet, even though the matter ended so well for the Cerrmor side, Nevyn was heartsick. As the endless war dragged on, he could see the kingdom tearing into pieces around him.

On a day wet with autumn rain, Nevyn went up to the tower

to see Mael, who was, as usual, working on his commentaries. As such projects will, this one had grown far beyond the simple introduction to Ristolyn's thought that Mael had originally planned.

"This aside is going to end up a cursed chapter!" Mael stuck his pen into the inkwell so hard that the reed nearly broke.

"So many of your asides do, but good chapters, withal."

"It's this question of what constitutes the greatest good, you see. For all its brillance, Ristolyn's argument doesn't quite satisfy me. His categories are a bit limited."

"You philosophers are always cursed good at multiplying categories."

"Philosopher? Ye gods, I wouldn't call myself that."

"By the hells, what else are you?"

Mael's face went slack in openmouthed amazement. When Nevyn laughed, he sheepishly joined in.

"Naught else, truly," Mael said. "For twenty years I've thought myself a warrior, chafing at the bit like a warhorse and lusting for the freedom to fight once again. I've been deluding myself for at least ten of them. Here, I wonder if I even could ride to war now. I can see myself, sitting there on horseback, wondering what Ristolyn meant by the word 'end' as someone knocked me right off mine."

"You don't look displeased."

Mael wandered over to the window, where the rain slashed down as silver-gray as his hair.

"The view from here is a different one than I ever had before. You don't see things as clearly in the dust of a battlefield." Mael leaned his cheek against the cool glass and looked down. "Do you know what the cursed strangest thing of all is? If I didn't worry so much about Gavra and the children, I'd be happy here."

Nevyn felt a dweomer-touched slap of knowledge. It was time for Mael to be released. Because he had accepted, he could go free.

"Tell me somewhat. If you were free to do so, would you marry Gavra?"

"Of course. Why shouldn't I? I've no place at a royal court anymore. I could legitimatize our children, too—if I were free to to do so. Truly, I am a philosopher. I'll even debate the hopeless and the impossible."

When he left Mael's chamber, Nevyn was considering the

weather. Since it rarely snowed along the seacoast, travel was a possibility, though an unpleasant one, all winter. He went straight to his chamber and contacted Primilla through the fire.

Gavra's shop occupied the front half of a house just across the street from her brother's tavern. Every morning, when she came out to set to work, she would look around at the shelves, stacked with herbs, the barrels, the jars, the dried crocodile hanging under the eaves. My house, she would think, and my shop. I own it all, just me. It was a rare woman in Cerrmor who owned property in her own name rather than in that of a husband or brother. With winter coming, she had plenty of customers with fevers and congested lungs, chilblains and aching bones, and she worked long hours in the front room. She also had another pressing matter to tend with: Ebrua's betrothal. Although she herself had let love rule her, she was determined to make a solid, conventional arranged match for her daughter.

Fortunately, the lad that Ebrua herself favored was a decent lad of sixteen, Arddyn, the younger son of a prosperous family who dealt in tanned hides. After she discussed the formal betrothal with the lad's father, she went up to the dun to consult with Mael. In a way, the trip was foolish; he'd never met Arddyn's family and had only seen his daughter from a great distance. But Mael listened gravely, turning his brilliant mind to the problem with such intensity that she knew he wanted to pretend, as she did, that they had some kind of a normal life together.

"It sounds like a good match for people like us," Mael said at last.

"Oh, listen to you, my royal love. People like us indeed!"

"My lady forgets that I'm naught but a humble philosopher. Here, when I finish my book, the priests at the temple will have fifty copies written out by the scribes, and I'll get a silver coin apiece. That, my love, is my sole fortune in the world, so let us hope that Arddyn's clan won't be greedy about the dowry."

"I'll think they'll take her interest in my shop, and maybe a bit of silver."

"Cursed good thing. It's an unlucky lass who has a philosopher for a father."

As Gavra was leaving the dun, she met Nevyn, who companionably slipped his arm through hers and escorted her down to the shop. Since the children were making the evening meal in the kitchen, they could talk in private. Nevyn laid a couple of big logs into the hearth and lit them with a snap of his fingers.

"Chilly today," he remarked. "I've got somewhat truly important to tell you. I think I have a very good chance of getting Mael released."

Gavra caught her breath with a gasp.

"Don't tell him yet," the old man went on. "I don't want to raise his hopes only to dash them, but you need to know. You'll have much to settle before you leave."

"Leave? Oh here, is Mael going to want me to go with him?"

"Now, if you ever doubted that for a minute, then that's the first stupid thing I've ever seen you do."

Suddenly Gavra had to sit down. She perched on a stool near the fire and wove her shaking hands together.

"I'm afraid there's no choice but to send him back to Eldidd," Nevyn said. "Do you want to go?"

She looked at the shelves, at the room, at everything she'd worked for so long to have. She'd be leaving her married daughter behind, too, and what was Dumoryc going to say when she introduced a stranger as his father?

"You know," Nevyn said, "it's likely that you'll end up living on the western border of Eldidd, and there's not a decent herbwoman out there for miles."

"I see. Well, then, I could build up a new shop for Dumoryc, and leave Ebrua this one. It would be a splendid dowry. We could cursed well write the marriage contract as we wanted it if I did that."

"Just so. And most likely you'll end up supporting your brilliant husband, too."

"Eldidd begins to sound interesting." She looked up with a smile. "And of course, I love my man, too."

For a variety of reasons, Nevyn decided to secure Mael's release in the spring. For one thing, the Kings of the Wildfolk warned him that the winter would be full of bad storms. The most pressing reason, however, was Mael himself, who would refuse to leave his imprisonment until he saw his book properly copied, a task that would take months. While the scribes down at the temple of Wmm worked on the book, Nevyn worked on the King, whose honor was the councillor's biggest ally. Generous man that he was, Glyn found Mael a profound embarrassment, too pathetic to murder, especially now that the learned priests praised him as a brilliant scholar and an ornament to the kingdom. When he judged the time was right, Nevyn asked Glyn outright about releasing Mael and letting him return quietly to Eldidd.

"It would be best, councillor, truly. Try to scheme out some reason for his honorable release. Cursed if I'll have Eldidd sneering at my weaknesses, but I can't stand the thought of that prince moldering up in the tower any longer."

In the end, it was the Pyrdon rebellion that provided the necessary reason. Since Eldidd desperately needed a quiet summer if he were to bring his rebels to heel, he offered Glyn gold to refrain from raiding. Not only did Glyn take the bribe, he solemnized the occasion by offering to release his captive in return for a token ten horses. After many an exchange of heralds and some peculiar stalling on Eldidd's part, the deal was set and signed. Only then did Nevyn tell Mael of his good fortune, when winter was already lightening into spring.

When Nevyn went up to the tower room, he found Mael caressing a copy of his book, leather-bound and neatly written in the spiky temple hand. The prince was so eager to show it to him that it took almost half an hour before Nevyn could get to his real business.

"The real marvel is that the King's going to subsidize another twenty copies," Mael finished up. "Do you know why?"

"I do. It's his way of solemnizing your release. He's setting you free next week."

Mael smiled, started to speak; then his face froze in disbelief. His fingernails dug into the soft binding of the codex in his hands.

"I'll be riding with you as far as the Eldidd border," Nevyn went on. "Gavra and your son will meet us outside Cerrmor. Ebrua will stay here, but then, you can hardly blame her. She loves her husband, and she's never even met you."

Mael nodded, his face so pale that it looked like snow.

"Oh by the Lord of Hell," he whispered. "I wonder if this caged bird remembers how to fly?"

Although Prince Ogretoryc and his wife now lived in a splendid suite of apartments at court, they had never forgotten the times when Primilla had been the only person to pay court to them, and they were usually willing to receive her in those moments they set aside for craftspeople and merchants. The prince was a tall young man with raven-dark hair and cornflower blue eyes, good-looking in a rough sort of way and inclined to be expansive as long as he wasn't crossed. That particular morning, Primilla brought him a present, an expensive little merlin for his favorite sport of hawking. The prince immediately took the bird on his wrist and chirruped to it.

"My thanks, good dame. He's a lovely little hawk."

"I'm most honored that he pleases his highness. When I heard about his highness's father being released, I thought a celebratory gift was in order."

His eyes suddenly dark, Ogretoryc began paying great attention to the merlin, who turned its hooded head his way as if it recognized a kindred soul. In her chair by the window, Camlada moved restlessly.

"Of course," she said with a carefully arranged smile. "We're ever so pleased about Mael's release. But how odd to think that my father-in-law's become a scribe."

Ogretoryc shot her a sidewise glance that could have meant any number of furious things.

"My thanks for the gift, good Primilla," he said. "I'll take him straightaway to my falconer."

Since it was clear that the audience was over, Primilla curtsied and withdrew to the public area of the royal great hall, crowded with various suppliants and the merely curious. As she talked with the councillors and scribes she knew, she picked up a number of hints that a good many important people would be glad to see Mael reinstated in his old place and his son reduced to being merely the heir. Perhaps it was for reasons of sentiment or honor that they felt so. Perhaps. Primilla sought out Councillor Cadlew and asked him outright why some were eager to see Mael return as liege lord of Aberwyn and Cannobaen.

"You seem cursed interested in Mael's affair," Cadlew remarked.

"Of course. The guild needs to know where to spend its gifts. We don't care to curry favor from the wrong lord."

"True spoken. But here, don't spread this any further, will you? The princess Camlada's given herself airs ever since her husband became Aberwyn. There's more than a few who'd enjoy seeing her in a reduced state. And there are some widows, too, who'd fancy themselves consoling a prince in his later years."

"So. This is all a woman's matter?"

"Far from it. The princess has offended more than the ladies in residence, and the widows have brothers who see a chance at influence."

"I see. Do you think Mael will be reinstated?"

"I hope not, for his sake. It would doubtless be very dangerous for his continuing good health, and you won't get one more word out of me, good dame."

It was quite enough, Primilla reflected. She made sure to contact Nevyn immediately, because she had no desire to see Mael come home only to be poisoned by his kin.

From the window in Mael's chamber, the ward of Dun Cerrmor looked as tidy and small as a child's toy. Little horses trotted across barely visible cobbles; tiny men strode around and disappeared into little doors. Only the loudest noises drifted up to his window. That afternoon, Mael was leaning on the windowsill and studying the familiar view when he heard the door opening behind him.

"Glyn, King of all Deverry, approaches," the guard sang out. "All kneel."

Mael turned and knelt just as the King strode in. For a moment they studied each other in a kind of bemused shock that they both had aged so much since their last brief meeting.

"As of today," Glyn said at last, "you're a free man."

"My humble thanks, Your Highness."

Glyn glanced once around the chamber, then left, taking all the guards with him. Mael stared at the empty doorway for a long time, until at last Nevyn appeared in it.

"Get up, my friend," the old man said. "It's time to try your wings."

As Mael followed him down the dark winding stairway, he stared at the walls, stared at the ceiling, stared at every person they met. When they went out into the ward, the sunlight rushed over him like water. He looked up and saw the wall of the dun rising above him, not below, and suddenly he was physically dizzy. Nevyn caught his arm and steadied him.

"The mind's a cursed strange thing," the old man said.

"So it is. I feel bewitched or suchlike."

At first, the noise and the confusion were overwhelming. It seemed that the entire ward was filled with men, shouting, laughing, leading horses by in a great clatter. Maidservants hurried back and forth with buckets of water, loads of firewood, armfuls of foodstuffs. The bright red and silver colors of Cerrmor were everywhere, troubling his recluse's sight. Yet after a few minutes, Mael's dizziness turned to greed. He walked slowly, savoring every sight, from a splendid lord on horseback to a pile of old straw by the stables. When one of the King's boarhounds graciously allowed him to pat it, he was so pleased that he felt like an idiot child, whom everything delights because he can place a value on nothing. When he remarked as much to Nevyn, the dweomerman laughed.

"And who's to say that the idiot child's not the wisest of us all?" Nevyn said. "Let's go along to my chambers. Gavra should be joining us soon."

But Gavra was already waiting in Nevyn's sparsely furnished reception room. Mael ran to her, swept her into his arms, and kissed her.

"Oh my love," he said. "I'm afraid to believe this. I keep thinking we'll wake on the morrow and find it only a cruel dream."

"It cursed well better not be, after all the trouble I've gone to over the shop! Getting it transferred to Ebrua gave me such a headache that I had to take some of my own herbs."

Nevyn estimated that it would take them about four days to reach the Eldidd border where, or so it had been arranged, an honor guard from the Eldidd court would be waiting for him. Yet on the third night, when they were making camp about ten miles west of Morlyn, a different sort of party came to meet them: Primilla and two young men, carrying quarterstaves. With a shout of greeting, Nevyn hurried over just as they were dismounting, and Mael trailed after him.

"What's all this?" Nevyn said.

"Well, I'm afraid I've come with some possibly ominous news."

"Indeed?" Mael broke in. "Is the court going to want me poisoned?"

"I see the philosopher remembers his old life as a prince very well indeed," Primilla said. "But I'm not sure if he's in any true danger. It's merely that it's never wise to take unnecessary

chances. We came to escort you to a safe place until I'm quite sure
we can meet the court on our terms, not theirs."

"My thanks, then," Nevyn said. "I haven't saved the lad's life
from the rope only to lose it to a vial of poison."

"Don't worry. We're going to slip through the woods as sly as
foxes, and then . . ." She paused for a smile. "And then, hole up
like badgers."

All week, since the farmers had been bringing in wagonloads
of firewood to pay their spring taxes to the Cannobaen light,
Avascaen was always up and around long before sunset, helping
them unload the wood and stack it in the long sheds. On that
particular day, when he saw dust coming down the road, he
assumed that another wagonload was on the way.

"Here come the lads," he told Egamyn. "Run and see which
shed's got the most room left."

With a sigh for the tedium of it all, Egamyn strolled slowly
away while Avascaen swung the creaking, complaining gates
open. With his hand still on the rusty bar, he froze and stared at
the party in the road. Riders—pack mules—that strange woman
with the blue hands—and behind them—it couldn't—it had to
be, gray hair or not. With a shout bordering on a sob, Avascaen
raced out into the road to welcome Prince Mael home. When he
caught the prince's stirrup as a sign of fealty, Mael bowed to him
from the saddle.

"Look at us, Avascaen! When I rode away, we were both lads,
and now we're all gray and grizzled."

"So we are, my prince, but the sight of you gladdens my
heart, anyway."

"And it gladdens mine to see you. Will you shelter us?"

"What? Of course, your highness. Why, you've come at the
perfect time. Scwna's just been airing out your chambers, you
see, like she does every spring, so they'll be nice and clean for
you."

"Has she now? Every spring?"

"Every spring. We're like badgers, my prince. We hold on."

Mael swung down from his horse, grabbed Avascaen's hand,
and shook it hard. When he saw the tears in the prince's eyes,
Avascaen began to feel a bit rocky himself.

"I'm not a prince anymore," Mael said. "And I count myself

honored to call you friend. Here, I've got my new wife and son with me, and let's pray that this time, I'm home to stay."

As the party filed into the ward, Egamyn, Maryl, and Scwna ran out of the broch to greet them. Avascaen gave Egamyn a smug smile.

"And didn't I tell you he'd be back?"

He had the satisfaction of seeing his bigmouthed son speechless.

After a companionable afternoon and celebratory dinner, Avascaen went out to tend the light. Just as the sky was fading to a pearly gray, he struck sparks from his steel, set the dry tinder burning, then blew on it until the sparks licked around the kindling. He added logs until, at last, the beacon burned strong and sent its warning out to sea. He walked to the edge and looked at the broch, the windows cheerful with lantern light. The prince was home. I didn't forget him and he didn't forget me, he thought, just like badgers, both of us. The world was a satisfying place, filled with justice. Later, when the full moon was at its zenith, Mael came up to the tower. Panting, out of breath, the prince leaned against the guardrail.

"You must have cursed strong legs," Mael said.

"Oh, you get used to it after a bit."

They leaned side by side onto the rail and looked at the sea, the waves foaming silver in the moonlight as they crashed onto the tiny strip of pale beach.

"Did I tell you that I was kept in the top of a tower during my imprisonment?"

"Well, fancy that. So there you were, looking down, and here I was, doing the same."

"Just that, but this view is a cursed sight wider than the one I had. I want to stay in Cannobaen for the rest of my life, but that depends on Prince Ogretoryc. The demesne is his to dispose of now, not mine."

"If he's got the gall to turn you out of it, then he'll have to find himself another lightkeeper." Avascaen considered the problem for a moment. "Now here, my brother's got more land than he can farm by himself. He'll take us in if things come to that."

"My thanks. I can earn some coin as a letter-writer, too."

For a few minutes they shared a companionable silence.

"By the way," Mael said, "have there even been any ships out here?"

"Cursed few, but you never know when someone will need the light."

Since Primilla's entire strategy was to portray Mael as someone utterly unfit for courtly affairs, she urged him to make his letter to his son as blunt as possible, and she was pleased with the result.

"To Ogretoryc, Prince of Aberwyn and Cannobaen, and my son, Mael the philosopher sends greetings. Although we have never spoken two words together, Your Highness, it behooves a father to be blunt with his own flesh and blood. I know full well that you wish to keep your positions and your honors at the court of my brother the king. I have no desire for anything but to see you do so. I have become a humble scholar, unfit for the duties of war and rulership after my long imprisonment. All I want is to live out the remains of my life in my old country lodge of Cannobaen, or, if His Highness prefers, as a common villager. You may send word to me through Primilla, head of the dyer's guild. I fear for my life in court circles. I have no desire to taste freedom only to taste poison a few weeks later. Your father, Mael the philosopher."

When she finished reading, Mael leaned back in his chair and gave her a quizzical smile.

"It should do splendidly," she said.

"Good. You know, it's a strange thing to be humble to your own son. If it's not enough for them that I've been disclaimed, now I've abdicated. Should keep things all nice and tidy, as our Avascaen would say."

When Primilla returned to Abernaudd, she waited a day before delivering the letter in order to hear the current gossip. Since the court—indeed, the whole city—was as full of rumors as a wasp's nest is of stings, all her friends had plenty to tell her. The King had indeed sent an honor guard to the border to receive Mael, but they'd found Nevyn the Cerrmor councillor and Prince Cobryn of Cerrmor there instead, telling them that Mael had decided to travel alone. Everyone suspected treachery, but on Ogretoryc's part, not Cerrmor's.

"Now I say they're wagering on the wrong horse in this race," Cadlew said. "If there's treachery, the princess is behind it, not the prince. Some of her loyal men might have taken a warband out after Mael."

"Indeed? Now, suppose the philosopher isn't dead. Does anyone have any idea of where he might be?"

"There's plenty of guesses, but the tale making the rounds is that Mael's gone over to the rebels in Pyrdon, who'll shelter him for the chance to make trouble here in Eldidd. Fortunately, they're too weak to back him in a drive for the throne—too weak as yet, anyway. After all, once a man's been a prince, who's to blame him if he wants it all back again?"

On the morrow Primilla made her visit to the prince and princess. Camlada's face was so drawn that it seemed she hadn't slept in nights; Ogretoryc merely looked baffled.

"Your Highness, I have a letter from your father to you."

Ogretoryc was up like a bow shot. Camlada crouched in her chair and stared wide-eyed as Primilla handed over the message tube.

"And where have you seen my father?"

"On the roads. His Highness knows that I often travel. He seemed much distressed and asked me to take the letter when he found out that I was going to Abernaudd."

"It's the seal of Aberwyn, all right." Ogretoryc was looking over the tube. "It must be the one he had with him when he was captured."

While he read the letter, Camlada watched with eyes that revealed far too much fear to be becoming.

"Well," Ogretoryc said at last, "this should put a stop to those rumors that we had him murdered on the road. I fear I forget myself, good dame, but my heart has been heavy this past few weeks."

"Of course, Your Highness. Doubtless concern for your father's life was hard to bear."

"It was." The way he spoke convinced her of his sincerity, as was the disdainful way he threw the letter into his wife's lap.

With a toss of her head, Camlada picked up the letter and read it. Primilla could see the currents in her aura, where fear and suspicion whirled around like demons.

"And is my lady satisfied?" Ogretoryc spit out.

"And is my lord thinking that I would be anything else?"

When their eyes locked, Primilla turned away and busied

herself with admiring a floral arrangement. After a moment, Ogretoryc broke away with a small snarl under his breath.

"Allow me to escort you to the door, good dame," he said. "You have my thanks for bringing the letter."

The prince didn't speak again until they were well out of the princess's hearing.

"Can you tell me where Mael is?" he said.

"In Cannobaen, Your Highness."

"I thought he might be, but hear, don't tell another soul until I have things arranged. My beloved wife can just stew over it a little longer."

Every morning, Mael and Gavra went for a long walk along the cliffs and looked at the ocean. Since memories of Cannobaen had haunted his imprisonment, it still seemed unbelievable that he was really there, feeling the sun warm on his back and breathing in the sharp clean smell of the sea. Often in the afternoon he would climb the tower and sit by the ashes of the beacon as he kept watch on the road. As the time slipped past, he began to wonder how many days of contentment were left to him. Every day without an answer from Abernaudd was an evil omen of court intrigue.

Yet when the answer did come, he was taken by surprise. He was in his chamber, using a stylus to rule lines onto parchment, when Avascaen's son Maryl burst in.

"Your highness, there's twenty-five men at our gates, and your son with them."

Hardly thinking, Mael grabbed his tiny penknife for a weapon and ran outside, but the men were dismounting in a friendly sort of confusion. Mael had no trouble picking out the prince in the bustle, simply because his son strikingly resembled him. Smiling, Ogretoryc strode over and held out his hand.

"It gladdens my heart to see you, Father. All my life I've heard tales about you, and now at last we meet."

"And so we do." Mael took the offered hand.

"Your letter ached my heart. You've got nothing to fear, I swear it."

"Then the court must have changed since last I rode there."

"I've had plenty of impious advice, if that's what you mean, but I'll kill any man who raises his hand against you."

He spoke so sincerely that Mael nearly wept with relief.

"Then you have my thanks."

Ogretoryc turned, looking up at the broch and the tower. "I've never been here before, you know. When I was a child, Mother never visited it, because thinking of how much you loved this place made her weep. When I was grown, I was off at war much of the time. It's yours again. I've made it over to you, and the King's most graciously bestowed a title with it. I've got the letters patent in my saddlebags."

"By the gods! And that was generous of you."

He shrugged, still looking away.

"There's one thing I've got to say," Ogretoryc went on. "Some years ago, when they sent the letter of disclaimance, everyone was sure Glyn would hang you. I would have begged the King not to send the letter, but I was away from court." At last he looked at Mael. "My wife arranged for me to be away from court during the councils when the King made his decision. I found that out much later."

"Well, I wouldn't ache your heart over it overmuch. I doubt me if the King would have listened to your plea. But I'll ask you a favor, that I never have to meet your lady."

"I'm putting her aside. She can live out her life in some quiet place of retirement."

The malice in his voice told Mael that he'd picked the best possible way to punish his wife.

On the morrow, Ogretoryc took his leave early with the promise to return soon if the summer's fighting allowed. Mael waved him out of the gates, then went looking for Gavra, whom he found studying the ward near Scwna's kitchen garden.

"What are you doing?" he said.

"Thinking of taking up these cobbles so we can put in a herb garden. Scwna tells me there's lots of sun out here."

"I can see it now. For years the folk will talk about the eccentric Lady Gavra of Cannobaen and her herbs."

"I can't be a lady. I refuse."

"Can't refuse. You sealed your fate when you married me. You know, many a lass has won a title with beauty, but you're the first one I ever heard of who won hers with a decoction of febrifuges."

When she laughed, he kissed her, then merely held her tight, free in the warm sunlight.

THREE

In the summer of 797, in his fiftieth year, Glyn, Gwerbret
Cerrmor and would-be King of All Deverry, died of a congestion
of the heart. Although Nevyn had been worrying about the
King's health for some time, the suddenness of it caught him off-
guard. One morning Glyn rode out at the head of his men; at
noon, they brought him home dead. He'd been stricken while
mounting his horse and died within minutes. While his sobbing
wife and her serving women washed and laid out his body, his
eldest son, Camlan, assumed the kingship before his loyal vassals
in the great hall, where the head-priest of Bel first blessed him,
then pinned the enormous ring brooch of kingship onto his plaid.
As the vassals came forward, one by one, to kneel to their new
liege lord, Nevyn slipped away from the confusion and went to
his chambers. The time had come for him to leave Cerrmor.

Late that night, Nevyn was in the midst of packing when the
new king sent for him. Camlan had already moved into the royal
apartments and stood by the hearth where Nevyn had so often
watched his father pace restlessly. At thirty, the new King was
heavily built, but he was just as handsome as his father, and he
stood as straight and as tall.

"I hear you plan to leave us," Camlan said. "I was hoping
that you'd serve me as you served my father."

"My liege is most kind." Nevyn sighed at the necessary lies
ahead of him. "But your father's death has dealt a heavy blow to
one as old as I. I have no more strength for court duties, my liege.
I only wish to eke out my last few years honoring your father's
memory."

"Most nobly put. Then it would please me to settle some land
near Cerrmor upon you, as a reward for your long years of service."

"The King is most generous, but he should save such favors
for a younger man. I have kin who will shelter me, and it's to his
kin that an old man's mind turns."

When he left Cerrmor, Nevyn rode to Cannobaen to see
Mael and Gavra. Although there was open warfare along the
Eldidd border, in his guise of shabby old herbman he easily
slipped the lines and made his way along the Eldidd coast. Late
on a golden summer day, when the wild roses bloomed along the
road, he reached the dun. Over the gates the old crest of the

princes of Aberwyn had been taken down, and a new device hung there, a pair of grappling badgers and the motto: *We hold on.*

When Nevyn led his horse and mule inside, Mael ran to greet him with a shout. He was tanned and vigorous, grinning as he grabbed Nevyn's hand and clasped it between both of his.

"What are you doing here, away from all the important affairs of the kingdom?" Mael said. "It gladdens my heart to see you."

"Well, Glyn's dead, and I left the court."

"Dead? I hadn't heard the news."

"You look sad, my friend."

"In a way, I am. Whatever his reasons, Glyn was the most generous patron a scholar ever had. He fed me for twenty years, didn't he? Many a lord's gotten a fulsome dedication for a cursed sight less than that. But come in, come in. Gavra will be pleased to see you, and we've got a new daughter to show you."

Besides the new daughter, Mael had another treasure to share, a very rare book indeed, which he had found at the temple of Wmm during one of his rare visits to Aberwyn. At night, they took turns reading aloud from this early translation of a dialogue by the Rhwman sage Tull Cicryn, and stayed up late many a time discussing these rare thoughts from the Dawntime age.

"I spent a cursed lot of coin on this," Mael remarked at one point. "Gavra thought I was daft, and mayhap she's right. But the priests said it's the only book of Cicryn's that came over in the great exile."

"It is, and it's a pity that we don't have more. The old tale runs that Cicryn was a man much like you, a prince of the Rhwmanes who fell from power because he backed the wrong claimant to the Rhwman throne. He devoted the rest of his life to philosophy."

"Well, I hope his exile wasn't too harsh, but it was worth it to have these *Tuscan Talks* of his. I intend to include his argument against suicide in my new book. That central image of his is most apt and striking, where he says that we're like watchmen for an army, appointed by the gods for reasons we can't know, and so to kill yourself is deserting your post."

"As I seem to remember pointing out to a very young prince a very long time ago."

Mael laughed easily.

"So you did, and my tutor was right enough. Here, I've been meaning to remember to tell you somewhat. You're welcome to stay here the rest of your life if you want. I can't offer you courtly splendor, but Cannobaen's warm in the winter."

"Most generous of you, and truly, I'm tempted, but I have kin to go to."

"Kin? Of course you must have kin. Here I've been thinking that dweomermen must spring full grown from the ground."

"Like frogs from warm mud? Well, we're not as strange as all that—not quite, anyway."

When Nevyn left, he slipped out early one dawn before the family was awake, simply to spare everyone a bitter parting. As he rode away, he looked back to see the pale glow of the Cannobaen light, high on its tower, and knew that he would never see Mael again. He wished that he really did have kin to go to, but, of course, what distant relations he did have were all at one or the other of the warring courts, which he would have to avoid for a time. Quite simply, he needed to pretend to die. After a good many years, another Nevyn the herbman could reappear in places that had once known him without people asking embarrassing questions about his unusually long life.

He decided to head for some outlying place in Cantrae territory, where he could bring his skills to the commonfolk of the torn kingdom. He wondered where he would find Brangwen again and if perhaps she was already alive somewhere in a new body. He could do nothing but follow his intuitions and let the chance that was more than chance guide him. With a long painful sigh, he turned his horse onto the north-running road. For all that his long life would have seemed wonderful to other men, he was very tired.

And as for Mael, Lord Cannobaen, he and his wife lived many a long happy year, finally dying within a few days of each other of old age and nothing more. As his reputation for wisdom grew, he became known as "Mael the Seer," being given the title of that class of men known as "vates" in the Dawntime. Although in Deverry folk would have called him Mael y Gwaedd, in the Eldidd way of speaking his name became Maelwaedd, a title passed to all his descendants down the long years.

Summer, 1063

You must never speak of "binding" a spirit into a
crystal or a talisman. If the spirit chooses to serve
you in this way, well and good, because it will gain
knowledge and power as its reward. Let us leave
this talk of binding and subjugation to the dark path.

The Secret Book of Cadwallon the Druid

It was a beautiful sunny day, and the sun sparkled on the waters of the River Lit. Lord Camdel, once Master of the King's Bath, sang as he rode beside the river, just snatches of songs, jumbled in no particular order, because he was having a great deal of trouble remembering the words. He was, in fact, having trouble remembering anything at all, such as the reason that he was riding through the lonely hills of the province of Yr Auddglyn. From time to time, the question would occur to him, but no matter how long he pondered it, he never found an answer. It merely seemed perfectly correct that he would be there, hundreds of miles from court, with a mysterious packet of jewels in his saddlebags. He knew that he'd stolen the jewels, but he could no longer remember why or who their owner was.

"I must be drunk," he said to his chestnut gelding. "But why am I drunk out here?"

The gelding snorted as if wondering the same thing.

A few miles on, the river road curved sharply, and as he rounded the bend, Camdel saw three men on horseback. In his muddled way, he knew that they were waiting for him. Of course, it was Sarcyn and Alastyr, and that third man had to be Sarcyn's brother! Doubtless he was here to buy some opium with those jewels. At last it all made sense.

"Well met, my friend," Alastyr said. "Are you ready to come with us?"

Camdel started to agree, but suddenly a thought came into his mind. Don't! it said, they'll hurt you! The thought was so urgent that without a moment's pause he wrenched his horse's head around.

"Here!" Sarcyn spurred his mount after him.

Run! screamed the voice in his mind.

Obediently Camdel kicked his horse hard, but just as it sprang to a gallop, it screamed in agony and reared. Camdel was thrown forward hard; he clung to its neck as it staggered. He saw a sword blade flash up and slit the horse's throat. Barely in time, he kicked his feet free of the stirrups and rolled off as the gelding went down. He staggered up, groping for the hilt of his sword. Then a sharp blow caught him across the back of the head, and he crumpled into darkness.

"Good work, Sarcyn," Alastyr said. "Evy, get those saddlebags! We've got to get on our way fast."

"Cursed nuisance about that horse," Sarcyn said, kneeling down by Camdel. "We'll have to steal him another one."

"I've been thinking that we should just kill him and be done with it. Things are much more dangerous than I thought they'd be. Don't forget, with this cursed war going on around here, we might meet a patrol or suchlike on the roads."

Sarcyn looked up with a flash of mutiny in his eyes.

"I know I promised, but—" Alastyr hesitated, remembering the Old One's warning that his apprentice hated him. "Ah well, he doesn't weigh much. You can tie him onto your horse until we get another."

"My thanks, master. Besides, we can use him for the ritual."

"So we can, and tonight. Ye gods, I'm exhausted."

Evy hurried up with the saddlebags. Although Alastyr was tempted to open them and gloat over the jewels then and there, time was short. Nervously he glanced around, half afraid of seeing some noble lord and his full warband riding toward them. Camdel was going to be a cursed nuisance. He felt hurt, he realized, that Sarcyn would hate him, after all he'd done for the little gutter rat! Still, there was no time to worry about such things now, and hatred or not, Sarcyn was too useful to get rid of.

His head throbbed, blinding him, and there were arms around him. But where was he? On horseback. Somewhere. Camdel opened his eyes and saw green meadow around him.

The Auddglyn. He'd tried to escape. With a groan, he twisted in the saddle and realized that his ankles were tied to the stirrups.

"Awake, are you?" Sarcyn said.

Camdel realized, then, that Sarcyn was riding behind him and holding him on the horse. He heard the sound of other horses following them. The green meadows danced and shifted in his tormented vision.

"My apologies for the blow on the head," Sarcyn went on. "But we couldn't have you just riding off like that. You'll feel better in a bit, little one."

"Why? What do you want me for?"

Sarcyn laughed, a little mutter under his breath.

"You'll find out tonight."

He was too exhausted to ask more. Although he was thoroughly trained in weapon craft, and had indeed won several tournaments, Camdel had never ridden to war or indeed exerted much of any kind of energy in his life. The pain took over his mind for the rest of the long, miserable ride.

At last they rode up to a farm, which had been deserted for some time, to judge by the crumbling earthen wall around it and the sparseness of the thatch on the roof of the farmhouse itself. When the others dismounted, Sarcyn cut Camdel's ankles free and pulled him down from the horse, then shoved him along inside to a big half-round room that had once been a kitchen. There was travelling gear scattered around on the floor and a pile of blankets by the hearth.

"Lie down and rest," Sarcyn said. "But I'm tying your hands and feet to make sure you stay here."

Once he was bound, Camdel lay very still and tried not to move his throbbing head. The others came in, talking among themselves about their booty, then moved on to another chamber. Although Camdel tried to drift off to sleep, he suddenly heard a howl of rage.

"It's gone! It must have fallen out when his cursed horse got killed! Everything's here but the Great Stone of the West. Sarcyn, get your horse saddled and get back there to search."

The Great Stone of the West. What was that? Camdel vaguely remembered the name, but the pain in his head was making it too hard to think. He drifted off into unconsciousness, only to have a frightening dream that Alastyr was questioning him about this mysterious stone.

When he woke again, it was night, and a fire was burning in the hearth. Nearby Alastyr, Evy, and Sarcyn sat on the floor and talked quietly among themselves in a cold fury. When he realized that they probably hadn't found the stone, he was pleased. Although he gave an involuntary groan when he tried to move, the pain in his head was bearable.

"Give him somewhat to eat and drink," Alastyr said. "I want to work the ritual straightaway. All this astral traveling I've been doing has left me drained, I don't mind telling you."

Camdel's heart started pounding like a drum. Every tale of evil magicians he'd ever heard came back to him as Sarcyn strolled over.

"Oh, we're not the opium-runners you thought we were," Sarcyn said as he knelt down. "Soon you'll learn more of the truth, little one. At first you'll hate what I'm going to do to you, but in a while, I think me you'll develop a strange taste for it."

When Sarcyn cut his hands free, they shook so badly that Camdel could barely hold the waterskin he was handed, but he was so thirsty that he forced them steady and drank in long gulps. Sarcyn watched with a small smile that made his flesh creep.

"Hungry?" he said.

"I'm not." Camdel gasped out the words. "Please, just let me go. My father's rich, he'll ransom me, by the gods, please, let me go!"

"Oh, you'll never see your father again, lad. You're coming with us to Bardek, and when I tire of you, you'll be sold as a slave. I think you'd best try to please me and make sure that I don't tire of you straightway."

All at once, Camdel understood his implication. Involuntarily he shrank back as Sarcyn laughed at him.

"He probably couldn't get food down," Alastyr broke in. "Cut his ankles free and bring him along."

When Sarcyn hauled him to his feet, Camdel staggered. He'd been bound so long that it was hard to walk. The apprentice half shoved, half carried him into another chamber, where a piece of black velvet, embroidered in strange signs and sigils, hung on one wall. Candle-lanterns hung glowing from hooks, and in one corner was a small bronze brazier, giving off a soft cloud of incense. In the middle was a stout iron ring set into a trapdoor, which doubtless led down to a root cellar or some mundane thing.

"We've had everything ready, just waiting for you to wake," Alastyr said, and Camdel hated his oily voice more than ever. "Now, if you struggle too much, you could be hurt, so lie quietly."

At that, Sarcyn shoved him face-down on the floor so hard that he gasped for breath. Quickly the apprentice bound his hands to the ring, then stepped aside. When Camdel looked up, he saw Alastyr standing at his head not more than three feet away. His hands were raised, palms forward, about shoulder high. In the dancing candlelight his eyes seemed to glitter as he stared into Camdel's own. All at once, he couldn't look away, even though he struggled to. Alastyr's eyes had him caught, pinned there, and he felt as if the old man were sucking life out of him, draining him in some mysterious way that he couldn't understand.

Then Sarcyn knelt down beside him and began pulling off his brigga, reaching under him to unlace them and to fondle him. He struggled, thrashing like a caught fish, but the apprentice was too strong. Shivering in fear, he lay half-naked and stared up into Alastyr's eyes while Sarcyn spread his legs apart and knelt between them. The old man began to chant in some incomprehensible tongue, a soft rhythmic mutter that was the more frightening for being done so slowly, with such perfect control.

Then he felt Sarcyn's hands grasp his buttocks. When he realized what was about to happen to him, he wanted to scream, but no sound would come.

In the gray humid dawn, the camp began to wake—the men yawning and cursing, the horses rousing themselves and pulling at their tether ropes with soft snorts. At his guard post down by the stream, Rhodry sheathed his sword and rested his shield on the ground while he waited for the captain to come release him from duty. On the other side of the stream stood a crop of spring wheat, turning pale gold and ripe for the harvest. Summer's here, Rhodry thought. My first cursed summer as a silver dagger.

Finally the captain released him with a shout and a wave. Rhodry hurried back to camp, dumped his shield beside his bedroll, and went down to the wooden carts to get his horse some oats and himself some breakfast. The twenty other men in the warband were already there. He took his place in the provision line behind Edyl, a square-faced young rider who was, so far at least, the only man in the warband who'd talk to a silver dagger.

"Morrow, Rhodry. I take it you didn't see any enemies creeping toward us, or were you asleep out there?"

"Oh, it was easy to stay awake, what with the lot of you snoring and farting."

With a laugh, Edyl gave him a friendly cuff on the shoulder. Up at the cart, Lord Gwivan's portly manservant shoved himself in at the head of the line to fetch his lordship's breakfast.

"How far are we from this Lord Daen's dun, anyway?" Rhodry said.

"Just about fifteen miles. If these horse dung carts don't break down again, we'll be at his side tonight."

"Think we'll get pinned in a siege?"

"Well, that's the rumor, isn't it? Let's pray it isn't true."

Since he'd ridden into the middle of this war in the Auddglyn, Rhodry was still trying to sort out exactly what was happening. As far as he could tell, Lord Daen and a certain Lord Laenrydd had a feud going of long standing, and some little incident had set it off. Each lord had called in all their alliances to muster as big an army as they could. Rhodry had been hired by Daen's ally Marclew, but since Marclew only owed Daen twenty-one men, he'd stayed at home and sent his son, Gwivan, to lead the warband. The shame of it ate at Rhodry constantly. Only last summer he'd been the cadvridoc of a large army; now he was just a silver dagger, hired to spare another man from riding to war.

They broke camp smoothly and were on the road by two hours after dawn. Half the warband ambled along with their lord at the head of the line; the carts jerked and jolted in the middle; the rest of the riders formed a rear guard. As a silver dagger, Rhodry rode at the very end and breathed everyone else's dust. He found himself thinking about Jill and wondering if she were safe, back in the dun with the rest of the warband and, for that matter, the widowed lord himself. His jealousy was a constant riding partner, gnawing him, taunting him with memories of just how beautiful she was. When they'd ridden away together, he'd managed to forget that they'd be separated for weeks and months at a time, when he would have no way of knowing if she were faithful to him.

Slowly the straggling line wound through the low hills, scrubby with trees and underbrush. Methodically Rhodry recalled every man at the dun and wondered if she would find him tempting. That every man who saw her would want Jill was a foregone conclusion in his mind; the question was, would she take someone up on it? All at once, the sound of a silver horn cut through his black brooding. With an involuntary shout, he rose in the stirrups and looked around. Far ahead down the road was a warband, armed and ready, drawn up across their line of march.

"Enemies, lads!" Gwivan yelled. "Arm!"

While he unlaced his shield from his saddle peak and pulled it up on his left arm, Rhodry guided his horse with his knees, turning it out of line and urging it up past the carts. The line of march dissolved into a swirling, cursing confusion as the other men did the same. Just as he reached the front line, another horn sounded, and down from the hills swept a second warband to cut them off from behind. Rhodry began to wonder if he'd ever see Jill again, faithful or not. Swearing under his breath, he pulled a javelin from the sheath under his right leg just as the enemy warband began to walk their horses forward.

"Gwivan!" the leader called out. "Surrender, you young dolt."

The lord urged his horse a few paces ahead of his grim and joustling men. Since Rhodry estimated that there were forty men behind them and thirty in front, he braced himself to die fighting if Gwivan refused to surrender.

"Use your wits, lad!" said the enemy lord. "It's not even your feud. Let your father ransom you and your pack. As long as you don't reach Daen's side today, I don't give a pig's fart about killing you. There's no dishonor in surrendering to this kind of odds, and besides, we can use the coin."

Behind him his warband laughed at the jest.

"That's all well and good, Ynryc," Gwivan called back. "But what about Lord Degwyc?"

"He's not riding with us, and I'll give you my solemn word of honor that you'll be safe from him while you're under my charge."

Gwivan considered for so long that Rhodry wanted to curse in frustration. His life was hanging in a web of other men's feuds, and he didn't even know who they were.

"Done," Gwivan said at last. "I'll take your pledge."

Rhodry sighed sharply in relief.

Slowly the waiting enemies rode forward and surrounded them. Ynryc took up a position by one cart and watched as one at a time, Gwivan and his men rode up and disarmed. Rhodry came at the very end. He threw his javelins into the cart first, then slowly and reluctantly drew his sword, a beautiful blade of the finest steel, with a handguard worked in the shape of the dragon of Aberwyn. It was the one thing he loved as much as Jill, and laying it down on the pile hurt.

"That's a fine sword, silver dagger," Ynryc remarked. "Battle loot?"

"It wasn't, my lord, but a gift from a man I served well." Rhodry was thinking of his father, who had given it to him.

"You must have fought like a fiend from hell to have earned a blade like that." Ynryc turned to Gwivan, sitting sullenly on horseback beside him. "Your father must be serious about his obligations if he'd actually part with coin to hire a silver dagger."

Gwivan set his mouth in a tight line.

"Ah, it's no fault of yours that your da's a cursed miser," Ynryc went on. "Think he'll pay the ransom for this lad?"

"My father is an honorable man," Gwivan snarled. "And he's *not* a miser."

"Merely a bit careful with his coin, eh?

When Ynryc roared with laughter, Gwivan's face went scarlet with shame. Rhodry felt a cold, sinking dread. If his lordship didn't pay over the ransom, Rhodry would be reduced to little better than a bondsman, Ynryc's virtual property for years until he worked off the debt.

Lord Marclew was in such a rage that everyone in the great hall could hear the news. With a flustered scribe and chamberlain trailing after him, he strode back and forth and bellowed out curses on Ynryc's name, clan, and masculinity. In the curve of the wall, Jill stood with a cluster of serving lasses and watched the lord, an enormous man, still hard-muscled for all the gray in his hair. He clutched Ynryc's message in one massive fist and shook it at the scribe as if the poor man were responsible for writing, not merely reading, it.

"The gall!" Marclew snarled. "Taking my son on the road by a sneaking pissproud bastard's trick, and then mocking *me* for a miser!" He threw the parchment at the scribe, who caught it and ducked back out of reach. "What was that bit again, the whoreson?"

The scribe cleared his throat and smoothed out the message. "I know his lordship values his coin, hugging it tight the way most men prefer to hug a wench, but doubtless his own son means enough to him that he will part with some of his treasures. We have set his price at two Deverry regals, a regal each for his men, including the silver dagger, and for the servants—"

"The gall!" Marclew howled. "Do they truly expect me to pay full ransom for a stinking silver dagger? They're doing it to mock me, and cursed if I will."

With a growl, Marclew went back to his pacing. The chamberlain turned Jill's way and beckoned, inviting her to come plead with the lord, but Jill shook her head in a no and stalked out of the great hall. One of the serving lasses followed and caught her by the arm.

"What are you doing?" Perra said. "Why won't you plead?"

"Because I've got the coin to ransom Rhodry out myself. In all my years on the long road, I've never been treated so shabbily by a lord, and cursed if I'll stand for it anymore. If I were a bard, I'd make a satire about Marclew."

"Oh, plenty of bards already have, but it hasn't done any good."

Jill went down to the stables, where she'd been sleeping in an empty stall next to her horse. A groom helped her saddle up and told her how to get to Ynryc's dun, about a day and a half's ride away.

"Now be careful, lass," he said. "There's going to be as many warbands in the hills as fleas on a hound."

"I will. Can you spare me some oats for my horse, or will your tightfisted lord beat you for it?"

"He'll never know. You want to take good care of a horse like that one, you do."

As if he knew he were being praised, Sunrise tossed his head and made his silvery mane ripple over his golden neck. Rhodry had given her this Western Hunter, back when he'd been able to bestow valuable gifts on those who served him.

Jill rode out without extending Marclew the courtesy of a farewell and galloped the first mile or so, just to put the dun well behind her. When she reached the broad, grassy banks of the River Lit, she slowed to a walk to let Sunrise cool down. Suddenly her gray gnome appeared on her saddle peak and perched there precariously.

"We're going to get Rhodry and then get back on the long road," she told him. "Marclew is a swine."

Grinning, the gnome nodded agreement.

"I cursed well hope he's being well treated. Did you go take a look at him?"

The gnome nodded a vigorous yes to both questions.

"You know, little brother, there's one thing I don't understand. Here's Rhodry with his elven blood, but he can't see you."

The gnome pensively picked his long blue teeth while he considered, then shrugged and disappeared. Apparently he didn't understand it, either.

The road wound through low hills, sometimes leaving the river when the water ran through a deep canyon, then rejoining it in the valleys. To either side stretched mile after of mile of scrubby pastureland, rolling through the hills. Here and there Jill saw herds of white cattle with rusty-red ears, tended by a cowherd with a pair of big gray-and-white hounds. Late in the day, Jill had just come round a large bend in the river road when she saw ravens off to the right. Out in the tall grass they waddled awkwardly around, or suddenly broke to fly and circle, only to settle to their feeding again.

Jill assumed that the corpse was a dead calf, born too weak to live, or even maybe a cow who'd gotten ill and died before the cowherd found her, but all at once, the gray gnome reappeared. He grabbed a rein with bony fingers, shook it hard, then pointed at the ravens.

"Do you want me to take a look?"

He nodded yes in great excitement.

Jill tied Sunrise to a bush by the road, then followed the gnome over. At their approach, the ravens flew up, squawking indignantly, and settled in a nearby tree to keep watch over their prize. In the tall grass lay the carcass of a horse, still carrying saddle and bridle, the leather straps cutting deep into the swollen flesh. Although she circled round it, the birds had eaten so much that she couldn't tell how the horse had died. The saddle and bridle bothered her. If a horse belonging to a warband had merely broken a leg, the men would have taken the gear after they put the poor beast out of its misery.

Holding her breath, she moved in a little closer. Silver and gems winked and gleamed on the bridle.

"By every god and his wife! Who would have left gear like that behind?"

The gnome, however, wasn't listening to her. He was rootling round in the grass, parting it with both hands to peer through it, his skinny little face screwed up in concentration. As Jill watched him, she realized that someone else had searched the area, because the grass was trampled and torn a good ways around the horse. When she walked toward the gnome, a wink of gold caught her eye. She picked up an arm bracelet, a semi-cylinder of pure gold, worked all over in an elaborate pattern of spirals and rosettes. Although she'd never seen anyone wear this sort of jewelry, she'd heard tales where the great warriors of the Dawntime did. It had to be some family heirloom passed down for centuries, and doubtless worth twenty times the weight of its gold.

"Here, is this what you're looking for?"

His eyes narrowed in confusion, the gnome came over. He touched the bracelet with one finger, sniffed it with his long nose, then suddenly smiled and did a little jig of victory.

"Well and good, then. We'll take it along."

The gnome nodded, then disappeared. As Jill wrapped the arm bracelet in her spare socks and put it into her saddlebags, she was wondering who had killed the horse and what had happened to its rider. All at once, she felt a dweomer-warning, a cold shudder down her back as if someone had stroked it with a clammy hand. Something dangerous was at work here, something far beyond her understanding, but she could smell it as clearly as she could smell the dead horse. That afternoon she rode on a good long ways before she made camp, and she barely slept that night, drowsing between sleep and keeping watch.

That same night, Nevyn was staying in a small inn about a hundred miles west. For the past two weeks, he'd been tracking Camdel down, ever since one of the spirits who were attached to the stone had come to him to tell him of the theft. Since he rarely slept more than four hours a night, he was awake late, brooding over this appalling theft, when Jill's gray gnome appeared in front of him.

"Well, good eve, little brother. Is Jill close by?"

The gnome shook his head no, then danced around, grinning from ear to ear.

"What's this? Good news of some sort?"

It nodded yes, then did an elaborate pantomime, using its

hands to describe some small round thing and staring into the shape as if it were scrying.

"Oh ye gods! Do you mean the Great Stone of the West?"

It nodded agreement, then pantomimed searching for something and finding it.

"You've found it? Oh here, do you mean Jill's got it?"

The gnome nodded yes again. For a brief moment, Nevyn felt sick with terror.

"Do you realize this means she's in terrible danger? Those men who stole it want the thing cursed badly. They'll kill to get it."

Its mouth opened wide, and it actually made a little whimper of sound, a difficult thing for one of the Wildfolk to do.

"You get back to her. At the first sign of danger, come tell me, do you hear?"

The gnome nodded, then disappeared. In something as close to panic as his disciplined mind could get, Nevyn turned to the charcoal brazier standing in the corner of the chamber. At a wave of his hand, the Wildfolk of Fire set the coals to glowing red. Nevyn stared into them and thought of Jill.

Almost immediately he saw her, keeping a lonely camp by a riverside amid rolling hills. Although she was asleep, she was sitting up with her back to a tree, and her sword was clasped in her hand. At least she seemed to realize that she was in danger, but he knew that the sword would do her little good against this kind of enemy. And where by all the gods was Rhodry? Irritably he switched his thoughts and saw the lad, lying on his blankets on the floor of a badly overcrowded barracks. All of the men packed in there looked sullen and shamed. Nevyn widened the focus, made his mind walk through the barracks door, and saw armed men on guard outside. So Rhodry had been captured while riding in some war or other. Jill was out on the road alone.

Nevyn swore so vilely that he nearly lost the vision, but he recaptured it and sent his mind back to Jill. What counted now was where she was. Using her camp as a starting point, he enlarged the vision and circled round in ever-widening sweeps until he saw enough to know that she was in the central part of Yr Auddglyn. He broke the vision and resumed his restless pacing while he made plans. He had to travel fast. He would buy a second horse, he decided, because he could make more miles a day if he switched his weight between two mounts.

"I've got to reach her in time," he said aloud. "And by every god I swear I will, even if I have to founder every horse I get my hands on."

Yet his fear swelled, because the dark master behind the theft had to be closer to her than he was. He went back to the brazier and took up a watch over her through the fire.

The mirror lay on a cloth of black velvet, embroidered with reversed pentagrams, that evil symbol of those who would tear down the very order of nature. Two candles stood to either side, their light caught and focused in the center of the curved surface. Alastyr knelt over it, bracing himself with his hands and wishing that he had a proper table. Since he had never actually seen the Great Stone of the West, he couldn't scry for it in the normal, easy manner. He took a deep breath and called on the evil names of the Lords of Husks and Rinds. At the names, he felt spirits gather, but just beyond his mental reach.

"Show me the stone," he hissed.

In the center of the mirror, shadowy shapes came and went, but nothing resolved itself into a clear image. No matter how hard he cursed the spirits, they fled from him, as they'd been doing all day.

"We need blood," Alastyr said, looking up.

Sarcyn smiled and went to the corner of the kitchen, where Camdel sat crouched in terror. When Sarcyn hauled him to his feet, he began to whimper, but the apprentice slapped him into silence.

"You're not going to die," Sarcyn said. "You might even like this. You're coming to see how well pain and pleasure blend, aren't you, little one?"

Slack-mouthed, the young lord half leaned against Sarcyn as the apprentice dragged him to the mirror-cloth. As Evy came up with the thin-bladed ritual knife, Sarcyn stood behind Camdel and began to fondle him. Chanting, Alastyr summoned those spirits that he had trained to do his will. Three black, twisted gnomes and a sprite with a huge mouth of blood-red teeth materialized in front of him.

Evy slashed the black of Camdel's hand. The lord moaned, but he leaned back into Sarcyn's embrace as the blood dripped down. The deformed Wildfolk clustered round, catching the drops on their tongues. Although they would get no nourishment from the blood itself, they were soaking up the raw magnetism that both the blood and Camdel's state of sexual arousal were exuding. Slowly the shallow wound staunched. The gnomes stretched clawed hands out to Alastyr.

"No more until you show me the stone. Then more."

The spirits dematerialized. Although Camdel was trembling, close to his climax, Sarcyn took his hand away.

"Later," he whispered in his pet's ear. "Later we'll work the ritual again. You'll end up liking that—in spite of yourself. I pleasured you good last night."

Camdel looked at him, his face torn between lust and loathing. Alastyr ignored them and knelt down by the mirror again.

"Show me the stone!"

In the light-struck mirror clouds formed, swirled, and turned slowly to darkness. Smiling, he leaned closer as the darkness resolved itself into solid shapes: hills under the night sky, a horse standing at tether near a tree. Pacing back and forth under the tree was a lad with a sword in hand. Not a lad—it was Jill, the warrior-lass who'd interfered with his plans of the year before.

"The stone," he whispered. "Where is the stone?"

The vision swooped down and focused on her saddlebags.

"Now, show me exactly where she is."

The vision flickered, then began to expand, to swoop out—and suddenly vanished in a blaze of white light. Half-blinded, Alastyr nearly fell forward onto the mirror as the Wildfolk appeared. From their terrified faces, he could guess that someone had banished them. A person with great dweomer-power was watching over that lass, then, and he could guess who that someone must be.

"The Master of the Aethyr," he whispered.

Nodding, the gnomes agreed with him, then disappeared. Alastyr sat back on his heels and considered simply giving up his quest for the stone. Yet he'd worked years, finding informants, laying his snares, then expending much power on ensorceling Camdel and keeping up the ensorcelment for weeks. He refused to run again, not until he had the stone in his hands. Besides, he'd seen Jill in the flesh last summer, when she and her famous father had been sitting in an Eldidd tavern. At the time, he'd thought that sight of her was merely a piece of luck, but now he was sure that the Lords of Husks and Rinds had guided him there. Since he'd seen her, he could scry her out normally, and Nevyn would have no way of detecting him. He looked up to find Sarcyn watching him.

"I've seen who's carrying it," he said. "And we should be able to kill her easily."

After a few hours of sleep, Jill woke in the morning feeling stiff and sore. The sun was already well over the horizon, and she felt an irrational dread at having lingered so long. At least Sunrise had finished his morning graze. She gave him a nosebag of oats, then ate her bread and cheese standing up. It was a beautiful sunny day, but she felt cold all over, as if she were about to take a fever. She packed up her few possessions in a hurry, and Sunrise had barely nibbled the last oat before they were on their way.

That morning her road took her away from the river. As she jogged along, the dark line of mountains that separated Yr Auddglyn from the province of Cwm Pecl loomed closer and closer, like clouds on the horizon. Toward noon, she was trotting through a small valley when she saw dust on the road ahead. As the dust resolved itself into six armed men, she loosened her sword in her scabbard, but when they met, the riders hailed her with a friendly wave.

"Hold a moment, lad," the leader said. "Are you riding a message from Lord Marclew by any chance?"

"I'm not, but I'm going to Lord Ynryc's dun, sure enough. That silver dagger he's holding for ransom is my man."

The riders leaned forward in their saddles and stared at her.

"And isn't that an evil Wyrd to fall upon such a pretty lass, to have a silver dagger for a husband!" the leader said, but with a pleasant smile. "Won't old Marclew ransom him for you?"

"Will Hell turn warm and grow flowers? I've come to haggle with your lord myself. Will you let me pass by?"

"Ah, we'll escort you back. You'll find our lord a cursed sight more generous than Marclew, but I'll warn you: he's short up for coin right now."

Although Jill stayed on her guard at first, the six of them treated her gallantly, commiserating with her on her difficult situation. The war had yet to reach the stage when men rape as casually as they kill. She had to admit to herself, too, that she was glad of this armed guard, even though she couldn't say why she was so sure that she needed one.

Ynryc's dun was another four miles on, perched at the crest

of a hill behind an ourter earthwork and an inner ring of stone. Inside loomed a massive stone broch, almost as wide as it was high, a thing Jill had never seen before, and the usual collection of huts and sheds. The cobbled ward was full of horses, tied up outside for want of enough stables. At the edge of the herd Jill saw Rhodry's blood-bay warhorse, tied up to one side as if a silver dagger's horse shared his shame.

One of Jill's impromptu guards, a stocky blond named Arddyr, took her into the great hall, which was as crowded as a town on market day. Among extra tables and piles of bedrolls, nearly two hundred warriors stood or sat, drinking ale and talking over the fighting to come. At the table of honor four men in the plaid brigga of the noble-born sat studying a parchment map. When Jill followed Arddyr over, a paunchy, grizzled lord turned their way.

"Lord Ynryc?" Arddyr said. "May this lady trouble you for a moment? Do you remember Rhodry the silver dagger? This is his wife, and Marclew's refusing to ransom him out for her."

"The old pig's turd!" Ynryc turned to another lord. "Well, Maryl, I've won our wager, and you owe me a silver piece."

"So I do. My faith that Marclew might have a scrap of honor left has just cost me dear. But here, lass, I've never heard of a silver dagger with a wife before."

"Doubtless I'm the only lass in the kingdom stupid enough to ride off with one, my lord, but he means the world to me. I don't have a Deverry regal, but I'll give you every copper I've got to have him back."

Ynryc hesitated, chewing on the edge of his mustache, then shrugged.

"A silver piece as a token," he said. "And naught more."

"If I were a bard, my lord, I'd praise your name for this."

In some five minutes, Arddyr led in Rhodry, who was carrying his saddlebags slung over one shoulder and his bedroll tucked under his arm. He dropped his gear on the floor and knelt at the lord's feet. When Jill handed over the token silver, Ynryc gave Rhodry back his sword and bade him rise.

"You're a lucky man to have a brave woman like this," Ynryc said. "Promise me you'll never ride against me in this war."

"I swear it from the bottom of my heart," Rhodry said. "Do you think I'm stupid enough to ride for Marclew again?"

All the lords laughed aloud.

Since Ynryc was as generous as a lord should be, he let Jill and Rhodry eat among his servants that night and gave them shelter in his dun. After much searching through the crowded fort, a servant found them a place to sleep in a storage shed. Among strings of onions and barrels of ale Jill spread out their blankets while Rhodry held his sword up to the lantern-light and examined every inch of it.

"It's not nicked, is it?" she said.

"It's not, thanks be to the gods of war." He sheathed it and laid the sheath down beside him. "Oh my love, you're too good for a dishonored man like me."

"Horse dung."

Smiling, he put his hands on her shoulders, stroking her, drawing her close.

"I've never even thanked you properly for my ransom," he whispered. "Come lie down with me."

As soon as his mouth touched hers, Jill could think of nothing but him, but later, when she lay clasped in his arms, both of them half asleep, she felt fear ripple through her mind again. She was glad that they were safely inside a dun, with a small army around them.

"As far as I can tell," Alastyr said thoughtfully, "they're about a day and half's ride ahead of us. Now that we've got a horse for your pet, we should be able to push ourselves for speed."

"Just so, master," Sarcyn said. "Can you reach her mind and send some spell to muddle her?"

"It may come to that, but for now, I'd prefer not to. Nevyn could detect that, you see."

Sarcyn did see. Although he'd been left behind in Bardek the summer before to tend to the master's affairs there, he'd heard many a tale about the Master of the Aethyr and his vast powers.

"And here's Rhodry again," Alastyr went on thoughtfully. "I'll have many an interesting thing to tell the Old One when we see him."

If we live to see him, Sarcyn thought to himself. He felt all their careful plans coming apart, just as when a farmer loads too much in an old sack, and the cloth shreds away rather than simply rips. Yet he never would have dared voice such doubts to the master. Uneasily he looked around their camp, Camdel curled in a blanket like a small child, Evy sitting by the fire and staring into it. Although his brother had carefully arranged his face to show no feeling at all, Sarcyn knew him well enough to know that he too was frightened. Alastyr got up and stretched.

"Tell me somewhat, Sarcco," he said. "Do you ever have the feeling that someone's scrying us out?"

"I've had a thought that way, once or twice. Do you think it's the Master of the Aethyr?"

"I don't, because if he knew where we were, he'd be after us like a snake striking. But if it's not him, then . . ."

Sarcyn shuddered, finishing the thought in his mind: then it has to be the Hawks of the Brotherhood. Half-assassins, half-dweomer-apprentices, the Hawks served the ruling council of the dark dweomer and enforced its commands. Although the Brotherhood was too loosely organized to have a code in any real sense of the word, it did require a means of dealing with traitors.

"And why would they be watching us?" Sarcyn said.

"I failed last summer, didn't I?"

"But the Old One laid no fault upon you."

"That's true." Alastyr hesitated, sincerely puzzled. "Then, maybe it's some minion of Nevyn's?" Again the hesitation. "I'm going out into the darkness where I can meditate upon this."

As the master strode away, Evy looked up, watching him with numb eyes.

"Oh here, young brother," Sarcyn said. "We'll pull this chestnut out of the fire yet."

"Will we now?"

Sarcyn merely shrugged. Evy went back to staring into the fire.

"Are you scrying somewhat out?" Sarcyn said.

"I'm not. Just thinking. Wishing I'd never gotten involved with dweomer at all."

"What? With all the power it offers a man?"

"Oh truly, and it's worth the danger."

Yet Sarcyn knew that Evy was merely saying what he wanted to hear. He began brooding himself, wondering what he would do if Evy became so weak that the master ordered him killed.

He wasn't sure if he would obey or not.

"Well, I've sworn not to take a hire in this war," Rhodry said, yawning. "So which way shall we ride?"

"Oh, we could go east to Marcmwr," Jill said. "This time of
year there's always caravans going to Dun Hiraedd."

"Oh ye gods, I'm sick to my heart of stinking merchants and
their stinking mules! I wasn't raised to be a nursemaid to a pack of
common-born traders."

"Rhoddo, you've only guarded two caravans in your entire
life."

"Two were too many."

Jill put her hands on either side of his face and kissed him.
"If it's bloodshed you're after, there are bandits in those
mountains. That's why the caravans need guards."

When they left Ynryc's dun, they rode east, heading for
Marcmwr. The road climbed steadily through the hills, and they
let the horses walk slowly. As the land rose, the grassy pastureland gave way to stands of the scrubby, twisted pines peculiar to
this part of Deverry. As they rode through the dark, silent forest,
Jill suddenly remembered the arm bracelet in her saddlebags.

"Rhodry? A cursed strange thing happened when I was on
my way to Ynryc's."

As she told the tale, he grew troubled, agreeing with her that
somewhat strange was afoot since the horse gear had been left.

"Why didn't you tell Ynryc about this?" he said at last. "That
horse could have belonged to one of his allies."

"You're cursed right." She felt a shudder of cold down her
back. "Why didn't I? I . . . well . . . I just forgot."

Rhodry turned in the saddle to look at her.

"That's a peculiar sort of thing to just forget."

"I know." She shivered convulsively. "There's dweomer at
work here. Do you think I'm daft for saying that?"

"I only wish I could dismiss it so easily." He halted his horse.
"We'd best get back to Ynryc with this tale."

Jill agreed, but as she was turning her horse, the gray gnome
materialized in the road in front of her. The little creature was
frantic, rolling its eyes in fear and waving its hands at them to
stop.

"What's wrong?" Jill said. "Shouldn't we go back?"

It shook its head no so hard that it nearly fell over.

"What's all this?" Rhodry said. "Your gnome?"

"Just that, and he doesn't want us to go back. He's terrified,
Rhoddo."

The gnome vanished, then appeared again in Rhodry's lap.

It reached up and patted him imploringly on the cheek. Although he couldn't see it, he could feel the touch.

"Well, the Wildfolk saved my life once," he said. "If he thinks that there's danger behind us, I'll take his word for it."

The gnome grinned and patted his hand.

"Besides," Rhodry went on, "we can turn the thing over to the tieryn in Marcmwr."

Shaking his head no, the gnome pinched his arm.

"Do you want us to keep it?" Jill said.

Relieved, he smiled and nodded yes, then vanished. Jill and Rhodry sat on their horses for a moment and stared at each other in bewilderment.

"Here," Rhodry said finally. "Let me just get my mail shirt out of my saddlebags. I wish to the gods that you had one."

"I think we should buy me one in Marcmwr. Since Ynryc was so generous about your ransom, we've got the coin."

"We do, do we? And here you've been telling me that we barely have a coin to our name!"

"If you'd drunk it all away, I couldn't buy mail now."

"True enough. Ah, you must truly love me, if you'd actually spend silver to ransom me!"

She leaned over and gave him a hard cuff on the shoulder.

After Rhodry had armed, they rode out at a faster pace, both of them with sword in hand and shields ready at the saddle peak. The road snaked through the hills, always climbing. Rhodry kept looking back the way they'd come. His elven-touched eyesight was an ally, she knew, because he could see much farther than an ordinary man and would spot their enemies long before the enemies spotted them. Ahead the mountains loomed, black with pines and streaked here and there with sandstone outcrops like the knuckles of a giant fist. Every little valley or canyon that they came to seemed to hide an ambush, yet always they passed safely by.

Finally they climbed one last hill and looked down on a narrow plain, hemmed in by mountains to the east and hills to the west. Beside a river stood Marcmwr. About three hundred round houses clustered together in the middle of a large open space inside the high stone walls, as if they had shrunk together in fear, but in truth, the open land was simply pasturage for the horses and mules of the merchant caravans that passed through.

"I've never been so cursed glad to see a town in my life," Rhodry remarked.

"Me, either."

Yet she didn't feel entirely safe until they rode through the massive iron-bound gates with armed town guards standing nearby.

"They almost turned back, curse them!" Alastyr snarled.

"It's that gnome of hers, master," Sarcyn said. "I saw it warn them when I was scrying."

"Indeed? Then we'll do somewhat about that."

It occurred to Alastyr then that his feeling of being watched at times might simply come from the gnome or other Wildfolk spying upon him. It was time, then, to set an example and scare them away.

For two days Rhodry and Jill stayed in Marcmwr, in a crumbling inn by the north gate, the only one in this trade town full of inns that would sell shelter to a silver dagger. Since in a town that size there was no such thing as an armorer's shop, on the first day they rode to the dun of the local tieryn and haggled with his chamberlain for an old mail shirt for Jill. On the second, Rhodry worked the town in earnest, looking for a hire. Finally he found one in Seryl, who had contracted to take a caravan of weapons and luxury goods to Dun Hiraedd.

Dun Hiraedd was an odd sort of city and a new one, too, having been founded only eighty years before. Originally it had been given the splendid name of Privddun Ricaid, the "chief royal fort," but the first warband garrisoned there called it "Fort Homesick," and the name stuck. Existing by royal charters, its sole purpose was to provide a legal and military center for Cwm Pecl, which was slowly being colonized by Deverry's expanding population. In Jill and Rhodry's time, the far valley was still a lonely sort of place, and it never could have paid enough taxes to maintain a gwerbret if the King himself hadn't helped supply it. Every summer, royal agents hired men like Seryl to take caravans of goods to the gwerbret's city.

Since Seryl was spending the King's money rather than his own, he was generous about Rhodry's hire, offering him two silver pieces a week and making no quibble about feeding Jill and her horse as well.

"And I'll want you to round up four other lads," the merchant said. "A silver piece a week for them."

"Done, then. I shouldn't have any trouble finding guards in a town like this."

Rhodry went back to the inn with a heavy heart. He had some very good reasons for never wanting to see Dun Hiraedd again, but he was desperate for coin, because buying Jill's mail had left them with only a handful of coppers. The innkeep, a skinny fellow with greasy brown hair, was in fact waiting for him at the tavern door.

"Well?" he snapped.

When Rhodry handed him the silver piece he'd gotten as earnest money, the innkeep turned all smiles and went to fetch him a tankard of ale. The smokey half-round of the tavern room was crowded with young men who watched him pay off his bill with great interest. They were a tattered lot, unwashed, poorly dressed and cheaply armed. All over the kingdom one found men like them, looking for a place in a lord's warband, taking guard work while they did, all of them driven by the dream of battle glory that lies in the hearts of most Deverry men. Rhodry let them speculate for a little longer and sat down by Jill, who was nursing a tankard at a table where she could keep her back to the wall.

"You found one?" she said.

"I did. Guarding one of the royal caravans."

Distracted with some thought of her own, she merely nodded.

"Is somewhat wrong?" he said.

"I'm cursed worried about my gnome." She dropped her voice to a whisper. "He hasn't come to me since we hit this stinking town, and while you were gone, I tried to call him. He's always come to me before, but I couldn't raise him."

"Oh well, who knows what goes on in their little minds?"

"This is serious!" Her voice shook with worry.

"My apologies, then, but what possibly could have happened to him?"

"I don't know, but considering what we found?"

She meant, of course, that there was dweomer all around them. Rhodry patted her hand to reassure her, but he could think of nothing comforting to say.

Everywhere was redness, and he could not move. He hated it, and he raged, desperately trying to move, until at last he felt merely hopeless. Although he had no words, he could remember pictures and feelings, of sailing free in his true home, of others appearing, ugly ones, twisted and cruel, who caught him and dragged him down. He remembered terror and a man's voice chanting. Then there was only this redness, and he could not move. A picture of her face came to him. He was washed in terror and love, mingled to an ache. The only word he could say filled him: Jill, Jill, Jill.

On a hot airless morning the caravan assembled at the east gate. Jill kept Sunrise off to one side and watched as Seryl and Rhodry conferred about the line of march in the middle of a swirling, braying confusion. There were forty mules, laden with the King's bounty, and fifteen muleteers, armed with quarter staves, four guards with swords, and Seryl's young manservant, Namydd. Rhodry disposed his men along the caravan, told Jill to ride at the head with the merchant, then took the dangerous rear guard for himself. After Seryl offered a prayer to Nwdd, god of traders, they ambled off under the hot sun while the mules brayed in protest. Ahead the mountains rose dark, streaked with pale stone, and as jagged as a mouthful of fangs.

With the heat and the steep road, it took the caravan a full day to travel ten miles. Climbing steadily, the road twisted and snaked through the rocky hills and thick stands of twisted pines that offered a thousand good places to lay an ambush. When the caravan made camp for the night, Jill tagged along as Rhodry set three men on guard. Although she offered to stand a turn on the watch herself, he turned her down. He did, however, pick out three muleteers to augment the watch, but even though he had Seryl's authority behind him, the men turned as sullen as their mules.

"Listen, silver dagger," one said, "you're the one who's paid to stay awake, not us."

"You'll get plenty of sleep in the Otherlands if we're caught by bandits. Are you following my orders or not?"

"I'm not taking orders from scum like you."

Rhodry punched him in the stomach with his right fist and clipped him under the jaw with his left. Jill admired the way the muleteer folded in half and hit the ground like a sack of grain. Rhodry glanced around at the gawking circle of his fellows.

"Who's next to argue?"

They looked at the man on the ground, then at Rhodry.

"Well, now," a man piped up. "I'll take a turn on watch. When do you want us out there?"

After a peaceful night, the caravan moved out about two hours after dawn and began its slow climb to the dangerous Cwm Pecl pass, where more than one caravan had been slaughtered by bandits. Once they were through, the danger would lessen, because Blaen, Gwerbret Cwm Pecl, kept patrols of riders on his side of the mountains.

"Now, bandits don't usually attack royal caravans," Seryl told her as they rode, "because they know the gwerbret will be out in force to hunt them down. After all, it's his goods they'd be stealing."

Yet Seryl didn't truly look reassured by his own words. When, just at noon, they reached the pass, Jill decided that it lived up to its evil reputation. About ten miles long, it was a sheer-sided gap strewn with enormous boulders that forced the line into single file.

"It's going to be hard on the stock," Rhodry said. "But we're not stopping until we're through."

Even the mules seemed to smell danger in the air, because they kept walking fast without a single blow or curse from the muleteers. Rhodry kept moving up and down the line, speaking to each guard in turn. After a few miles in, the road began to widen, but still it twisted through piles of fallen rock. Every time Jill glanced at Seryl, he merely nodded her way, then returned to watching the road ahead. Finally Rhodry came up beside them.

"Get back in line, good merchant. I'll stay up here now."

"Expecting trouble, silver dagger?"

He nodded, looking up at the boulder-strewn cliff top far above them.

"I've ridden in enough wars to smell trouble coming," Rhodry said. "I smell it now."

With a moan, Seryl turned his horse out of line and headed back to a safer position. When Rhodry began unlacing his shield from his saddle peak, Jill did the same.

"Do I have any hope of convincing you to get back and stay out of this?" he said, pulling a javelin.

"None." Jill glanced back and saw that he'd positioned all the guards directly behind them. "After I killed Corbyn, I never wanted to ride to war again, but by Epona herself, I'll cursed well fight for my own life."

He gave her a tight smile, as if he'd been expecting no less from her. For another mile the road snaked on, growing slightly wider. The dust they were raising hung in the windless air like a banner to announce that they were coming. Jill felt a little coldness in the pit of her stomach. She knew what riding to battle meant. In her hand, her sword winked bright, the blade that her father had given her. Oh Da, she thought, it's a cursed good thing you taught me how to use it.

Then the road made a sharp turn, and Jill saw them, a pack of some twenty armed men, blocking the road about thirty feet ahead. Behind her the caravan turned into a shouting mob as the muleteers pulled the mules to a halt and tried to get through with their staves. With an automatic shout of his old war cry, "For Aberwyn!" Rhodry threw the javelin in his hand and drew his sword on the follow-round as the war dart arched up. Screaming, the bandits charged, but their leader's horse staggered to its knees and fell with Rhodry's javelin in its chest, rolling its rider under the hooves of his own men. Jill kicked Sunrise forward as Rhodry led his ragged handful of men out to meet the charge.

They were outnumbered, sure enough, but the pass was too narrow for the bandits to mob them with their superior strength. The enemy was poorly armed, too, mostly wearing tacked together bits of leather and splint, with only here and there a bit of chain. They had also never faced a berserker like Rhodry, who howled and yelped with laughter as he slashed into them. In utter silence Jill faced off with one man, slashed under his clumsy strike, and caught him full on his unarmored chest. Blood welled up through his shirt as he fell over his horse's neck. The horse beside him reared, trying to avoid the corpse, but her battle-trained Sunrise merely danced by and pressed on. As the rearing horse came down, Jill gave a good strike at its rider. She stabbed him in the side just next to the edge of his leather cuirass.

Suddenly she felt a hard blow on her back, turned by the mail, but it half knocked the breath out of her. She had gone in too far. Blindly she swung around and caught a second blow on her shield just barely in time. While Sunrise tried to turn in the pressing fray she slashed out, parrying more than striking. When

she heard Rhodry's demon laughter coming toward her, she
fought even harder, swinging this way and that in the saddle,
parrying every blow that came her way, while Sunrise dodged
and bobbed and bit viciously at the horses around him. The
laughter howled closer and closer, shrieking above the shouts
and the war cries; then the man at her flank went down, his neck
split by Rhodry's sword. He was through, and they fought side by
side, stabbing as they worked free of the pack. Suddenly a bandit
pulled free and fled down the pass away from Rhodry's god-
touched laughter. Screaming, another followed. With all the typical courage of their kind, the bandits broke, shoving and
joustling each other as they turned from the fight.

"Let them go!" Rhodry yelled. "Fighting behind!"

His laughter wailed again as they wheeled and charged back
to the caravan, where a few bandits had broken through the line.
Jill saw one of their young guards fighting desperately to keep
between Seryl and a hard-slashing bandit. Just as Sunrise carried
Jill up, the bandit killed the lad. With a howl of rage, Jill avenged
him with a stab in the back that knocked the swine off his horse.
As the other bandits tried to flee, Rhodry and the last two guards
were there to cut them down. Jill grabbed the reins of Seryl's
horse. His left arm was bleeding from a long slice, and he was
slumped over his saddle peak.

"I never thought I'd see the day when a lass would save my
life," he whispered. "But my thanks, silver dagger."

Calming the panicked mules was almost a harder fight than
the battle, but at last those of the muleteers left alive beat them
into some kind of order, a huddled, miserable herd in the middle
of the pass. Jill did what she could for the wounded while Rhodry
and the guards searched through the corpses for anyone left
alive. Their own men they brought to her, but the bandits they
killed, slitting their throats as calmly as the King's executioner.
Jill had just finished bandaging the last wounded muleteer when
they carried over Seryl's manservant. He'd fallen from his horse
and been trampled. Although he was still alive, he was splitting
up blood, and both his legs were broken.

"Ah ye gods!" Seryl groaned. "My poor Namydd."

The lad looked up with eyes that obviously didn't recognize
him.

"We can't move him," Seryl snapped. "It would kill him."

"He's going to die anyway," Jill said. "I'm sorry, good sir, but that's the hard truth of it."

Seryl groaned again and ran his hand through the lad's hair. Jill left him to his grief and went to join Rhodry, who was kneeling beside the last of the wounded bandits with his blood-dripping silver dagger in his hand. The lad, who couldn't have been more than fifteen, whimpered so piteously that Rhodry hesitated.

"Hold your hand," Jill said. "He's dying anyway."

When the lad turned his face away and wept, she knelt down beside him.

"I can staunch that wound and save you. Will you spill what you know if I do?"

"I will. Ah ye gods, it hurts so bad."

The cut on his groin was so deep that it took Jill a long time to staunch it. By then he was so weak that he could barely talk, but she did find out that he was new to the band, a runaway apprentice who'd stolen from his master, and that there were thirty-one bandits in all. Ten had been left behind to guard their camp, an ominous piece of news.

"They're bound to come back," Rhodry said. "They'll lick their wounds tonight, but on the morrow . . ."

"We killed twelve out of the thirty-one."

"True enough, but we've lost two swordsmen and six muleteers, too. Well, at least we know what we're facing. It's a good thing you decided to save that lad."

"It wasn't just that. It seemed like there was somewhat else he should have been able to tell us."

"What's this? More of your cursed dweomer?"

"Just that. Ah by every hell and its ice, I wish my gnome would come back. I swear he knows somewhat about all this."

Rhodry shuddered like a fly-stung horse. Jill looked up at the clifftops. She knew that they were being watched—she had never been so sure of anything in her life—but nothing moved among the silent, brooding mountains.

Just at sunset, Namydd died, coughing away his life from his crushed lungs. Jill said what words of comfort she could to the merchant, then wandered restlessly through the camp. The muleteers sat huddled together, unspeaking, exhausted, like frightened sheep waiting for the wolves to come finish them off. It's not far to the Cwm Pecl border, Jill thought, but it might as well be on the other side of the Southern Sea for all the speed this lot can make. Then she got the idea, reckless, utterly foolhardly, but the only chance they had. When she told Rhodry, he swore at her.

"Don't be a dolt!" he went on. "For all we know, the rest of the scum are camped along the pass. I'm not letting you ride off alone, and that's that!"

"Getting a message to one of Blaen's patrols is the only hope we have, and you're forgetting that I have Sunrise. Even if they saw me, by the time they saddled up and got down into the pass, they'd never catch a Western Hunter. I don't weigh that much, and even though he's tired from the fight, Sunrise has had a good afternoon's rest."

All the time she was saddling and bridling the gelding, Rhodry swore, argued, and threatened, but in the end, she got her way, simply because she was right about it being their only hope. The full moon was rising as she rode out, letting Sunrise pick his way among the boulders with his long, easy stride. She rode with her shield at the ready and her sword in her hand.

For a long time Rhodry stood on the edge of the camp and looked in the direction Jill had gone. Finally he wept, a brief scatter of tears for the danger that she was in, then went back. The men had built a little fire, but most of the muleteers were asleep already, drowning their terror the only way they could. The two guards, Lidyc and Abryn, rose when he walked up and looked at him in a blind hope that maybe this battle-wise silver dagger would save them yet.

"Get some sleep," Rhodry said. "I'll stand the first watch."

They nodded. Abryn started to speak, then merely shrugged. Rhodry got his shield and helm, then walked about a hundred yards down the pass. In the moonlight, he could see as clearly as if it were day, even the colors of things—part of the legacy of his elven blood. Guard duty was tedious at the best of times, and now, with his worry over Jill, the time crawled past. In the tricky shadows, it seemed that things moved. Rabbits, maybe, or ferrets? When he stared toward the movement, it would stop, but whatever it was, it was very small and doubtless no threat. Finally, when the moon's position showed that it was well past midnight, Lidyc came out.

"You should have woken me earlier."

"I don't get as tired as most men. When you come in to change the guard, tell Abryn to wake me well before dawn."

Lidyc smiled, as if he thought Rhodry was merely pushing himself to spare his men, but it was the simple truth that Rhodry could go long hours without sleep, another gift from his wild blood. As he walked back into camp, he passed the wounded bandit, who was moaning aloud. When he knelt down beside the lad, he decided that Jill's efforts to save him had been a waste of time. The bandit's face was flushed so scarlet that it was obvious that infection had set into the wound.

"Which silver dagger are you?" he whispered.

"Rhodry. Why?"

"Where's the lass?"

"Gone for help."

"Does she truly have the jewels?"

"The what?"

"The jewels. The ones the old man said she had. We were supposed to take her alive and get the jewels."

Rhodry grabbed him by the shoulders and shook him.

"Tell me the truth!" he snarled. "What old man?"

"The one who hired us." His words were slurred and faint. "I don't know his name. But he hired us to get the lass."

"What did he look like?"

When he didn't answer, Rhodry shook him again, but he'd passed out. With an oath, he got up and left him. It was too late to go after Jill now. He wept again, then went out to take the watch back from Lidyc. It would be hours before he would be able to sleep with this new fear preying upon him. He'd let her go alone, when she was the true prize the entire time.

By midnight Sunrise was tiring badly. Jill dismounted to spare him her weight and led him on, both of them stumbling weary. Although her back ached like fire from the weight of the mail, she decided against taking it off. All she could think of was sitting down to rest, but she knew that if she did, she would fall asleep. In another mile, she came to the highest point of the pass. Beside the road was a rough-cut stone pillar carved with a rearing stallion, the blazon of the gwerbrets of Cwm Pecl.

"The sight of that's as good as an hour's sleep. It can't be much farther now."

Sunrise snorted wearily, his head hanging. She leaned

against the pillar and let him rest for a few minutes. All at once, she knew that she was being watched, felt it as a cold shudder down her back. Sword in hand, she dropped the reins and took a few steps out into the road, then turned slowly in a circle, scanning the cliff tops. Nothing moved; there were no silhouettes of enemies against the moonlight. She grabbed the horse's reins and went on, walking faster with a second wind of fear.

The feeling grew until sweat ran down her back. She was being watched. Any moment now, just beyond that bend in the road, or just behind that cluster of rocks, was the ambush that meant her death. Yet another mile passed, and the ambush never came. The steep cliffs began to wear away, and the road grew wider, clearer, easier footing, a better place for an attack. Still those eyes followed them as she walked beside her horse and patted his sweaty neck, encouraging him with soft words.

Finally he stumbled and almost went down. She let him stand, head hanging almost to the road, and considered leaving him behind. Then she felt the watcher leave her. Dazed, she glanced around and saw, not a hundred yards away beside the road, a broch tower behind a low stone wall. It could only be one of Gwerbret Blaen's famous patrol stations, a small warband quartered close to the border and ready for trouble, an expense no other lord in Deverry cared to undergo. She threw back her head and laughed.

"Come along, old friend. We can make a few more yards."

Stumbling, Sunrise let her lead him up to the iron-bound gates, carved with the stallion blazon. She prayed that someone would hear her when she yelled, but she saw a wink of silver in the moonlight—a horn, chained to the gate ring. She grabbed it and blew, a long desperate note, while Sunrise tossed his head and snorted in triumph.

"Who goes?" a voice answered from inside.

"A silver dagger. There's bandits in the pass."

The gates creaked open, and a man from the night watch grabbed her arm and led her in to safety.

"We're just going to wait here?" Seryl said.

"It's for the best," Rhodry said. "We can fight with our backs to the cliff."

Nodding agreement, Seryl stared at him like a starving child stares at its father, sure against all reason that Da will find food even when all hope is lost. In the gray dawn light, they circled the camp while Rhodry fought with his grief. He was sure that Jill was dead. His own death he could face calmly, but not hers. His one comfort was knowing that soon he would have a chance to avenge her by taking a few of the bandits with him to the Otherlands. The camp was fortified as well as it could be. The mule packs were heaped up in a rough wall with the muleteers behind, their backs to the cliff, with the mules tethered nearby. Rhodry repeated his orders. After he and the other two swordsmen were killed fighting on horseback, the muleteers were to panic the stock and send the herd into the midst of the bandits. The confusion would probably bring a few down.

"And fight to the death," he finished up. "Because you won't get mercy."

Rhodry, Lidyc, and Abryn mounted, then sat on their horses in front of the improvised barricade. Although the lads were pale, they were holding steady, determined to die like men. Slowly the sun brightened; slowly the minutes crept by. Rhodry realized that he was impatient, wanting to get his dying over with and eager to join his beloved in the Otherlands. Finally they heard hoofbeats and the jingle of tack, the sound of many men riding hard toward them. With a flick of his sword, Rhodry led the others out to meet them. At a fast trot, the warband turned around the bend in the road, twenty men, mailed, mounted on good horses, and on their shields was the red and gold blazon of Cwm Pecl. Rhodry heard the camp behind him explode with cheers and hysterical laughter, but he said nothing, his heart too full to speak because he now knew his Jill was safe. The warband's captain trotted over to him.

"Well, silver dagger," he said with a grin. "Sounds like everyone's glad to see us."

"I've never seen a man I liked more on first meeting, truly. When did the other silver dagger reach you?"

"About an hour past midnight, and he's a tough lad, for all that he looks about fourteen. He was practically dropping where he stood, but he kept saying he wanted to ride back with us."

"He's like that, true enough." Rhodry was more than willing to let them go on thinking Jill a lad. "Did you bring a chirurgeon? We've got wounded men." He pulled off his helm and pushed his mail back from his face.

"We did, at that." Suddenly the captain stared at him. "Well, my lord, I mean."

"Ah by a pig's cock! So you've seen me before, have you?"

"Many a time, my lord."

"Never call me that again. My name's Rhodry and naught else."

The captain nodded in a silent sympathy that was infuriating. Rhodry turned his horse and led the warband back to camp, but as he was dismounting, the captain hurried over to hold his bridle for him.

"Stop it! I meant what I said."

"Well and good, then. Rhodry it is, and naught else."

"That's better. Here, how far is it to your patrol station? I'm going to have a word of praise for our young silver dagger."

"Just about five hours ride on a fresh horse, but the lad won't be there when we get back. I sent him down to Dun Hiraedd, you see, with a message asking for reinforcements. He said he'd leave at dawn."

Rhodry swore aloud. The captain was obviously still thinking of him as Lord Rhodry Maelwaedd, because he hurried to explain.

"I had to bring every man I had with me. These scum almost never attack the king's caravans, because they know we'll be out in force if they do, so somewhat cursed strange is afoot here."

Rhodry was hardly listening. Jill was out on the road alone, and she knew even less than he did about the danger stalking her.

"She just slipped out of my grasp," Sarcyn said. "I was only a mile behind when she reached the patrol station."

"I know," Alastyr said. "I was scrying you out."

"If you'd thought to scry her out earlier . . ."

There it was, a flash of his all-too-familiar arrogance, but Alastyr let it pass, because they were in too much danger to risk fighting among themselves. Although Evy and Sarcyn were both good swordsmen, there were nineteen angry bandits standing around them, and Alastyr could never ensorcel them all. The newly elected leader of the pack, an enormous red-haired man named Ganedd, strode over, his arms tightly crossed over his chest.

"You never told us that the lass could fight like a fiend from hell!"

"I warned you that she was battle skilled."

Ganedd snarled alarmingly. Alastyr pulled out the pouch he had ready for them.

"I said that you'd be well paid and I meant it. Here."

When Ganedd spilled the pouch into the palm of one hairy hand, his face brightened with a wide gap-toothed smile at the sight of a Deverry regal, twenty pieces of silver, and a square-cut ruby as big as his thumbnail.

"No hard feelings, then," he said, turning round. "Well and good, lads. We've got a jewel here that we can sell in Marcmw, and we'll live like kings for months."

As the bandits cheered, Alastyr and his apprentices mounted their horses and rode away, leading Camdel behind them. Although the bandits might try later to ambush men they now thought rich, Alastyr could use his dweomer to hide them from such an unpleasant occurence. As they rode, he felt like cursing in frustration. They'd come so close to getting the lass! He was sure that if he could take Jill alive, he would be able to trade her to Nevyn for a promise of safe passage out of Deverry—with the stone.

Although Jill wanted to wait at the patrol station for Rhodry, no silver dagger could refuse a direct order from a gwerbret's captain to take an important message to the gwerbret himself, not without getting flogged, at any rate. Since Sunrise was still tired, the groom gave her a sturdy black to start her journey. The captain had already given her an official token; as long as she was riding on his grace's business, any of Blaen's vassals would give her a fresh horse and a meal to speed the message on its way.

"Now listen," Jill said to the groom. "Sunrise had cursed well better be here when Rhodry arrives."

"And what do you think we are, horse thieves?"

"There's many a great lord who's 'traded' for a horse whose owner had no mind for a trade, and Sunrise is a cursed valuable animal."

"He is, but he's safe enough. I'll tell you somewhat, silver dagger. We men of Cwm Pecl hate horse thieves the worst of all the thieves in the world. A horse thief doesn't just get his hands cut off. He gets fifteen lashes and a public hanging."

"Splendid. Then I'll be on my way with a peaceful heart."

Jill left the patrol station at a fast pace, alternately walking and trotting until she was free of the mountains. On the easier slopes of the foothills, she could gallop every now and then. Just before noon, she came to the dun of a noble lord, got her meal and a fresh horse, and galloped on again. Quickly the hills fell away behind her, and she was in the rolling meadowlands of Cwm Pecl. Although much of the province was unfit for farming, it was perfect for stock. In the well-watered meadows among stands of white birches, she saw plenty of horse herds, grazing peacefully while mounted herdsmen kept watch, or white cows with rusty-red ears lying in the shade to chew their noontide cuds.

On the flatter land, she could keep up a gallop-trot pace, and she changed horses twice more. The city was a good fifty miles from the patrol station, a distance that only a speeded courier like herself could hope to cover in one day. By her third change, the sun was low in the sky, and the lord who was giving her the fresh horse remarked that gwerbret's courier was welcome to shelter the night. Jill considered, but one of her dweomer warnings cut through her like a knife. She had to go on, and as fast as possible.

"My thanks, my lord, but this message is truly urgent."

"No doubt you know best, then, silver dagger."

When she left, she rode out at a full gallop, and the dweomer-cold rode with her. Someone knew where she was, and that someone was following her to work her harm. After her broken night, she was half asleep in the saddle, but she kept rousing herself and pushing the horse hard. Whenever she passed anyone on the road, she would yell at them to clear the road in the gwerbret's name. With startled shouts they would move aside and let her by.

At last she crested a low hill and saw below her the gwerbret's city of Dun Hiraedd, spreading on either side of a river and surrounded with high stone walls. The river was glittering so brightly in the sunset that Jill could barely look at it with her exhausted eyes. Sunset. The town gates would be closing for the night. She kicked a burst of speed out of her horse and charged, dashing up to the gates just as they were swinging shut.

"A message for the gwerbret!" she yelled. "From the Cwm Pecl pass!"

The gates held open. As a guard ran out to meet her, she swung down and presented the token with a flourish.

"Well and good, silver dagger," he said, taking it. "I'll take you up to the dun straightaway."

As the gates swung shut behind them, Jill felt a relief so strong that she knew it had to be dweomer-inspired. Here, for a little while, she was safe.

The city guard led her quickly through the maze of cobbled streets and close-packed round houses. Windows shone with lantern light; people were hurrying home after a day's trade; here and there a scent of cooking drifted from a house and made Jill's stomach growl. At the far side of town was a low artificial hill, ringed with stone walls. There were more gates, more guards, but the token brought them into the ward of Blaen's enormous dun, where a triple broch towered over sheds and stables. After a page took Jill's horse, the city guard led her inside the great hall.

The room was bright with firelight and candles. Jill stood blinking by the door while the guard went to speak to the gwerbret. Down at one hearth, servants were putting out the evening meal for a warband of a hundred men at long tables. Near the honor hearth, the gwerbret was dining alone. As she looked at the elegant stonework, the fine tapestries, the silver goblets and candalabra on the tables, Jill felt profoundly embarrassed. Why hadn't the stupid patrol sent the message to the gwerbret's captain, instead of making her barge in like this on a great lord at his dinner? A dirty silver dagger like her should have been waiting outside in the ward.

Blaen himself was hardly reassuring. When the guard spoke to him, he rose, tossing his head arrogantly and standing with a proud set to his shoulders. He was far younger than she'd expected, about two-and-twenty, and he reminded her strikingly of Rhodry, with dark blue eyes and raven-dark hair, although, of course, he was nowhere as good-looking as her man.

"Come here, silver dagger," he snapped. "What's this message?"

Jill hurried over and started to kneel, but she was so saddle-weary that she lost her balance and nearly fell spraddled.

"Your pardon, Your Grace," she stammered. "I've been riding for two days and fought a battle before that."

"By the asses of the gods! Then get up off the cursed floor and have a chair. Page! Get some mead! Get a trencher! Move! This lad must be half starved."

Before the startled pages could intervene, Blaen grabbed her by the shoulders, helped her up, and sat her down in his chair. He shoved a goblet of mead into her hand, then perched on the edge of the table, his meal forgotten behind him.

"I'll wager I can guess," he said. "There's been trouble in the cursed pass again."

"Just that, Your Grace."

While Jill told the story, Blaen's captain came over to listen. He was a heavyset man in his thirties with a faded scar slashed across one cheek. When she finished, the gwerbret turned to him.

"Comyn, take fifty men and a change of horses and leave tonight. I—here, wait a moment." Blaen grabbed a slice of roast beef from a golden platter and tossed it to Jill. "Help yourself to bread, lad. Now listen, Comyn. Chase these whoreson bandits into Yr Auddglyn. If Gwerbret Ygwimyr has the gall to complain about it, tell him it means war if we don't have their heads on pikes in a week or two."

"I will, Your Grace, and I'll send back a messenger the minute there's somewhat to report."

Jill went on eating as they worked out the details. When Comyn left to pick out his men, Blaen took his goblet of mead and gulped a good bit down as fast as if it were water. A waiting page stepped forward smoothly and refilled it.

"Looks like you've barely touched yours, lad," Blaen said. "What kind of a silver dagger are you to drink so slow? What's your name, by the way?"

"Gilyan, Your Grace, and I'm not a lad but a lass."

Blaen stared, then tossed back his head with a laugh.

"I must be growing old and blind," he remarked, still smiling. "So you are. What makes a lass take to the long road?"

"The man I love's a silver dagger, and I left my kin to follow him."

"Now that was stupid of you, but then, who knows what you women will do!" He dismissed the problem with a shrug. "Very well then, Gilyan. We can't have you sheltering out in the barracks, so I'll give you a chamber in the broch for the night."

Earlier that same day, the patrol of Cwm Pecl riders escorted what was left of Seryl's caravan back to the border station before they rode out again to go bandit-hunting. Rhodry helped carry Seryl to a bed in the barracks, saw to it that his guards and the muleteers were properly fed, then went out to the stables to make sure Sunrise was safe. The groom told him that Jill had indeed ridden out at dawn as a speeded courier.

"So she'd be reaching Dun Hiraedd about now." Rhodry glanced out the door at the sunset.

"Just that. Been in our city before, silver dagger?"

"Once or twice. Well, I'm going to get my dinner."

After he ate, Rhodry checked on the wounded bandit, who had been locked in a storage shed. The precaution turned out to be unnecessary, because the lad was dying. Not only was he too feverish to talk, but Rhodry could smell the stench of his septic wound even through the bandages. He gave the lad a drink of water, then sat back on his heels and considered him. Never in his life had he seen a bad wound spread so fast (and he'd ridden in many battles), almost as if the cut had been deliberately poisoned. Since bandits weren't known for eating like lords, no doubt the lad had been badly fed for some time and thus abnormally weak. Yet still, the foul humors should have spread more slowly, especially since Jill had put a proper bandage on the wound right after he'd gotten it. If someone had wanted to shut the lad's mouth, they couldn't have been luckier.

"And was it just luck?" Rhodry said aloud.

The dying lad moaned and gasped for breath in his fevered sleep. Although Rhodry'd been ready to slit his throat the day before, he felt a sudden pity for him.

Jill woke late in the morning and looked around blankly, unsure of what she was doing in this luxurious bed with embroidered hangings, until she finally remembered Blaen's hospitality of the night before. When she pushed the hangings aside, she found sunlight streaming through the windows and a page hovering uncertainly in the doorway.

"My . . . uh . . . lady?" the boy said. "The gwerbret requests your presence at the noon meal. Shall we fetch you a bath? There's just time."

"A bath would be splendid. Noon? Ye gods! Here, will His Grace's lady be at table? I don't even know her name."

"It's Canyffa, but she's visiting her brother for a while."

Jill thanked the gods for that. She hadn't been looking forward to having a noblewoman scrutinizing her table manners. After her bath, she got her other shirt, which was clean, out of her saddlebags, then decided she'd best change her socks, too. All at once she remembered the armband, which should have been wrapped up in her spare clothes. It was gone.

"By all the ice in all the hells! One of those cursed muleteers must have stolen it."

Irritably she hunted through both saddlebags, but the armband simply wasn't there. Down at the bottom of one, however, caught under the stitched flap, was something small and hard. She pulled it out to find a sapphire finger ring, a fine large stone set in a band of gold, with two tiny dragons curled around the setting. Jill stared at it in utter disbelief.

"How did you get into my gear? Did the Wildfolk steal the arm bracelet and leave you in its place?"

The sapphire gleamed softly in the sunlight. Jill felt an utter fool, talking to a ring as if it could understand her. She found a scrap of rag and wrapped it up carefully. There was no time to worry about it now, not with a gwerbret waiting for her.

It turned out that Blaen was extending her the honor of having her eat at his table because he was curious about her life on the long road. Since she knew that having people talk about his exile made Rhodry feel shamed, she did her best to say little about him while they talked, a job made easy when she mentioned that her father was Cullyn of Cerrmor.

"Is he now?" Blaen said with a grin. "Well, then, no wonder you can bear up on the long road so well. Here, Jill, I met your father once. I was just a little lad, six or seven, I think, and my father gave him a hire. I remember looking up at him and thinking that I'd never met a more frightening man."

"Da takes people that way, truly."

"But a splendid warrior he was. I don't quite remember how the thing worked out, but my father ended up giving him a beautiful scabbard, all trimmed with gold, as an extra reward beyond his hire. Now here, is he still among the living?"

From that point, Jill could fill the time with tales of her father's various deeds over the years. When the meal was over, Blaen gave her a careless handful of coins as her pay for riding the message.

"And when will this caravan of yours ride in, do you think?" the gwerbret said.

"Not for at least three more days, Your Grace. Some of the men were wounded."

"Ah. Well, when they do, have the caravan master come to me."

Jill collected her gear and carried it out of the dun into the busy streets of the city, which was the only settlement worthy of that name in the entire far valley. Under arches in the walls, the river flowed through town and divided it into a west side for the well off and the gwerbret himself, and an east for the ordinary townsfolk. The riverbanks themselves were a green commons, where some cows were grazing in the hot afternoon sun. Over by the east gate, Jill finally found an inn called the Running Fox that was desperate enough to take her custom. As soon as she was alone in her filthy, small chamber, she opened her saddlebags. The ring was still there, but now only one dragon coiled around the setting.

"I can't be going daft. You must be dweomer."

The stone glowed brightly for a moment, then dimmed to just the shine of an ordinary gem. Jill shuddered, then wrapped it up again, putting it into the pouch she wore around her neck, where all but a few coppers of her coin were stored. When she went down to the tavern room, she got herself a tankard of the darkest ale available to calm her nerves. Ye gods, here she was, in a strange town with a dweomer gem in her possession and Rhodry miles away! Nevyn, oh Nevyn, she thought, I wish to every god in the sky that you were here!

He's coming, a thought sounded in her mind. He'll come save us both.

Jill choked so hard on her ale that she coughed and sputtered into her tankard. The innkeep hurried over.

"There wasn't no fly in that, was there?" He pounded her on the back.

"There wasn't. My thanks."

With a sympathetic nod, he hurried away. That's the last feather off this hen! Jill thought. I've got to find out somewhat about this gem. Although there were bound to be several jewelers in a town this size, she had no intention of talking openly about a gem that could shapechange and send thoughts to peo-

ple's minds. There were, however, always other sources of information for a person who knew how to look for them.

The tavern room was crowded. At one table sat a gaggle of
blowsy young women who were eating breakfast porridge rather
late in the day; at another, a handful of aspiring caravan guards;
at a third, some young men who might have been apprentices to
shopkeepers. When the innkeep came to refill Jill's tankard, she
did a bit of deliberate bragging, praising Blaen's generosity and
saying she'd never been so well paid for riding a message. Of
course, she paid the man from the pouch she wore openly at her
belt, not the well-stuffed one around her neck. Then she went out
to walk around the streets.

The afternoon sunlight lay thick on the well-swept cobbled
streets. Prosperous tradesmen hurried by on business or strolled
along, gossiping idly. Women with market baskets or water buckets glanced at Jill's silver dagger and pointedly crossed the street
to avoid her. Jill turned down all the narrow alleys she could find
and strolled slowly, as if lost in thought. Finally, in an alley between a bakery and a cobbler's shop, her hunt brought game. As
three young men passed, one of them bumped into her. He made
a gracious apology and began to hurry on, but Jill swirled and
grabbed his wrist. Before he could squirm away, she slammed
him into the stone wall of the cobbler's shop and knocked the
breath out of him. His two friends ran for their freedom as the
thieves' code allowed them to do. Jill's catch, a skinny little fellow
with pale hair and a warty nose, stared up at her and gasped for
breath.

"My pardons, silver dagger, I never meant any insult."

"Insult? The Lord of Hell can take the insult. Give me back
my pouch."

The thief kicked and made a dart sideways, but Jill grabbed
and twisted him face-forward against the wall. While he whimpered and kicked, she got her hand inside his shirt and retrieved
her pouch of coppers, then took for good measure his wicked
little thieves' dagger out of its hidden sheath. When she hauled
him round to face her, he moaned and went limp in her hands.

"Now," Jill said. "If I take you to the gwerbret's men, they'll
cut your hands off in the marketplace."

The thief's face went dead-white.

"But if you tell me who's head man in this town, I'll let you
go."

"I can't! That would cost my life, not just my hands."

"Oh by the hells, what do you think I'm going to do? Run and tell the gwerbret? Listen, I've got money to give to your king. If you hadn't made a stupid try at robbing me, I'd have asked you nicely." She held out the dagger hilt first. "Here, have it back."

As he considered, the color came back to his face. Finally he took the proferred dagger.

"Ogwern," he said. "Down at the Red Dragon Inn, on the east side of the river near the commons. You can't miss it. It's right next to the candlemaker's."

Then he turned and ran, as fast as a startled deer in the forest. Jill strolled slowly after, letting him get back to Ogwern with news of her before she announced herself. She found that he was right about the candlemaker's shop: it was indeed hard to miss. Out in a sunny yard in front of a long shed were heaps of tallow, quietly stinking in the heat. Just across a narrow alley was a little wooden inn with balding thatch on the roof and unpainted warped shutters at the windows. Unlike most inns, its door was tightly shut. When Jill knocked, the door opened a bare inch to reveal a dark suspicious eye pressed to the crack.

"Who are you?" said a deep male voice.

"The silver dagger who was asking for Ogwern. He'll be cheating himself out of coin if he won't speak to me."

With a laugh the questioner swung the door open. He was enormously fat, his belly swelling out his shirt, his jowls hanging around his bull's throat.

"I like your gall. I'm Ogwern. Come in."

The half-round tavern room reeked of old straw and wood-smoke, and it sported four battered and unsteady tables. At Jill's insistence, they sat down where she could keep her back to the wall. An innkeep, as pale and skinny as Ogwern was fat, brought them tankards of surprisingly good ale, which Jill paid for.

"So then, fair lady," Ogwern said. "For fair you are, though truly, you can't be a lady if you know so much about the likes of us. What brings you to me?"

"A simple matter. Probably you know that I rode a message for his grace from the Cwm Pecl pass."

"Oh, I do hear what tidbits are worth knowing."

"Well and good, then. I rode into town on a horse belonging to one of the gwerbret's vassals, but my own mount is coming along behind with a caravan that I was guarding. He's a valuable horse, and I don't want him stolen. I was thinking that a bit of coin in the right place would keep him nice and safe."

"Naught could be simpler, and you have indeed come to the right place. What kind of horse is it?"

"A Western Hunter, a gelding, and he's gold."

"Battle-trained?"

"He is."

Ogwern considered, waggling one fat hand in the air.

"Well, if it was a stud, it would cost you a gold piece," he said at last. "But for a gelding, we'll say fifteen silvers."

"What? Ye gods! Highway robbery!"

"Kindly don't use such nasty terms. They trouble my fat but precious heart. Thirteen, then."

"Ten and not a copper more."

"Eleven. Let me remind you that there's a considerable market for such a valuable animal."

"Done, then. Eleven—six now, and five when we leave town safely."

"Ten if you hand it over now. I swear to you that my men take my orders. Fat I may be, but I rule Dun Hiraedd like a gwerbret."

"Well and good, and I'll stand you another tankard to seal the bargain."

While Jill paid over the protection money, Ogwern considered her with shrewd brown eyes.

"Let me give you a bit of a tip," he said, pocketing the coin. "Our cursed gwerbret's set up a squad of town wardens, a patrol of six at all times, prowling the streets with naught better to do than to stick their snotty noses into other men's affairs."

"By the black hairy ass of the Lord of Hell!" She feigned disgust. "And do they patrol at night?"

"They do. Revolting, I calls it. Ah, Blaen's father was a splendid man—easygoing, much distracted with war, and rather stupid. Blaen, alas, takes after his clever mother, and life has been grim since he inherited the rhan."

"A true pity, although I'll admit to being pleased that he does his best to wipe out bandits."

"True. Cursed louts, I hate them! I sincerely hope that you killed a few when they attacked that caravan of yours."

"Now here, you sound like one of the gwerbret's men."

"Kindly don't be rude." Ogwern laid a plump hand on the

mound of flesh approximately over his heart. "Bandits are blood-thirsty dolts, cluttering up the roads and forcing honest men to hire guards. Why, if it weren't for them, a true thief could go sneaking up on a caravan for a bit of real sport. Besides, they won't pay taxes to the guilds."

"Oho! So that's the true thorn in your side, is it?"

Ogwern snorted in feigned hurt, then went on studying her. Jill began to realize that there was something that he wanted out of her as much as she wanted something out of him.

"Just an idle wondering," he said at last. "I heard, of course, that the caravan was coming from Yr Auddglyn. I don't suppose you were in Marcmwr."

"I spent a couple of days there. Why?"

For a moment he frowned into his tankard.

"Well, here," he said at last. "I don't suppose a silver dagger would have any interest in stealing jewels."

Jill's heart thumped once in excitement.

"Not in the least," she said. "I know we're all cousins to thieves, but that's not the same as being a brother."

"Just so. I heard a bit of interesting news from down Deverry way, you see. A certain fellow was supposed to be riding up into Yr Auddglyn with a cursed large packet of stolen jewelry. He sounds like an utter dolt, by the way. Here he is, trying to pass himself off as a merchant, but his horse has a saddle and bridle fit for a gwerbret—a warrior's saddle at that."

Jill did her best to look only mildly interested. Ye gods, she thought, you've had a silver dagger's luck indeed.

"Now, if the stones are still in Yr Auddglyn," Ogwern went on, somewhat meditatively, "it's none of my affair. But some of the lads there were trying to find this so-called merchant, of course, to relieve him of the weight he was carrying. They tracked him to the Aver Lit, and by the hells, there he vanished."

"Aha, and so you're wondering if perhaps he's come into your territory. He must have been carrying some valuable things indeed if every thief in the kingdom was keeping track of him."

"Very valuable. They say the stones belonged to the King himself."

"Now here, how could anyone steal from the King?"

"A good question, silver dagger, a very good question indeed. I'm only repeating what I've heard. But one of these gems is a ruby as big as your thumbnail. Do you know what a gem like that would be worth? And then there's supposed to be an opal the size of a walnut. Now, usually an opal's not worth as much as other gems, but one that size is rare enough to cost a fortune."

"No doubt. I did hear someone talking about a sapphire ring when I was in Marcmwr. Do you think it's part of this same hoard?"

"Could well be." Ogwern's eyes gleamed bright from folds of flesh. "What did you hear?"

"That it was supposed to be cursed." Jill was thinking fast, trying to put talk of dweomer-stones into terms he could understand. "It would send thoughts to your mind, they said, and its gleam came and went strangely. Probably naught but horse dung."

"Now listen, never mock cursed gems. I've handled many a stone in my fat but precious life, and you'd be surprised at the kind of power some of them have. A truly fine gem has a life of its own. Why do you think men covet them so much?" He paused, drumming his fingertips on the table. "A cursed gem, huh? That might explain somewhat. One or two of the lads did make a try on this fellow, but they both came to bad ends doing it. One fell to his death from a high window, trying to climb in, just like someone pushed him, said his partner. I don't know what happened to the other."

The thought in her mind sounded again: the bad Wildfolk tripped him and sent him into a river.

"Is somewhat wrong?" Ogwern said sharply. "You look pale."

"Oh, naught, naught. I'm still tired from my long ride."

By then the tavern room was filling up. A few at a time, nondescript young men slipped in the door, got tankards of ale, and stood together quietly in the shadows. At the hearth, the skinny innkeep slipped roast chickens off of a spit.

"Stay and have dinner," Ogwern said to Jill. "The food here is a cursed sight better than at the Running Fox. The kitchen lass there has been known to pick her nose while stirring the stew."

The food was indeed a good bit better than Jill would have guessed. The innkeep brought her a trencher with a half a bird and some fresh bread, and one for Ogwern with a whole fowl and a loaf. While they ate, one thief or another came up to say a few words to Ogwern or to hand him a few coins. Finally the warty young man whom Jill had caught slipped in. Ogwern waved him over with an imperious flick of a chicken leg.

"This is Jill," he said to the thief. "And Jill, this is the Heron. I trust there's no ill will between you?"

"None on my part," Jill said.

"And none on mine." The Heron made her a small bow. "Here, since you've been over in Yr Auddglyn—"

"We've been discussing that," Ogwern broke in. "And she—"

Someone knocked loud and hard on the door. As the innkeep hurried over, some of the lads moved close to the windows. The innkeep peered out, then shook his head in a no. Everyone relaxed.

"It's not the wardens, you see," Ogwern whispered to Jill.

The innkeep stepped back, admitting a tall, broad-shouldered man in plain gray brigga and a sweat-stained shirt, pulled in by a heavy sword belt with an expensive-looking scabbard and sword. The easy, controlled way he moved told her that he knew how to swing his blade, too. When he strode over to Ogwern's table, the Heron hastily moved out of his way. Jill could understand his reaction. She'd never seen eyes like this blond stranger's before, ice blue, utterly cold, utterly driven, as if he'd looked on so many sickening things that there was naught left to him but to see the world with contempt. Hardly thinking, she laid her hand on her sword hilt. When the stranger caught the gesture, he smiled, a thin twitch of his lips.

"Er, good eve," Ogwern said. "I take it you wish to speak to me?"

"Perhaps. It depends on what this silver dagger has to say."

His voice was not particularly unpleasant, merely cold and dry, but Jill shivered when he turned to her.

"I don't believe we've met, good sir," she said.

"We haven't. But I understand you're carrying a stolen jewel. I'll pay you for it in gold."

Jill was aware of Ogwern watching in amused surprise, as if thinking she'd duped him earlier.

"You're wrong," Jill said. "I don't have any jewels for sale. What do you think I have?"

"An opal. A rather big opal. I know you thieves haggle, but I promise you I'll pay a good bit more than any midnight jeweler. It's in that pouch around your neck. Get it out."

"If I had this opal, I'd sell it to you." Jill felt another force put words into her mouth. "But the only piece of jewelry I have is a ring brooch."

The stranger's eyes narrowed in annoyance. Jill brought out the pouch, opened it, and took out—a ring brooch, just as she'd known would be there, a rather plain brass one, at that, set with glass for want of gems.

"Don't trifle with me, lass," the stranger snarled.

"I swear to you, this is the only piece of jewelry I own."

The stranger leaned onto the table and stared directly into her eyes. His glance pierced her in a way that reminded her of Nevyn, as if he were boring into her very soul.

"Is that truly the only piece of jewelry you own?"

"It is." She found it very hard to speak. "It's the only piece I have."

His eyes seemed to darken, and she felt then that he was trying to go even deeper into her soul. With a wrench of will she broke away, tossing her head and taking up her tankard, ready to heave it at him if he tried tricks on her again. The stranger set his hands on his hips and looked around, honestly baffled.

"Now what is all this?" Ogwern snapped. "Jill's telling you the truth."

"I know that, hog fat! Do you have the stone? Do you know where it is?"

"What stone?" Ogwern laid down his chicken leg and wiped his hands on his shirt. Jill saw the little gleam that meant he'd palmed his dagger. "Now here, you can't come blustering into an honest inn like this. Kindly state your business, and we'll see if we can help you."

The stranger hesitated, spitting Ogwern with his glance.

"Very well," he said at last. "I'm in the market for a particular opal, as big as a walnut but perfectly polished. Now don't try to tell me you haven't heard of it. These things spread around."

"So they do, and I won't lie to you. The last I heard it was in Yr Auddglyn. If it was anywhere in Cwm Pecl I'd know, and it's not. I wouldn't mind having a look at it myself."

Again he hesitated, glancing around him with those driven eyes. For all that he was keeping himself tightly under control, Jill could feel a trace of fear in him, feel it so clearly that she knew he'd attempted to make some kind of bond between them when he'd stared into her eyes. She felt as revolted as if she'd reached into a nest of spiders.

"Now listen you," he said to Ogwern. "It has to be on its way to Dun Hiraedd. When it comes through, you get your fat paws on it, and you sell it to me. I'll pay you well, but I'm the man who gets it, or you die. Do you understand?"

"My good sir! All I'd want from it would be the profit, and since that's what you offer me, you'll have it for sure. No need to threaten."

"You might well be approached by someone else. Understand? Sell it to anyone but me, and I'll cut you open and trim out some of that lard while you beg me to let you die."

The calm way he spoke made it clear the threat was no idle one. His jowls trembling in terror, Ogwern nodded agreement.

"I'll return every now and then to see if you have it. Save it for me. It should be soon."

The stranger contemptuously turned his back and stalked out, slamming the door behind him. The Heron tried to speak, but only gulped.

"By the hells," Ogwern whispered. "Did I truly see that?"

"I'm afraid you did," Jill said. "I hope he's not staying at the Running Fox. I don't want to go back only to find him in the tavern room."

"We'll find that out easily enough. Heron, take a couple of lads. Don't risk following the bastard; just ask around."

"Someone must have seen him," the Heron said. "I'll wager he stands out in a crowd."

With a couple of friends, the Heron left by the back window. Ogwern sighed and contemplated the remains of the fowl.

"I've quite lost my appetite," he said. "Do you fancy a bit of this, Jill?"

"None, my thanks. It's a marvel and a half if you're not hungry."

"Kindly don't be rude." He laid his hand over his injured heart and sheathed his dagger with the same gesture. "A man can only take so many insults. Lard? Hah!"

It was over an hour before a more than usually furtive Heron returned. His face was quite pale as he told Ogwern that search as they might, he and the lads had found no trace of the stranger.

"Are you daft?" Ogwern sputtered. "Dun Hiraedd's not all that big."

"I know, but he isn't here, and no one ever saw him come in or nothing. And here's the cursed strangest thing. We caught one glimpse of him, walking toward the city wall. Then he turned down an alley and just seemed to melt away somehow. Ogwern, I swear it! He just disappeared."

"Oh by the pink asses of the gods," Ogwern said feebly. "Let us pray that this jewel turns up soon so we can take his wretched gold and be done with him."

Soon after Jill went back to her inn. She walked quickly, keeping close to buildings and looking constantly around her, pausing at the door to make sure that the stranger wasn't waiting for her before she went inside. Once she was up in her chamber, she barred door and shutters alike from the inside. Although she slept with her sword beside her on the floor, nothing disturbed her but her dreams, which were full of severed heads, dark caves, and the eyes of the stranger, glaring at her.

Rhodry passed that same day in a fury of impatience. There was Jill, off alone and in danger, and here was he, honor bound to play nursemaid to a wounded merchant and his stinking mules. Since he'd given his word to Seryl that he'd escort them to the city, he saw no alternative but to stay with him until he was fit to ride. Toward noon, the wounded bandit died. Rhodry helped bury him just to have something to pass his time. Finally, about an hour before sunset, the patrol returned.

"We followed them toward Yr Auddglyn," the captain said. "I can't go over the border without authorization, so we'll have to wait until his grace gets a message to us."

"Then by every god in the Otherlands, I cursed well hope it gets here soon."

The message arrived more quickly than anyone expected. Just as the patrol was sitting down to dinner, Comyn led in fifty men with as many spare horses. In the confusion, it was easy for Rhodry to slip away. The last thing he wanted was for Comyn to recognize him. For want of a better hiding place, he went into the kitchen hut, where the frantic servants were too busy getting fifty unexpected meals to notice him standing in the curve of the wall by the hearth. The fire blazed up hot as a servant stuck a spitfull of pork chunks on to roast, and grease dripped down.

Rhodry watched the dancing flames and cursed his wretched Wyrd. Here he was, hiding from a man he respected and who once had honored him. The golden play of flames seemed to mock him as they flickered this way and that, flaring up only to die in an instant, just as a man's honor and glory could do. The glowing coals seemed to form pictures, as if in them he could see Aberwyn and his beloved Dun Cannobaen. As if he could see Nevyn. Rhodry suddenly felt a cold shiver down his back. He *could* see Nevyn, or rather a clear image of the old man's face, floating above the fire. Then a thought came to his mind, the sound of the old man's voice.

"You're not going daft, lad. I truly am talking to you. Think your answers back to me."

"I will, then. But what is all this?"

"No time now to explain. Our enemies might be able to overhear us. But you've got to get to Dun Hiraedd. Jill is in grave danger. Leave tomorrow at dawn."

"What? I'll leave tonight!"

"Don't!" Nevyn's image turned grim. "It's not safe for you to be on the road alone at night. Do you hear me? Wait for dawn, but ride!"

"Of course I will. Oh ye gods, she doesn't even have her gnome with her."

"What? What do you mean?"

"The little creature disappeared somewhere along our way. Jill was worried sick over it."

"As well she might be. I'll look into it."

Suddenly the image was gone. Rhodry looked up to find a servant glaring at him.

"Somewhat you need, silver dagger?" he snapped.

"Naught. I'll just get out of your way."

As he went outside, Rhodry was wrestling with his honor. For all that he'd given Seryl his sworn word, he knew that Jill was the one thing in the world that would make him break it.

Over the last few days, Nevyn had at times wondered why the gray gnome hadn't come to him, but he'd assumed that the faithful little creature was merely afraid to leave her side. Now he could guess that it had fallen afoul of the dark master. That night, he was camping by the road down in Yr Auddglyn, with a cheerful campfire burning for his scrying. In his heart he thanked the gods for the lucky chance that had made Rhodry stare into that other fire so far away. Although Rhodry had no true dweo-

mer talent, his elven blood made him highly susceptible to dweomer worked upon him from outside. For just that reason, Nevyn
was as worried about him as he was Jill.

Nevyn turned his mind firmly to the task at hand and laid his
worry aside for the moment. When he called upon the Wildfolk
who knew him, they appeared immediately, crowding round, an
obese yellow gnome, blue sprites, gray gnomes, green gnomes,
sylphs like crystal thickenings in the air, and salamanders leaping
up in the fire.

"Do you know your little gray brother who follows Jill
around the kingdom?"

They nodded, a vast rustle of tiny heads.

"And you know the bad man I'm chasing? Well, I'm afraid
he's gotten hold of your brother."

A faint sound of anguish swept over him.

"Try to find where he is, but stay very very far away from the
bad man. Do you hear me? Be very careful."

Suddenly they were gone, and the fire was only a normal fire
again. Nevyn turned his attention to it and thought of Jill. He saw
her easily, sitting in a filthy tavern next to an enormously fat man,
but try as he might, he couldn't get her attention, couldn't influence her enough to make her look toward the fire. He could feel,
however, how frightened she was, and her fear fed his own.
Finally he banished the vision and got up to pace restlessly back
and forth.

It was some time later that the Wildfolk returned, grinning
and dancing in triumph. Nevyn hastily counted heads to make
sure that they were all safe.

"I take it you found him."

Rubbing his stomach, the yellow gnome stepped forward
and nodded a yes. When he held up thumb and forefinger to
define something small and square, Nevyn could guess his meaning easily.

"The bad man bound him into a gem."

The gnome nodded agreement.

"Now for the hard part, my friends. I have to know where
the gem is. Does the bad man still have it?"

When the gnome indicated no, Nevyn sighed in relief. The
gnome pointed to a salamander's red face.

"It's a red gem."

It was, indeed. As the Wildfolk put on elaborate pantomines

and clever mimickings, Nevyn finally understood all that they had to tell him. The gnome's elemental spirit was bound into a ruby stolen from the King himself; the dark master had given it to a bandit with red hair; that bandit had taken it to a town to sell. Although the name of the town was difficult, finally a sprite rode on a gnome's shoulders while others indicated something big.

"Marcmwr! A big horse!"

In a swirl and dance, they spun around him, then disappeared. Feeling a little weary from all that guessing, Nevyn sat down by the fire. It was just like a dark master to bind a spirit into a gem and then give it to someone who knew naught of such matters, thus trapping the poor thing there for all eternity. Fortunately, he would reach Marcmwr by noon on the morrow.

"And then on to Cwm Pecl," he remarked to the fire. "It's a good thing that I know faster ways through those mountains than that wretched pass."

By staying in the stables, where he was sleeping, Rhodry managed to keep out of Comyn's way all evening. Once the captain and his weary men were settled in the barracks, Rhodry went back to the broch, where Seryl had been given a chamber on the second floor. The merchant was awake, staring blankly at the candlelight dancing in the room.

"Here, good sir," Rhodry said. "I've come to beg you a favor. I know I swore to stay with you, but one of the gwerbret's men brought me a message from Jill. She's in some kind of trouble down in the city."

"Then by all means you'd best ride tomorrow." With a sigh, Seryl raised himself up on one elbow and looked round the room. "Do you see that pouch lying on my cloak? Take the lot, silver dagger, and my thanks with it. I'd be dead if it weren't for you."

Although Rhodry's honor nagged at him, he took the heavy pouch of silver. He and Jill might need it soon. As he left the chamber, he realized that he'd lied to Seryl, the very first lie he'd ever told in his life. He was starting to think like a silver dagger, and such a black hiraedd swept over him that he nearly wept.

That night, he had trouble falling asleep. Since he was determined to reach Dun Hiraedd by sunset of the next day, he thought out his plan carefully. Not only was his own horse well rested, but he had Sunrise. By changing his weight back and forth between them, he could make good speed, and if the bay gelding tired too badly, he could trade it for another horse, perhaps, at some lord's dun.

Yet the next morning, Rhodry woke to the sound of rain. Although he left anyway, willing to ride wet for Jill's sake, he could no longer travel fast. As he slopped and sloshed his way down the muddy road, he cursed his luck and wondered if it were only bad luck. If someone had wanted to keep him from reaching town by sunset, they couldn't have found a better way.

"That should slow the cursed silver dagger down," Alastyr remarked, looking up from the fire. "The road's turned to muck, good and proper."

"Splendid, master. Then I should be able to catch him on the road a good long ways from town," Sarcyn said. "Are you sure that I shouldn't just kill him? I know he's the better swordsman, but I can ensorcel him and slow him down."

"I'm tempted to tell you to just go ahead and get him out of our way, but the Old One ordered me to leave him alive."

There was no arguing with that, of course. Sarcyn felt fear clutch his stomach with icy hands. Although he tried to keep up hope, every day that the stone eluded them was a day that brought them closer to failure, a failure that could mean their deaths, whether at the hands of the dweomer of light or of their own brotherhood, which never tolerated the weak and the failed for long. Alastyr looked haggard, as if he too were thinking such unpleasant thoughts.

"Well, Rhodry might well have the gem," the master said. "After all, they travel together; things get shifted from one piece of gear to another all the time. If only I could scry the cursed thing itself out! Now, we know that she had it at one time. The Wildfolk were definite on that. If Rhodry doesn't have it, I'll simply have to summon them again, but ye gods, with the Master of the Aethyr keeping watch, it's cursed dangerous."

"So it is. For all we know, the cursed gem fell out of her gear during that fight with the bandits."

"Just so. Well, go look up our fat thief first, and then get on the road after the silver dagger. If all else fails, I'll slip into town and try to ensorcel Jill myself. I'd forgotten that she must have dweomer talent."

"And a strong one, master. She brushed me aside like a fly."

Alastyr snarled and stared into the fire. Sarcyn saddled his

horse, told Evy to keep a good eye on Camdel, then left their
camp among the trees and rode out through a dweomer-induced
rain to Dun Hiraedd.

On Nevyn's side of the mountains, the weather held clear
and warm, and he reached Marcmwr well before noon. Since he
kept track of every smith in the kingdom who served the silver
daggers—and that sort of smith usually traded with thieves—he
knew exactly where to go, a rundown little shop on the east side
of town. Hanging just below the filthy thatch was a sign with a
faded picture of a silver goblet upon it. When he opened the
door, silver bells tinkled above him, and Gedryc came out to
greet him from an inner chamber. A skinny fellow with enormous hands, the silversmith was going quite badly bald.

"Well, if it isn't old Nevyn!" he said with a smile. "What
brings you to me, good herbman?"

"A matter of some stolen property you've received."

Gedryc went pale.

"Now, don't waste my time," Nevyn snapped. "I'm not
about to turn you over to the laws if you just give me the ruby."

"The square one as big as a thumbnail?"

"The very one. I figured it would pass through your hands."

"Right you are. Here, if I'd known it was yours, I wouldn't
have touched it."

"It's not mine, and anyway, I'm cursed glad you've got it.
Have you cut it yet?"

"I was going to this afternoon. Make it a little less recognizable, like, but it ached my heart to spoil a stone like that. You
know, I paid a cursed lot for it."

"I'll give you the price back. Just bring it out. Time's cursed
short."

Nevyn was traveling with coin scraped together by the dweomerfolk to buy back the King's gems as he found them. Although only the opal was dweomer, the rest, stolen to make
Camdel's crime look more credible, were valuable enough for
the King to promise a high reward to anyone who fetched them
back. Although Nevyn had no interest in a monetary reward, he
was hoping to gain a bit of direct influence with the King and
perhaps a win a post at court for one of the younger dweomermen, who could then root out the corruption that had al-

lowed this theft to happen. Yet the rest of the gems troubled him little. His true goal was protecting the Great Stone of the West.

When Gedryc returned, Nevyn gave him a gold regal, then cradled the enormous ruby in his palm. With his second sight, he saw a faint crystalline pattern of force lines, the bound spirit within.

"My thanks," Nevyn said. "And if any more spectacular gems come your way, save them for me whole. You'll get a good price."

"Gladly. Uh, I don't suppose you could tell me what all this is about?"

"You're quite right. I can't. Good day, good smith."

With the ruby clutched in his hand, Nevyn stalked out of the shop. Once outside, he paused beside his horses, gave a quick glance around, and saw that no one was nearby. He opened his hand and stared into the ruby. Unlike truly inanimate matter such as earth or leather, the crystalline structure of jewels gives them an extremely dim, extremely rudimentary consciousness, which can be influenced by a dweomer-master who's done the necessary long years of training. This influence is a subtle thing, a matter of making the gem vibrate to a certain feeling, normally, and then release that feeling back to a human mind, as when a dweomerman makes a talisman of courage, for instance. Those who are highly trained can make the gem vibrate in exact sympathy with a certain elemental spirit, to the result that the gem sucks the spirit up and traps it within. Releasing the spirit again is usually a difficult process, but to Nevyn, it was the work of a minute to persuade the gem to let its unwilling inhabitant go. He saw the lines of force in the ruby dim and wink out. All at once the gray gnome was clutching him by the legs and staring up, his face contorted with joy and gratitude.

"There you go, little brother," Nevyn whispered. "Now, never go near that bad man again. Get back to Jill. She misses you."

The gnome gave him one last hug and disappeared. Nevyn slipped the ruby into the pouch at his neck, then mounted his horse, caught the lead rope of the other, and rode out of town fast. Although he was low on food, he decided to wait to buy provisions, because he knew a place to get better than those Marcmwr offered.

As soon as he was well out of town, Nevyn left the main road and turned his horse's head north, directly into the foothills. For several hours he threaded his way along narrow tracks through the pines while the hills grew steeper and more rocky around him. At last he came to an outcropping of pale rock that towered over him in a sheer cliff some hundred feet high. At its base were enormous boulders, scattered as if by a giant hand. Nevyn dismounted and led his horses through them until he stood at the base of the cliff. Since it had been many years since last he'd passed this way, he studied the various ridges and furrows in the stone for some time until at last he found the right pattern and pressed it hard with the heel of his hand. Although he could hear nothing, he could imagine the enormous bell inside booming as it turned over. Then came a wait while he fretted impatiently. Finally he heard a scraping sound above and looked up to see a shutter of stone swing open, revealing a suspicious, bearded face.

"Tarko!" Nevyn hailed him. "I need to use your road, if your people will allow it."

"And when have we ever denied anything to the Master of the Aethyr? Stand back a bit, my lord, and I'll open the door."

Nevyn got the horses out of the way, and Tarko disappeared back inside. In a few minutes pebbles began to bounce down; rock dust plumed like smoke on the cliff face. With a grinding rasp, an enormous door into the mountain swung open. A lantern in his hand, Tarko beckoned Nevyn inside. He was tall for a dwarf, about five feet, and even more heavily muscled than most of his folk. His gray beard was neatly trimmed close to his chin.

"Haven't seen you in years, my lord," he remarked as Nevyn coaxed the nervous horses into the tunnel. "In fact, we haven't even been using this door much now that your folk are living so close by. You're lucky, truly. A party of the lads went out hunting, and so I was here to let 'em in again."

"You can't know how grateful I am that you were. I need to reach Dun Hiraedd in a hurry fit for the Lord of Hell."

"Well, the big road runs straight enough."

So it did. In just twenty-five miles, Nevyn would be free of the mountains, and the road would bring him out only thirty more from the town.

"These horses are going to be exhausted by the time I'm through," Nevyn remarked.

"Leave them with us and take a pair of ours."

"My thanks. Then I can ride all night tonight, too."

Nevyn mounted, and with a wave to Tarko set off, the hoof-beats echoing under the high arched vault of the tunnel, lined with perfect blocks of stone and lighted by carefully cultivated phosphorescent fungi and mosses. Soon he would come to one of the great caverns where airshafts let in sunlight, and there he could buy enough food to see him on his way.

Because of the drowsy sound of the rain on the roof, Jill slept late that morning. When she woke, she lay in bed for a while and debated going down to the tavern room. She was in for a terrible day, she knew, one spent in a boredom that was full of dangers, rather like marching to war. In her mind she could still see the driven eyes of the stranger, threatening her. Finally she got up and dressed. She was just buckling her sword belt when the gnome appeared.

"Thanks be to every god!"

When she threw open her arms, he rushed to her, leaping up to twine his skinny arms around her neck. She held him tight and rocked him like a baby while tears ran down her cheeks.

"You little beast, I've been so frightened! I was afraid some harm had befallen you."

He pulled back to look at her and shook his head in a solemn yes.

"Somewhat terrible did happen?"

He flung himself against her and shook in terror.

"My poor little creature! Thanks to the gods you're safe now. Here, how did you escape whatever the danger was?"

In an agony of concentration he looked away, obviously trying to figure out a way to show her.

Nevyn saved him, you dolt, said the voice in her mind, *who else?*

"Listen, you beastly gem! Don't you insult me! If it weren't for you, I wouldn't be in this pile of horse dung up to my neck."

I know, but I'm worth it.

"Bastard."

Well, if that's the way you're going to be, cursed if I'll tell you one jot more.

Jill was too pleased to have her gnome back to care if the dweomer-stone spoke or not. For a long time she sat on the floor with him in her lap and fussed over him. When he finally did disappear, it was slowly, as if he hated to leave but had to go: a bit at a time he faded, became transparent, then at last was a smudge in the air that turned to nothing.

Smiling to herself, she went down to the tavern room and got a bowl of suspiciously lumpy barley porridge. She was picking her way through it, looking for weevils, when the Heron came in. He strolled idly past her table, glanced at her as if he'd never seen her before, then whispered "To the Red Dragon" under his breath. Jill got her cloak from her chamber, then hurried through the drizzle to the inn, where she found a pale, sweating Ogwern sitting at his usual table. His vast paws were shaking so hard that he had to raise his tankard to his mouth with both hands.

"What's so wrong?" she said.

"You remember that fellow from last night? Well, he came back. He walks in here not an hour ago, as bold as brass and twice as solid, and sits himself down beside me without so much as a by-your-leave. If I don't find that opal for him, he says, he'll turn me into sausages! The gall!"

"Gall and twice gall. He must want this thing cursed bad if he'd risk contacting you in broad daylight."

"Oh, I doubt me that he's putting himself at any risk." Ogwern paused for a comforting gulp of ale. "Now here's the cursed strange part. I know it'll sound daft, but Jill, I swear it's true on my fat but precious self. When he left, I decided to follow him. It was easy enough, because the street was crowded, and he walked right along without even a look over his shoulder. So he strolls along, and I trail him from a good bit back. He goes right down to the commons by the river. Do you know that clump of birches by the bridge?"

"I do."

"Well, he walks into the trees and disappears. I mean, he truly disappeared! He walks into the trees, you see, and I wait. And wait and wait. I never see him come out, and birch thickets aren't dense like hazels or somewhat, you know. So finally I walk into the thicket, and he's not there."

"Now here! You're letting your nerves get out of hand. You must have just missed seeing him leave."

"Would I have the position I do if I couldn't even see a man in broad daylight? And don't tell me I'm getting old. That would be cursed rude."

Jill shuddered in cold fear. He has to be dweomer, she thought. She knew how dangerous dweomer could be in the hands of a madman; now she was faced with a man coldly using it for evil ends.

"I want to offer you a hire," Ogwern went on. "Guarding precious me. A dagger won't be much good against this fellow, and if I have a sword at my side, that sword had better be in someone else's hand if it's going to do me any good. A silver piece a night, silver dagger."

"I'm on, then. He might have eyes like the Lord of Hell, but I wager he bleeds like any other man."

"Let us profoundly hope that we don't have him bleeding all over my floor. Ugh! How I hate all these nasty threats."

A rainy sundown caught Rhodry a good twenty miles from Dun Hiraedd. Mindful of Nevyn's warning about traveling at night, he offered a farmer a couple of coppers for the right to sleep out in the cowbarn. For two coppers more, the farmer's wife threw in a bowl of good stew and a chunk of bread. Rhodry accepted them gratefully and ate with the family at a long plank table before the hearth. The gray straw on the floor smelled of pigs, and the farmers ate with dirty hands, saying not a word to each other or to Rhodry until the last crumb was washed down with watery ale, but much to his surprise, Rhodry was glad of their company. When he was finished eating, he lingered awhile, idly listening to the talk of the next day's hard work, staring into the fire while he both hoped for and feared another message from Nevyn. None came.

All at once the dogs leapt up from the straw and charged through the open door in a barking, snarling pack. The farmer glanced at Rhodry's sword.

"You're a good bit more welcome than I thought. Come outside with me, silver dagger?"

"Gladly."

The farmer grabbed a pitchy torch, shoved it briefly into the fire to light it, then hurried out with Rhodry right behind, his sword in hand. Down by the gate in the earthen wall, the dogs were barking furiously at a man standing outside. He was leading a horse, and Rhodry noticed that he was wearing a sword. When the farmer swore at the dogs, they stopped barking, but they snarled and growled with bared teeth at the stranger the entire time he reamined. No amount of kicks or curses could silence them.

"What's all this?" the farmer said.

"Naught that concerns you, my good man," the stranger said with an unpleasant smile. "I just want a word with this silver dagger."

Rhodry felt a little coldness in his stomach. How had this fellow known where he was? The stranger looked him over with a twisted intensity. All at once Rhodry realized that the fellow was sexually interested in him; he'd probably smiled like that himself at many a pretty lass. He was so revolted that he stepped back.

"I'm looking for a stolen gem," the stranger said. "I had a tip from someone in Marcmwr that you might be carrying it."

"I'm not a thief."

"Of course not, but if you've got this opal, I'll give you a gold piece for it. That's more than you can get from any midnight jeweler."

"I'm not carrying any gems."

The stranger leaned forward and stared him full in the face. For a moment, Rhodry felt as muddled as if he'd had too much mead.

"You're not carrying any gems?"

"I'm not."

With a brisk nod, the stranger stepped back and released him.

"So you're not," he said. "My thanks."

Before Rhodry could say another word, he mounted and rode away. The dogs snarled until he was well out of sight.

Sarcyn had found a big wooden shed, doubtless built for the various cowherders who wandered with their stock. Although it stank, it was dry and had a little hearth in one wall. He stabled his horse at one end, then built himself a fire. When he thought of Alastyr, the master's face appeared instantly. Apparently he'd been sticking close to his own fire and waiting for the news.

"He doesn't have it," Sarcyn thought to him.

"I was afraid of that." Even Alastyr's thoughts sounded weary. "Well, I'll have to force the spirits to scry it out. If the lass has it, I'll send Evy into town."

"Now, wait. He's not strong enough—"

"Don't you question what I do."

Alastyr's image vanished. Although Sarcyn tried for some

time, he couldn't summon him again. There was no use in trying
to reach Evy, because the master was doubtless having him assist
at the scrying ritual. He got up and walked to the door of the shed
to stare out at the falling rain. Of course, by all the principles of
the Dark Path, if Evy were weak enough to fail, he deserved to
pay whatever price his failure brought. Besides, having a weak
member in their little band was endangering all of them. Yet, in
spite of himself, he was remembering a rainy day in Cerrmor
long years past, when they were still living out on the streets. Evy
had a fever, and as he watched his brother tremble with cold, he
wept, thinking of their mother.

"I tried to take care of him, Mam," he whispered to the
falling rain in Cwm Pecl.

Then he cursed himself soundly for being such a weak-
hearted idiot that he would talk to himself. In something close to
rage, he turned back to the fire and stared into it, seeing nothing
but the flames, leaping and falling. Apparently Evy was still at
Alastyr's side and thus under his astral seals. All Sarcyn could do
was hope that the Great Stone of the West was lying in the mud of
the Cwm Pecl pass.

Jill and Ogwern stayed at the Red Dragon through the evening meal because Ogwern had to receive the various taxes and
dues owed him by the other thieves. While the guildmaster
worked his way through an entire joint of lamb, Jill picked at her
food and considered contacting the town wardens. Yet what
could she do? go running to the gwerbret with chatter about
cursed gems and evil dweomermen? Blaen would probably have
her arrested for public drunkenness if she tried.

After they ate, Jill and Ogwern fetched her gear from the
Running Fox, then went to Ogwern's lodgings, a pair of small
rooms over a tailor's shop. In one was a bed; in the other, a
wooden chest, a small table, and two benches. He told her that he
lived so cheaply to prevent the wardens from proving that he
had more income than his half-ownership of the Red Dragon
would allow. Jill spread her bedroll in front of the door and sat
down on the blankets, but Ogwern paced about, lighting tin
candle-lanterns, waddling over to the window to peer out the
crack between the shutters, then waddling back to the hearth
with heavy sighs.

"Oh come now," Jill said at last. "Do you think our nasty

friend is going to drop out of thin air into the middle of your bed?"

"It wouldn't surprise me in the least." Ogwern lowered his bulk to a bench with one last sigh. "I'm very upset. If I liked this sort of thing, I'd have been a silver dagger myself."

"It might have kept you leaner."

"Kindly don't be rude. A man can only take so many insults. Sausages, indeed! The gall of . . ." He paused, listening.

Someone was coming up the stairs with a heavy tread. Jill loosened her sword in her scabbard as she got up. Someone pounded on the door, paused, then pounded again.

"I know you're in there." It was a different voice than they'd been expecting. "Open this door, or I'll smash it off the hinges."

Although a real rage ran under the voice, it inspired no fear, merely annoyance. Jill and Ogwern exchanged a puzzled glance.

"Who are you?" Ogwern snapped. "What do you want?"

"Just to talk with you . . . on a matter of business." The voice changed, frightened now, pleading. "My brother's spoken to you before."

With a shrug, Ogwern unbarred the door and opened it a bare crack. Jill heard a grunt as their visitor smashed into it and shoved the vast thief out of his way, then slipped in and slammed the door behind him. His features were so familiar that he obviously was indeed the brother of the man who'd been seeking the opal, but his eyes lacked the hideous intensity of the other's. He glanced this way and that, manoeuvered carefully to keep his back to the wall, and the droop of his shoulders and dark shadows under his eyes testified to a soul-numbing weariness.

"There's been no sign of the opal," Ogwern said.

"I don't believe you." He turned to Jill. "You have to have it. It's been seen in your gear."

"Seen? Scrying, I'll wager you mean, but somewhat's gone wrong for you. You have enough dweomer to know that I'm speaking the truth when I tell you that the only jewelry I have is a ring brooch, and a cheap one at that."

"Gods, it doesn't make sense! You have to—my master—"

"Here!" Ogwern squeaked. "What are you two talking about? I don't understand a cursed word."

Ignoring him, the stranger took a step toward Jill, looked her straight in the eye, and tried to capture her will in such a clumsy attempt that she laughed at him. He snarled once, then snatched at his hilt. As his sword sprang clear, Jill drew, dropping to a fighting crouch.

"Ogwern! Call the town watch!"

Since she was between him and the door, the stranger hesitated, backing up a step to give himself room to manoeuvre. Ogwern ran to the window and threw open the shutters. At the sound, the stranger lunged at Jill, but she parried his first strike so easily that he gasped in surprise. She feinted in, drove him back to the wall, just as Ogwern began to scream "Help! Murder!" at the top of his lungs. Like a trapped animal, the stranger charged. He was no clumsy bandit, but her equal. Jill was fighting for her life, the steel ringing, blade on blade, as they danced and dodged around the tiny chamber.

Footsteps came pounding up the stairs, and a voice yelled "Open in the gwerbret's name!" The stranger made a desperate strike, but for one brief moment, he was distracted. Jill dodged in and cut him hard on the right shoulder, then swung back and up, catching his blade and sailing it out of his limp hand. With a yelp, the stranger threw himself back against the wall just as six wardens, tabarded in red and gold, threw open the door and shoved their way into the room.

"Ah by the gods, good Cinvan," Ogwern said. "Never has an honest citizen been gladder to see you than I am."

"Indeed?" The leader, a stout man with graying dark hair, allowed himself a contemptuous smile. "What is all this? Here, it's that cursed silver dagger who's a lass!"

"So I am, and I beg you, take us to the gwerbret straightaway."

"You needn't worry on that account," Cinvan said.

Panting for breath, the stranger leaned against the wall. He laid his left hand over the wound and pressed hard, trying to staunch the blood running down his arm. When he glanced Jill's way, his eyes were tortured by a dark ache far beyond the pain of his wound.

"Staunch that man's wound," Cinvan barked. "And disarm the silver dagger, too."

Jill handed over her sword and dagger to one warden while another started looking around Ogwern's chamber for a rag. The stranger never took his eyes from her face. All at once he smiled, as if he'd made some decision. He took his hand away from his

wound, dragged it across his shirt as if to wipe it, then raised it to
his mouth.

"Stop him!" Jill lunged forward.

Too late—he'd swallowed whatever poison it was. Rigid in a
half circle he fell back, slammed his head against the wall, then
twisted, still rigid as a strung bow, and fell to the floor. His heels
drummed on the wood; then he lay still, a trickle of bitter-smell-
ing gray foam running from his mouth.

"By all the gods!" Cinvan whispered.

Gouts of sweat running into his jowls, Ogwern lumbered
into the bedchamber. They all heard him retching into a chamber pot and let him be. The youngest warden looked as if he
wished he could do the same.

"Come along, lads," Cinvan said, a trifle too loudly. "Two of
you carry his body. We'll hustle our innkeep here along to see his
grace."

"By your leave!" Ogwern returned in trembling indignation.
"Is this how an honest citizen gets treated when he's nobly called
the gwerbret's wardens?"

"Hold your tongue," Jill hissed. "For your own sake, Ogwern, you'd best pray that his grace can come to the bottom of
this little matter."

Ogwern looked at her, shuddered, then nodded agreement.
Jill felt sick. What had he been afraid of, that he would smile
when he made up his mind to die?

It was a grisly little procession that filed into the torchlit
guardroom out behind Blaen's broch. While Cinvan went to
fetch the gwerbret, his men dumped the still-rigid corpse onto a
table and made Jill and Ogwern kneel nearby. In a few minutes
Blaen strolled in, a goblet of mead in hand. He glanced at the
corpse, had a good swallow of the drink, then listened thoughtfully while Cinvan made his report.

"Very well," Blaen said when he'd done. "Now, silver dagger, what were you doing in the midst of this?"

"Working a hire and naught else, Your Grace." Jill hesitated;
for all that she respected Blaen, as a silver dagger her loyalties lay
closer to the thieves' guild than to this living symbol of the laws.
"Ogwern told me that someone had been threatening his life,
and he offered me a silver piece to guard him."

"And why was he threatening you?" Blaen turned to Ogwern.

"Ah well, Your Grace." Ogwern wiped his sweaty face on his capacious sleeve. "You see, the original threats came from another man, not this one. I own part of the Red Dragon Inn, and this fellow swore I'd cheated him in the tavern room. So I hired Jill, and lo and behold, this perfect stranger . . ." He waved one hand at the corpse. ". . . came barging into my chambers saying he'd come to settle the matter of his brother's debt."

As well he might have been, Blaen looked puzzled by this ambiguous little tale.

"His brother?" the gwerbret said at last.

"Just that, Your Grace," Ogwern said. "I can only assume that this fellow was the brother of the man who swore I cheated him."

"Hah!" Cinvan snorted. "Robbed him, more like."

"My good sir!" Ogwern gave him a wounded look. "If he thought he'd been robbed, he would have come to you."

"True spoken," Blaen said. "Now here, you mean the man who had the complaint against you is still at large somewhere?"

"Just that, Your Grace, and truly, I still fear for my fat but precious self. I have witnesses to the threats, Your Grace, all most reliable."

Blaen considered, sipping the mead while he studied the bluish gray corpse. "Well," His Grace said finally. "There's no doubt that a fellow who carries poison in his shirt is up to no good. On the morrow we'll have a formal hearing on the matter in my chamber of justice. As for now, Ogwern, you may go. Cinvan, detail a warden to stand guard at his doorway all night. The malover will be about two hours after noon, so bring your witnesses with you."

"I will, Your Grace." Ogwern rose and made a surprisingly graceful bow. "I'm most humbly grateful that Your Grace provides so much safety for us honest poor folk of your city."

Ogwern walked backward, bowing all the way, out of the dreaded gwerbret's presence. Jill assumed that he would run all the way out of the dun. Blaen turned to Cinvan.

"Come now, Warden," he said. "Do you truly think that fat fellow is the king of Cwm Pecl thieves? I find it cursed hard to believe, myself."

"I know Your Grace has doubts, but I swear it, someday I'll catch him with enough evidence to convince a whole roomful of councillors."

"When you do, we'll cut his hands off, but not before. Now as for you, silver dagger, I don't want you sneaking out of town the moment the gates open. Cinvan, we'll take her under arrest."

"But Your Grace," Jill stammered, "he drew on me first."

"No doubt, but I want you at the malover to say that in person. Listen, lass, it's not like I'm charging you with murder or suchlike. He poisoned himself, after all. It's just that I know how little silver daggers think of the laws."

"As it pleases Your Grace, then, but meaning no offence, Your Grace, if I'm to be put on trial for somewhat, I have the right to have some of my kin at my side."

"On the morrow we'll have naught but a hearing, but you're right enough. If I think matters warrant full malover, then we'll wait until you summon any kinsman within a reasonable distance."

"I was thinking of my man, Your Grace. Rhodry should be here with that caravan soon enough."

"Rhodry?" Blaen gave her an oddly sharp look.

"That's his name, Your Grace, Rhodry Mael—I mean, Rhodry of Aberwyn."

Cinvan made an odd choking sound, but Blaen tossed back his head and laughed.

"You started to say Rhodry Maelwaedd, didn't you?" the gwerbret said. "By the gods, Jill, he's my cousin, my mother's sister's son."

"Then no wonder that he looks so much like you, Your Grace."

"Just that. All the great clans are as inbred as a herd of Bardek horses. Here, get up off that floor! A fine way I have of treating my cousin's wife! It's going to be cursed good to see Rhodry again. When I heard the news of his exile, I was furious, but Rhys was always a stiff-necked little bastard, and I know he'll never listen to me about his folly. Cinvan, find the lady a chair."

The only chair the guardroom could offer was a wooden stool, but Jill took it gratefully.

"Well, in truth, Your Grace," she said, "I'm neither a lady nor Rhodry's legal wife."

"He hasn't married you decently, has he? Well, I'll speak to him about that. Where's your gear? Cinvan, send one of your lads after it. Gilyan will be staying in the broch tonight."

After the warden was sent on his way, Cinvan got down to

the grim job of searching the corpse. Blaen studied Jill with a small paternal smile. Among the noble-born, a man's cousins were far more important to him than his brothers, who were rivals for land and influence. You've had a silver dagger's luck, Jill told herself, but I wonder what Rhodry's going to think of all this? Suddenly and profoundly she wished that he were there, so she could throw herself into his arms and forget about all this evil dweomer.

"Now here," Blaen said. "Since we're practically kin, tell me honestly. You know more about this fellow than you're willing to admit."

"Your Grace is going to think me daft, but I'll swear to you that he had dweomer. He came shoving himself into Ogwern's lodgings to cause trouble. When I tried to stop him, he looked in my eyes and cursed near ensorcled me. For a minute I could neither think nor move."

Behind them Cinvan swore aloud.

"Begging your pardon, Your Grace," he said. "Look at this."

The warden held up a medallion, dangling from a chain. It was a thin circle of lead, graved with a reversed pentagram, a Bardek word, and three strange sigils.

"It was around this bastard's neck. I doubt me if Gilyan's talk of witchcraft is as daft as it sounds."

In his scrying fire Alastyr watched Evy die, saw the corpse still drumming and twitching reflexively as the pale blue etheric double separated out and rose, floating over the dead matter below. Alastyr gasped for breath, his head swimming, and a hazy golden fog crackled in front of his eyes. He had to exert all his trained will to push that fog away and keep from fainting. He had been bound to Evy by a link between their auras, so that he could siphon off the apprentice's vitality at will to feed his own. The breaking of the link hit him like a sword thrust. Bound on the other side of the fire, Camdel stared terrified as Alastyr lay down on his back. Although he felt utterly drained, he knew he had to cauterize this wound.

When he shifted to the second sight, he could see his own aura, pulsing feebly, a reddish egg-shaped cloud, shot with fine black lines. From it dangled a broken line of light, flopping like a headless snake. He concentrated upon it, started to withdraw it into his aura, then thought of Camdel. With his sight still opened, he staggered to his feet and considered the cowering lord. Camdel's aura was pale and shrunken around him. To drain more vitality from him might kill him, and he was still a useful tool. Alastyr sat down, his head bent over his knees, and absorbed the line of light back into himself, then closed down the sight. He had to rest.

It was then that he felt Sarcyn's mind touch his, demanding that Alastyr contact him. The apprentice's rage was almost palpable, sweeping over him like a tide of fire. When Alastyr set personal seals around himself, the tide receded, then disappeared. He lay down again and fell asleep.

Sarcyn, of course, had also scryed out the events in Ogwern's chamber. When Alastyr refused to contact him, his rage drove him to grab a heavy stick of firewood and smash it against the wall. The whinney of his frightened horse brought him to his senses. By force of will he calmed his breathing and his mind with it. Since he was twenty miles away from Dun Hiraedd, there was naught more he could do for his brother. Although a better-trained dweomerman could have travelled there in the body of light, Sarcyn was only a beginner at that dangerous technique, and a river ran through town, too, a dangerous torrent of force on the etheric capable of tearing an unwise traveller apart.

There remained, however, revenge. Although he was tempted to simply ride away and leave Alastyr, he knew that he wasn't strong enough to seize Jill by himself. For a little longer, at least, he would have to put up with the master, until he'd glutted himself with vengeance. With a smile that would have been horrifying to see, he sat down by the fire again to scry her out. Twenty miles away or not, he had a few tricks at his disposal. Her very talent for the dweomer made her vulnerable.

Since Blaen insisted on treating Jill as if she were his beloved cousin's legal wife, his chamberlain gave her a large chamber with its own hearth, a lushly embroidered bed, and silver sconces set along the walls. After a page brought her hot wash water, she had a satisfying wash, set the bowl of dirty water outside for a page to take away, then barred the door from the inside. Since she had done very little all day, her brief sword fight had left her merely nervous, not tired. For a while she paced around, watching the flickering candlelight dance along the walls. The room, the broch, were utterly silent, but all at once she was certain that she wasn't alone.

No sound, not even that subtle difference in a room that means an extra body is soaking up sound—but she could feel someone watching her like a tangible presence. Feeling like an utter fool, she drew her silver dagger and prowled slowly around the chamber. She found not so much as a mouse in the corners and spun around to see nothing but candlelight and shadows. Yet something was there; she'd never been so sure of anything in her life, that someone was stalking her.

One cautious step at a time, she went over to the windows and threw open the shutters. No one was climbing up the smooth stone tower; far below, the dark ward was empty. When she glanced up, she could see the stars, the great spread of the Snowy Road far above her—light, but cold, indifferent to her or to any human being's plight. All at once, she felt despair, a black sorrow in her heart, as if nothing mattered, not her honor, not her life, not even her love for Rhodry, nothing, since all that human life could be was a little fleck of light against the all-embracing dark, like one of those pinprick stars, indifferent and cruel. She leaned on the windowsill and felt the despair spreading, leaching away her energy and will. Why fight? she thought. The night always wins; why fight it?

Far off on the horizon, beyond the sleeping city, the last quarter moon was rising, a pale glow against the black. Soon the moon too would slip into darkness and be gone. But she rises again, Jill thought, she rises full on her return. The moon was a promise in the sky, returning and growing into a great silver beacon, shedding her light on all, good men and evil alike, when her dark time was done. Only to fade yet once again, a thought whispered in her mind. Yet the thought came in some other voice, not hers. Only then did she realize that she was fighting, battling an enemy she couldn't see with weapons she'd never used.

The realization snapped the despair, sending it breaking the way a rope stretched too tight snaps. She spun around, her eyes searching the chamber. No one was there, yet she spoke aloud.

"By the Goddess herself, the light wins in the end!"

She was alone in the chamber. The presence was gone, but for all she knew, it would return to torment her, perhaps in her dreams, where she would be helpless against it. In a little flurry of tears, she sat down on the edge of the bed and pressed her shaking hands between her knees. None of her much-praised swordcraft would help in this battle. Only dweomer could fight dweomer, and she was untrained and weak. She saw then that denying her dweomer-power had left her helpless, that continuing to deny it meant that she would constantly be drawn into contact with strange things beyond her power to influence or control. It was then that she remembered Nevyn, and that he was on his way.

Many a time she had seen the old man contact other dweomer-masters through a scrying fire. For all she knew, only a master could do such a thing, not some ignorant like her, but she rose and walked slowly over to the candles, massed in their sconce. At this, her first conscious attempt to use dweomer, she first felt foolish, then embarrassed, and finally frightened, but she forced herself to stare into the flames and think of Nevyn. For a moment she was aware only of a blankness in her mind, then an odd sort of pressure, building against some unexplained thing, just as when a person temporarily forgets a name that he knows well and searches his mind in utter frustration at the lapse.

Her fear built, fear of using dweomer, fear of whoever was stalking her, built and built until all at once she remembered what she had somehow always known, that the fear was her key, that some strong feeling will break down the walls in the mind.

"Nevyn!" she cried out. "Help me!"

And there, dancing over the candle flames, she saw his face, a clear image, his bushy eyebrows raised in surprise, his eyes troubled.

"Thank every god you called to me," his voice sounded in her mind. "I've been trying to reach you for days."

He sounded so matter-of-fact that she giggled in near-hysteria.

"Try to be calm or you'll lose the vision," he thought to her, and sharply. "Think of it as a sword fight, child. You know how to concentrate your will."

She realized that she did, now that he'd pointed it out. It was much the same as the cold, deadly concentration she summoned when she watched an opponent move.

"I was scrying you earlier and saw that fellow poison himself," Nevyn went on. "No wonder you're so troubled. Now listen, our enemies seem to be cursed strong. Do you realize what they want?"

"That opal I'm carrying, or at least, I think I have the opal. The arrogant little bastard keeps shape changing on me."

He chuckled with such humor that she felt her fear vanish.

"It's the opal, sure enough, and I'll admit that the spirits who tend it can be irritating at times. The thing is a talisman of the noble virtues, you see, and they take the virtue of pride a bit too seriously. But here, has the shade of the dead man been troubling you?"

"I don't know. Someone was. I called to you because thoughts kept appearing in my mind, and I felt someone stalking me."

"Then it's not him. Don't worry. I'll set a seal over you. Go to sleep and rest, child. I'm almost to Dun Hiraedd."

His image vanished. Although Jill did indeed lie down, she kept the candles burning and her silver dagger beside her on the pillow. She was sure that she would never sleep, but suddenly she woke to a room full of sunlight. Outside in the corridor she heard a page whistling, and that simple human sound seemed the most beautiful music she'd ever heard. She got up and went to look out the window. Sunlight poured down on the men who strolled across, laughing and talking. It seemed impossible to believe in dweomer battles now. Yet she knew that she had summoned her will and spoken to Nevyn through the fire. With a shudder she left the window and hurried to get dressed. She wanted other people around her.

Once she was down in the great hall, the memory of her fear slunk to the edge of her mind. At their tables, the warband were eating breakfast and joking with one another, while servants hurried back and forth. Blaen himself was in a sunny mood, chatting with Jill as if he'd quite forgotten about poisoned strangers in his city. The high officials of his court, the chamberlain, the bard, the councillors and the scribes, came and went, stopping to bid their lord a good morning and bowing gravely to Jill. Blaen broke up a loaf of sweet nutbread and handed Jill a chunk with a courtly gesture. She was pleased to see that his grace was drinking ale, not mead, with his breakfast.

"Ah, it's going to be good to see my cousin again," the gwerbret said. "We had a lot of good times when we were lads. We were pages together in Dun Cantrae, you see, and the old gwerbret there was rather a stiff-necked sort, so we were always pulling one prank or another." He paused, looking up as a page hurried over. "What is it, lad?"

"There's the strangest old man outside, Your Grace. He says he's got to see you straightaway on a matter of the greatest urgency, but he looks like a beggar and he says his name is nobody."

"Nevyn, thanks be to every god!" Jill burst out.

"You know this fellow?" Blaen said with some surprise.

"I do, Your Grace, and for Rhodry's sake as well as mine, I'll beg you to speak to him."

"Done, then. Bring him in, lad, and remember to always be courteous to someone old, shabby or not."

As the page hurried away, Jill shuddered, feeling that the sunny, bustling hall had suddenly turned unreal. As if he'd picked up her mood, Blaen rose, watching the doorway with a small frown as Nevyn strode in, his tattered brown cloak thrown back from his shoulders and swirling behind him. He knelt to the gwerbret with an ease that many a young courtier would have envied.

"Forgive me for demanding your attention, Your Grace," Nevyn said. "But the matter's very urgent indeed."

"Any man's welcome to my justice upon demand. What troubles your heart, good sir?"

"That fellow who poisoned himself last night."

"Ye gods!" Blaen said, amazed. "Has the tale spread as fast as all that?"

"It has to those with the ears to hear it. Your Grace, I've come to spare you the expense of burying that fool. Does his lordship know where the corpse lies?"

"Here, is he kin to you?"

"Well, since every clan has its black sheep, you might say that he is."

Puzzled, the gwerbret glanced at Jill.

"Please, Your Grace?" she said. "Please do what he asks."

"Well and good, then. Can't be any harm in it."

Doubtless consumed by curiosity, Blaen escorted Nevyn and Jill out to the ward and hunted up a warden. It turned out that the corpse had been wrapped in a blanket and laid in a small shed usually used for storing firewood. Between them, Nevyn and Jill dragged it outside onto the cobbles. Nevyn knelt down beside it and pulled the blanket back to study the corpse's face.

"I don't recognize him," he said at last. "Which is a bad sign of sorts."

He sat back on his heels, rested his hands on his thighs, and looked at the corpse for a long time. From the slack way he sat and the drowsy look of his eyes, Jill suspected that he was in a trance. Every now and then his mouth moved soundlessly, as if he were speaking to someone. Finally he looked up with a toss of his head, and he seemed deeply sad as he got to his feet.

"A poor little fish, that one," he announced. "And caught in a net not of his making. Well, we'll send him to his rest."

Motioning Jill and Blaen back out of the way, he stood at the head of the corpse and raised his arms high as if he were praying to the sun. For a long while he merely stood, his face set in concentration; then slowly he lowered his hands, sweeping them down in a smooth arc until his fingertips pointed at the dead thing on the cobbles. Fire burst out in the corpse, an unnatural, ghastly fire, burning blue-silver in peaks and leaps. When Nevyn called out three incomprehensible words, the flames turned white hot and leapt high, too bright to look upon. With an oath, Blaen threw one arm over his face. Jill covered her eyes with both hands. She heard a tormented moan, a long sigh of terror, yet oddly enough, mingled with relief, just as when a wounded man knows that his death is near to free him from his pain.

"It is done!" Nevyn called out. "It is over!"

Jill looked up in time to see him stamp three times on the ground. Where the corpse had been lay only a handful of white ash. When Nevyn snapped his fingers, a little breeze sprang up and scattered it, then died down as abruptly as it had come.

"There," the old man said. "His soul is freed from his body and on its way to the Otherlands." He turned to the gwerbret. "There are strange things afoot in your rhan, Your Grace."

"No doubt," Blaen stammered. "By the black hairy ass of the Lord of Hell, what is all this?"

"Dweomer, of course. What did it look like?"

Blaen took a step back, his face pale, his mouth working. Nevyn gave him a gentle, patient smile of the sort mothers give to children who've stumbled onto something they're too young to understand.

"It's time that everyone in the kingdom learned the truth

about the dweomer," Nevyn said. "His Grace may congratulate himself on being one of the first. Would his lordship allow me and Jill to take our leave of you for a little while? I have an urgent matter to attend to in the city."

Blaen looked at the cobbles, still shimmering with heat, and shuddered.

"If my lord wishes." The gwerbret abruptly elevated Nevyn's rank. "I should be willing."

Nevyn caught Jill's arm through his and led her firmly away.

"I'm so cursed glad to see you," she said. "I've been so frightened."

"As well you might be. Now here, child, the danger's not over yet. You've got to understand that. Stay close to me and do exactly what I say."

Jill nearly wept in disappointment, because she'd been certain that once he arrived, she'd be safe.

"When I scryed, I saw you guarding Ogwern the thief," he went on. "Take me to him. If you had a bad time last night, I'll wager he did, too. Someone was tormenting you to get some revenge for Evy's death."

"Evy? How did you know his name?"

"He told me just now, of course. Since he'd been dead some time, he couldn't tell me much more, because his shade was already beginning to break up and weaken. So I just sent him on to his judgment, much as I would have liked to squeeze some more information out of him."

Jill felt herself turn rigid with fear at this talk of ghosts.

"Now, now," Nevyn said. "It's a perfectly ordinary thing, but it's not the right time to explain it all to you. Let's see what's happened to Ogwern."

When they arrived at the Red Dragon Inn, they found out that Nevyn was quite right to be concerned. The frightened innkeep told them that Ogwern had been taken ill the night before and that he was in his chambers. As they hurried over to the tailor's shop, Jill kept to the back alleys out of a natural suspicion of the gwerbret's wardens combined with a fear of Evy's brother. When she knocked on Ogwern's door, the Heron opened it.

"I heard Ogwern was ill," Jill said. "I brought an herbman we can trust."

"Thank every god in the Otherlands," he said with sincere

piety. "This has been horrible, it has. I never thought I'd be grateful to a cursed warden, but if His Grace hadn't set that great strong fellow at the door for a guard, Ogwern would have thrown himself out of a window, I swear it."

Nevyn nodded grimly, as if he'd been expecting just that. They went in to find Ogwern lying in bed with a frayed blue blanket pulled up around his massive neck. Although he was staring at the ceiling, he looked more terrified than ill.

"Last night was like being in the third hell," the Heron said. "We were having a tankard in the Red Dragon, and all at once he started shaking and raving."

"I don't want to hear of it." Ogwern pulled the covers over his head. "Leave a dying man in peace, all of you."

"You're not going to die," Nevyn snapped. "I'm an herbman, good sir, so pull the blanket down and tell me your symptoms."

The blanket receded until Ogwern's dark eyes peered over the edge.

"I'm going mad. Oh doom doom doom! I'd rather die than go mad, so brew me up some kindly poison, herbman."

"I'll do nothing of the sort. Stop ranting and tell me about these ravings."

"Well, I don't truly know what to say. All at once I was terrified, good sir, and I started shaking and sweating buckets. I knew I was doomed, you see, that I was going to die, no matter what I did." Ogwern let his voice trail off weakly. "I've never felt such terror in my life."

"And then he started screaming that it would be better to die fast than slow," the Heron broke in. "He grabbed his dagger, so we jumped him, and me and a couple of the lads got him here about the time the city warden shows up. After he tried to jump out the window, we tied him to the bed, but he went on raving and yelling about wanting to die."

"Ah, I begin to understand," Nevyn said. "Then at dawn, he was suddenly calm."

"Just that." Hope dawning, Ogwern sat up, revealing that he was fully dressed under the blankets. "It was so sudden that it was like a fever passing off."

"Exactly, but it wasn't a fever, but a poison. Now here, Ogwern, you must have an enemy in town who put a particular herb in your drink: *oleofurtiva tormenticula smargedinni.*" Nevyn rolled off this imposing name with a flourish. "Fortunately, your bulk saved you from a fatal dose. This poison unbalances the humors, giving the victory to the hot and moist over the cold and dry, which support the rational faculties. Then, as the body feels the poison work, the mind can't understand what's occurring and can't take rational steps to combat it, and thus the clever poison doubles its own effects."

"Ye gods!" Ogwern whispered. "Fiendish, good sir."

"You must guard yourself very carefully from now on. For the residual poison, eat only cool, dry foods for two weeks, cracker bread, apples, the white part of fowl, taken cold. This will cleanse the humors."

"I will, good herbman. Ye gods, what a close call!"

Since he wasn't dying after all, Ogwern got out of bed and insisted on giving Nevyn a silver piece for the consultation.

"It's a pity in a way that I'm not ill," he said gloomily. "Now I'll have to face the cursed gwerbret this afternoon. Now listen, Jill, say as little as possible. Stick to the tale about being only my bodyguard and leave the rest to me."

"We spent hours on this story," the Heron put in. "It's a beauty, it is."

When they left, Nevyn insisted on going to the temple of Bel down by the river, so that he could put Ogwern's stolen coin into the cauldron of donations for the poor. As they walked along, Jill kept nervously looking around, half expecting that enemies would spring out of the walls.

"Nevyn, how did Evy's brother get that poison into Ogwern's ale?"

"What? Oh here, I can lie as well as a silver dagger if you believed all that nonsense. I just made up the medical lore on the spot to ease Ogwern's mind. He needs to be on his guard, but I couldn't tell him the truth, because he wouldn't have believed it."

"You mean it's not a real poison?"

"It's not. The name's in the ancient Rhwman tongue, and it means emerald-colored little torment for fat thieves."

"Then what did happen?"

Nevyn glanced around at the riverbank. Down by the water's edge were a couple of boys, guarding the cows that grazed there. Otherwise they were alone on the commons.

"Evy's brother was working on Ogwern's mind the way he tried to work on yours," Nevyn said. "I doubt if he would have

driven you to suicide, because if he had, Blaen would have taken
your effects into custody, and then they wouldn't have had a
chance to get at the opal. But he did want to torment you, to
make you suffer. Since there's somewhat of a link between us, I
could set seals over you from a distance, but there was naught I
could do for our poor thief until I got here. I'll make sure he has a
peaceful night tonight."

Jill felt so ill that it must have shown on her face, because
Nevyn laid a steadying hand on her shoulder.

"Do you see why I glossed the matter over for Ogwern with
a babble of comforting words? Ah by the hells, child! Never did I
wish such evil things to come upon you. I've tried to leave you
alone to work out your Wyrd in your own way, but now your
Wyrd seems to have brought you to a strange thing indeed."

"So it seems. Was it truly my Wyrd that brought me here?"

"Let's put it this way. It was sheer chance that brought you
to that dead horse in the Auddglyn, but it was your Wyrd that
showed you the gem in the grass. If the Wildfolk didn't trust you,
you never would have seen it. Now let's get back to the dun. I'm
not going to say one word more out here in public."

It was about two hours after noon when Rhodry finally
reached the south gate of Dun Hiraedd. He dismounted, then led
his two horses through behind a small crowd of farmers, carrying
in produce and chickens to the daily market. Lounging just inside the gate were a pair of city guards. As he passed by, he
noticed one mutter something to the other; then they stepped
forward and blocked his way. Out of the shadow of the wall
stepped two more; one caught the horses' reins, the other his
sword arm.

"Silver dagger, are you? No trouble now, lad, but you're
coming with us."

"What in the hells is this?"

"His Grace's orders, that's what. Keep watch for a silver
dagger who looks like an Eldidd man and bring him along. We've
had enough trouble in town lately from your kind."

"And her a lass at that," said another guard. "Makes you
wonder what the kingdom's coming to."

"What's Jill done?"

"Oh, you know her, do you?" the first guard said with an
unpleasant grin. "She seems to have somewhat to do with a man

who got himself killed, that's what. His Grace should be holding malover right about now, so we'll take you right along."

Rhodry was too worried to protest when the guards disarmed him. As they marched him through the streets, he kept a sullen silence. He'd been hoping to avoid Blaen, who (or so he thought) doubtless despised him as a dishonored outcast, and now he was faced with the prospect of seeing him again only to beg for Jill's life. And what's Jill done? he thought, if I get her safely out of this, I'm going to beat her black-and-blue! In the ward of the dun, the guards turned his horses over to a page, then shoved him inside the broch. Rhodry hadn't been inside Dun Hiraedd for two years, when he'd come for Blaen's wedding. He looked around dazed at the great hall where once he'd dined as an honored guest; then the guards hustled him up the spiral staircase to the second floor. The heavy oak doors of the chamber of justice stood open, and he and the guards stepped just inside and waited.

In the curve of the wall, under a rank of windows, Blaen sat at a table with a scribe at his left hand and two councillors at his right. Since there were no priests in attendance, Rhodry could tell that this was merely some sort of hearing, not full malover. Kneeling on the floor in front of the gwerbret were Jill, a couple of unprepossessing young men, and an enormously fat fellow. Wardens stood around with quarter-staves in their hands. In the corner where the round stone wall met a wickerwork partition sat Nevyn in a half-round chair. Rhodry felt profoundly relieved, knowing that the old man would never let Jill come to harm.

"Very well, Ogwern," Blaen was saying. "I admit that the dead man's threats were sufficient for you to want a bodyguard."

"It was most horrible, Your Grace," the fat fellow said. "And a poor but honest innkeep like myself has no time to train with a blade."

"Even a porker should have tusks."

"His Grace is ever a quick man with his jests, but I'd rather hire tusks than grow them. Truly, the silver dagger was an excellent bargain, seeing as the nasty fellow actually drew on me."

Blaen nodded, then glanced at Jill.

"Well, silver dagger, I begin to think you were justified in drawing first blood."

"My thanks, Your Grace, and truly, I had no way knowing that the fellow was going to poison himself."

At that peculiar statement, Rhodry forgot himself enough to step forward. With an oath, the guards grabbed him and pulled him back. Blaen turned toward the interruption.

"Bring him forward. So, you caught this miserable lout of a silver dagger, did you?"

"Riding in the south gate as bold as brass, Your Grace," said a guard. "And he's got a Western Hunter with him that I'll wager is stolen."

"No doubt. He always was too fond of other people's horses."

Although Blaen was trying to suppress a grin, Rhodry caught him at it.

"Blaen, you bastard!" Rhodry snapped. "This is one of your cursed jests."

Although everyone in the room gasped at the insult, Blaen burst out laughing and rose, striding across the chamber to grab his cousin's hand.

"Well, so it is. I thought we'd have a laugh by arresting you like the silver dagger you are. Ah by the gods, it gladdens my heart to see you."

As they shook hands, Rhodry felt like weeping.

"It gladdens my heart to see you, too," he said. "But what are you doing with my woman?"

"Naught, I assure you. I've got more honor around women than some of my kin I could mention."

With a grin, Rhodry punched him on the shoulder. Everyone in the chamber was staring at them, and Blaen suddenly remembered that he had a judicial proceeding on hand.

"Go stand with old Nevyn, will you? Let's finish this cursed thing up."

When Rhodry did so, Nevyn gave him a thin, dry smile, but the old man's eyes were deeply troubled. He began to find out why when the warden stepped forward to give evidence about a stranger who took poison rather than face the gwerbret and who wore some sort of witchcraft talisman around his neck. Blaen considered the matter for a moment, announced that he found no fault with anyone over the death, then closed the hearing.

"Doubtless Dun Hiraedd is better off without him," he said cheerfully. "So that's that."

Ogwern and his witnesses rose, bowed to the gwerbret, then made a frank dash for the door. As the puzzled councillors gathered round Blaen to ask questions about this poisoning, Rhodry strode over to Jill and caught her by the shoulders.

"Ye gods, my love! What is all this?"

"I don't truly know. Rhoddo, you can't know how much it gladdens my heart to see you."

When he threw his arms around her and pulled her close, he felt her shaking with fear. Since he'd never seen her afraid of anything before, he felt a cold knot form in his stomach.

"Well, my love," he said. "We've ridden together in some hard battles before. We'll win this one, too."

"You cursed well better be right."

His back against a birch tree, Alastyr sat very quietly on the ground and tried not to panic. He had just tried to scry Jill out and had seen nothing at all, no matter how hard he bent his will to the task. It could only mean one thing: Nevyn was there to put a seal over her. When he heard hoofbeats coming his way, he jumped to his feet, half thinking that the Master of the Aethyr was riding for him, but it was only Sarcyn, dismounting near the camp, then leading his horse into the trees. Alastyr braced himself for a difficult scene, but his apprentice seemed perfectly in control of himself as he walked over.

"I know you're troubled over Evy's death," Alastyr said. "But I sent him in there as a test, and he failed it. That's the way of the warrior's path, lad."

"I know that, master." Sarcyn spoke mildly. "My fondness for him was only holding me back, anyway. You were right when you warned me that a man has to be utterly alone to gain true power."

"Oh." He felt himself relax. "Splendid. Then I'm glad you can finally see things so clearly. Now, how tired is your horse? If we're going to pull this chestnut out of the fire, we have to have some place to hole up for a while. We can't go on camping like brigands on the road. This morning I went out on the etheric and took a good look around the countryside, and I think me I've found the perfect place."

"Good. I can ride Evy's horse and just lead mine alone."

"Then switch over your tack. I'll saddle my horse myself. We've got to make all speed."

When Alastyr hurried away, Sarcyn stood for a moment and stared at his master's broad back. Well and good, so far, he told himself. The cursed old fool actually believes I've forgiven him.

No bard or gerthddyn had ever had a more attentive audience than Nevyn did that afternoon, and he couldn't resist playing up to it. In Blaen's private chamber, a plain little room that held a hearth, five chairs, Blaen's shield, and nothing more, Rhodry, Jill, and the gwerbret himself were sitting and watching him as he stood by the hearth and lounged against the mantle. After the inevitable mead had been served and the page sent away, Blaen gestured at him with his goblet.

"Here, good sorcerer," the gwerbret said, and firmly. "You owe me an explanation of this matter."

"So I do, Your Grace, and you shall have it. Jill, give me that bit of jewelry you've got in your pouch."

When she handed him a cheap ring brooch, he laid it on his palm and held it out for all to see, then thought a brief instruction to the spirits attached to it.

"This, Your Grace, is called the Great Stone of the West."

"That ugly thing?" Blaen sputtered.

At that precise moment, the stone shapechanged, glowing, wavering, seeming to dissolve. Suddenly an enormous opal, the size of a walnut, lay in Nevyn's hand. It was so beautifully polished that its surface gleamed, catching the light from the window and turning it to fire in its deep-running veins, while a rainbow of iridescence played upon it. When his audience gasped aloud, Nevyn could feel how smug its spirits were. They were a higher type of spirit than the Wildfolk, of the order commonly called planetary spirits, though their connection is not with the actual planets themselves, but rather with the forces the planets represent.

"Oh ye gods!" Jill said. "Is that what I've been carrying around?"

"This is its true form. There are spirits who guard it, you see. They can shapechange it when they have to, and also move it around, not far, but enough to hide it when there's danger. Our cursed enemies didn't realize those two things, and that's why we've managed to thwart them so far."

Nevyn let everyone chew over this information while he slipped the stone into the pouch at his neck. The spirits sighed in

relief, an audible sound in his thoughts, at being so close to him
again. Several times Blaen started to speak, then thought better
of it. Finally the dweomer-master nodded politely at him, giving
the gwerbret permission to speak in his own dun.

"And who, good sorcerer, are these enemies?"

"Men who follow the dark dweomer, of course. You'll notice,
Your Grace, that I keep saying 'our' enemies. You see, this gem
belongs to the High King himself, and the dark dweomer wanted
it to work him and the kingdom harm."

Blaen and Rhodry both swore aloud in rage. Though one was
the honored lord, and the other the dishonored exile, they'd both
sworn oaths of personal fealty to their liege. Nevyn was well
pleased to see that they honored their vow.

"The King lives in the middle of the best fortress in all
Deverry," Blaen snapped. "How could anyone steal from him?"

"With great difficulty. I suspect that they've been plotting
this for a very long time indeed. The opal is one of the greatest
dweomer-gems the world has ever seen. About a hundred years
ago, a certain dweomerman shaped it and asked spirits to inhabit
it, then gave it to the royal line." Nevyn sighed a little, just from
remembering the long hours it took him to polish and grind the
thing into a perfect sphere. "I'm forbidden to tell you all its
powers, as I'm sure you'll understand. To keep it safe, various
dweomermen are appointed as its guardians. When one of us
dies, another takes its place. It's now my turn to hold that post."
There, he almost slipped and said "my turn again." "The secret
of the gem is passed down from King to Marked Prince, and so
the kings know enough to guard it well. They keep it within their
own chambers, not the royal treasury. No thief would have a
chance to outright bribe the loyal men and women who have
access to the royal apartments, of course. There are, however,
more ways to work on a man's mind than gold. Here, Your Grace,
and Rhodry, too, did you ever meet a man named Camdel at
court?"

"I did," Blaen said. "The Master of the King's Bath, wasn't
he? A skinny sort of fellow as I remember, but the Queen seemed
to favor him for his well-spoken ways."

"He was an arrogant bastard," Rhodry broke in. "I won a
mock combat from him once, and he sulked all day."

"That's the man," Nevyn said. "He's the younger son of the
gwerbret of Blaeddbyr. I'm afraid his arrogance was only one of

his faults, but still, he doesn't deserve what's happened to him. The dark dweomermen have taken him over, mind and soul, and they've been using him like a farmer uses a mattock—to dig out a stone."

"What?" Blaen said. "I can't imagine Camdel stealing from his liege!"

"Of his own will he never would have, Your Grace. Now, I still don't know how the dark dweomermen got in touch with him. I have a friend who's up in Dun Deverry right now trying to find out. But once they did get a hold over him, Camdel had no control over his own actions, none. I'll wager that the last few months have all seemed like a dream to him, one long confused waking dream that ended in a nightmare."

"So," Blaen said, and there was a growl in his voice. "My sword and my warband are at your disposal, good sorcerer. Do you know where these men are?"

"I don't, and here, Your Grace, you see the limits of the dweomer. I can keep these poisonous dolts from scrying me out, but alas, they can do the same to me."

Blaen shuddered at all this talk of scrying and dweomer. Although Nevyn disliked telling so many secrets, he truly did have no choice. For all he knew, he might need to take Blaen up on his offer of the warband.

"Until this morning," Nevyn went on, "they couldn't have been more than a day's ride from Dun Hiraedd, but for all I know, they may be fleeing for their lives. If I catch them, I'm going to wipe them off the face of the earth for this."

"Well," Blaen said, thinking, "if we split the warband into squads, we can start scouring the countryside. Some farmer or suchlike must have noticed if peculiar strangers have been riding around the rhan."

"It may come to that, Your Grace, but I'd like to hold off for awhile. Because of Camdel, you see. If this dark master should scry out your men riding his way—and the dolt is bound to be keeping such a guard—then he'll just slit Camdel's throat and ride out fast. If I possibly can, I want to pull our young lordling out of this alive. I have a few more tricks at my disposal, too."

Blaen nodded gravely, taking this reassurance on trust. Nevyn himself was more worried than he wanted to show. Although he could ask the Wildfolk to find the dark master, to do so would expose them to the chance of grave harm. Likewise, he could go out into the etheric in the body of light, but to do so meant risking open battle with his enemies. From piecing together what Jill had told him, he could guess that this dark master had apprentices with him; he simply didn't know how many. If he should be slain in an astral battle, then Jill and Rhodry would be defenseless against the dark ones, who would doubtless take a horrifying revenge. Although he had called upon other dweomermen for aid, it was going to take days for the nearest one to reach him. By then, Camdel might well be dead.

"Ah well," Nevyn said at last. "This cursed mess is just like a game of Gwiddbwcl, Your Grace. They have Camdel—their king's peg—and are trying to move him off the board while we place our men and try to stop them. Unfortunately, I'm not sure if the next move is ours or theirs. Jill, come have a private talk with me. I want to hear every detail of the days you spent alone, and there's no need to bore His Grace and Rhodry with it."

Obediently she rose, looking at him in a desperate hope that he would keep her safe. Deep in his heart, he prayed that he could.

As the chamber door closed behind Jill and Nevyn, Blaen drained the rest of the mead in his goblet in one long swallow, and Rhodry had a good slug of his, too. For a moment they looked at each other in an understanding that had no need for words. Rhodry knew perfectly well that they were both terrified. At last Blaen sighed.

"You're filthy, silver dagger. Let's have the pages draw you a bath. I could use some more mead, too."

"You've had enough drink for an afternoon."

Briefly Blaen looked furious; then he shrugged.

"So I have. Let's go get you that bath."

While Rhodry bathed in the elegant chamber he would share with Jill, Blaen perched on the edge of the bed and handed him the soap like a page. As he splashed around in the wooden tub, Rhodry wished that he could wash all this talk of dweomer away as easily as the dirt from the road.

"Are you thinking that I've got cursed strange taste in women?" Rhodry said at last.

"You always did. But truly, Gilyan suits you well enough, and the life you're leading. Ah by the hells, it aches my heart to see that silver dagger in your belt."

"It's better than starving on the roads. There wasn't a cursed lot else I could do."

"True spoken. I talked with your most honored mother the last time I was at court. She asked me to urge Rhys to recall you, but he wouldn't listen to a cursed word I said."

"Don't waste your breath again. He always wanted me gone, and like a dolt, I gave him his chance."

Rhodry got out of the tub and took the towel Blaen handed him.

"I have no formal alliance with Aberwyn," Blaen said. "I can offer you a place here with me. You could marry your Jill and be my equerry or suchlike. If Rhys doesn't like it, what's he going to do? He's too cursed far away to start a war with me."

"My thanks, but when I took this dagger, I swore I'd carry it proudly. I may be an exile, but cursed if I'll be an oath-breaker, too."

Blaen raised one quizzical eyebrow.

"Ah by a pig's cock," Rhodry sighed. "The truth is, I think it'd be worse, living on your charity, watching the honored guests sneering at Aberwyn's dishonored brother. I'd rather ride the long road than that."

Blaen handed him his brigga.

"Well, I'd feel the same myself," he said. "But by the black hairy ass of the Lord of Hell, you're always welcome here."

Rhodry said nothing, out of fear that he'd weep and shame himself. While he dressed, Blaen pulled the silver dagger and fiddled with it, hefting it, testing the edge with his thumb.

"The cursed thing is sharp," he remarked.

"Dishonor or not, it's the best dagger I ever had. Cursed if I know how the smiths mix the metal for it, but it never tarnishes."

Blaen threw the dagger at the firewood stacked near the hearth, the blade whistling straight to the target and biting deep.

"A splendid blade, right enough. Well, everyone knows that the silver dagger brings shame with it, but I never knew it brought dweomer, too."

Although Rhodry knew he was only jesting, the thought struck something in his mind. It was odd, now that he considered it, that first the dweomer had brought him the silver dagger, and then, his first summer on the long road had taken him to the dweomer in return.

"Somewhat wrong?" Blaen said.

"Naught, truly."

And yet he felt his Wyrd call to him, a whistling on the wind.

Although Salamander had passed through Dun Deverry several times, he rarely stayed long, because a gerthddyn had too much competition in the busy streets of the capital. At that time, the city was a spiraled maze of streets stretching halfway around Loc Gwerconedd; the largest city in the kingdom, it sheltered nearly three hundred thousand people, all of whom demanded more sophisticated entertainment than a few tricks with scarves. In the many open parks and market squares tucked away all over the city, one found gerthddynion and acrobats, minstrels from Bardek, people with performing bears or trained pigs, jugglers and wandering bards, all earnestly trying to part the passersby from their coin. In this pack no one noticed another gerthddyn, even one who asked the occasional question about the opium trade.

Since he was trying to avoid undue attention, he had compromised his standards and was staying in a middling sort of inn in the old part of town along the Aver Lugh, a district of small craftsmen and respectable shopkeepers. The Wheatsheaf had another advantage, too, in that many of the wandering entertainers stayed there, and he could pick up all the gossip there was. Not that hearing gossip about Lord Camdel's crime was difficult; even though it was some weeks after the theft, the city was still buzzing over it.

"They say that the King's sent messengers to every gwerbret in the kingdom," Elic the innkeep remarked that afternoon. "What I want to know is this, how does one man slip through all those warbands and suchlike?"

"He might be dead," Salamander said. "Once the news got out, every thief in the kingdom was probably keeping an eye out for him."

"Now that's true spoken." Elic considered, sucking on the edge of his long mustaches. "He might be, at that."

There was one patron of the Wheatsheaf who kept pretty much to himself, for the simple reason that he was a Bardek man who spoke little Deverrian. Enopo was about twenty-five, quite dark of skin, and he wore no face paint, which meant that his family had kicked him out of their house and clan for some reason. He was wandering the Deverry roads with a wela-wela, a complex Bardekian instrument that lay flat in the performer's lap and had some thirty strings that were plucked and strummed with a quill. Since he knew Bardekian quite well, Salamander had been cultivating the minstrel, who was almost pathetically glad to find someone who knew his native tongue. At the end of their day of performing, they would meet back in the tavern room to compare their day's take and complain about the niggardliness of the folk in the richest city in the kingdom.

That particular day, Salamander had done remarkably well, and he stood them a flagon of fine Bardek wine. When they settled into a table by the wall to drink it, Enopo savored each sip.

"A fine vintage," he pronounced. "Ah, but it brings back bitter memories of home."

"So it must. Here, you don't have to answer if you don't want to, but—"

"I know." He flashed Salamander a grin. "Your storyteller's heart is aching with curiosity about my exile. Well, I don't care to go into all the details, but it had to do with a married woman, very high-born, who was far too beautiful for the ugly and old rich man she married."

"Ah. It's not an uncommon tale."

"Oh, no. Far from it." He sighed profoundly. "Ugly or not, her husband had great influence with the archons."

For a moment they drank in silence while Enopo gazed away as if he was remembering the beauty of his dangerous love. Salamander decided that if Enopo would tell him the reason for his exile, he now trusted the gerthddyn enough for Salamander to make his next move.

"You know, wine isn't the only fine thing Bardek produces," the gerthddyn casually remarked. "When I visited your lovely and refined homeland, I enjoyed a pipe or two of opium."

"Now look." The minstrel leaned forward earnestly. "You want to be very careful with the white smoke. I've seen men become so degraded over it that they've sold themselves into slavery just to ensure they got more."

"Really? Ye gods, I didn't know that! Will just a pipeful every now and then do that to a man?"

"Oh, no, but as I say, you've got to be very careful. It's like drink. Some men can drink or go dry; others turn into sots. But the white smoke has a stronger pull than any drink I've ever known."

Salamander pretended to be considering this carefully while Enopo watched with a slight smile.

"I know what you're thinking of asking me, gerthddyn," he said. "And I don't know anyone who has the stuff for sale."

"Well, if it's as dangerous as you say, it's doubtless for the best, but I was wondering."

"From what I understand, in fact, it's only the noble-born men in this city who use it."

"Indeed?" Salamander sat bolt upright. "Where did you hear that?"

"From a man of my people, a merchant, who came through here about . . . oh, a month ago, I guess it was. He looked me up for my father's sake, just to see if I was well and all, and he gave me some money my brothers had sent, too. We had a fine dinner with lots of wine." He looked wistful at the memory. "But at any rate, old Lalano and I were talking, and he mentioned the white smoke. Merchants back home were starting to sell it to Deverry men, he said, just now and again. He was troubled about it, because the trade's disreputable enough back home, and he knew it was against your laws here. So as we talked about it, it occurred to us to wonder who would have the money to buy smuggled goods."

"Who but the noble-born, true enough."

"Or an occasional rich merchant, maybe, but these so-called lords of yours are certainly good at keeping a merchant poor."

Now isn't this interesting? Salamander thought to himself. If Camdel had been smoking opium, it would certainly explain how the dark dweomermen had gotten their claws into him. He decided that over the next few days, he'd do a little discreet asking around, as if he were interested in buying the stuff himself. At that point he felt the little tug on his mind that meant some other dweomer-person was trying to contact him. Casually he stood up.

"Excuse me a moment, Enopo. I've just got to go the privy out back."

With a wave of his hand, the minstrel dismissed him. Salamander hurried out and went round to the stableyard, where a watering trough stood, catching the afternoon sun. He stared into the dappled water and opened his mind, expecting to see Nevyn. Instead, Valandario's beautiful but stern face looked up at him. He was too startled to think anything to her.

"So there you are," she said. "Your father's asked me to contact you. He wants you to ride home straightaway."

"I can't. I'm running errands for the Master of the Aethyr."

Her storm-gray eyes widened.

"I can't tell you what, exactly," he went on. "But dark and dangerous deeds and doings are—"

"Less chatter, magpie! I'll tell your father you'll be delayed then, but come home as soon as you can. He'll be waiting down by the Eldidd border, near Cannobaen. Do not disobey him this time, please."

Then her face was gone. As he always did when confronted by his old teacher in dweomercraft, Salamander felt guilty, even though this time he'd done nothing wrong.

At dinner that night, Blaen insisted on treating his cousin as an honored guest. Every time a page called him "my lord," Rhodry winced, and hearing a servant use one of his old titles, Master of Cannobaen, brought tears to his eyes. All this well-meant courtesy only made him think of his beloved Eldidd, her wild seacoasts, her vast oak forest, untouched since time immemorial. He was profoundly glad when he and Jill could take their leave of the gwerbret's table and go to their chamber.

By then, it was late, and Rhodry was more than a bit drunk and much more tired than he cared to admit. While he struggled to pull off his boots, Jill opened the shutters at the window and leaned out, looking at the stars. Candlelight danced shadows around her and made her hair gleam like fine-spun gold.

"By every god and his wife," Rhodry said. "I wish you'd left that cursed bit of jewelry in the grass when you saw it there."

"And a fine lot of good that would have done. What if this dark master had found it?"

"Well, true spoken. I guess."

"Oh, I know, my love." She turned from the window. "All this talk of dweomer aches my heart, too."

"Does it now? Truly?"

"Of course. What do you think I'm going to do? Leave you for the dweomer road?"

"Uh well." All at once, he realized that he'd been afraid of just that. "Ah, horse dung, it sounds stupid now that I hear you say it aloud."

She looked at him, her mouth slack as if she were debating

what to say next, then suddenly smiled. She bent down and held out her hands to something, then picked up what he assumed was her gray gnome and cradled it in her arms.

"Is somewhat wrong?" she said. "It's not? Good. Did you just come to see us, then? That's sweet, little creature."

Seeing her speak to something that he couldn't see yet knew existed was eerie, troubling him further. As he watched her in the candlelight, he was remembering being a tiny lad, and thinking that maybe the Wildfolk were real, and that maybe he could see them. At times, when he was out in his father's hunting preserve it would seem that maybe there was an odd creature peering at him from under a bush or up in a tree. Yet even as a very small child, Rhodry had dismissed the Wildfolk as only something his nurse spoke about to amuse him. His hard-bitten father had made sure that his son had no trace of whimsy about him.

But now he knew that they were real, and he smiled, imagining Tingyr Maelwaedd's square jaw dropping in surprise at the truth. Jill carried the gnome over to the bed and sat down next to him.

"Here's Rhoddo," she said. "Say 'good eve' to him."

Rhodry felt a little hand clasp his finger.

"Good eve," he said, smiling. "And how does our good gnome fare?"

All at once, he saw it, a dusty sort of gray, with its long limbs and warty nose. It was grinning at him while it held his fingertip in one spiky hand. Rhodry caught his breath in a gulp.

"You see him, don't you?" Jill whispered.

"I do, at that. Ye gods!"

Jill and the gnome exchanged a smile of triumph; then the creature disappeared. Rhodry stared openmouthed at her.

"I asked Nevyn this afternoon why you couldn't see the Wildfolk," she said, as calmly as if she were discussing what to serve her man for dinner. "And he told me that you probably could, with that trace of elven blood and all, but that since you didn't think you could, you wouldn't. So I thought, well, if I made sure you knew just how real they are, it would come to you."

"And right you were. By the hells, my love! I don't know what to say."

"Oho, it has to be a strange thing indeed to turn you dumb!"

"Oh, hold your tongue! And why is it so important to you that I see them?"

"Well, it could come in cursed useful." She looked away, suddenly troubled. "They'll take messages and suchlike, if we get separated again."

There it was again, the truth that he didn't want to face: there was dark dweomer stalking them. He drew her tight into his arms and kissed her passionately, just to drive his fear away.

After their lovemaking, Rhodry slept like a dead man for most of the night, but toward dawn he had a dream so troubling that he woke abruptly, sitting bolt upright in bed. The chamber was gray with dawn, and Jill was still asleep beside him. He got up and put on his brigga, then went over to look out the window, just to chase the feeling of the dream away. When someone tapped on the door, he yelped aloud, but it was only Nevyn, slipping into the chamber.

"Here, lad, I was wondering if you had any strange dreams last night."

"By the great god Tarn himself! I did, at that."

With a drowsy yawn, Jill sat up and looked blearily at them.

"Tell me about the dream," Nevyn said.

"Well, I was standing a night watch at the gates of some small dun. Jill was inside, and I had to guard her. Then this swordsman came up to the gates, and he wouldn't answer me when I called for the password. He was taunting me, calling me every low name I ever heard and throwing my exile in my face. I've never been so cursed furious in my life. So I drew, and I was going to challenge the bastard, but then I remembered that I was on guard, so I held my place at the gate. Finally I thought to call for the captain. Here's the cursed strange part. When the captain came running, it was you, with a sword in your hand."

"So it was."

"Oh now here!" Jill chimed in. "Did Rhodry have a true dream?"

"More true than most," Nevyn said. "You know, Rhodry, you've got a lot of honor in your heart if you'll hold to it even in your sleep. The dream was showing you a true thing by using a fancy like in a bard's song. The dun was your body, and the man you felt yourself to be was your soul. That swordsman was one of our enemies. He was trying to lure your soul away from your body, because when a man's asleep, his soul can slip out into the

Innerlands. But if you'd gone after him, you would have been
fighting on his ground, and a very strange place it is. He would
have won."

"And what then? Would I have been dead?"

"I doubt it." Nevyn thought for a moment. "Most likely he
would have trapped your soul and taken your body over for
himself. You would have felt like you were dreaming the whole
time, you see, while he had it under his control. Humph, I wonder who he wanted to kill: me or Jill? Maybe both. Either way,
eventually you would have woken up to find yourself with a
bloody sword in your hand and one of us lying dead at your feet."

Rhodry felt as sick as if he'd bitten into rotten meat.

"Fortunately, I keep a strict guard," the dweomerman went
on. "But from now on, if you have a dream or even an idle fancy
that troubles you, tell me straightaway. Never be in the least
embarrassed about it."

"Done, then."

"Good." The old man began pacing back and forth. "Well,
I've just learned an important thing. Our enemies aren't retreating. That dream was a challenge, Rhodry. They're going to stand
and fight me over this."

After his unsucessful attempt to take over Rhodry's body,
Alastyr was tired and more than a little puzzled. He had never
expected the silver dagger to have such strength of will, although, as he thought about it, a hardened warrior would have to
develop a certain power of concentration to survive in battle.
The most puzzling thing, however, was the simple feel of
Rhodry's mind and the way his dream-self looked on the astral
plane. Given Rhodry's strength of mind, however untrained it
was, his dream-projection should have been unusually solid, but
it had flickered constantly, at times looking more like a man-
shaped flame than a body. Somewhere in his stock of lore was the
explanation for that. He sat quietly, letting his mind wander as it
would from one flickering thought to another tenuous connection.

"By the dark power itself!" he said abruptly.

Startled, Sarcyn looked up and turned to him.

"I just realized somewhat," Alastyr went on. "I'm willing to
wager that Rhodry's father was no more Tingyr Maelwaedd than
he was me. I swear that lad is half one of the Elcyion Lacar."

"Indeed? Then it's no wonder that all the Old One's predictions and starcraft were wrong."

"Just so. Well, he's going to be interested to hear that."

"If we live to tell him."

Alastyr started to make some reply, then merely shrugged. Yet once again he wondered if they should simply kill Camdel and flee for their lives. But there was the stone. If only he had the Great Stone of the West, he could subjugate its spirits and tap untold power for his own use and to further the plans of the dark powers. From years of study, he knew that the Great Stone had a direct link with the mind of the High King, a link that could be used to drive him slowly mad and plunge the kingdom into chaos. Then could the dark masters work as they pleased in Deverry. Sarcyn was watching him with dark, unreadable eyes.

"Are you thinking of escaping on your own, lad?" Alastyr growled. "I have ways of finding you if you try."

"Naught of the sort, master."

Alastyr's dweomer told him that the apprentice was speaking the truth, but still he felt some other thought, hiding below the surface of his mind. It was time, he decided, to put his apprentice in his place a bit.

"Take care of the horses and your pet," he said. "I need to be alone to do a working."

Sarcyn went out to the stable of the isolated farm they'd appropriated by the simple means of killing the old farmer who owned it. Crouched in the straw of an empty stall was the farmhand, whom they'd left alive because he looked useful. A solid middle-aged man of about forty, he was so thoroughly ensorceled that he rose to his feet obediently the moment Sarcyn snapped his fingers.

"Feed and water the horses," the apprentice said. "Then come into the kitchen for my next order."

He nodded agreement, swaying as if he were drunk.

The kitchen was a big quarter-round room, set off from the rest of the house by wickerwork partitions. It was an old-style house, with one hearth in the middle under a smokehole in the thatched roof. In the straw on the floor, Camdel lay curled up like a baby. When they were rummaging through the farm, Sarcyn had found an iron chain with a cuff that had been doubtless used at one point for restraining an ox. Now it coupled Camdel's ankle to an iron ring for hanging a pot by the hearth. When Sarcyn unlatched it, Camdel moaned and sat up.

"Want some breakfast, little one? There's proper barley porridge."

Unshaven and filthy, the lordling nodded. Later, Sarcyn decided, he would let his pet bathe. He touseled Camdel's hair with one hand and smiled at him.

"The worst is almost over," he said with a bravado he didn't feel. "Once we're back in Bardek, we'll have a good place to live and get you some decent clothes and suchlike."

Camdel forced out a tremulous smile. It was odd, Sarcyn thought, how men differed. Some fought his domination to the very end; others found that they had a taste for the strange sexual pleasures that he introduced them to. In a very satisfying way, Camdel was one of the latter. As he watched the lord eat his breakfast, Sarcyn realized that he was glad of Camdel's tastes. He felt an odd emotion gnawing and nagging at him, so unfamiliar that it took him a long time to identify it: guilt. All at once he remembered being a small child and weeping over Alastyr's rape. *It was worth it*, he told himself, *because he brought me to the warrior's path.* The reassurance rang hollow even to him.

"Tell me somewhat," Camdel said. "Do you mourn your brother?"

"You've heard me tell Alastyr how I feel."

"So I have, but do you mourn him?"

Sarcyn looked sharply away.

"You do, don't you?" Camdel said. "I thought so."

Sarcyn slapped him across the face, then rose, stalking to the door. The farmhand was walking up. With a sway he knelt at the apprentice's feet. Sarcyn sent out a line of light and fastened it around his aura, then sent the aura spinning.

"You're going to fetch us more food. You're going to say naught but the tale we told you. Look at me, man."

The farmhand looked up and stared into his eyes.

"I'll go get the rabbits," he whispered. "I'll say naught but the tale you told me."

"Good. Then get on your way."

The farmhand rose and shuffled away to the stables. When Sarcyn went back inside, Camdel was eating his porridge. Ignoring him, Sarcyn walked through the little chambers, fanned out around the hearth, into the storeroom. There he stopped, grunting in surprise. Alastyr stood before the window, and the corpse of the dead farmer was standing, too, a pale thing, gray and bloodless, but moving nonetheless, swaying on awkward feet. Alastyr shot his apprentice a sour smile of triumph.

"I bound Wildfolk into it. They'll keep it alive for some time, and it'll do our bidding. Now tell me, you little dog, can you match my power in that?"

"I can't, master, truly."

"Then mind what you say to me, or you'll end up the same way one fine day."

Sarcyn felt a revulsion so strong that he wanted to turn and run from the chamber, but he forced himself to stare at thing calmly while the master gloated over it. He had the brief thought of taking Camdel and trying to escape, but he realized then that he was in this dark muck too deep to get out.

Nevyn insisted that Jill and Rhodry have breakfast with him in his chamber, and when a page came, saying that the gwerbret wanted his cousin to come sit with him, Nevyn sent back the answer that the silver dagger was otherwise occupied. Although he doubted that Alastyr could form a link with a rider in Blaen's warband or indeed, anyone else in the dun, things were too dangerous to take chances. All it would take was one crazed kitchen lass with a cleaver and the unnatural strength of ensorcelment to bring his plans to an abrupt end. As he thought about it, it was strange that the dark master had been able to work on Rhodry's dreaming mind. He began to think that the enemy he was facing was the same man who'd caused the war in Eldidd the summer before, someone who'd seen Rhodry and had had the chance to study him.

Later that day he had another piece of evidence to feed that suspicion. He was perched on the windowsill and watching Jill and Rhodry dice for a pile of coppers. As soon as one had won the lot, they would divide it in half and start all over again. To distract himself, Nevyn began using his second sight to see which one would win each particular game. He had just proppesied to himself that Rhodry's luck was turning when Blaen himself came into the chamber.

"Comyn's back from the Cwm Pecl pass," he announced. "They wiped out those bandits, and he's brought back a prisoner. He might know somewhat of interest."

"So he might," Nevyn said. "I think I'll run the risk of leaving here to watch the interrogation. Come along, silver daggers. I don't want you out of my sight."

Out by the warden's guardroom was a small, squat tower that served as a dungeon keep for local criminals awaiting trial or punishment. When they came into a small room, ill-lit by one tiny window, they found that the wardens had been busy. Bound to a stone pillar was a man, naked to the waist. Nearby an assortment of irons and pincers lay on a table. A stout man with arms as muscled as a blacksmith's, the executioner was laying bits of charcoal into a brazier and blowing on the coals.

"Should be nice and hot in a minute, Your Grace," he said.

"Good. So, this is the rat my terriers dragged in, is it? Rhodry, have you ever seen him before?"

"I have. He was one of the pack who attacked us, sure enough."

The bandit laid his head back against the pillar and stared so desperately at the ceiling that Nevyn could guess he was wishing that he was dead with the rest of his band. Although Nevyn disapproved of torture on principle, he knew that nothing he could say would convince the gwerbret against it. Blaen strolled over and slapped the bandit across the face.

"Look at me, swine. You have a choice. You can die mercifully and quickly, or slowly, in pieces."

The bandit set his lips tightly together. When the executioner set a thin iron into the brazier to heat, the charcoal hissed and exuded the smell of burnt flesh. With a yelp, the bandit squirmed until Blaen slapped him into silence.

"We know someone hired you to attack the caravan. Who?"

The executioner took the iron and spat on it. The spit sizzled.

"I don't know much," the bandit stammered. "I'll tell you everything I do."

"Good." Blaen gave him a gentle smile. "Then kindly proceed."

"Our leader's name was the Wolf, and he was down in Marcmwr, just seeing what he could see about caravans and suchlike. Well, he comes back and says he has a bit of work for us. This old merchant type wanted us to get the lass who was riding with this caravan. Sounds easy, the Wolf says, so we'll take the old fart's coin for it. He had this plan. We'd hit the caravan, and the Wolf and a couple of the lads would grab the lass, and then the rest of us would just pull back, like, before we lost any men. We didn't know she could fight like the Lord of Hell. Don't harm her, he says. Horseshit! As if any of us could have." He paused to shoot Jill a venomous look.

"Keep talking." Blaen slapped him again.

"And we weren't supposed to harm the silver dagger, either, if we could help it, anyway." He looked at Rhodry. "He knew your name. Don't harm Rhodry, says he, unless you have to to save your life. He's not as important, but I'd hate to see him dead. After you killed the Wolf like that, we cursed well forgot what the old man said, too, you bastard."

Rhodry merely smiled. Oh indeed? Nevyn thought, it must be the same dark master, then! But why did he want Rhodry alive? He'd wanted Jill, most likely, to bribe Nevyn to let him go, but why Rhodry?

"So anyway, Your Grace," the bandit said, "we couldn't get her. So we elected a new captain and went to meet the old man. We were thinking of killing him, see, for vengeance, but he gave us so much coin that we let him be."

"What was he like?" Nevyn stepped forward. "Was he a Bardek man?"

"He wasn't, but one from Deverry. He dressed like a merchant, and mostly he looked like he came from Cerrmor way. He had this oily little voice that rubbed my nerves raw. One of his men called him Alastyr. He had these two swordsmen, see, and one of them fair creeped my flesh. He looked us over like he'd like to slit our throats just to watch us die."

"He probably would have enjoyed it, at that. Did they have a prisoner with them?"

"They did, this brown-haired fellow tied to a horse. His face was all bruised up real bad, and he wouldn't look at nobody. He was a slender kind of lad, the sort who reminds you a bit of a lass, like."

"Camdel, sure enough," Blaen broke in.

"I'm afraid so," Nevyn said. "Very well, Your Grace. I'm afraid there's no more ale to be squeezed out of this turnip."

"Hang this vermin publicly at noon tomorrow." Blaen turned to the executioner. "But make sure he dies an easy death."

With a sudden stink of urine, the bandit fainted.

As they left the tower, Nevyn mulled over the bandit's information. He remembered the shipmaster in Cerrmor, saying that the passenger he'd taken to Bardek also had an oily voice and looked like a typical Cerrmor man. It was quite unlikely that there were two dark dweomer-masters who seemed so similar. And this Alastyr had had only two apprentices, which meant there was only one left. The battle odds seemed more and more in his favor.

He realized, too, that he'd been thinking that he knew his opponent, only to find out that he was wrong. He had an old enemy, a dark master with whom he'd crossed swords several times in the last hundred years, a Bardekian who was particularly skilled in reading omens of future events. The war last year in Eldidd, the attempt on the dweomer opal, even leaving Rhodry alive as a kind of experiment—it would all have fit Tondalo perfectly. Of course, he reminded himself, Tondalo might be behind it from a distance. By now, the Bardekian would be some hundred and fifty years old, and likely too weak to travel far. Although dark dweomermen can keep themselves alive by unnatural means, they have no way of remaining healthy, especially toward the end. Nature herself tries to thwart them, simply because they go counter to her principles, like water trying to flow uphill.

Caught in Alastyr's strong grasp, the brown and white rabbit struggled, trying to work its hind feet free to rake him, but he knocked its head against the kitchen table until it went limp. He slit its throat with his knife, then leaned over to suck the hot blood directly from the wound. Even though he'd done it for years, the procedure always disgusted him, but unfortunately it was the only way to ensure that he got all of the blood's magnetic effluent. He could never understand why other masters of the craft left killing their meat to their servants. As he drank, he felt the magnetic strength flow into him in a small rejuvenation. He wiped his mouth carefully on a rag, then set about skinning the rabbit and cutting it up.

As he worked, he felt his fear like a pounding in his blood. Although he wanted to flee, he was afraid to return to the Brotherhood with another failure on his hands. The Old One might well forgive him, especially since he'd know that Rhodry's elven blood was the factor that had ruined his calculations, but the other masters of the dark path would see him as weak. Once a man weakened, he was likely to be attacked, torn apart, and drained of his power. Suicide would be a better fate than that. The thought of death made him tremble all over. After all, it was simply the fear of dying that had made him turn to the dark craft all those years before. Soon he would have to decide whether to flee or fight. Soon. Very soon. Although the dweomer sends no warnings of danger to those on the dark path, simple logic told him that time was short.

He looked up from his brooding to find Sarcyn watching him.

"What do you want?" Alastyr snapped.

"I only wanted to butcher the rabbit for you, master. It's my place to wait on you."

Alastyr handed him the knife, then washed his bloody hands in a bucket of water. Nearby Camdel sat crouched in the straw.

"If we do make a run for it," Alastyr said, "Camdel has to die. He'll only slow us down."

Whimpering, the lordling shrank back. Sarcyn looked up with the knife in his hand, and his eyes were murderous with rage.

"I won't let you kill him."

"Indeed? And who are you to let me do or not do anything?"

Alastyr sent a wave of hatred down the link between his aura and Sarcyn's, followed it up with a twist of rage. With a gasp, Sarcyn dropped the knife as the emotions translated themselves into pure physical pain. Writhing he fell to his knees, his face twisted as he tried to keep the pain from showing there. With a snarl, Alastyr released him, shaking on the floor.

"Now hold your tongue until you're spoken to," he snapped. "I have to think."

He paced over to the window and stared out blindly, feeling his fear clutch and pulse within him. Once he glanced back to see Sarcyn and Camdel clasped in each other's arms. Fools! he thought, maybe I'll kill them both!

When time came for the evening meal, Jill ate up in Nevyn's chamber with the old man and Rhodry. Although she had no appetite, Rhodry packed away roast beef and fried onions like the true warrior he was, eating cheerfully before a battle because he knew he might never get another meal. And what am I, then? she thought, a coward, sure enough. As much as she hated the word, she had to admit that she was terrified at the thought of dark dweomer wanting to capture her for reasons of its own. Finally she couldn't stand to watch them eat any longer and went to the window.

Looking out on the golden sunshine of a summer evening reminded her that the real, solid world was still there, untouched by dweomer, yet she knew that she would never see that world in the same way again. A question haunted her, almost as frightening as the dark dweomer itself: how do I know so much about all of this? Although she'd been caught up in events that would have baffled most people, she'd known so many things instinctively, that the jewel could shapechange, that the apprentice had the dark dweomer and could use it to see if she were speaking the truth, that she could reach Nevyn through the fire. Reluctantly, slowly, fighting all the way, she was being forced to realize that she had not only dweomer talent, but a strong one.

Clenching her hands on the sill, she leaned out of the window and reassured herself by watching the ordinary bustle of servants in the ward below. Then she saw the Heron, lurking by the main gate of the dun and peering around him. He must want to talk with me, she thought. And why had she gone to the window at just the proper moment to see him?

"Is somewhat wrong, child?" Nevyn said. "You've gone a bit pale."

"Oh, it's naught, but the Heron's at the gates, and I think we'd best speak with him."

Nevyn insisted on sending a servant to bring the Heron up to their chamber rather than going down to the ward. The poor man was so nervous at being inside the gwerbret's broch that he couldn't bear to sit down. He paced restlessly back and forth, clutching the tankard of ale that Jill poured him.

"Here, good herbman," he said. "Are you truly sure we won't be overheard?"

"I swear it. I'll lie to the gwerbret's face if I have to to protect you."

"Well and good, then." He had a gulp of ale. "I think we've found the men who tried to poison Ogwern."

It took Jill a moment to remember the lie that Nevyn had told the thieves, but the dweomerman himself sat bolt upright in his chair and smiled.

"Oh have you now? Here, tell me everything."

"After you warned us, you see, we did some hard thinking. It had to be a stranger who put that oily-fur-what's-it into Ogwern's ale, because he's as fair as fair when it comes to splitting swag and levying taxes, and none of the lads would want him done away with. So we figure another guild's trying to move in on us. So we all spread out, like, marking any strangers we saw and following them. We spread a bit of coin around, too, for information. And so just before noontide I had a bit of luck when this fellow comes into town to buy at the market fair. Someone told me he was a farmhand, but he was buying a cageful of rabbits. Now I ask you, why would a farmer spend coin on rabbits when his fields are full of free ones?"

"A better question than you can know, my friend."

"So I took one of the guild horses and followed the man out. I was being as careful as careful at first, but he never even looked back once. From the way he sat on his horse, all slumped over, like, it looked like he was ill or suchlike, so I could follow pretty close. He goes to a farm, all right, and I begin to think I've got a false trail. But I'm out there and all, so I spread a few coppers around in the village nearby, and I hear a strange tale. That farm belongs to an old widower, who's gotten a bit strange over the years. Now, everyone thought he didn't have a soul in the world, but all of a sudden, like, he's got guests. One of the village lads was chasing a lost cow up that way, and he saw a fellow saddling up an expensive horse out in the farmyard. Fortunately the lad had to keep after his cow, so he didn't go down to ask nothing."

"Fortunate and twice fortunate," Nevyn said softly.

"That's what I was thinking, too," the Heron said with a nod. "Because I'll wager those guests belong to some other guild, and the poor old man's gone to join his wife in the Otherlands."

"I have the nasty feeling you're right." Nevyn got up and joined the Heron at his pacing. "Tell me exactly where this farm is and everything you can remember about the countryside."

The "everything" turned out to be a great deal. Apparently the Heron could look a place over and memorize it as a clear picture in his mind, because as he talked, he stared off into space, his eyes moving as he examined an image that no one else could see. The farm was up in the hills and quite isolated; once a month or so a neighbor would go up to see if the old man was all right, but otherwise, the villagers rarely saw him.

"A perfect place for men to hide when they've got murder

on their minds," Nevyn said when he'd finished. "Now listen, tell the guild to leave this to me. I can't explain why, but these lads are far more dangerous than you think."

"I will, then. Here, good sir, Ogwern swears that you're dweomer."

"Does he now? Isn't dweomer just embroidery in a bard's tale?"

"Oh, you see many a strange thing when you work in a guild. I know lords and merchants and suchlike scoff, but they're not out in the streets at the bottom of things."

"So they're not. Well, Ogwern's a shrewd man, for all his fat, and I'm going to prove it to you. You want to get out of here without being seen, don't you?"

The Heron groaned as he remembered where he was.

"Well and good, then," Nevyn went on. "If you swear to me that you won't steal anything while the spell lasts, I'll make you cursed near invisible for a few minutes."

Although the Heron swore in perfect sincerity, Jill was shocked. She'd never seen Nevyn be so open about his powers when there was no true need. When the old man led the Heron out into the shadows of the corridor, the thief suddenly turned into an oddly blurred figure. He had only scuttled off a few paces before he seemed to disappear. Rhodry swore aloud. Grinning broadly, Nevyn shut the door.

"The hunt is up," Nevyn announced. "The masters of the dark dweomer are known for eating raw meat but not for their skill at snaring rabbits. I'll wager that farmhand is ensorceled, too."

"They're right at hand!" Jill snapped. "The arrogant bastards."

Rhodry was staring the closed door, his mouth set tight and a little twisted, as if he'd eaten something bitter.

"What's so wrong, my love?" she said.

"That man's a thief, that's what, and so's Ogwern."

"Oh come now, my innocent one, did you only just realize it?"

"Don't tease, curse it! He's given us the help we need, and I should be rewarding him, but by the hells, I'm honor-bound to turn him over to Blaen."

"What! You can't!"

"Now, here, lad," Nevyn broke in. "I despise thieves myself, but I've known about Ogwern for years and haven't given evidence. Do you know why? Because as thieves go, he's very small beer indeed. He keeps his lads in line, he never murders, and he does his best to prevent murders in his kingdom. With him gone, who knows what vicious sort might come to power?"

"That's all well and good," Rhodry said. "But here I am, my cousin's guest, when by rights he could have turned me out on the road. I can't hold my tongue and make a mockery of his justice."

"You dolt!" Jill felt like grabbing him and shaking him. "Why are you making a fuss over this now? There's dark dweomer all around us."

"That's got naught to do with it. It's the honor of the thing."

"Now, now." Nevyn laid a paternal hand on Rhodry's shoulder. "I know it's a hard road you've got to ride, lad, choosing between two dishonors. Just look at me, will you? There, my thanks. Now, you're not going to say a word to Blaen about the thieves. You've forgotten already, haven't you? The Heron isn't a thief, and neither is Ogwern. They just owe me a few favors; that's why they helped us. You'll remember that, lad."

When Nevyn took his hand away, Rhodry blinked like a man walking out of a dark room into strong sunlight.

"Who was that fellow, anyway? A pot boy down in Ogwern's inn?"

"Just that," Nevyn said. "You know I'm always willing to heal the poor for free."

"True, but it was cursed good of him to run that risk, anyway. I'll make sure Blaen gives him a reward."

It took all of Jill's will to keep a normal expression on her face.

"Rhodry, would you go fetch Blaen up here?" Nevyn went on. "I think we'll be taking him up on his offer of the warband after all."

As soon as the door closed behind him, Jill turned to Nevyn.

"Here!" she burst out. "You told me that ensorceling someone is a wrong thing."

"It is, but not when it's the only way to save someone's life. When the word got out that Rhodry had turned the king and the prince of the Cwm Pecl guild over to the gwerbret, how long do you think your lad would have lived?"

"Not very. I was going to use that argument next, truly. The thieves wouldn't think of him as an honor-bound man."

"Exactly. He would have been just a traitorous silver dagger to them. You know, child, I'm cursed glad I never swore a vow that I'd never lie. Many dweomerfolk do, and it gains you the favor of the Lords of Wyrd, but I prefer to be a little more flexible about such matters."

He looked so sly that she had to laugh.

"That's a better mood," he said. "Now, would you stand guard at the door? I've got to scry."

After the Wildfolk lit the firewood in the hearth, Nevyn knelt down and stared into the leaping flames. Since he knew the settled parts of Cwm Pecl quite well, he'd recognized the farm in question from the Heron's description. In fact, once he'd ridden there to treat a sick child, many years ago. When he called up the memory of following the path on a sunny afternoon, immediately the image in the flames changed to the path as it looked now in the darkening light outside. In vision he followed the road up to the spot where the farm should have stood. Nothing was there but wild meadow, not a house, not a wall, not even a cow grazing nearby. So Alastyr had set an astral seal over it. With a snap of his fingers, he put out the fire.

"Did you see them?" Jill said.

"I didn't—which means they're there. Oh, Alastyr can hide from me, sure enough, but he forgot what it means to make enemies of men who trust their eyes, not the dweomer." He smiled gently. "He's about to remember."

Now that his mind was made up, Alastyr felt much calmer. He strode into the kitchen and found Sarcyn and Camdel sitting at the table. Sarcyn looked up with a satisfying cringe.

"We're leaving at the break of day," Alastyr announced. "I'd rather take our chances with the Brotherhood than with the Master of the Aethyr."

"Well and good, master. I'll pack some of the gear tonight."

"Good." He turned to Camdel. "As for you, if you cooperate with us, you can stay alive. We're traveling fast, and if you cause the least bit of trouble, you die. Understand?"

Camdel nodded a cowed agreement. Alastyr turned on his

heel and strode back to the ritual chamber. He had to keep up his guard.

The plan was risky, Nevyn knew, but he had to act fast. Sooner or later Alastyr would realize that it was dangerous to stay so near to Dun Hiraedd and would move on. As he sat on horseback in the torchlit ward with Jill and Rhodry, Nevyn shuddered. The battle ahead would be a hard one against two opponents if this apprentice had the skill to fight beside his master. Around him, twenty-five of Blaen's best men were saddling their horses while the gwerbret walked through, speaking to a man here and there. Although Nevyn was throwing his dice on a long wager by taking His Grace along, he needed to have something to use as a distraction.

"Now remember what I told you," he whispered to the two silver daggers. "At a certain point, we're slipping away from the warband."

They nodded agreement. With a jingle of tack and scabbards, the warband mounted. Motioning to Jill and Rhodry to follow, Nevyn rode over to the gwerbret.

"Your Grace is sure he knows how to find the farm?"

"By the hells, a blind man could find it from the instructions you gave. Don't worry, good sorcerer. We'll dig these rats out of their holes."

When the warband rode out, Nevyn kept Rhodry and Jill with him at the very rear. He tossed his reins to the lad and told him to lead his horse along. Since he was going to have to go into a light trance, it would be difficult enough to stay in the saddle without worrying about guiding his horse. As the warband clattered down the night-dark road, Nevyn slowed his breathing and withdrew his consciousness from the world around him. To an observer he would have looked half asleep, his head bobbing in time to the horse's motion. Through half-lidded eyes he watched the warband and set to work.

First he called upon the Great Ones and saw a beam of imagined light come to him. He meditated upon it, saw it ever more clearly in his mind, until at last it lived apart from his will, a great swathe of light shaped like a sword. In his mind he caught it by the hilt and used the blade to trace a mighty sphere of light around and above the warband. Because of the motion of the horse and the noises around him, it was a hard struggle to con-

centrate, but eventually he got the sphere solid and the seals—
the five-pointed stars of the Kings of the Elements—set at each
ordinal point and at zenith and nadir. As soon as it was glowing
brightly, he invoked the great Light that shines behind all the
gods and begged permission to meddle with darkness. Slowly,
carefully, he withdrew the light from the sphere while leaving its
structure until there was nothing left but a solid sphere of darkness, invisible to normal eyes but a shield against scrying.

With the sphere created, Nevyn could bring his mind back
to the normal world. He was shocked to find that the warband
had traveled a good three miles; working dweomer on horseback
was even harder than he'd expected. For the next hour or so, he
merely rested, until they were about three miles from the farm.
He went briefly back into his trance, called up the light, and let it
stream back into the waiting sphere, but he cast a new wrap of
darkness over Jill, Rhodry, and himself. Now he could only hope
that Alastyr had the common sense to keep a scrying watch. If he
was, he would see that sphere, blazoned with the sigils of the
light, riding straight for his hiding place. Nevyn wanted him to
panic, and panic thoroughly.

"Jill, Rhodry," he whispered. "Now!"

They slowed their horses to match his pace, tagging after the
warband for a few hundred yards until there was a good distance
between them and the unsuspecting gwerbret. With a quick
wave of his hand, Nevyn led his two silver daggers off the road at
a trot. They turned down a side lane that led to the farm by a
narrow but more direct route than the road, galloped into a stand
of birches, then made their hidden way through the trees. By the
time Blaen noticed that they were gone, they would be well
ahead of the warband.

At length, when they came to a little stream running in a
valley between two hills, Nevyn pulled his tiny warband to a halt.

"Very well, silver daggers. The farm lies just on the other
side of this hill. Here are your orders. I'm going to lie down and
go into a deep trance. You two tie up the horses, then stand guard
over my body. It's just possible that Alastyr will send his apprentice out to try to kill me."

"They'll never get past my sword," Rhodry said quietly.

"Well, if I lose this battle, we'll meet someday in the Otherlands." He turned to Jill. "If I die, child, pray with all your heart

and soul to the Light that lies behind the Moon, and don't you tell me that you don't know what I mean."

Jill caught her breath with a gasp, but even though his heart ached for her, Nevyn had no more time for words. He spread his cloak out on the ground, lay down on his back upon it, and folded his arms over his chest, laying each hand on the opposite shoulder. First he invoked the Lords of Light, then lay quietly, gathering strength. Nearby Jill and Rhodry stood with drawn swords. As he closed his eyes, he wondered if he'd ever see them again.

Slowly and carefully within his mind, Nevyn summoned his body of light, a pale blue simulacrum of his own form, but stripped down to the essentials and joined to his solar plexus by a silver cord. When Nevyn transferred his consciousness over to it, he felt as if the physical body were dropping sharply away. For the briefest of moments he felt nauseated; then there was a click like a sword striking a shield, and he was looking out of the simulacrum's eyes. His physical body lay below him in a world filled with the blue light of the etheric plane. Since he'd withdrawn from it, his own body looked like a lump of dead flesh and nothing more, but he could see Jill and Rhodry as two egg-shaped whorls of flame, their auras pulsing around them. The trees and the grass glowed dull red with vegetable life force.

Nevyn rose about ten feet above his body, the silver cord paying out behind him like a fisherman's line, and looked around. The stream that flowed through the valley might well be useful, he decided, because crossing running water in the body of light is dangerous in the extreme. In the blue light, the stream ran silver, and above it drifted its elemental current, visible as a troubled, shifting wall of smoky stuff, a snare if only he could get his weasel into it. He rose higher and drifted toward the crest of the hill. It was time to throw his challenge.

Down on the other side of the hill was a grassy meadow, and in it lay the farmstead, a crumbling roundhouse behind an earthen wall, some sheds, a few fruit trees so old that their life glow was more a brown than a red. Nevyn smiled to himself. Since the seals were down, Alastyr must have scried out the warband and let them fall in panic. All at once he saw a man run out of the house and head toward a shed with his arms full of saddlebags. He decided that he'd best keep his enemies too busy to think of killing Camdel.

Out of the glowing blue light Nevyn fastened a spear shape

with his mind, then threw it hard for the running man's dark-shot aura. When it struck, the fellow dropped the saddlebags and screamed aloud. Although his physical body would feel no pain, his trained mind must have felt it searing like hot iron. With the swoop of a striking falcon, Nevyn flew over the farmhouse as the man ran back inside.

"Alastyr!" he called out in a long exhalation of thought. "Alastyr, I've come for you!"

He heard an answering howl echo through the blue light. Like a snake striking up from the ground, Alastyr rushed to meet him. His simulacrum was a huge, black-robed figure, hung with rich jewels and woven with sigils. The silver cord was wrapped thrice about his waist like a kirtle and hung with severed heads. The face that peered through the hood was pale and cruel, the eyes a glitter of dark in a white ghost. Nevyn called upon the Light and felt his own body of light pulse and glow with its power. In answer, Alastyr swelled up and blackened as if he would suck up every light in the universe and put it out. The battle was joined: to see who could break up the other's body of light and drive the soul within, naked and helpless, into the power of the greater forces behind each warrior.

Nevyn struck first with a wave of light that made Alastyr bob and float like a bit of jetsam on the sea. He thrust again, sending his enemy swooping up, but as he followed, he felt Alastyr's own forces working on him—a decay, as if a thousand claws pulled at him and tried to tear him apart. Much of his will was diverted to keeping his simulacrum together, pulling down more and more light and building it up as fast as Alastyr could rend it. The rest of his power went for attack, a rain of golden arrows and long spears that drove Alastyr this way and that as Nevyn circled round, edging, pressing him with light that beat against the darkness and shrank it back.

His whole strategy was to force Alastyr out of the blue light and into the first sphere of the Innerlands proper, where he would have mightier forces to command. As yet, Alastyr was too strong. Nevyn kept hammering him, striking with spears of light, while Alastyr sent out wave after wave of darkness to claw and bite him in return. The dark eyes within the hood burned and raged. When Nevyn struck hard enough to tear some of the pompous sigils off the black robe, Alastyr howled like an animal and pulled back. Nevyn risked trying to build a gate behind him, using part of his will to pin the dark enemy and part to open a path to the Innerlands. Too soon—Alastyr slipped away and sent out a flood of darkness like a wild sea.

For a moment, Nevyn plunged and fell. He felt his simulacrum loosening around him like a slipping cloak and desperately called upon the Light. All he could do was struggle to heal himself and fend off the worst of Alastyr's blows as the dark enemy pressed in closer and closer. Like boulders of palpable darkness the blows hit home. All at once Nevyn saw the water veil over the stream coming closer, too close! He wrenched around and flew up fast, dodging past before a startled Alastyr could react. Yet he'd barely repaired his shattered body of light when the enemy was after him with a darkness like a spew of poison.

Straight into his face Nevyn hurled a wall of light that tore and dissolved the severed heads on his kirtle, yet he could feel himself weakening as the enemy pressed ever on, the darkness pouring from twisted hands. All at once Alastyr screamed, the thought-sound echoing in the blue light, and swooped this way and that like a swallow coursing a field for gnats. Below him his silver cord dangled, broken. Someone had killed his physical body, and Nevyn could only assume that it was Jill or even Blaen.

But there was no time to indulge his shock at this unexpected aid. Alastyr's simulacrum was breaking up, revealing the pale blue etheric double underneath. While the dark master fought against the inevitable decay, Nevyn built up a gate to the Innerlands, two pillars, one black, one white, with an indigo void between them. As soon as they held steady, he sent a blast of light that shoved Alastyr through, then rushed after. Although he'd lost the first battle, the enemy was far from crushed, and Nevyn knew it.

Nevyn threw himself through the gate after the fleeing dark master, both of them rushing, gliding, falling down the path, blown like scraps of parchment on a livid indigo wind, while all around them were voices, laughter and screaming and torn scraps of words blown past them on the indigo flood, and images —faces, beasts, stars—swirling and beating against them like a flock of manic birds. Nevyn threw waves of light ahead of him, pounding Alastyr, stabbing him over and over until the last of the black robe tore away and whirled past, torn with rents that opened into the void. The wind blew them onward, rushed them, threw them headlong at last into a glow of violet light, where a river flowed far beneath, tenuous, shifting water of a kind that no stream on earth has ever known and no man ever tasted. A silence here, the wind gone, and around stretched fields of flowers, or the shapes of flowers, moon-gossamer things, white and deathly.

Shaken, Alastyr's etheric double swooped and fluttered, desperately trying now for escape, not victory. The Moon Land where they fought is the gate to many others, Nevyn's own Green Land, the Orange of the world of form, the shining home of the Great Ones; here, too, abuts the proper sphere of the dark dweomer, the Dark of Darkness, the Land of Husks and Rinds. If Alastyr could escape there, his soul would live on, working harm for aeons to come. Nevyn could see him trying to open a gate, his hands fluttering, the words of the rite pouring gibbering from his mouth. Nevyn sent a spear of light that slapped and flung him high just as the first pillar formed, then shattered the half-made gate.

Howling, Alastyr tried to flee, but Nevyn swooped up and rained down fiery light to trap him. With one hand Nevyn flung spear after spear and pinned Alastyr in a cage of light, while the etheric double threw itself against the shining bars and bit them in panic. With his enemy pinned, Nevyn built up another gate, this one with the golden pillars of sun, and between them opened the pure blue of a summer sky.

"Not mine the judgment!" Nevyn called out. "But yours!"

Through the pillars sped an enormous shifting shimmering arrow of light, flying straight and true, striking Alastyr so hard that the double shattered into a thousand pitiful shreds. There was a shriek, then the whimpering of a tiny child. For the briefest of moments Nevyn saw the child, flickering like a candle flame, a mewling babe with Alastyr's raging eyes. Then the light swelled, enveloped the tiny form, and swept it through the portal and up the path to the Hall of Light, where it would be judged.

"It is over!" Nevyn cried out. "It is finished!"

Three great knocks, three claps of thunder, boomed through the violet light, while down below the death-white flowers nodded. Nevyn knelt and bowed his head, not in worship, but as a sign of fealty, then let the portals fade away. In his exhaustion he felt the silver cord tugging on him, pulling him back to his body, which lay at a great distance but no true distance at all.

Sarcyn pulled his dagger free of Alastyr's heart and wiped it clean on his dead master's face.

"Vengeance," he whispered. "And honey sweet it is."

Hastily he rose and ran into the kitchen just in time to see the farmhand bolting out the back door. Sarcyn let him go; there was no time to waste chasing someone who knew so little about them. Whimpering under his breath, Camdel lay in the straw by the hearth. When Sarcyn knelt beside him, he shrank away from the knife.

"I'm not going to kill you, little one," Sarcyn said, sheathing it. "I'm going to unchain you. We've got to ride fast."

When Camdel moaned aloud, Sarcyn hesitated, caught by a feeling that he couldn't quite understand. His pet lordling was going to have a miserable life ahead of him, no matter how much sexual pleasure he took in his master's torments.

"Ah horseshit!" Sarcyn said abruptly. "You're going to see your cursed father again after all."

Cursing himself for a fool for succumbing to the first feeling of pity that he'd felt in years, Sarcyn got up and grabbed the leather bag that held Alastyr's books.

"Fare you well, little one," he said.

Camdel let two thin trails of tears slip down his cheeks in an agony of relief. Sarcyn ran out of the room and into the farmyard, where his horse was waiting, saddled and ready. After he put the precious books into a saddlebag, he mounted and rode out fast, turning the horse away from the main road into the hills. Ever since they'd moved into the farm, he'd been planning escape routes. He'd gone about a quarter mile when he heard the jingle of tack that meant the gwerbret and his cursed men were coming. Quickly he dismounted and held his horse's mouth shut as the jingle grew louder, passed him, then slowly died away.

"So much for that dolt," he whispered.

Yet as he remounted, he knew that the danger was far from over. Once the Brotherhood learned of Alastyr's fate, assassins would come seeking him. He would have to stay on the run, always hiding, moving constantly, while he studied the books and grew in power. Maybe he could keep ahead of the Hawks just long enough to garner enough power to save his life. Maybe. It was the only hope he had.

As soon as Nevyn went into his trance, Jill moved back among the trees while Rhodry stayed close to the old man. The pale moonlight shone on the stream and turned the white birches into ghost trees. In the dweomer-touched silence, she was painfully aware of the sound of her own breathing. Nevyn lay so still that she kept wanting to kneel down beside him to see if he were alive. All at once she heard a sound behind her and spun, her sword raised and ready.

"Only a rabbit," Rhodry said.

Since she knew that he could see in the dark, she turned back, keeping her eyes on the crest of the hill, looking for a movement that would mean enemies moving through the night. Suddenly Nevyn moaned. Jill stepped forward just as he flopped over onto his side. With a muddled thought that he'd been poisoned, she flung herself down beside him. He half sat up, then flopped sideways, but all the time his eyes were shut tight and his breathing slow and deliberate. He kicked out, narrowly missing Rhodry, then heaved himself onto his stomach with a scuttling motion like a crab that carried him a foot away. When his head barely missed a rock, Jill grabbed him by the shoulders and tried to pin him, but his trance-strength was far beyond her. Easily he flung her off and pitched to one side. Swearing, Rhodry flung himself down to help.

For what seemed a grotesque eternity they wrestled with Nevyn's body as he twisted, jerked, and flung his arms around. Once he landed Rhodry a hard blow on the jaw, but although Rhodry swore even louder, he hung on. Jill could only pray to the Goddess to keep away any enemies that might be approaching. At last Nevyn went limp, and she could just see him smile in the moonlight. His mouth worked as if he were speaking; then he lay utterly still.

"Oh ye gods," she said. "Is he going to die?"

Just then he opened his eyes and grinned at her.

"What have I been doing?" Nevyn said. "Flopping around?"

"Like a fish on a riverbank." Rhodry let go his hold.

"It happens now and then in trances." The old man sat up, looking around as if he were a bit dazed. "Did one of you kill Alastyr's body?"

"We didn't," Jill said. "We stayed with you."

"Then Blaen and his men must be at the farm already. No time to explain. We've got to hurry."

And yet, they reached the farm just at the same time as Blaen and the warband. At the head of his men, the gwerbret trotted over to them. In the gray dawn light, he looked profoundly annoyed.

"Thanks be to every god that you're safe," Blaen snapped. "We scoured the hills for you."

"I owe you an apology, Your Grace," Nevyn said. "But the battle's already over."

Camdel heard them all ride into the farmyard. He went tense, every muscle in his body spasming in panic when he realized that he wasn't going to starve to death but be rescued. With a moan he heaved himself to his knees, the ankle chain clanking. It was just long enough for him to stand and take a few steps. Lying on the kitchen table was a long-bladed knife, which would do to slit his throat or his wrists if only he could reach it. He wanted death, lusted for it, the one thing that could wipe away his shame and make him forget the hideous truths about himself that Sarcyn had taught him.

The chain let him reach the table, but the knife lay at the end of its six foot span. He leaned over the edge, stretched out, couldn't get up far enough to lie on it, stretched and stretched but could just brush the handle with his fingertips. From outside came voices, and two that he recognized: Gwerbret Blaen and Lord Rhodry of Aberwyn, here to see what had become of the Master of the King's Bath. With a stretch that ached his shoulder he touched the knife. He could just close two fingers on the handle scissorlike, but as he began to pull it toward him, his aching hand spasmed and knocked the knife to the floor. It bounced on the edge of the hearthstone and lay far out of his reach.

Sobbing, gasping for breath, he let himself fall from the table and crouched in the straw. Why hadn't Sarcyn killed him? Perhaps his master knew he wanted to die and left him alive as the last torment of all. Blaen will hang you, he told himself, because you stole from the High King. He clung to his one comfort, that soon he'd be dangling from a rope in Dun Hiraedd's market square. Outside the voices came closer.

"I only pray we find Camdel alive." That was Blaen, who doubtless wanted the pleasure of hanging him.

"So do I," said an unfamiliar voice. "But I warn you, Your Grace, he might be mad."

"Ah, the poor lad!" Blaen's voice was full of pity. "Well, no man can hold him accountable for this, from what you've told me."

Camdel felt his head jerk back. Blaen wasn't going to hang him. He was forgiven, and he would have to live with what he knew about himself. He began to scream, over and over as he tossed himself from side to side. Dimly he heard men shout and running footsteps, but he went on screaming until someone knelt in front of him and grabbed him by the shoulders. He looked up into Blaen's face, twisted in horror and pity both.

"Kill me," Camdel stammered. "For the love of every god, I beg you to kill me."

Although Blaen's mouth worked, he couldn't speak. An old man with a thick shock of white hair and piercing blue eyes knelt beside the gwerbret.

"Camdel, look at me," he said. "I'm a healer, and I'm going to help you. Just look at me, lad."

His voice was so kind that Camdel did what he asked. The blue eyes swelled to fill the world, as if he were looking into a lake of clear water. When the old man laid a hand on his arm, he felt warmth running into his blood, a soothing, calming warmth that made all his cramped muscles ease into peace.

"Later we'll have to talk about what's happened to you, but for now, there's no need for you to remember all that."

Camdel felt drunk, a pleasant, giggling sort of drunk.

"You're forgetting already, aren't you, lad? Of course you are. You only know that you're very ill, and that we're going to help you."

Camdel nodded in agreement, thinking that his long illness had left him fevered and confused. He clung to the old man's hand and wept in gratitude for his rescue.

As soon as he saw how broken Camdel was, Rhodry backed out of the kitchen in a hurry. The man was mad, his mind torn to pieces and the pieces scattered forever—or so Rhodry saw it. Death in battle he could face, but this misery? Feeling sick to his stomach, he wandered around to the main door of the house, where a pair of Blaen's men were keeping guard.

"Did they find him, my lord?" Comyn said.

"Never call me that again."

"My apologies, silver dagger."

"Well and good, then, but find him they did, and it's not pretty."

Comyn shivered.

"I sent some of the lads out to search the farmstead," the captain remarked. "Just in case there's someone lurking around, like."

"Good idea. Has anyone been inside yet?"

"No one wants to go, and I can't order a man to do somewhat I'm afraid to do myself."

"Well, you've got a silver dagger riding at your orders. I'll volunteer. Better than letting Blaen do it and put himself at who knows what dweomer-soaked risk."

Comyn hesitated, then handed Rhodry his shield.

"Don't know what you'll find in there, do you now?"

"I don't." Rhodry settled the shield on his left arm. "My thanks."

Rhodry drew his sword as Comyn kicked open the door. The farmhouse was big, about sixty feet in diameter, and like most houses of its type it was cut up like pie into small wedge-shaped chambers, divided from one another by wickerwork partitions. Rhodry stepped into what had been a parlor of sorts with two wooden chairs, a carved chest sitting under a window, and on the wall a wooden shelf that proudly displayed three painted earthenware plates. The dust lay so thick on the floor that he left footprints.

In either wall were openings, hung with blankets. Since the one to his right would lead to the kitchen and Camdel, Rhodry decided to go left. He approached the opening cautiously, then flicked up his sword and pulled the blanket down. As it crumpled, he saw into a bedchamber, with fresh straw on the floor and a couple of hay-filled pallets. He walked in, spotting several bedrolls and piles of saddlebags, all strewn about as if someone had recently searched through them. Although it looked like perfectly ordinary gear, he refused to touch it. For all he knew, it was filled with strange magicks.

The blanket over the next opening was pulled to one side. He peered into a chamber, far bigger than the last two, that had plowshares, old horse gear, and a couple of pieces of broken furniture lying about. Sitting by the doorway on the far side was a corpse, a gray, puffy thing dressed in farmer's clothing and holding a woodcutter's ax in both hands. Rhodry assumed that the farmer must have tried to defend himself as the dark dweomer overwhelmed and slew him.

"Well, old man," he said as he walked in, "we'll get you a proper burial."

The corpse raised its head and looked at him. Rhodry yelped aloud and stood frozen for a moment as it slowly lurched to its feet. Although its eyesockets were empty, it raised the ax and staggered toward him just as if it could see. Rhodry wanted to gag, but he flung up his shield and stepped aside as a clumsy blow swung down and missed him. When the thing turned toward him, he swung his sword up under its slow parry and caught it full across the throat. There was a gush of some dark liquid with an acrid smell, but the corpse calmly raised the ax again and stepped forward.

Rhodry's berserker laugh rose in his mouth. Sobbing and chortling, he dodged, lunged, and hacked into the corpse's armpit. Although more stenching liquid spewed, the thing came on and swung down at him. When he caught the blow on his shield, he heard the wood crack: the unnatural warrior was strong. His laughter rose to a howl as he swung up hard and cut the thing's right arm half off. It merely shifted the weight of the ax to its left hand and swung again. With a dodge, he darted round and stabbed it in the back. Slowly it turned to face him.

Distantly Rhodry heard voices yelling, coming closer, but he kept all his concentration on the ax as the thing swung it from side to side as if it would cut Rhodry down like a tree. He dodged, caught a blow on his shield and sliced its arm open, but still it swung. He was hampered by the clutter in the room as they went round and round. All at once he slipped; the ax sailed by a bare inch from his head. He jumped up, shrieking with laughter, and put all his berserker's strength into the blow. The sword bit deep and cracked bone as it caught the thing on the back of the neck.

Its head dangling from a strip of skin and muscle, the corpse swung the ax full into Rhodry's shield. The wood and leather split and cracked to the boss, and half the shield fell away. Rhodry ducked and dodged, then swung at its left arm. Although it dropped the ax at last, still it kept coming for him. He leapt back fast. It seemed that being touched by its fingers would be worse than the blow of a blade. Desperately he sliced its abdomen open. No guts spilled, and still it came for him.

"Halt in the name of the Master of the Aethyr!"

The tattered, oozing corpse stood stock-still. As Nevyn came in, Rhodry flung sword and shield down, dropped to his knees, and vomited, uncaring of who might see him. He heard other voices, then, as men crowded into the chamber. Comyn knelt down beside him just as he was wiping his mouth on his sleeve.

"Are you all right, silver dagger? By the Lord of Hell's asshole, what was that thing?"

"Cursed if I know, but I've never been more grateful for the loan of a shield in my life."

As he got up, he heard Nevyn chanting in a strange language. When the old man came to the end of it, the corpse buckled, its knees giving way, and settled rather than fell to the floor. Nevyn stamped thrice on the floor. Rhodry saw ugly and deformed Wildfolk dancing on the corpse; then they vanished.

"After this, Rhodry lad," the dweomermaster said, "you might ask my advice before poking around in strange places."

"You have my sworn word on that."

And yet, the worst horror of all still lay before him. Nevyn walked to the opening in the last chamber and pulled down the blanket to reveal a tiny, windowless room with a piece of black velvet hanging on the curved wall. On it was embroidered an upside-down five-pointed star and some other marks that Rhodry couldn't recognize. The chamber stank of incense and a fishy sort of smell.

Lying in the middle of the floor was the body of a stout, gray-haired man, his arms outstretched on either side. He looked like an ordinary Cerrmor man, but someone must have hated him, because he'd been stabbed in the chest over and over, so many times, truly, that he must have been long dead before the final blow fell. Although seeing the corpse meant little to Rhodry, merely looking into the room terrified him, so much so that when Nevyn walked in, he wanted to scream at the dweomerman to stay out. He forced himself to follow, but only because he was sure that Nevyn needed guarding. In the dim light it seemed that things moved, half-seen, silent. Nevyn nudged the corpse with the toe of his riding boot.

"Well, Alastyr," he said, "at last we meet in the flesh. You've been cursed clever, because I don't remember ever having seen

you before." He glanced at Rhodry. "This is the man who wanted
you dead, the one who stood behind Loddlaen in the war."

More in bewilderment than rage, Rhodry stared at his old
enemy. Since he'd been picturing the dark master as a fiend in
human form, he was oddly disappointed to find him so ordinary-
looking. Yet the room was fiendish enough. His irrational terror
grew until Nevyn laid a reassuring hand on his shoulder.

"There's no more danger here," the dweomerman said. "It's
the touch of elven blood in your veins that makes you so sensitive."

"Truly?"

"Truly. This is the chamber were Alastyr worked his foul
perversions of the dweomer, you see. Ah ye gods, poor Camdel!"

"Did they make him watch or suchlike?"

"Watch? Hah! They used him for their rituals. He was repeatedly raped in here."

"Oh pig's cock!" Rhodry was trying to deny what he was
hearing. "How can you rape a man?"

"Don't pretend to a naïveté that a court-raised man doesn't
have. You know cursed well what I mean. They cut him when
they were doing it, too, to spill blood for their twisted spirits."

If Rhodry had had anything left to heave, he would have
vomited again. Nevyn was watching him thoughtfully.

"Blaen and I are minded to tell the King that Camdel's
dead," the old man said. "Will your honor allow you to keep our
secret?"

Rhodry glanced around the chamber and wondered how it
would look to a man thrown down on the floor.

"Maybe Camdel was a thief," he said at last. "But I for one
don't have a cursed word more to say about that."

Nevyn helped Blaen get Camdel onto one of the horses
they'd found left behind in the stables. Although the young lord
swayed drunkenly in the saddle, he was conscious enough to be
able to ride. Later, Nevyn would remove the ensorcelment—
much later, once he had another dweomer-person there to begin
healing Camdel's mind.

"Now here, good sorcerer," Blaen said. "Are you sure you're
going to be safe out here alone?"

"Quite sure. The work I have to do won't take that long. I
should return to the dun in time for the noon meal."

"No doubt you know your own affairs best, then, and I don't care to know what they are."

As the warband mounted up, Nevyn had a chance to say a few words to Jill, who was yawning in the saddle.

"Camdel will sleep for some hours when you get back. Can I ask you to go sit with him when he wakes?"

"I will, truly. We don't want him to be all alone, in case he remembers somewhat of what he's been through."

Nevyn's heart ached. If only the little dolt could see it, he thought, she'd make such a splendid healer! Yet never could he force her Wyrd upon her, and he knew it. Until the warband was well out of sight, he waited, yawning some himself in the warm morning sun. Even his unnatural vitality had its limits. Somewhat wryly he reflected that tonight, he'd have his first full night's sleep in fifty-odd years. Then he went back into the house.

Blaen's men had already buried Alastyr and what was left of the farmer's corpse up in the hills. Nevyn went to the ritual chamber, tore down the piece of velvet, then threw it into the hearth for the Wildfolk of Fire to dispose of. While it smoked and crackled, he rummaged around and found the farmer's store of precious salt in a little crock and a couple of thin splints of wood of the sort used for transferring fire from a hearth to a candle. Since he had no incense, plain smoke would have to do.

When he returned to the chamber, the atmosphere already seemed a bit lighter, just from having that blasphemous symbol down from the wall. Although he wanted to do the banishings immediately, the chamber had secrets to tell him which would be lost once he did the working. He sat down cross-legged in front of a brown stain of Alastyr's blood, laid the salt and splints aside, then slowed his breathing until his mind was perfectly focused. He built an image of a six-pointed star until it glowed as two interlaced triangles, one red, one blue. Slowly he pushed the image out of his mind until it seemed to stand in front of him.

In the center hexagon, he visualized Alastyr's corpse as he'd first seen it at dawn, then sent his mind backward in time, at first only imagining the room as it would have looked by candlelight. Since the murder was so recent, true vision replaced his imagination in only a few seconds. He saw the blond apprentice kneeling on guard at his master's head. His mouth was twisted into a small, terrifying smile as Alastyr twitched and writhed in his trance; then his hand went to his belt and drew his dagger. For a while he paused, as if savoring the moment, then plunged the dagger into the helpless man's heart, over and over. Since he didn't care to watch the blows, Nevyn broke the vision and withdrew the star into himself.

"So that was my unexpected help, was it? And he must be the one who took Alastyr's books and other ritual objects, too. Well, assuming that he had any with him."

The Wildfolk crouched in the corners all nodded to indicate that, indeed, Alastyr had traveled with all the usual impedimenta of a dark master. They were a pitiful lot of spirits, all twisted and deformed by Alastyr's meddling.

"And yet he left the cloth behind. Was he in a hurry because we were coming?"

Again they told him yes.

"Is that why he didn't kill Camdel?"

They shook their heads no. One black gnome with protruding fangs lay down on the floor and pretended to cower in fear, while another stood over him, clawed hand raised as if it held a knife. Then it pantomimed kneeling down, sheathing the knife, and patted the other gnome gently on the shoulder.

"By the hells! Do you mean he *pitied* Camdel?"

They nodded a solemn yes.

"Now, I never would have thought that! Huh. Well, my friends, it's no affair of yours. Soon you'll be free of those ugly shapes. Help me perform the banishings, and then you can go to your kings."

When they leapt up, he felt their joy, washing over him as tangibly as water.

"Is he awake?" Rhodry said.

"Sort of." Jill sounded doubtful. "It's hard to tell."

Rhodry walked into the chamber and forced himself to look at Camdel, who lay on top of the bed with his shirt off. He was filthy, bruised, and sliced here and there with thin lines of scabs. At last he opened his eyes and looked up warily, as if he expected Rhodry to give him a few more scars.

"Do you want somewhat to eat?" Jill said.

"I don't," Camdel whispered. "Water?"

All the time that Jill was filling a cup from a pitcher, Camdel stared at Rhodry in wide-eyed fear.

"Oh here, don't you remember me from court? Rhodry Maelwaedd, Aberwyn's younger son."

At that, a faint smile flicked on his mouth, and he sat up to take the cup of water. Holding it in both hands, he sipped it slowly while he looked around the chamber. The late afternoon sun slanted in the windows and picked out the dust motes dancing in the golden shafts. As pleased as a child, Camdel smiled at the sight. Rhodry felt his revulsion rise and looked away. What if the dark masters had gotten hold of his Jill? Would they have done something similar to her? In his heart he made a solemn vow that if ever it was in his power to rid the world of any dark dweomermen, he would risk his life if necessary to stamp them out like crawling insects.

"Rhoddo, would you call a page?" Jill said. "I want them to fetch up water so he can have a bath."

"A bath?" Camdel sounded drunk. "I'd like that."

Rhodry left the chamber gratefully. Although he didn't blame Camdel for a thing, he couldn't bear the sight of him.

After he sent the pages on their errand, Rhodry joined Blaen at the honor table. Blaen was, of course, drinking mead, and for the first time in his life Rhodry decided to try to keep up with him. While his cousin watched with a small smile, he gulped down as much as he could in one swallow.

"Does a man good," Blaen remarked. "Wipes things away."

"It does, at that. Did you hear what . . ."

". . . happened to Camdel? I did."

Rhodry had another swallow of mead. Neither of them spoke again for hours.

In the foothills on the western side of Cwm Pecl, Sarcyn led his weary horse along a narrow track through stands of pine trees. He'd fled west blindly, seeking some isolated spot where he could hide for a day or two, but now it occurred to him that he'd better keep moving. Both the gwerbret's men and, worse yet, the Master of the Aethyr would be hunting him down. Yet in his weariness he wondered if it might not be better to let the gwerbret hang him than to fall into the hands of the Dark Brotherhood. They would make his death last for weeks.

"But I have the books," he whispered aloud. "Someday I'll have the power to stand against them."

Near sunset he found a valley with a stream and plenty of

grass for his horse. He made camp, then scrounged some dead wood from the forested hillside and lit a small fire with his flint and steel. Although his stomach was growling, he ignored his hunger. He'd already had one meal that day, and he needed to eke out his meager store of provisions. For a while he stared into the fire and brooded over his plans. Scattered around the kingdom were a number of people who might shelter him for a few days at least. A few days were all he could afford to spend in one place, no matter how much he needed time to study Alastyr's books. All at once he was too weary to think—remarkably weary and muddled, as he would realize later.

Like a child, he curled up on his blankets and fell asleep by the fire. When he woke, it was suddenly, at the touch of hands on his arms. He cried out, then struggled, kicking and writhing, but a leather cord slipped round his wrists and pulled tight, and a man fell across his knees and pinned him. By the light of the dying fire he could see his assailants, two light-skinned Bardek men in Deverry clothes. One lashed his wrists tight; the other, his ankles, even as he threw his weight this way and that. At last they were done, and he lay panting on the ground while they stood over him.

"So, little one," said the taller. "You've slain your master, have you?"

Sarcyn went rigid with terror, a coldness that started at the base of his spine and rippled upwards.

"I see you know who we are," the assassin went on. "The Hawks of the Brotherhood have you, sure enough. The Old One sent us to follow Alastyr and keep an eye on him. We've been scrying you out all along, little one, but never did we think to see a murder."

"I'll wager the Old One suspected somewhat of the sort," said the second. "He never tells a man all his thoughts."

"It may be, at that." He kicked Sarcyn hard on the side of the head. "But you'll pay, little one, and slowly, after you've told the masters everything you know."

Although the world danced like fire from the blow, Sarcyn bit his lip hard and kept from crying out. Even though fear was making him tremble, he swore himself a solemn vow: he would tell them nothing at all, no matter how cleverly they tortured him, because he would get no mercy from them even if he obeyed them. As the Hawks went to get their horses, hidden somewhere in the trees, he shrank into himself and clung to his will. It was all he had left, his ability to concentrate his will and drive himself with it. He forced the fear away, stopped trembling, and lay as limply as a netted deer while he stared into the fire.

Although Nevyn had returned around noon, Jill had no chance to talk with him until sunset, because the dweomerman worked on Camdel all afternoon, washing and treating his various wounds as well as soothing his mind. After dinner he sent a page to fetch her to his chamber, where the last blaze of light poured in the window. Jill sat down on a chest while he paced restlessly back and forth.

"How's Camdel?" she asked.

"Sound asleep, the gods be thanked. I had him tell me some of what's happened to him, but I made sure he won't remember doing so. He's too weak to face his memories just now."

"No doubt. Why did they . . . well, use him like that?"

He cocked his head to one side and considered her in an oddly sly way.

"By rights, I shouldn't tell you," he said at last. "Besides, I thought all this talk of dweomer ached your heart."

"Oh, Nevyn, don't tease! You know cursed well that what's aching my heart is curiosity."

"So I do." He paused for a smile. "Very well, then. Well, when two people bed down together, a certain amount of a substance called magnetic effluent is given off. I know you don't know what that is, and I'm not going to explain it further to someone without more knowledge, so take what I say on faith. This effluent has many a peculiar property, but it's basically a kind of life stuff. It's also present in blood. Now, the dark dweomermen are trained in ways of sucking up the effluent if it's present and using it to restore their own vitality. When his apprentice was using Camdel, Alastyr was basically feeding off their lust."

Jill felt sick to her stomach.

"Disgusting, isn't it?" Nevyn remarked. "Now here, though, that reminds me of somewhat. The apprentice—Sarcyn his name is, or so Camdel told me—did escape. You and Rhodry are going to have to be very careful when you ride out."

"I've been brooding over that all day, truly."

"I'm planning on hunting him down, or I'd insist that you two stay with Blaen, no matter how shamed it makes Rhodry feel. As it is, he's fairly weak, and eventually he'll have worse enemies than me. When news of Alastyr's murder reaches his foul brotherhood, they'll send assassins after our Sarcyn. I expect he'll be too busy to worry about revenging himself on you. Still, stay on guard. He's got a head start on me, and of course, I can't scry him out. I've never laid eyes on him in the flesh."

As soon as Jill had her idea, it seemed obvious, except that she had no idea of how she knew what she did. She sat very still, thinking it over, feeling her fear grow, not only a fear of Sarcyn, but of deliberately and coldly using the dweomer. If she voiced her idea, she knew she would be taking the first step on a very strange road. Or was it truly only the first step? Somewhat puzzled, Nevyn watched her until at last, she made her decision.

"I've seen him in the flesh," she said. "You can scry through me, can't you? I don't know why I'm so sure of this, but can't you use me like a pair of eyes?"

"By the hells! You're right enough, but are you sure you'd let me? It means my taking over your will."

"Of course I'd let you. You should know that I'd trust you with my life."

Nevyn came close to weeping. Hastily he turned away and wiped his eyes on his dirty sleeve while she wondered at it, that her good opinion would mean so much to a man of his powers.

"Well, my thanks," he said at last. "Let me just get some wood from a servant, and we'll build a fire."

By the time that the fire was burning steadily, the twilight was deepening to a velvet dark. Nevyn had Jill sit in a chair in front of the fire while he stood behind her. Although she was frightened, with the fear came the same kind of exaltation she felt just before a battle. When he laid his hand on the back of her neck, just where the spine meets the skull, at first his fingers seemed normally warm; then the warmth increased and seemed to flow into her very veins, to spread along them through her face and mind, until at last it centered itself between her eyes as a peculiar twisting sensation.

"Look into the fire, child, and think of Sarcyn."

As soon as she did, she saw him, lying asleep by a campfire somewhere in hilly country. The image was small at first; then it swelled to fill first the hearth, then her whole mind, until she hovered above the scene the way she did in a true dream. As she floated over the valley, she saw two men leave the trees up the hill and begin to stalk the unsuspecting sleeper. Slowly they moved, and quietly, gliding along low to the ground like ferrets. Even though she'd hated Sarcyn not a minute before, she was suddenly terrified for him.

In her vision-trance she tried to cry out and wake him, but no sound came. She swooped down and grabbed his shoulders, but her incorporeal touch couldn't shake him awake. Just as the two men pounced, she darted away and stood on the other side of the fire as the Hawks bound and taunted their prisoner. All at once, she heard Nevyn's voice in her mind.

"Come back now! They have the power to see you if they should look your way with the second sight. Think of me, child. Come back to the room."

She pictured his face, the room; suddenly her eyes were open, and she was looking into the fire. Nevyn was no longer touching her. She got up, stretching a peculiar stiffness away.

"I never dreamt they'd be following Alastyr along like that," Nevyn said. "I've got to work fast if I'm going to pull our apprentice out of this particular trap."

"What? Why do you want to save him, after all the foul deeds he's done?"

"He'll pay for those crimes, sure enough, but under the laws."

"But he's the most hateful swine I've ever—"

Nevyn held up his hand flat for silence.

"Why don't you go down to the great hall and your Rhodry? I've got some hard thinking to do."

As soon as Jill left, Nevyn resumed his restless pacing while he considered what was to be done. He was determined to save Sarcyn from the Hawks more for the good of the kingdom than for that of the apprentice. If he died cursing and screaming under torture, his hatred and pain would infill his next life, making him a twisted threat to everyone around him.

"If we can pull him out, anyway," Nevyn remarked to the fat yellow gnome, who was basking by the fire. "Doubtless they're heading for Bardek. I wonder how they'll smuggle him onto a ship? Probably a large chest or suchlike would do."

The gnome scratched its stomach thoughtfully. Nevyn considered asking Blaen to send a warband after them, but the Hawks had a long head start. Besides, since they were dweomer-trained, they would only see the pursuit and be able to hide quite effectively. *I could ride with the warband, though,* he reminded himself, *if we can catch up.* It was going to be slow going for the Hawks, after all, as they picked their way through the mountains.

The mountains. All at once Nevyn chuckled to himself. He knelt down by the fire to contact the one dweomer-master in the kingdom who could help him now.

After the Hawks tended their horses, they returned to the campfire. Sarcyn lay unmoving and listened to them talk until he finally puzzled out their names. Dekanny was the taller, the one with the yellowish-brown eyes that bespoke some Anamura blood in his veins, while the other, who also seemed to be in charge, was Karlupo. Once they'd eaten, Dekanny knelt down beside Sarcyn and grabbed his wrists to haul his arms up over his head, then pulled up his shirt until it covered his face, blinding him. He lay still, summoning his will and listening to the Hawk humming to himself while he did something at the fire. Finally he came back.

"I'm holding a dagger. I heated it."

Sarcyn braced himself with every ounce of his will. Dekanny giggled like a girl, then laid the heated steel on Sarcyn's right nipple. Although the pain seared into his very heart, he made no sound.

"I'm turning it over now, little one."

The pain bit into his left nipple. He fought to choke back the scream that bubbled up from his throat. Suddenly he felt his bowels gush and empty.

"What a stink! I'll turn you over and mark your cheeks for that."

"No you won't!" Karlupo said from nearby. "You've done enough for one night. He's got to be in decent shape when he reach home, because the masters will want him to last as long as possible."

"Ah, he can heal on the ship."

"I said: enough."

Then the world spun around, and Sarcyn fainted. He woke in the middle of the night to find himself still lying in his own excrement. They'd pulled his shirt down, and the rough linen chafed on his burns, which oozed some sort of liquid. He lay awake for a long time, fighting to keep from moaning, before he fainted again. In the morning they kicked him awake and hauled him up to a sitting position. Karlupo had made barley porridge in a small kettle and brought a bowl over.

"I'll untie your hands so you can eat," he said. "But if you cause the slightest trouble, Dekanny will get some pleasure out of you before we ride."

Sarcyn turned his head away. He was determined to starve and weaken himself so that he'd die more quickly under the torture.

"You're going to eat," Karlupo snapped.

When he still refused, they knelt down on either side of him. Dekanny pried his jaws open while Karlupo shoveled in a spoonful. The stuff gagged him so badly that he had to swallow it out of sheer reflex. They fed him the whole bowl, and the humiliation hurt as much as his burns.

Yet once they were on horseback, the pain took over. The motion of the horse made his shirt rub on the raw burns, and in the hot sun he sweated, adding salt to the friction until he could think of nothing but dying and putting an end to the pain. About midmorning his bound wrists began to swell, making the thong cut into the puffy flesh. By the time they stopped for the noon meal, his lower lip hurt, too. He realized that in fighting the pain, he'd chewed it open.

"Are you going to eat, little one?" Karlupo said. "Or do you want us to feed you again?"

"I'll eat."

Karlupo untied his hands and stood over him with a drawn sword while he ate beef jerky and hardtack. Then it was back on the horses again, and more agony.

By then they were well into the mountains and following a narrow track that twisted through enormous boulders. Every now and then they forded a fast-rushing stream or rode by a cracked and crumbling cliff. Sarcyn barely noticed what they passed. He had a new discomfort to add to his pain: riding all day in his damp and filthy brigga was making his thighs and buttocks chafe raw. Eventually Dekanny dropped back to ride next to him.

"Soon we'll be making camp. I'll have a few minutes to play with you again. I want you to make a choice. I can either put the heated blade in your armpits, or in the small of your back—twice, of course. Tonight you tell me which one you want."

With that he dropped back to take up the rear guard and let Karlupo have the lead. Sarcyn trembled beyond all his will to stop. He knew exactly what Dekanny was doing. If he didn't choose, of course, he would get both tortures, but if he chose, he would be taking the first step into collaborating with his tormentor. They wanted him to begin to surrender his will, to become a partner in his own pain until at last there would be a dreadful, almost sexual complicity between the giver of pain and the receiver of it.

"Dekanny!" he called out. "I won't choose."

From behind came only a girlish giggle of excitement. They rode into a rocky defile, topped with scrub and brush. Once, when Sarcyn looked up, one of the bushes seemed to turn into a face. Hastily he looked away. If he became delirious, he would lose his will to resist. He concentrated on his breathing and tried to put his mind far away from his aching, throbbing body, while the shadows grew ever deeper and the night grew inexorably closer.

Two hours before sunset they camped in a valley so narrow that it was more a cleft between two hills. Sarcyn sat on the ground and watched every move Dekanny made as the two Hawks set up camp and gave the horses extra rations of oats to compensate for the lack of grass. Soon, very soon, he would feel the hot blade four times.

"Let him eat first," Karlupo said finally. "He won't be able to get anything down when you're done with him."

"Very well. I'll let him rest between each mark, too."

Sarcyn bit his bleeding lip and stared at the ground as if he could reduce the whole world to this little patch of rocks. All at once, he heard Dekanny shriek. He looked up to see the Hawk staggering with an arrow in his left shoulder and a swarm of men pouring into the valley. Short they were, about five feet tall at most, but massively built and armed as warriors. Their long axes swung efficiently, twice, three times, and Karlupo lay dead with his head knocked off his shoulders and both legs cut off at the knee. Although Dekanny tried to run, a great ax slashed up from below and drove deep into his crotch. Screaming he fell, to have his throat slit neatly with the barest edge of a blade. The warriors smiled at each other and gathered round to look at the corpses.

Only then did Sarcyn realize that none of them had uttered a sound during the unequal battle.

Taking off his pot helm, one of the warriors strode over to Sarcyn. He had a lined, tanned face, a thick gray beard, and bushy black eyebrows.

"You speak Deverry speak?"

"I do."

"Good. I speak Deverry speak. Not good good, but I speak. Others speak good good, back inside. Talk then. I Jorl. You stand up?"

"I don't know if I can. Here, good Jorl. I don't understand this. Who are you?"

"Mountain people. No worry, lad. We rescue. You safe."

Sarcyn let his head slump forward and wept, the tears pouring like a child's, while Jorl cut his hands free with a tiny dagger.

It took several dwarves to get Sarcyn back in the saddle. They collected the other mounts, then set off on foot, leading the apprentice along. Although he was dimly trying to figure out why they'd rescue him, it took most of his will and attention just to stay mounted. Finally, as the twilight was growing gray, they marched down a narrow valley and straight toward a cliff. As they came close, Sarcyn heard a grinding sound.

"Oh by the gods!"

A huge door was slowly opening in the cliff face. Just as they reached it, it held steady and open. When Jorl led his party into a high, square-cut tunnel, other men came forward, carrying lanterns and speaking in a language Sarcyn had never heard. He glanced back to see the door slowly being winched shut behind him. The sight of the disappearing crack of twilight made his head swim. Suddenly hands reached up and grabbed him to lower him gently down. Jorl's face leaned over him.

"We get litter. Carry you."

Sarcyn wanted to thank him, but the swimmy darkness enveloped him.

When he woke, he was lying on a narrow pallet in a pitch-dark chamber. His first reaction was panic, because there was not a crack or shimmer of light, not even the variations of darkness as in a normal nighttime chamber. Gradually he became aware that he was clean, naked under a soft blanket, and that his burns throbbed only slightly. His broken lip, too, had been smeared with some pleasant-smelling salve. In a few minutes, a door opened with a burst of light. A fellow who was about four feet tall walked in, holding up a lantern.

"The Wildfolk said you were awake," he announced. "Can you eat?"

"I think so."

"I'll bring you somewhat, then."

He set the lantern down on a little table near the door, then went out, shutting the door behind him. Sarcyn heard the sound of a heavy bar being dropped on the outside. So he was a prisoner, if a well-treated one. Although the room was only about ten feet on a side and carved out of the living rock of the mountain, it was far from being a cell. On the floor was a solid red carpet, and besides the pallet and the table there was a squarish chair with a high back and cushioned seat that looked like it would be quite comfortable—for someone with very short legs. Near the door, discreetly covered with a square of cloth, sat a chamber pot, and next to it were his clothes, washed, dried, and carefully folded.

Moving slowly, because his head was still light, he got up and dressed. He was not surprised to find that his sword was nowhere to be seen. He was just finishing when the fellow returned, bearing a wooden tray with two bowls on it.

"Do you like mushrooms?"

"I do."

"Good." He set the tray down on the table. "All the movables are a bit small for you, aren't they? Well, you won't be here long."

"Can you tell me where I'll be going?"

He paused, head tilted as he considered, then shrugged and went to the door. He held it a bit open so that Sarcyn could see the two heavily armed soldiers on guard before he spoke.

"The Master of the Aethyr's coming to fetch you."

Then he stepped out, slamming the heavy door shut just as Sarcyn leapt for it more in sheer terror than a rational attempt to escape. He slammed into it and leaned there spread-eagled, listening to the sound of the dropping bar, then began to sob in near-soundless gulps. Finally he pulled himself away and began to pace around and around the room. Up near the high ceiling was an opening that had to be an air vent, but it was only a foot square, far too small to squeeze through. Maybe he could pretend to be ill, then overpower his keeper—but there were the guards. Maybe he could withdraw his aura, slip out—if they ever opened that door again before Nevyn arrived. Or he could summon Wildfolk to create a distraction; maybe he could even get one to lift the bar on the door.

All at once, he stopped pacing as a thought went through him like an arrow: he didn't want to escape. He sat down very slowly on the floor near the table and considered it again and again: he had no desire to be free. He was weary, exhausted in his very soul, far too tired to run, and if he escaped, he would be always running, from Nevyn, from the law, from the Hawks, from the terror of his own memories, running always running, always lying, always on guard.

"The deer on a hunting preserve have more peace, truly."

He smiled, a bitter, twisted smile, at his own words. So he was going to die. Nevyn would turn him over to the gwerbret, no doubt, and he would be killed. It was better than being in the hands of the Hawks, of course. At the worst, he'd be broken on the wheel, but he'd seen and heard enough of Blaen to know that most likely he'd be given a merciful hanging. He felt a certain perverse pleasure, too, in realizing that all the crucial facts he'd gathered would die with him. The Old One would never know about Rhodry's mixed blood. When he smiled at the thought, he realized that he'd hated the Old One for years, hated them all, every dark master and apprentice and Hawk that ever he'd met, hated them as indeed, they must have hated him. Well, he'd be rid of them now.

When he held up his hands, he half expected to find them shaking, but they were perfectly steady. He wanted to die. He saw, suddenly, that his inevitable death would be not an execution, but an assisted suicide. For years he'd felt like an empty, hollow farce of a man; now the thin false shell he presented to the world would collapse and be swallowed up by the void inside him. The long weariness would be over. He smiled again, and as he did, he felt a warm calm envelop him, as if he floated in a hot perfumed bath, as if he floated a few inches off the floor, so light and calm and safe did he feel now that he wanted to die. No one would ever force him to go against his own will again; no one would ever hurt him again. Still smiling, he drew over the tray of food. He was perfectly calm and very hungry.

By the time he finished eating, the calm had become a weariness so deep that he could no longer hold his head up. He lay down on his stomach, pillowed his head on folded arms, and watched the shadows thrown along the floor by the lantern. At times he floated out of his body, then slid back, moving back and forth between the etheric and the physical without any conscious effort or control. He was out of the body, in fact, when the cell door opened and Nevyn strode in, accompanied by the dwarf who'd brought the food. Even though Sarcyn had never seen the old man before, he knew that he was facing the Master of the Aethyr by his aura, a near-blinding blaze of pale gold light.

"Worms and slimes!" the dwarf snapped. "Is he dead?"

"I doubt it." Nevyn knelt down by Sarcyn's body and laid a hand on the back of his neck. "He's not, but in a trance."

All at once Sarcyn felt the blue light swirl around him. He felt as if his body was sucking at him; no matter how hard he fought, it pulled him down the silver cord until at last he heard a rushy hiss and a click. With a grunt he opened his eyes and saw Nevyn leaning over him.

"Good," the dwarf said. "Well, I'll be right outside if you need me."

Sarcyn stared down at the floor until he heard the door slamming shut; then, very slowly, he turned his head and looked at his adversary. It seemed that he should say something, some cry of defiance, perhaps, or make the simple remark that he was ready and willing to die, but he was weary again, and no words came. For what seemed a long time Nevyn simply looked at him.

"I came here hoping to speak of restitution," Nevyn said at length. "But I think me it's far too late for that."

With a sigh the old man rose and started for the door. Sarcyn was asleep by the time he opened it.

Although Nevyn had insisted that he was capable of riding off and bringing back a dangerous prisoner on his own, neither Jill nor Rhodry had been willing to let him. Now, however, they understood why the dweomerman had refused to let any of Blaen's men accompany them. In silent awe they sat on a long stone bench near the wall of the enormous cavern and watched the dwarven market-fair. At least a hundred yards in diameter and easily twice that high, the cavern was lit by shafts of sunlight streaming in from far above. Directly across from them, water trickled down the rock and collected in artificial basins. Every now and then, a dwarf would fill a bucket at a pool and take it away again for some domestic purpose. Out in the center of the cavern, some hundred or so of the mountain people haggled and traded. Most of the stuff for sale was food spread out on rough cloths: mushrooms, bats, root crops furtively tended up on the surface, game hunted equally slyly.

"It's a hard life these people have," Jill remarked.

"Huh. They deserve it."

"Oh, here, my love. Try to take it with good grace."

Rhodry merely scowled. He was smarting, she knew, because the dwarves had taken one look at him, seen his elven blood, and instantly decided that he was a thief. Only Nevyn's intervention kept them from making him wait outside. Although every now and then someone would stroll over and say a few pleasant words to her, Rhodry they ignored, as if he were a wolf or some other dangerous pet she kept.

"Well, I understand now why Otho the smith was so nasty to you," she said.

"I only wish I'd been nastier in return."

Jill patted his arm in what she hoped was a soothing manner. Wearing a rough brown dress that came to her ankles, a tiny woman, no more than three feet high, came over. In a sling at her hip she carried a baby. Since Jill had no idea of how long these people lived or how fast they grew, she couldn't tell the child's age, but it sat up as straight and looked around as alertly as a human child of about a year old.

"Ah," the woman said. "You must be the lass who came with the Master of the Aethyr."

"I am, at that. Is your babe a lad or a lass?"

"A lass."

"She's a precious lambkin, truly."

At the praise, the baby dimpled and cooed. Although she had a low forehead under a mop of curly black hair and her nose was thick and broad, she was so tiny yet so vital that Jill longed to hold her.

"Can I ask you somewhat?" Jill went on. "Why do so many of your folk speak Deverrian?"

"Oh, we trade with the farmers in the foothills. They're a peaceable lot, and they keep our secrets in return for a bit of our silver. There's naught like precious metals for making friends— or bitter enemies."

With the last she gave Rhodry a pointed look, then wandered on, clucking to her baby.

"I wish to every god that Nevyn would get himself back here," Rhodry snarled.

His wish was granted in a few minutes when the dweomer-master emerged from a tunnel on the far side of the cavern. With him was the dwarf named Larn who was in charge of guarding the prisoner, and as they strode over they were talking urgently.

"Where's Sarcyn?" Rhodry got up to greet them.

"I left him in the cell," Nevyn said. "He's gone mad. Completely and unreachably mad."

"Serves the cursed little bastard right."

"I suppose. Oh truly, your point has some justice in it, but I—" Nevyn hesitated, then shrugged. "It matters not. He's mad, and there's an end to it."

Jill knew that the dweomerman was hiding something from them, that he had some reason for wanting Sarcyn sane, but she also knew that he would never reveal it until he chose to.

"Nevyn?" she said. "You're not just going to let him go, are you? That would wrench my guts, to see him free."

"As vengeful as always, aren't you? But truly, I'm not. He's as dangerous mad as he was sane, and besides, he was sane enough when he murdered that farmer and kidnapped Camdel. We'll take him back for Blaen's malover."

"Why?" Larn broke in. "I can have a couple of the lads drag him outside and slit his throat. Save us all a lot of bother."

"I'm no man to judge him and order his execution. Only the laws can do that."

"Have it your way, then," the dwarf said with a shrug. "I'll have him brought out."

Floating above the fire, the image of Salamander's face was grinning broadly. Nevyn heartily wished that just once the gerthddyn would take something seriously.

"So," Salamander thought to him. "Camdel's evidence means that I was right about the opium."

"Just so. I want you to go to a certain Lord Gwaldyn straight away. He's associated with the King's Provost, and he knows me well. Have Gwaldyn take this Anghariad under arrest as soon as he can, and tell him to guard her carefully. I'll wager there's plenty of the noble-born at court who're going to want her poisoned to stop her tongue from wagging."

"I'll go to him first thing on the morrow. How long should I stay in Dun Deverry?"

"Until I arrive. Liddyn the apothecary—you've met him, I think—is on his way here from Dun Cantrae. I'll be giving Camdel into his care, then set out to return the Great Stone to the King. Do you mind waiting there?"

"Not in the least. In fact, your asking me to stay is somewhat of a boon, because my beloved and esteemed father wants me to come home."

"Well, now, if he needs you, I can send someone else to the capital."

"Don't trouble yourself, oh Master of the Aethyr." Salamander turned melancholy in a most dramatic way. "I can guess exactly what this is about: he wants to berate me for my wandering ways. I said I'd return in the fall. That'll be soon enough to hear yet another carefully composed and precisely pointed lecture on my faults, all delivered in full bardic voice."

After they finished their conversation, Nevyn put out the fire, for the summer night was warm, and sat by the fading coals to wonder yet again if there was anything he could do about Sarcyn. On the morrow at dawn he would hang in the market square, would die with a mind as confused and wordless as an animal's when the farmer raises the ax for slaughter. And how would that carry over to his next life? Nevyn had no detailed idea, but he knew that the end result would be bad, twisting Sarcyn's soul just a bit more to the paths of evil. Yet he had tried talking to the apprentice and gotten nowhere, because Sarcyn in his madness was incapable of understanding complex ideas such as restitution and free choice. On the other hand, Nevyn wondered if the apprentice would have been able to understand those ideas even when he was sane, or if he'd have chosen to change. Most likely not, he supposed, but it saddened him to think of a soul throwing itself down into darkness when there was no need.

On the hearthstone nearby sat Alastyr's three books, which the dwarves had handed over him. One was simply a copy of the *Secret Book of Cadwallon the Druid*; the others, in the Bardek tongue, were called *The Way of Power* and *The Warrior's Sword*, half pretentious garbage, half exceedingly dangerous procedures and rituals. Idly Nevyn opened *The Warrior's Sword*.

"Yea, for all things shall be dominated by the Will of the true

Warrior, down even unto the secret places of the Darkness, for it is most admirable and recondite a truth that they who fight under the Sigil of the . . ."

With a snort Nevyn slammed the book shut and tossed it aside.

"I wonder why those people can never write decently," he remarked to the yellow gnome. "Recondite, indeed!"

The gnome scratched its stomach, then grabbed a handful of charcoal from the hearth and scattered it all over the carpet. Before Nevyn could grab it, it was gone. He was picking up the last of the bits when there was a knock at the door.

"It's Jill."

"Come in, child, come in."

She stepped in, shutting the door, then leaning back against it as if she were weary.

"I've come to say farewell. Rhodry and I are leaving on the morrow."

"Ye gods! So soon?"

"So soon. It's the way Blaen treats Rhodry. All the generous things he does only make Rhoddo feel more shamed. Sometimes I don't understand the honor-bound at all."

"They have a rocky field to plow. But I'd hoped you'd linger here until I finished up my affairs, at least."

"So did I. I'll miss you."

"Will you now?" He felt his throat tighten. "I'll miss you too, but you can always reach me through the fire."

"So I can." She was silent for so long that he came closer to look at her. "I've been thinking. At times I wish I'd just gone with you when you wanted me to study herbcraft, but now it's too late."

"Because of our Rhodry?"

She nodded agreement, thinking something through.

"But well," she said at last. "One of these days, he's bound to get me with child, and I won't be able to ride with him. If I went back to Dun Gwerbyn to be with Da, he couldn't even visit because of his exile. But cursed if I'll end up a tavern wench like Mam. So I was wondering, you see, if maybe—"

"Of course, child!" Nevyn felt like jigging in sheer glee. "There's no reason that you and I and the babe couldn't settle down somewhere where the folk need an herbman and his apprentice."

She smiled in such sunny relief that she looked more a child than a woman.

"If it weren't for Rhodry's stubborn honor," he went on, "we could do it straightaway, but I can't see him being willing to grub among the herbs like a farmer."

"He might—on the night when the moon turns purple and falls from the sky."

"Just so. But well and good, then. We'll keep it in mind. Up in the northern provinces there are a number of towns that need an herbman enough to ignore the fact that a silver dagger is wintering with him."

After Jill left, Nevyn stood by the window for a long time and smiled to himself. At last! he thought. Soon his Wyrd would begin to unknot; soon he could begin to lead her to the dweomer. Soon. Yet even in his joy, he felt a cold warning, that nothing in his dweomer-wound life would ever be simple again.

Epilogue
Winter, 1063

The wild wind of a man's Wyrd twists his life.
Untamed it is, unknown its turning.
Dread the dolt who declares he sees his, sun
sparkling. In mirror-murk, Wyrd watches him.

From the Gnomic Stanzas *of Gweran,*
Bardd Blaedd

Why didn't you have Valandario order Ebañy home?" Calonderiel said. "It's been months since the Master of the Aethyr had any need of him."

"Because in my heart I was hoping that he'd do something just because I asked him," Devaberiel said. "Just once."

Calonderiel considered this gravely. They were sitting in Devaberiel's tent, and a fire burned under the smokehole in the center of the roof. Every now and then, a drop of rain slipped past the baffles and hissed in the flames.

"You know," the warleader said at last, "you rant and rave at the lad too much. I swear it, bard, when you're in full voice and yelling at a man, it makes his head ache."

"And did I ask your advice?"

"No, but you've got it anyway."

"Coming from you, of all men—"

"Ah, I know us both very well. Isn't that why you're angry at me now?"

Devaberiel stifled a furious retort.

"Well, yes," the bard said at last. "I suppose it is."

Calonderiel smiled and passed the mead skin. For a change, the warleader was tactful enough to let the subject drop.

By then, autumn was drawing to a close. The weary sun hauled itself up late and stayed for only a scant six hours before setting among rainclouds. Most of the People had ridden farther west to the winter camps, but Devaberiel and a few friends waited on the Eldidd border, driving their horses from meadow to meadow in search of fresh grass, hunting the gray deer and the feral cattle left from the days when Eldidd men had tried to claim the borderlands. For all his bluster, Devaberiel was worried about his son. What if Ebañy had been taken ill in the filthy cities of men or been killed by thugs or bandits?

Finally, just two days before the darkest day, when rain poured down and wind howled around the tents, Ebañy rode in, dripping wet and shivering with cold, so miserable that Devaberiel didn't have the heart to berate him straightaway. He helped his son tether his horses with the others, then brought him into the warm tent and had him change his clothes. Ebañy huddled by the fire and took a skin of mead gratefully.

"And have you run enough errands for one summer?" the bard said.

"Oh yes, and a strange business it was." Ebañy wiped his mouth on the back of his hand and passed the skin to his father. "There. I am braced, oh esteemed parent. You may lecture, scold, berate, and excoriate me to your heart's content. I realize that I've arrived in the autumn only in the most limited, restricted, and weaseling sense of the word."

"I was just worried about you, that's all."

Ebañy looked up in surprise and reached for the skin with a flourish.

"Well," Devaberiel went on, as mildly as he could, "Deverry's a dangerous place."

"That's true. I'm sorry. I found this lass up in Pyrdon, you see, on my way home, who found my humble self very amusing indeed."

"Oh. Well, that's a reasonable excuse."

Again Ebañy stared at him in wide-eyed shock. Devaberiel smiled, enjoying the effect he was making.

"Don't you want to know why I called you home?"

"Well, I assumed you wanted to take me to task for being a wastrel, scoundrel, lazy sot, or perchance total fool."

"Nothing of the sort. I've got important news. This spring, I discovered that you have a half-brother I didn't even know existed. His mother is a Deverry woman like yours, and he's ended up a silver dagger."

"Rhodry."

"That's his name, sure enough."

"Ah by the Dark Sun herself, I met him, and just this spring. I kept staring at him and wondering why I thought I knew him. Here, Da, he looks a cursed lot like you."

"So I've been told. Do you remember that silver ring, the one with the roses on it? It's for him. Now look, I can't go riding around the kingdom, so when spring comes, will you take it to him?"

"Of course. After all, since I've met him, I can scry him out easily enough." Then suddenly he shuddered.

"It looks to me like you've taken a chill. I'll put more wood on the fire."

"It's not that. The dweomer-cold took me."

Devaberiel felt like shuddering himself. Realizing that his son was one of those persons that the elves call "spirit friends" always creeped his flesh. He busied himself with finding the leather pouch and tossing it to Ebañy, who shook the ring out into his palm.

"It's a strange trinket, this." Ebañy slipped into Deverrian when he spoke. "I remember when you showed it to me, all those years ago. I wanted it so badly, for some reason, and yet I knew it wasn't mine."

"Do you still covet it?"

"I don't." He closed his fingers over the ring and stared into the fire. "I see Rhodry. He's up in the north somewhere, because he's riding through snowdrifts. The ring quivers in my hand when I watch, so it's his, true enough. Oh, it longs for him, it does, but I think me that in the end, it might bring his death."

"What? By the barbarian gods, maybe I should just chuck the thing into a river."

"It'd only find a man to fish it out again." Ebañy's voice was soft, half-drunken. "And he'll not die, our Rhodry, till his Wyrd comes upon him, and what man can turn that aside? Not even his own father, and you know it well."

Yet Devaberiel felt heartsick, that his son saw some grave thing come toward them from the future.

It was a long time before the Old One fully pieced together the story of the summer's debacle in Deverry. When the appointed time for Alastyr and the Hawks to return came and went, he knew that something had gone seriously wrong and sent spies off to the kingdom. Before they could return, however, he received alarming news from more ordinary sources. Over in

Deverry, the king's men and the gwerbret of Cerrmor's men swept in and arrested several of their most important agents in the opium trade. Fortunately, Anghariad had been poisoned before she could babble secrets under torture, and Gwenca knew little of dark dweomer besides superstitious ramblings that the gwerbret disbelieved. Still, the arrests were a severe blow to the opium trade, which provided the dark brotherhood with a significant part of its income.

Yet the worst news of all arrived with the shaken spies. As the Old One had long believed, Alastyr and his apprentices were dead, and the books of power in Nevyn's hands. The Old One longed to know what Sarcyn had told the old man before his public hanging; he simply couldn't believe that Nevyn would waste a chance to torture every possible scrap of information out of the apprentice. The thing, however, that made him rage and swear for long hours was that Nevyn had pulled a final trick on them. When in his gratitude at having the Great Stone returned the King had offered the dweomerman a boon, Nevyn had asked for a court appointment for his "nephew" Madoc, the Master of Fire and a man of considerable power. With him there on guard, the dark dweomer would never be able to meddle directly at court again.

For several days the Old One shut himself up in his study and poured over the astrological data and the written records of his meditations. Somewhere in them had to be subtle indications of trouble that, it seemed, he'd missed before. Yet he found nothing to indicate the role Rhodry had played in disrupting Alastyr's plans. Jill was even worse, a complete cipher to him, because he had neither her birth time nor that of her parents, whose low status made it likely that the precious times were unrecorded and thus forever lost. Finally he decided that he had made no mistake, that something was at work to disrupt all his carefully laid workings, something beyond his control.

With a sigh that was close to a growl, he heaved his bulk out of his chair and waddled to the window. Outside, trembling in the coolish winter wind, flowering vines splashed scarlet over the garden wall. Two slaves moved across the square of lawn, raking fallen leaves. He barely saw them, his mind ranging far to Deverry. If only he could have travelled there! Impossible, of course; not only was his health so poor that the sea journey would have killed him, but also he was too well known to the Master of the Aethyr. For a moment he was close to panic. His delicate position in the Brotherhood depended on successful predictions, not advice that led to disaster. What if the other members of the ruling council decided that he'd outlived his usefulness? Then he steadied himself, reminding himself that he still had power beyond most, that he was far from defeated yet.

He went to the door, rang the gong for his majordomo, and told the slave that he was not to be disturbed for anything short of the house being on fire. Then he settled himself in his chair and let his breathing slow while he prepared for the working. The Old One had discovered and elaborated a most curious form of meditation over his long years that was the source for many of his most accurate predictions. In Bardek at that time, when parchments and writing materials were extremely expensive, learned men had developed a clever system of training their memories to store information. First the student learned to visualize clear mental images of ordinary objects, say a silver wine flagon. Once he could hold this image in his mind for a moment or two and see it as clearly as if it sat before him, he went on to doing the same thing with more and more elaborate objects, until at last he could hold an entire room, filled with furniture, in his mind and have that room be exactly the same every time he recalled it.

At this point he began to build a memory house, imagining and visualizing it one room at a time. Into each room he placed objects symbolic of things he wanted to remember, and these images were usually amusing or grotesque the better to stimulate the memory. For instance, a spice merchant would have a room in his house where he stored information about certain important customers. If a rich woman detested black pepper, say, he would put in a statue of her sneezing violently. If at a certain point he remembered that she had a special quirk, he would mentally walk into the room, look around, and see the picture, which would remind him to bring her a present of some other spice.

Now, it's obvious that this method of memory training has a great deal in common with the beginning steps of a dweomer apprenticeship, and the Old One had realized it as soon as he began his dweomer-studies. As a young man, he'd been trained as a government clerk, a job that required the memory method above all else, because in those days the very simple idea of filing papers and information in alphabetical order had yet to be invented. In his mind the young slave eunuch who was still known as Tondalo had built a vast archive, into which he could walk and find the location of every important document in his care. Once he had bought his freedom and made himself a rich man by squeezing every drop of the rich juices of a civil service run mostly by bribes, he had spent an intensely pleasurable afternoon burning that archive down to the precisely imagined ground.

The technique, however, had remained extremely valuable, especially once he'd chanced upon a way to expand it. It had happened, some hundred years earlier, that he'd been working on a particularly difficult problem for the dark guild, a question of whether or not to assassinate a certain archon. As spies brought him information about the archon and the political situation in his city-state, Tondalo had stored them in a memory room, because they were far too scandalous to write down. At one point, he returned to that room to find that certain of the objects had changed. A statue of a naked young boy (representing the archon's true love in life) was holding a bowl that the Old One hadn't placed there, and next to the boy stood a weeping woman. Spurred by the change, Tondalo saw the solution to their problem: the boy was holding poison in a bowl; the woman was his mother. One of the dark guild's more presentable members had worked on the mother's mind until she was furious enough to denounce the archon publicly for his vices. After the mob was through with him, the dark guild had no need to send an assassin to the archon's door.

That particular set of symbols had changed only out of intuition; the Old One had seen that clearly, that just as in a dream, one part of his mind had solved a problem while his consciousness was looking another way. But it had given him an idea. What if he made a special room, a temple, even, and filled it with dweomer-charged symbols? Would they perhaps change as tides from the future touched them and tell the secrets of time to come? Although it had taken him years, in the end the Old One had made the idea work.

That afternoon he sat in his chair and called up his temple of Time. Since this working was a purely mental one, he was fully awake, merely concentrating with an intensity beyond the reach of an untrained mind. The first building was a tall, square tower, made of white stone, that stood on a hill; one side of the hill was in

full sunlight, the other, in moonlight. He walked round to the
moonlit side and went in one of the four doors that opened into
the first of twelve stories. Each wall had seven windows, and in
the center was a circular staircase of fifty-two steps. He went up,
barely glancing at the collection of objects that filled each room,
until he reached the twelfth floor.

Standing where he'd placed them around the staircase were
the statues of four elves, two male, two female, all with their
backs to the stairs as if they were staring out the windows. Beyond them was a statue of Rhodry, as close to the descriptions
he'd heard as the Old One could make it, except that he'd
dressed the statue all in red. At Rhodry's feet lay the silver and
blue dragon of Aberwyn. Nearby was a stylized statue meant to
represent Jill, a pretty blonde with a sword in her hand. Just
beyond her was—nothing. The Old One felt a shudder run down
his back when he realized that Alastyr's image had utterly vanished. He should have expected that, he supposed; it showed that
the temple was firmly linked to higher forces. All around were
various other symbols and objects, a statue of Nevyn, a broken
elven longbow, various Wildfolk holding things that had associa-
tions in the Old One's mind, but he ignored them at first and
crossed to one of the windows.

Outside a mist swirled, and he steadied his nerves before he
peered into it. Strange creatures sometimes came there, because
even though the temple had started out as a mental construct
only, over the many years he'd worked in it it had started to
acquire an astral reality as well, as any image will if ensouled with
enough force. Yet that particular day he saw only moonlight
swirling through the mist rather than cryptic images of future
events. He went round to all the moonside windows, but always
he was disappointed. As he turned back to the stairs, something
caught his eye, and he stopped to examine the statue of Rhodry.
There was a difference, some tiny thing—he looked it over until
at last he found the change. There were tiny roses growing
around the index finger of Rhodry's left hand, dead-white roses
so perfectly formed that their thorns had raised a drop of blood
on the statue's finger. Puzzled he turned away, only to stop and
stare again: the statues of the elves were laughing at him.

All at once he was terrified. He heard small noises, a rustling
at the windows as if something were trying to get in. As he
started down the steps he heard the distant laughter, heard mu-

sic playing like a whisper on the wind that suddenly blew around his tower. In panic he ran, clattering down the steps, leaping from floor to floor, till at last he reached the safe silence of the bottom story, where the statues of long-dead archons stared at him as if disapproving of his unseemly haste. There he calmed himself. The tower was only a mental image, his construct, quite unreal, and he'd been a stupid fool to give in to that inexplicable fear. All he had to do was open his eyes and the temple would disappear back into his memory. Yet he wondered then just how real the temple might have become, if perhaps he might find it— or some strange, distorted version of it—waiting for him on the astral plane if he travelled there to look. For a moment he was afraid to attempt opening his eyes in case he found himself trapped in the vision. Then he forced himself to walk out one of the sunlit doors, to look at the mental hillside—and to open his eyes.

His familiar room appeared to him, his desk, the litter of scrolls, the tiled floor, the open window. With a sigh that was closer to a gasp of relief, he got up and went on trembling legs to ring the gong for a servant. One of his well-trained young men appeared almost immediately.

"Bring chilled wine—white, but not one of the best vintages."

The slave bobbed his head, then ducked out of the room. The Old One waddled back to his chair and sat down heavily, cursing Rhodry Maelwaedd and his entire clan in his mind. Then he reminded himself that Rhodry was only a minor irritation compared to the Master of the Aethyr. It was Nevyn who had destroyed Alastyr, Nevyn who had trapped his apprentice, Nevyn who stood like a dun wall between the Old One and his ultimate goal, that of exciting such hatred and suspicion between Deverry men and the Elcyion Lacar that open war would rage between them. In the end, the men of Deverry would win. The elven race were few in number; they had few children, too, while human beings bred like rats. If things came to a long war, then the world would be rid of the elves.

It was not, mind, that the Old One hated the elves in any emotional sense. They were, quite simply, in his way with their instinctive honor and their affinity for the dweomer of light. He didn't need obscure predictions and image-workings to tell him that if ever their dweomer joined forces with the dweomer of

Deverry on any wide front, then his dark brotherhood was doomed. He had no intention of letting such a thing happen. The Maelwaedd clan, and especially Rhodry, were marked by the omens to be the reconcilers between elf and man in some convoluted way that the Old One couldn't fathom, and thus, they too must die. Yet, as he brooded over his wine that afternoon, his simple irritation that Rhodry had ruined his plans grew into something close to a hatred, and that rage grew until it spilled over onto Rhodry's clan and most of all, Rhodry's protector, Nevyn himself. Long did he consider, until at last he found the seed of a plan. Every man in the dark brotherhood was threatened by this summer's turn of events. No doubt he could call a meeting of the council and convince them to join forces to wipe the threat away. They would have to plan carefully, work slowly, and hide their actual dweomer until the end, but if all went well, they would win.

"Oh yes," he said aloud. "The Master of the Aethyr must die."

Appendix

Characters and Their Incarnations

Current	ca. 643	ca. 696	ca. 773
Nevyn	Galrion/Nevyn	Nevyn	Nevyn
Jill	Brangwen	Lyssa	Gweniver
Rhodry	Blaen	Gweran	Ricyn
Lovyan	Rodda	Cabrylla	Dolyan
Cullyn	Gerraent	Tanyc	Dannyn
Seryan	Ysolla	Cadda	Macla

Glossary

Aber (Deverrian) A river mouth, an estuary.

Alar (Elvish) A group of elves, who may or may not be bloodkin, who agree to travel together as a living unit.

Alardan (Elv.) The meeting of several alarli, usually the occasion for a drunken party.

Angwidd (Dev.) Unexplored, unknown.

Archon (translation of the Bardekian *atzenarlen)* The elected head of a city-state (Bardekian *at).*

Astral The plane of existence directly "above" or "within" the etheric (q.v.). In other systems of magic, often referred to as the Akashic Record or the treasure-house of images.

Aura The field of electromagnetic energy that permeates and emanates from every living being.

Aver (Dev.) A river.

Blue Light Another name for the etheric (q.v.).

Body of Light An artificial thought-form (q.v.) constructed by a dweomer-master to enable him or her to travel through other planes of existence.

Brigga (Dev.) Loose wool trousers worn by men and boys.

Broch (Dev.) A squat tower in which people live. Originally, in the Homeland, these towers had one big fireplace in the center and a number of booths or tiny roomlets up the sides, but by the time of our narrative, this architectural style has given way to regular floors with hearths and chimneys on either side the structure.

Cadvridoc (Dev.) A war leader. Not a general in the strict sense, the cadvridoc is supposed to take the advice and counsel of the noble born under him, but his is the right of final decision.

Captain (translation of the Dev. *pendaely.)* The second in command, after the lord himself, of a noble's warband. An interesting point is that the word *taely* can mean either a warband or a family, depending on context.

Conaber (Elv.) A musical instrument similar to the panpipe but of even more limited range.

Cwm (Dev.) A valley.

Dal (Elv.) A lake.

Dun (Dev.) A fort.

Dweomer (translation of Dev. *dwunddaevad)* In its strict sense, a system of magic aimed at personal enlightenment through harmony with the natural universe in all its planes and manifestations; in the popular sense, magic, sorcery.

Elcyion Lacar (Dev.) The elves; literally, the "bright spirits," Bright Fey.

Ensorcel To hypnotize a person by direct manipulation of his/her aura rather than by manipulation of the consciousness in order to affect the aura.

Etheric The plane of existence directly "above" the physical. With its magnetic substance and currents, it holds physical matter within an invisible mesh and is the source of life.

Etheric Double The true being of a person, that electromagnetic structure that holds the physical body together and that is the true seat of consciousness.

Geis A taboo, usually a prohibition against doing something. Breaking geis results in ritual pollution and usually death to anyone who firmly believes in the concept, either by their morbid depression or by some self-inflicted "accident."

Gerthddyn (Dev.) Literally, a "music man"; a wandering minstrel and entertainer of much lower status than a true bard.

Great Ones Spirits, now disincarnate but once human, who exist on an unknowably high plane of existence and who have dedicated themselves to the eventual enlightenment of all sentient beings. Buddhists call them Bodhisattvas.

Gwerbret (Dev.) The highest rank of nobility below the royal family itself. Gwerbrets (Dev. *gwerbretion)* function as the chief magistrates of their regions, and even kings hesitate to override their decisions because of ancient tradition.

Hiraedd (Dev.) A peculiarly Celtic form of depression, marked by a deep, tormented longing for some unobtainable thing; also and in particular, homesickness to the third power.

Javelin (trans. of Dev. *picecl)* Since the weapon in question is only about three feet long, the reader should avoid thinking of it as a proper spear or as one of those enormous javelins used in the modern Olympic games.

Lwdd (Dev.) A blood-price; differs from wergild in that the amount of lwdd is negotiable in some circumstances, rather than being set by law.

Malover (Dev.) A full, formal court of law with both a priest of Bel and either a gwerbret or a tieryn in attendance.

Melim (Elv.) A river.

Mor (Dev.) A sea, ocean.

Pecl (Dev.) Far, distant.

Rhan (Dev.) A political unit of land; thus, gwerbretrhyn, tierynrhyn, the area under the direct control of a given tieryn or gwerbret. The size of the various rhannau varies widely, depending on inheritance and the fortunes of war rather than some legal definition.

Scrying The art of seeing distant people or places by magic.

Sigil An abstract magical figure, usually representing either a particular spirit or a particular power or kind of energy. These figures, which look a lot like geometric scribbles, are derived by various rules from secret magical diagrams.

Spirits Living though incorporeal beings proper to the various planes and forces of the universe. Only the elemental spirits, the Wildfolk (trans. of Dev. *elcyion goecl*), can manifest directly in the physical plane. Others need some vehicle, such as a gem, incense, smoke, or the magnetism given off by freshly spilled blood.

Taer (Dev.) Land, country.

Thought-form An image or three-dimensional form that has been fashioned out of either etheric or astral substance by the action of a trained mind. If enough trained minds work together to build the same thought form, it will exist independently for a period of time dependent on the amount of energy put into it. Manifestations of gods or saints are often thought forms picked up by the highly intuitive or those with a touch of second sight.

Tieryn (Dev.) An intermediate rank of the noble-born, below a gwerbret but above an ordinary lord (Dev. *arcloedd*).

Wyrd (trans. of Dev. *tingedd*) Fate, destiny; the inescapable problems carried over from a being's last incarnation.

Ynis (Dev.) An island.

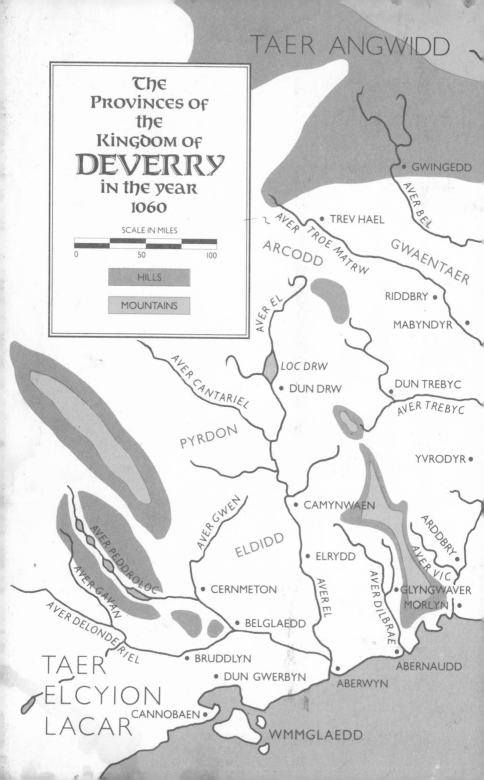

TAER ANGWIDD

The
Provinces of
the
Kingdom of
DEVERRY
in the year
1060

SCALE IN MILES

0   50   100

HILLS

MOUNTAINS

GWINGEDD

AVER BEL

AVER TROE MATRW

TREV HAEL

ARCODD

GWAENTAER

RIDDBRY

MABYNDYR

AVER EL

LOC DRW

DUN DREW

DUN TREBYC

AVER CANTARIEL

AVER TREBYC

PYRDON

YVRODYR

CAMYNWAEN

AVER GWEN

ELDIDD

ELRYDD

ARDDBRY

AVER VIC

AVER PEDDROLOC

CERNMETON

AVER EL

AVER DILBRAE

GLYNGWAVER

MORLYN

AVER GAVAN

BELGLAEDD

AVER DELONDERIEL

BRUDDLYN

ABERNAUDD

TAER
ELCYION
LACAR

DUN GWERBYN

ABERWYN

CANNOBAEN

WMMGLAEDD